D1021336

Other Titles by Catherine Coulter

BORN
TO BE
WILD

CATHERINE COULTER

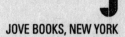
JOVE BOOKS, NEW YORK

THE BERKLEY PUBLISHING GROUP
Published by the Penguin Group
Penguin Group (USA) Inc.
375 Hudson Street, New York, New York 10014, USA
Penguin Group (Canada), 90 Eglinton Avenue East, Suite 700, Toronto, Ontario M4P 2Y3, Canada
(a division of Pearson Penguin Canada Inc.)
Penguin Books Ltd., 80 Strand, London WC2R 0RL, England
Penguin Group Ireland, 25 St. Stephen's Green, Dublin 2, Ireland (a division of Penguin Books Ltd.)
Penguin Group (Australia), 250 Camberwell Road, Camberwell, Victoria 3124, Australia
(a division of Pearson Australia Group Pty. Ltd.)
Penguin Books India Pvt. Ltd., 11 Community Centre, Panchsheel Park, New Delhi—110 017, India
Penguin Group (NZ), Cnr. Airborne and Rosedale Roads, Albany, Auckland 1310, New Zealand
(a division of Pearson New Zealand Ltd.)
Penguin Books (South Africa) (Pty.) Ltd., 24 Sturdee Avenue, Rosebank, Johannesburg 2196, South
Africa

Penguin Books Ltd., Registered Offices: 80 Strand, London WC2R 0RL, England

This is a work of fiction. Names, characters, places, and incidents either are the product of the author's imagination or are used fictitiously, and any resemblance to actual persons, living or dead, business establishments, events, or locales is entirely coincidental. The publisher does not have any control over and does not assume any responsibility for author or third-party websites or their content.

BORN TO BE WILD

A Jove Book / published by arrangement with the author.

PRINTING HISTORY
Jove mass-market edition / August 2006

Copyright © 2006 by Catherine Coulter.
Text design by Kristin del Rosario.

ISBN: 0-515-14239-5

JOVE®
Jove Books are published by The Berkley Publishing Group,
a division of Penguin Group (USA) Inc.,
375 Hudson Street, New York, New York 10014.
JOVE is a registered trademark of Penguin Group (USA) Inc.
The "J" design is a trademark belonging to Penguin Group (USA) Inc.

PRINTED IN THE UNITED STATES OF AMERICA

10 9 8 7 6 5 4 3 2 1

To my delightful niece
Roxie DeAngelis:
You light up the world.

Catherine Coulter

BORN TO BE WILD

ONE

Mary Lisa didn't want to puke up the two Ritz crackers she'd eaten for dinner. She swallowed hard, tasted bile, swallowed again, and held herself very still. No way was she going to get sick on this beautiful dark green satin Valentino gown Signore Malo insisted she wear this special night. She put an Eclipse lozenge on her tongue, felt the burst of weird sharp flavor, and continued not to move a muscle.

The applause slowly died as Christian Jules LeBlanc, who played Michael Baldwin on *The Young and the Restless*, walked off the stage beside Crystal Chappell, the Emmy for Outstanding Supporting Actor clutched in his hand.

Mary Lisa couldn't breathe. Her lungs were all hitched up. Forever went by. And then another six hours passed before Eric Braeden and Melody Thomas Scott, the two major staple stars from *Y&R*, strolled onto the stage, so confident, so beautiful, so very sure of their place in the sun.

Breath whooshed into her lungs. A good sign, surely, she was still alive. She felt Bernie's hand clasp hers tighter, felt Lou Lou's hand clutch her forearm. She could hear Elizabeth's sharp breathing behind her left shoulder.

"And the nominees for this year's Emmy for Outstanding Actress in a Drama Series are . . ."

I won't win, I can't win, how can I? I've won two times, it can't happen again. I won't vomit. Those two times were a fluke, a gift from God for something I must have done that I simply don't remember. It's all over. No more bursting sun. No one would vote for me again, not again. I'll be stoic. I won't get depressed. Those first two wins—the Nielsen ratings were skewed, everyone was fooled. But now they know the truth. Ohmigod, she just read out my name, she didn't stumble over it, and that's good. And she's reading out the four other actresses, all of them splendid, all of them— Fact is, I've tanked. I'll be out of a job, no, wait, I have a contract so they'll have to kill me off slowly over the next six months until my contract is up, or they can whack me close up and fast right at the end. I'm not going to vomit.

Clyde Dillard, *Born to Be Wild*'s producer, cupped her arm from the row behind her. And then Eric Braeden's beautiful deep voice filled the vast auditorium. No man, no matter what age, looked finer in a tux than Eric Braeden.

His lips moved. There was laughter. He must have made a clever remark, but Mary Lisa hadn't heard it. She shook her head to stop the buzzing. His voice deepened. She heard him say in Moses's voice, "And the winner for the Outstanding Lead Actress in a Drama Series is"—pause, long, long pause, Eric, master that he was, stretching it out to infinity—"for the third year in a row"—*third year in a row? No, impossible, he's made a mistake, he's going to correct himself now, say, I'm sorry, but I don't have my glasses on, no, wait, he does have his glasses on, he does! An aneurysm then, he's just blown something in his brain. No, wait, can it be? Really?*—"Mary Lisa Beverly, as Sunday Cavendish, FOX, *BORN TO BE WILD*!"

What?

Suddenly there were hugs, shouts, screams, and applause from the cast of *BTBW*, rocking the auditorium around her.

Then everyone else joined in, though understandably not with quite the same enthusiasm as the people on the show.

Bernie Barlow, executive producer and head writer of *BTBW*, pulled her to her feet, hugged and kissed her. "You did it, sweetie, you did it, oh, this is the best thing. We're golden, we're on top, we can do anything. Anything!" He gave her a little push. "Go get it, babe, you deserve it, but be fast, time is running down."

And from Lou Lou, who was patting her shoulder, not wanting to disturb her hair or makeup, "You look gorgeous. Go get 'em, tiger." Mary Lisa heard Elizabeth saying over and over, "I knew you'd get it, I knew you'd get it, you're the best—"

So many voices she knew congratulating her. Lou Lou lightly shoved Mary Lisa into the aisle.

All the tension, the gut-knotting terror, the cannonball of nerves gripping her stomach, all of it disappeared in a flash. She'd won. She couldn't believe it, but she had. She smiled hugely, right into the camera that was homed in on her face, and took her first step down the wide aisle. *I won't trip, I won't trip, nice and easy now, shoulders straight, glide, glide. I'm a gazelle, smooth and graceful. My dress won't fall down. I don't look like an idiot, do I? I am an idiot, wearing these four-inch heels. No, a gazelle wouldn't trip on her four-inch heels. They make the gazelle look awesome. Keep that smile. Oh my, oh my.*

The applause kept going, loud and sustained. This audience knew very well the last thing an actor or actress wanted was to have the applause die when there was another thirty feet or so to go before the stage. And there, overlaying all of it, the cacophony of hoots and whistles and cheers, and they were chanting her name—*Mary Lisa, Mary Lisa*, over and over again—most she recognized as the dulcet voices of the nineteen members of the *BTBW* cast, the directors, the stage manager, all the crew, the makeup and wardrobe people, all of them at full volume. Bless them. *Thank you, God, thank you, God, I can't believe it, I just can't believe it.* Her smile became bigger as she approached Eric Braeden, whose smile, like Sean Connery's, could fell a woman at fifty paces.

He kissed her cheek, whispered in her ear, "You want to come over to *Y&R*?"

She gave him a silly grin, and whispered back, "Only if I can marry you and have your baby," to which he kissed her again, whispered against her cheek, "I'll speak to Melody backstage, see what she thinks." Then he formally placed the Emmy in her hands. She turned to hug Melody Thomas Scott, so very beautiful and talented, who was smiling at her, congratulating her, and then Mary Lisa stepped to the podium. She looked out across the overflowing Kodak Theater at the beautifully dressed people, all of them looking back at her. She nodded happily at the many faces she worked with daily, basked for an instant in the presence of all those great stars she'd watched over the years. She drew in a deep breath, raised the Emmy high, and thought, *Damn, I'd sure like to thank three dozen people but there's no time.*

"I am so happy at this moment, so proud and thankful to all the wonderful people I work with on *Born to Be Wild*, that if I weren't wearing this tight dress I'd be clicking my four-inch heels together. Thank you, Bernie, Clyde, all our actors and actresses, our directors, the incredible makeup artists—all of you know who you are—thank all of you so very much."

She waved the Emmy, then carefully made her way back to her seat. She was so excited, her adrenaline level so high, she wouldn't be surprised if it geysered out of the top of her head. She felt hands patting her, murmurs of *Way to go! Congratulations! You deserve it.* And then shushes because there were only two minutes left and Juliet Mills was quickly reading out the names of the Outstanding Drama Series.

Then Steve Burton opened the envelope, studied it, and with perfect timing called out, ". . . And the winner is . . . *BORN TO BE WILD*, FOX, Bernard Barlow, Executive Producer and Head Writer."

Bernie's face flushed scarlet, he was close to hyperventilating, and he was shaking. Mary Lisa knew he was feeling exactly what she'd felt. She hugged him. "You're wonderful, Bernie, congratulations—but hurry, you've got one minute before they pull the plug on all the TV sets in the world."

Bernie made it to the stage in twenty seconds, accepted the Emmy after hugging Juliet Mills for a really long time (since he'd been in love with her for twenty years), accepted the Emmy from Steve Burton, saw the furiously blinking red light, and said into the microphone, "I've got the greatest group of writers in the universe, the most wonderful actors and actresses, and of course there are the countless experts who—" The red light blinked faster. "Thank you all from the bottom of my—"

To those watching the Emmys on TV, no one really complained about being cut off since they knew what his final word was. But they'd have been wrong. The audience in the Kodak Theater heard "Thank you from the bottom of my tap-dancing feet." And when they cut away to commercial, Bernie said, "This is for both Mary Lisa and me"— and he did a little jig.

TWO

Malibu, California

Mary Lisa was minding her own business, wearing big Audrey Hepburn sunglasses that covered most of her face, tatty plumber jeans that would have showed off a lot of stomach if she hadn't been wearing an equally tatty over-size Packers sweatshirt that pooled around her butt, and high-top sneakers. A Yankees baseball cap sat low on her head, her hair, too distinctive, as red as a violent sunset over the ocean, stuffed under the cap, unseen.

She was fretting over the upcoming plotline: *Should Sunday really go that far over the line to actually sleep with her weak, treacherous half sister's sleazy husband? Tit for tat—her half sister, Susan, had gone over the line, hiring that bozo to terrorize Sunday, something Sunday knew her mother was actually behind, but the two of them were like evil twins—but still, actually sleep with Damian? That was the best revenge they could come up with?*

She immediately took back that stupid question. In the world of soaps there were no lines the writers wouldn't cross. Well, maybe still a couple. On *Y&R* they'd cut off a budding interracial romance, and on another soap—she couldn't remember which one—a mother and son very nearly slept together, barely avoiding a kinky Oedipus deal. Hmm, maybe they'd flinch too at a relationship between athletic Nurse Markham, at Community Hospital, and her rescue Saint Bernard. Not a good visual. She stopped, burst out laughing.

Then she realized another reason she didn't want her character, Sunday, to sleep with her half sister's husband, maybe the real one. It was a case of art imitating life and it gave her indigestion. It had been three years since her sister Monica had married Mary Lisa's ex-fiancé, Mark Bridges, and left her hollowed out with bone-deep humiliation, and a goodly dollop of rage. What a fool she'd been. At least it had been more than a year now since she'd wanted to smash Mark's face.

Art imitating life, she thought again, and crossed the road between the Malibu Library, one of her favorite places in Malibu, where the staff was efficient, friendly, and still talked about how Robert Downey Jr. had been hauled into the court right next door in shackles. It was the corner building in the Malibu Civic Center.

Down the road a bit, across Civic Center Way, was the Malibu Country Mart, one of three small shopping centers in Malibu, all nearly within spitting distance of each other. It was only a block from Highway 1, or the Pacific Coast Highway, or simply PCH, as she'd learned to call it when she'd moved to the Colony in Malibu a year and a half before. She loved Malibu, not really a town, she'd tell visiting out-of-towners, but it was quite a place, loaded with movie stars and just plain rich folk who wanted privacy, a precious commodity, and they found it here because, she'd learned, most long-timers who worked here in Star Mecca didn't really care if you were Jennifer Lopez or Godzilla.

Malibu started out as a skinny strip of highway set between high bluffs on one side and the ocean on the other, until the cliffs receded making room for some scattered strip stores, inns on the water, lots of eateries, from Chinese to fat-heavy beach cuisine, the library and city hall, a small sheriff's station, and not much else except beautiful homes, outrageous sports cars, and truckloads of money. Besides the local high school, Malibu was home to Pepperdine University, just to the north, which had expanded to its current size in the early 1970s.

It was in the mid eighties today, the hazy sun scorching gold overhead. She'd walked to the library to check out the newest Harry Potter, and had it tucked in her huge tote.

Suddenly she saw a man duck into the shaded doorway of a small bagel shop—a paparazzo, a blight on the landscape, his camera at the ready. The paparazzi were everywhere, even in lovely private Malibu, the jerks. She'd bet the Baby Ruth in her tote it was Poker Hodges, her nemesis for years now. She called him Puker, ever since he'd caught her on film squeezing a roll of toilet paper at a local 24/7 six months ago and her photo had appeared in the *Star* the next week with some dumb caption that she thankfully couldn't remember. That must have appealed to his perverted brain because she was now his main target. He'd tracked and stalked her to the extent that she'd managed to get a restraining order to keep him at least one hundred feet away from her. That had helped, up to a point, but he was still there, whenever she happened to look up. Was that bagel doorway one hundred feet away? No, she'd bet it was no more than eighty feet. She knew he was taking photos of her with a telephoto lens. But who cared? Who would publish them if no one could recognize who she was? And thus her cap and huge sunglasses. She ducked into Luther's Army Salvage, caught by the sight of army combat boots piled high in a barrel. She looked through them but didn't find her size. Then she saw the pile of pea green knit sleeveless T-shirts, perfect for workouts and running on the beach. None of the three older guys in the store gave her a second look. She bought three identical pea green T-shirts, paid cash, pulled one on in a cramped dressing room, and slipped out the side door, then ran the block to PCH. She looked back, didn't see him. She turned right and ran at a steady pace on the side of the highway, her tote banging against her side. When she reached Webb Way, she paused at the red light, then charged across just as the light was changing, the traffic on PCH still idled. All she had to do was keep up a nice fast pace until she reached the kiosk at the entrance of the Colony just three blocks away.

No sooner had she gained the other side of Webb Way, right next to the Malibu Plaza, when she ran smack into an old woman pushing a grocery cart piled high with brightly colored afghans, all neatly folded. She apologized profusely, saw the woman eyeing her pea green T-shirt, reached into her store bag and pulled out another one. She thought the woman would kiss her, but she only nodded and gave her a stingy smile. Mary Lisa looked back to see the woman unbuttoning her ancient red blouse with its Peter Pan collar. She really didn't want to see the woman wear the T-shirt, she really didn't, not weighing two hundred plus pounds.

Mary Lisa looked around and didn't see Puker. Only another couple of blocks to go and she'd be safely through the gates into the sanctuary of the Colony. She began whistling, feeling quite fine, and found herself thinking again about where the writers were heading with the plot. She'd cornered head writer Bernie Barlow yesterday morning. "Listen, Bernie, Sunday doesn't even like Damian. She knows he's a jerk and a sleaze, that he's a fake, she knows he married her half sister for her money, knows he'd like to finagle his way into her mother's company. There's no way Sunday would ever sleep with him, no matter the provocation."

Of course the writers never listened to the actors although they tried hard to pretend they did. Bernie patted her shoulder, nodded enthusiastically, and said, "Good, good," but ended with, "Sweetie, Sunday sleeps with Damian for revenge against her half sister and her mother. It's that straightforward, at least that's the way it'll appear for a couple of weeks, then—well, we'll just have to wait and see."

She knew she should hang it up, stop pestering him about it, but where were they heading with this?

She paused a moment before crossing the gnarly Malibu Road, its name not posted to discourage outsiders. She didn't see a single car coming and crossed the road. She heard a gut-jerking song from *Phantom* at the same instant she heard the screech of tires and saw the flash of an old Buick LeSabre coming straight at her. For an instant her brain and her feet froze, then air whooshed out of her lungs as she hurled herself toward the opposite sidewalk. The car clipped her right side, sent her tote flying, and her crashing onto the sidewalk where she landed at the feet of a woman with a white toy poodle on a leash. The poodle barked maniacally in her face, his sequinned collar nearly blinding her.

The woman, wearing too-tight white Capri pants that barely covered her hip bones, and a tube top of bright lime green, wasn't, however, a sloucher. She fell to her knees beside Mary Lisa.

"Oh my God, that maniac tried to kill you! I saw it. Are you all right? What hurts? Are you bleeding inside? Sorry, you wouldn't know that. Don't move." She pulled out her cell phone and dialed 911. The poodle stopped barking at the sound of his mistress's voice telling the dispatcher what happened. When she punched off, the dog started licking Mary Lisa's cheek.

She didn't hurt yet, but she knew, somewhere deep where such knowledge resided, that pain would come, and it would be arriving soon and it wouldn't be good. She pictured a tsunami, nearly to her coastline. She looked up at the woman, but couldn't think of a thing to say. So she lay there listening to the woman talk to her while lightly patting her arm, as the dog's tongue scratched her cheek.

"An ambulance is on the way, you lie still, it'll be okay. My name is MacKenzie Corman and I'm an actress, but that isn't important now. Well, yes it is since I have an audition in two hours in Burbank, but I'll stay with you until the paramedics arrive. Calm down, Honey Boy, don't lick her face off. There, there, you'll be all right. Maniacs, they're everywhere, even here in Malibu. Damned fool. He wasn't a crazy boyfriend, was he? Do you hurt anywhere?"

Mary Lisa thought about that. "I don't hurt in one particular spot yet, and that's a relief. Thank you for helping me."

"That's okay." Honey Boy, now curled around Mary Lisa's head, occasionally licked her hair, pulled free of its French braid, her baseball cap having flown off her head when she'd gone airborne. MacKenzie sat down beside her and kept patting her shoulder.

Mary Lisa heard voices coming closer now, some low and worried, some excited and loud.

"Is she a drug overdose?"

"Is she dead?"

"Who is she?"

"I sure like that green T-shirt."

MacKenzie called out, "A car hit her. Everyone stay back, give her room. An ambulance is on the way."

Mary Lisa whispered, "Ask if anyone saw the car hit me."

MacKenzie asked, but no one had seen anything. Until an old man wearing a black bikini Speedo and black sleeveless shirt, a surfboard balanced easily over one wiry shoulder, jogged up. "Yeah, I saw the silly bastard, aimed right at her, did it on purpose, you ask me. I saw him do a big skid onto PCH going south. No cops around when you need 'em. I hope she didn't happen to owe Breaker Barney money, that wouldn't be good." He managed to step through the growing crowd of people, and gasped. "Mary Lisa! Oh my God, dear girl, oh my—"

Mary Lisa smiled. "Hello, Carlo. How are the waves today?"

"Fine, perfect actually. Hey, who'd you piss off?" Carlo squatted beside her and lifted her hand in his. Honey Boy growled at him, received a consolation kiss from his mother, and subsided again, wetting a hank of Mary Lisa's hair with drool.

"I'll be okay, Carlo. It happened so fast I didn't see the driver. I don't owe anyone any money. You know I'm not stupid enough to gamble with Breaker in his house of sin.

You know Breaker and I drink espresso most mornings over at Monte's. He likes me, says I'm cheap to keep."

Carlo thought about this and nodded. "This isn't Breaker's style anyway, particularly when his mark is female. It's okay, sweetie, you lie still. I'll stay here. Hey, who are you?"

"I'm MacKenzie Corman—nice name, don't you think?— and I'm an actress. I have an audition in an hour and fifty-one minutes in Burbank."

"You're gorgeous," Carlo said, giving her the professional and objective eye, "but so is every other girl I know in L.A. You'll need buckets of talent and O.J.'s luck. You related to a movie star, maybe a successful moneymaking director or producer? That'd be the ticket."

"Well, no, but I've really got this role down. I'm going to play Lena Cross, a noble dedicated nurse who's ministering to poor Indians in backward mountain villages when she happens to find out there's a gold treasure chest in an Andean cave."

"Low budget, huh?"

Mary Lisa moaned. She didn't mean to, it boiled up out of her throat. The tsunami had struck and pain ripped through her side. Carlo angled his surfboard so it shaded her face. "Hot sun today," he said to Mary Lisa. "I hear sirens, close now. You hang in there, baby doll."

Well, there was really nothing else she could do, Mary Lisa thought. She listened to all the conversations around her, not really understanding the words, and not really caring.

"You've called her three different names now. Which is it?"

A beautiful smile broke through Carlo's sun-seamed face. "She's my favorite bitch goddess." He looked back down at Mary Lisa. "You want me to call Bernie at the studio? Maybe Lou Lou or Elizabeth? What about that idiot agent of yours?"

Mary Lisa shook her head, closed her eyes against a sharp jab of pain in her side. "Not yet. Maybe a Band-Aid will fix me up. I don't want them to freak out."

MacKenzie went *en pointe*. "What do you mean, bitch goddess? What studio? You're not famous, are you? Maybe it's the same studio where I'm having my audition. All the stars dress like dog meat down here so they won't be recognized and have their photos plastered all over the fanzines. You don't mind?" And MacKenzie fingered Mary Lisa's curling red hair, pulled off her huge Audrey Hepburn sunglasses, and leaned down to study her face. "You look familiar. Who are you?"

Carlo grabbed the sunglasses and slipped them back over Mary Lisa's eyes. "Don't you watch *Born to Be Wild*? It's the best soap on TV, noon every day on Channel Five. Mary Lisa won the Emmy for Best Actress, the third year in a row. Never been done before."

MacKenzie shrieked. "Oh my God, you're Sunday Cavendish! Oh my, I see—the bitch goddess! But you don't look like her, you look like a regular person, kind of ratty, actually, but that's okay. You don't look like a bitch, but someone sure tried to run you down. Maybe it's revenge, you know? Oh goodness, Honey Boy, no, no, sweetie, don't lick her mouth."

Carlo's face faded from Mary Lisa's view, but he kept his surfboard above her to shade her from the sun. The pain in her hip started drumming big time now.

The tsunami had hit hard. She felt dizzy and light-headed, nauseated. She swallowed. No way was she going to vomit. She heard Honey Boy panting close to her ear. When she finally heard a paramedic shouting for people to move aside, she wanted to sing hallelujahs.

As they strapped an oxygen mask on her nose and loaded her gently onto a gurney to put her in the ambulance, she heard MacKenzie announce, "I helped save Sunday Cavendish's life. I'm a nurse by nature, Lena Cross, Angel of the Andes."

Honey Boy barked.

And suddenly Puker was there, snapping photos over a paramedic's shoulder, grinning down at her like a maniac.

"I've got a restraining order on you, Puker. I'm going to

put you in jail for this." She didn't know if she'd said the words out loud because Puker didn't stop clicking until a paramedic shoved him out of the way.

"Nah, the restraining order expired last week," Puker called out, and snapped more photos.

"Get out of the way, you moron," a woman said. "Not you, dear. You hang in there. We'll have you to the hospital in under twelve minutes." Mary Lisa felt a hand on her forearm. She felt it stroking her even as she floated away.

THREE

The first soap: In 1930, Chicago radio station WGN started a fifteen-minute daily serialized drama set in the home of an Irish American widow and her young unmarried daughter.

UCLA Medical Clinic in Santa Monica

Mary Lisa sat on the edge of the stainless steel gurney, her sneakered feet dangling. She felt wonderfully loopy. She wiggled her hip. No pain, not a single zing. Drugs were magic. She started singing Lennon and McCartney's "Yesterday." It didn't alarm her that she seemed to be watching herself from about three feet away, marveling at how silly she looked and how sweet her voice sounded, even though she wasn't in the shower. She lifted the hideous open-backed blue paper sackcloth and gingerly eased down her panties to look at the continent of bruises spreading on her hip. A little bit like Australia, she decided. Perhaps by evening, at the rate it was growing, she'd be a billboard for India. She knew, objectively, that the bruise was going to make her whimper once the drugs wore off, but for now, she fancied the fast-spreading green splotches were mountains. Maybe there would be a yellow blob right in the middle for Ayers Rock.

At least she hadn't needed stitches anywhere. But she could see the directors' eyes rolling back in their heads when they saw the scrapes and bruises on her arms and neck. Because of the grinding schedule, there were four directors now on *Born to Be Wild*, each responsible for one or more hour of airtime a week. Mavis in wardrobe, who loved to turn Sunday out with lots of skin showing, wouldn't be happy either. She studied the half dozen Band-Aids dotted here and there, and thought them very nicely designed.

Strange that they'd left her alone all of a sudden. They were probably waiting for the pain meds to kick in so they wouldn't have to hear her whine. She hadn't really whined much, she'd been pretty stoic, truth be told, only whimpered a bit.

She eased her panties back up and pulled the crinkly paper gown over her as best she could, not that she really cared. She threw back her head to finish giving her all to "Yesterday." When she was four years old, she hadn't understood it very well, but she'd had a great little memory.

A man stuck his head through the curtain, not a doctor, but a lovely slender man in a light sports coat and tan slacks. He was in his early thirties, black haired, with soft brown eyes that nonetheless looked quite shrewd. At the moment he also looked amused as he stood there politely, evidently waiting for her to finish the song. She grinned at him, cocked her head, and asked, "And you would be . . . ?"

He stuck out his hand, gently took hers. "Hello, Ms. Beverly. I'm Detective Vasquez of the Lost Hills Station in Calabasas. We handle any problems in Malibu. Let me say that I like how you sing that song, as do most of the people in the waiting room. In fact there was a bit of a singalong happening. Sounds like you're a happy camper."

"Ain't drugs great? And they're legal so you can't arrest me. Do you know what? I really like police officers." She realized she was still holding his hand. She didn't want to let go because his hand was big and warm. When he finally managed to get his hand back, he lightly patted her on the shoulder. "Hey, Deputy Lindstrom said you played kissy-face with a car."

"More like kissy-hip," Mary Lisa said and touched her fingertips to her side. "I'm growing a bruise the size of a continent, Australia, most likely. It's got mountains and valleys. Do you think it'd be okay if purple represented rivers?"

"Why not?" He stared at her, his eyes crinkling in amusement again, but his voice was quite serious. "The doctors say you were very lucky, that you're not really hurt." He smiled, showing white teeth and kindness. "You're an actress, right?"

She nodded. "Much of the time, yeah."

"There's a photographer out there, a skinny guy with sharp eyes who made me as a cop. I got rid of him, but he's probably a lurker. You know him?"

"His name's Puker Hodges and you described him perfectly. He's good at what he does. He can disappear behind a dead bush when he wants to. I saw him in Malibu today before that car hit me. The jerk snapped pictures of me when they were loading me into the ambulance. He must have followed the ambulance here. I wonder how long it will be before one of them shows up on the cover of the *National Enquirer*."

"If you're recognizable, not long at all, I would imagine. Puker?"

"That's what I call him. I think his real name is Poker. That's weird too, isn't it?"

Detective Vasquez pulled out a small notebook and a pen. "I hear you're a soap star."

She nodded. "I play Sunday Cavendish on *Born to Be Wild*."

He stared at her a moment, then grinned real big and shook her hand again. "A real pleasure, ma'am. I thought you looked familiar. *Born to Be Wild* is the soap of choice at the sheriff's department. We all get a kick out of the 'jugular' dialogue. You get amazing reactions. You're everyone's favorite."

She sat there, sneakered feet dangling, and preened, but only for a moment. Then she gave a deep sigh. "That's nice, thanks for telling me. Now, I don't suppose you caught the jerk who hit me?"

"Not yet, and that's why I'm here."

He'd dropped his voice a half octave and he sounded dead serious again.

"Oh dear. You stopped smiling and my hip started throbbing at the same time. Bummer."

Nurse Blenkens whisked back the flimsy curtain at the edge of the alcove and stopped short when she saw the man. "You must be the police officer, right?"

"Detective Vasquez, ma'am."

Nurse Blenkens said, "You'll have to leave for a moment. You can speak to her once I've helped her get dressed." She pointed unceremoniously toward the hallway and started untying Mary Lisa's gown.

"Sure thing. I'll be outside in the waiting room, Ms. Beverly." Bless her cop, he pulled the curtain closed on his way out.

When Mary Lisa was back in her clothes, Nurse Blenkens said, "I really like that T-shirt. There's just a little smudge on it. You're hurting again, aren't you? It's all right, I only gave you enough of the doctor's order to take the edge off, to see how you'd react to it. Since you're not driving, I can give you another shot before you leave, if you like."

She was soon rubbing Mary Lisa's arm where she'd pulled out the needle. "Now, here are the pain meds I promised you. You can take one every four hours. They should keep you singing—there was an old guy with a broken leg in the waiting room singing along with you. Nice. Now remember you promised to check with your doctor on Monday. Come back if you feel ill or the pain gets worse. There's going to be a big bruise on your hip, nothing for it except maybe some ice. The doctors all say it's superficial. You'll have to wait for it to fade, I'm afraid, actress or not. I'm sure all your makeup people can cover the smaller bruises on your face and shoulders. Oh, yes, would you give me your autograph? It's for my nephew, Tommy. He's a grotty little thirteen-year-old, but an excellent snow-boarder. Makes his parents hopeful."

Mary Lisa signed the back of a prescription form and slowly eased off the gurney. She was beginning to feel quite fine again. She touched her fingertips to the bruise on her hip. "Thanks for everything. Do you know, about my bruise, I'm now thinking India—lots of fine and varied to-pography," She shook Nurse Blenken's hand. "Have I told you how much I love drugs?"

"And they love you too. Just stay away from that stuff you shoot between your toes."

"The only thing I put near my toes is nail polish. Usu-ally a nice coral."

Nurse Blenkens nodded, but without a hint of a smile. Mary Lisa wasn't sure she'd believed her. "No, really, it's usually coral, but I'm leaning toward French now, same as my fingernails. What do you think?" She thrust her dirty hand toward the nurse and wiggled her fingers.

Nurse Blenkens studied her nails. "You're going to need some repair. Now, Ms. Beverly, you go home and take to your bed until tomorrow morning, all right? Since you've been so nice, maybe you could sign an autograph to Dr. Murray's wife, Marge. He was too embarrassed to ask. He said she hates Sunday and tapes all your shows."

"Sure," Mary Lisa said and signed the back of another prescription form. "I'm always telling the writers not to re-deem Sunday too often, my alter ego and I are having too much fun."

Ten minutes later Detective Vasquez helped Mary Lisa into his brown Crown Victoria.

"Hey, I've never been in a slick before. This is very cool."

He grinned at her. "You know the idiom. I don't know where that name came from. My old boss always called the detectives' cars 'plain wrapped,' since they're always one solid color, usually boring. Okay, I don't see Puker Hodges."

As he maneuvered out of the parking lot, he said, "I'm a little surprised that you weren't surrounded by people from the studio by now, your friends, your agent, people like that, insisting on taking you home."

"Actually you saved me from all that, and I'm really glad to be getting out of there without any press showing up. I wouldn't call the studio people unless I was on life support. As for my agent, thankfully, he's in Istanbul, taking a long-overdue vacation. I'll call my friends when my brain is less squirrelly."

"What's his name?"

"Marvin Leftwich, with Trident Media, in L.A."

He nodded and turned right onto the highway. He looked into his rearview mirror, frowned.

"What's wrong? Do you see something?"

FOUR

The first TV soap opera, a half-hour program, appeared in 1956 with the debut of *As the World Turns*.

"A dark four-door sedan. No, don't look back." He smiled. "It's okay, he turned off on Topanga Beach." He gave her a reassuring smile. "Stop worrying, let me do that. Okay, when I checked in with the station, they wanted you to know they have a weekly betting pool going about what Sunday Cavendish is going to do next. Detective Farber asked me to get the inside scoop."

"You can tell her I honestly don't know myself, but she should remember I'm bad to the bone."

Mary Lisa leaned her head back and closed her eyes. "And she knows they like to push the envelope with Sunday."

"And yet she remains sympathetic."

"Amazing, isn't it?"

"You feeling all right, Ms. Beverly?"

She said without opening her eyes, "Compared to lying on the sidewalk with a toy poodle named Honey Boy licking my mouth, yeah, I'll take it." Mary Lisa roused herself enough to call Lou Lou. When Detective Vasquez pulled up beside the Colony kiosk, she called out, "Chad, it's me. I was hit by a car, but I'm okay. This is Detective Vasquez. He'll probably be coming around again, so please let him in."

Chad came around to the passenger side of the car, poked his head in, examined her face. "I heard about some asshole hitting you, not two blocks from here. You sure you're okay?"

"Yeah, I promise, only temporary agony."

Chad frowned over that. "I also heard it was on purpose. Carlo saw it all."

Mary Lisa said to Detective Vasquez, "Carlo Spinelli is one of my neighbors. He used to own a computer company up in Silicon Valley, sold out ten years ago and moved down here. He's a great surfer, even gives some lessons. He came right after I was lying on the road."

"I know Carlo," Detective Vasquez said.

Chad backed away and waved them in. He called after them, "Cool slick you're driving, Detective!"

Detective Vasquez grinned and patted the dashboard of the Crown Vic.

The Colony, originally known as the Malibu Motion Picture Colony when it was established back in the 1920s, was now simply known as the Colony. Bing Crosby, Ronald Coleman, Gary Cooper, and Gloria Swanson were only a few of the early arrivals who built cottages on the beautiful, pristine stretch of beach. They came to play in privacy. There were two long rows of houses, all set close together, half of them on the ocean side, the others across a narrow street. The houses ranged from palatial to an occasional small cottage. The Colony extended all the way down to Malibu Lagoon State Beach, separated from the public land by a high rusted fence. Even though it was private, with only residents and their guests allowed in, anyone could duck under that fence and walk in. But no cars could get in, not unless the folk at the kiosk weren't paying attention, which rarely happened.

She directed Detective Vasquez about two-thirds down Malibu Colony Road to her small ocean-side beach house. "Another twenty houses and we'd be in the Malibu Lagoon

State Beach. Always lots of action there, big-time surfing. It's Carlo's favorite place. Actually, there's lots of action all over the beach."

"Nothing would surprise me in this town." Detective Vasquez paused a moment. "But you know, Malibu isn't a real town, which sounds strange, but I've always thought that."

She grinned. "Come on now, we have a mayor, we have a high school, we have chiropractors. But I know what you mean. Truth is I think of it as a special place, my own special place." She directed him into her driveway.

"Hey, nice house."

Mary Lisa beamed at him. She was still excited about her two-story cottage, all glass and redwood, built back in the early '80s, and all hers, her very first home, bought and paid for. "I purchased it from an older actress, a friend of Elizabeth Fargas—she's also a friend of mine—who gave me a good price. She wanted to move back to Nebraska. Go figure that. I step off my back porch and get sand fleas between my toes in under five minutes. And then I dive in the waves and the fleas drown."

He laughed. "An example of nature's balance." He pulled in behind a bright red Mustang convertible. He opened her unlocked door and walked directly into a large, high-ceilinged living room. He helped her ease down on a bright red-and-white-striped sofa. It was one of three colorful sofas set about the big room with at least half a dozen chairs and love seats interspersed among them. Bright geometric rugs were scattered on the oak floor. Pale light poured in through all the windows. "You've got lots of places to sit."

"I've got lots of friendly neighbors who are always dropping by. I started out with one sofa and chair and just kept adding."

Yes, he thought, she'd have lots of friends. She seemed just plain nice, and funny, at least when she was drugged up. He watched her look thoughtful and open her mouth, but she seemed to forget what she was going to say.

He said, "Nice and bright in here. Makes you smile, I'll bet. You're looking a bit peaked, Ms. Beverly. Your friend coming over soon?"

Mary Lisa nodded. "Her name's Lou Lou Bollinger, one of the makeup artists for *Born to Be Wild*. She's a bit freaked out so I'm hoping she won't get a speeding ticket getting over here."

"Interesting name."

"Wait 'til you meet her. She's the best, excellent at her job. I'm going to have her fix me up before anyone else sees me."

"There's more than one makeup person on the show?"

"There are at least twelve actors shooting any given day, so the four makeup people we have are kept busy, but Lou Lou always does me."

"Can I get you anything? Tea, water? All right then, you sit back and relax and we can get started if it's okay with you." At her nod, he took out his notebook again and sat down on the green patterned love seat facing her. "You told me you ducked into the army salvage store in the Country Mart to avoid Puker Hodges?"

"Yep. I bought this wonderful pea green T-shirt—"

He liked how that green T-shirt looked on her, noticed the dirt, and nodded for her to continue.

She went through it all slowly, he asked questions and she remembered more, then finally, ". . . I was lying flat on my back on a gurney, a paramedic placing an oxygen mask over my nose, and there was Puker, hovering over me, snapping photos. You know the rest."

He looked thoughtful. "I don't recognize the description of the bag lady you gave one of your T-shirts to, but someone will since we don't have many homeless people in Malibu. I'll check her out."

"She loved the T-shirt. I'll bet she's still wearing it."

"We'll locate her. Now, about Carlo. Well, everyone knows Carlo. Did you go to his birthday party last month? A cookout on the beach thrown by Ben Affleck?"

"I couldn't make it. A friend on *OLTL—One Life to Live*—had a baby shower. I heard Carlo gave midnight surfing lessons to fifty drunk naked people."

"Sounds about right. Carlo just turned seventy, can you believe that?"

Mary Lisa nodded. "He's taught a couple dozen stars how to surf over the years."

"Okay, let's get back to it. Carlo swore to my deputy that this guy ran you down on purpose, no way it was a hit and run."

"As best as I can remember how it happened, yes, it was on purpose. He wasn't weaving around like he was drunk. He came right at me."

"Now, MacKenzie Corman, the wannabe actress with the white poodle. I've seen her around. I'll speak to her as well. You're sure the dark car that hit you was a Buick LeSabre?"

"Lou Lou owns a powder blue LeSabre, a 2000 model. It was identical to hers as far as I could tell, except for the color. It was black, possibly, or really dark blue."

"Excellent. It was the front left fender that struck your side?"

Mary Lisa closed her eyes, pictured herself being knocked to the street in that frozen moment, and slowly nodded. "Yeah, it hit me pretty hard. You think maybe I left a dent in the fender?"

"Not likely, but who knows? We'll get a list of all dark four-door 2000 LeSabres registered in the area, see if you recognize any of the owners' names. You said you didn't see who was driving. No feeling if it was a man or a woman?"

She shook her head.

He paused a moment, then said matter-of-factly, "This might have been a hit and run, someone who was drunk, hit you and was afraid to stay. If I didn't know Carlo, how reliable he is, I'd be leaning toward an accidental hit. But the deputy told me Carlo swore the guy hit you on purpose. So until proved otherwise, we'll treat this as an intentional act. Now, do you know of anyone who might be dangerous, or have a problem with you—like an old boyfriend, a business associate, whatever?"

Lou Lou said from the living room doorway, "The moron who tried to run her down could have been Paulie Thomas. You know how weird he is, Mary Lisa. Half a dozen people at work believe he's going to poison Sunday Cavendish with a Danish."

FIVE

Before *Buffy the Vampire Slayer*, Sarah Michelle Gellar
played Kendall, the daughter of Susan Lucci's Erica Kane
on *All My Children*.

Detective Vasquez's eyebrows went straight up. "Really?
Have you asked to have him fired, Ms. Beverly? Surely you
have that kind of clout."

"Yeah, she does," Lou Lou said, "she just won't."

Mary Lisa slowly shook her head. "I really don't share
Lou Lou's opinion about him. Besides, I really like the
donuts he's always bringing in. So does everyone else. Oh,
I'm sorry. Detective Vasquez, this is Lou Lou Bollinger.
Lou Lou, this is Detective Vasquez. He's going to find out
who was driving that car."

Lou Lou held up her hand, and nodded to him.

"Is Lou Lou your real name, Ms. Bollinger?"

Lou Lou's chin went up. "You got a problem with my
name?"

"No, not at all. It's simply interesting and unusual."

Lou Lou was uncertain whether or not to believe him because she'd swear there was this sort of twinkle in his eyes.
"Hmmm," she said as she sat down beside Mary Lisa and
cupped her face in her palm, studying her. "You're doped

up and that's good. I'm seeing just a few scratches I can take care of easily, so don't worry about the cameras. You swear there's nothing serious going on here?"

"I swear."

"Okay. I left a message on Elizabeth's phone, told her what happened—and reassured her, so you'd better not be lying to me." She said to Detective Vasquez, "Mary Lisa sometimes laughs when she should be screaming. Drives us nuts. You look competent, Detective Vasquez. That's a relief."

"I'll keep that in mind, Ms. Bollinger. Okay, this Paulie Thomas, what does he do on *Born to Be Wild*? An actor? Stage crew? What?"

"Paulie's the nephew of one of the directors, Tom O'Hurley," Lou Lou said. "He's one of the prop guys. Locations are selected and the necessary props are all set up during the night before the various scenes are shot the next day. However, Paulie likes to come to the set during the actual shooting. I don't know when the guy sleeps. Everyone likes his uncle, so no one says anything."

Mary Lisa said, "Come on, Lou Lou, Paulie does make himself useful. Don't forget, he isn't paid for it." She cut her eyes to Detective Vasquez. "He's a gofer—he runs errands for everyone, scrounges for missing props, fetches ordered lunches, and brings in the best donuts, you know, the kind filled with cream or jelly, or the ones with sprinkles."

"Yeah, yeah, everybody loves his donuts, but don't forget he hates you, Mary Lisa."

"No," Mary Lisa said patiently, "it's Sunday Cavendish he can't stand."

Lou Lou said to Detective Vasquez, "Most of the people who see him scowling at her think it's funny. They think it's a tribute to how good she is. Fact is"—Lou Lou tapped her head—"Paulie isn't the sturdiest tree in the forest, lots of branches missing off the top."

Mary Lisa said, "Okay, so he's a little slow. What does that matter? The thing is, Detective Vasquez, Paulie's a fixture, sort of like a mascot."

Lou Lou interrupted her. "Yes, he feeds people sugar and they're happy, but he's got this thing for Margie McCormick— she plays Sunday's half sister, Susan Cavendish—and he was really angry when the word went around that Sunday might sleep with Susan's husband, Damian Sterling."

"What is Damian Sterling's real name?"

"Jeff Renfrew," Mary Lisa told him. "He's a nice guy, a really talented actor, a little goofy sometimes. He wouldn't be involved in something like this."

Still, Detective Vasquez wrote down his name. "Everyone's got two names. Do you ever get them confused?"

"Not really," said Mary Lisa, "but when you play the same role for such a long time, the characters sort of become your alter egos. You get to know them very well, even care about what happens to them, and you can slip into character on a dime."

Lou Lou grinned at him. "Like Jekyll and Hyde."

Detective Vasquez grinned back, and Mary Lisa realized he wasn't looking at Lou Lou through a cop's eyes. No, it was pure guy. And she knew what he was seeing. Lou Lou was nearly as tall as she was, a natural blond, although who knew or cared in L.A.? She had light blue eyes, a fit, curvy body, and the brightest smile in the universe.

Detective Vasquez suddenly turned to Mary Lisa, and now he was all business. "What about the rest of the cast? Anyone else I should talk to?"

Mary Lisa said slowly, "Well, there's Margie McCormick, who plays my half sister, Susan. She's about as different from Susan in real life as she could possibly be. Margie doesn't take grief from anybody, tells you exactly what she thinks, never suffers in silence. Her character, Susan, even though she acts weak and helpless, is really sly and manipulative. She's got both our mother and her husband fooled. But the person Susan hates all the way to her bones is her half sister, Sunday. It's a vendetta thing. Every chance she gets, she tries to knock Sunday out of the picture. For example, she and Sunday's mother hired this guy to terrorize Sunday; it went on for a good month before

Sunday actually shot him when he came to her house to kill her in her bed."

Lou Lou fanned herself. "Wow, was that ever a scene. It was so scary, Mary Lisa was so believable, I nearly wet myself."

Mary Lisa grinned. "Yep, but Sunday always rides again. So what happened today is a little like life imitating art, don't you think, Detective?"

"I can see why you'd say that, Ms. Beverly," Detective Vasquez said slowly. "Would you say that the actress, Margie McCormick, could be jealous of you and your success?"

"Nah, Margie's not the type. She doesn't ever slink around or lie to get her way. She's right out there. She knows what she wants and goes after it."

"How long has she been on the show?"

"Five, maybe six years."

"And you're telling me she isn't jealous that you show up and become the runaway star, win three Emmys in three years? An unknown to boot?"

"You want the truth?" Mary Lisa grinned. "I think everyone is deliriously happy because *Born to Be Wild* has the highest viewership in our time slot and that means the sponsors line up to pay big bucks to advertise, and those bucks mean security, money, and a solid future for everyone. The other actors might want more face time, more plotlines that put them front and center, but I'd say for the most part people on the cast feel very lucky to be a part of it all."

"Since Mary Lisa showed up, everyone smiles," Lou Lou said. "You can see it in the Nielsen ratings—when Mary Lisa is center stage, the ratings skyrocket. If she isn't—which is very rare now—they fall. Actually, *BTBW* is the most watched of all the soaps. I even saw the producer, Clyde Dillard, whooping and high-fiving everyone in the vicinity the other day when he landed a huge advertising deal, all because of Mary Lisa's latest big scene-chomping plotline. There's no one gonna want to knock off Mary Lisa. She's everybody's meal ticket. What's more, she's nice to everyone."

"Well, someone doesn't like me," Mary Lisa said, wishing it was time to take another happy pill. She peeked at her watch. No, not time yet. She said to Detective Vasquez, "The reason I mentioned Margie McCormick is not that I thought she might have been the one to hit me but because she might be able to give you insights on Paulie Thomas."

Detective Vasquez thought about this a moment, tapped his pen against his knee, then asked, "Does Paulie Thomas have a personal interest in Margie McCormick?"

Lou Lou said, "As a matter of fact, he asked her for dates a good half dozen times. She actually agreed to meet him off-set once—he is, after all, related to one of the directors and that couldn't hurt, but mainly, she felt sorry for him. It was maybe four months ago, after a nasty breakup with her boyfriend. She told me she wanted to let him down easy. It didn't go well, at least that's what Margie said when I was trying to get her eyebrows on straight the morning after."

Mary Lisa picked it up. "Margie said Paulie took her to Cartier on Rodeo Drive, wanted to buy her a diamond ring. She nearly freaked."

Lou Lou said, "The thing is, Detective, it seems to me Paulie might be having trouble judging reality like that when it comes to Mary Lisa too. He's pleasant enough to her whenever anyone's around, but he really hates Sunday Cavendish, calls her names under his breath, only it's not under enough, you know? He mumbles stuff about her whenever the script calls for Sunday to do something outrageous, especially when she fights with Susan, stuff like she should have her cheating heart cut out, that sort of thing."

"He sounds pretty dramatic himself. Why would the producer let someone like that around to bother their golden goose? Why have you allowed it, Ms. Beverly?"

Mary Lisa sighed. "He usually says stuff when he knows

no one else will hear him. Lou Lou didn't hear him—I told her what he'd said. Paulie's got problems, but the stuff he says about Sunday? She's a character, Detective, she isn't a person. What does it matter? There are lots of fans who say the same thing about Sunday."

"I'll be speaking to him, Ms. Beverly. I'm thinking that after what happened today, he might not be with the show much longer."

Mary Lisa sighed again. "The producers don't know about it. I guess I never thought of him as ominous or dangerous to me, just a little sad."

"Get rid of him, Ms. Beverly."

"We'll see."

"That's another thing," Lou Lou said. "Mary Lisa's got this gooey center." Lou Lou started to punch her in the arm, but drew back at the last second, looking horrified.

"It's okay, Lou Lou. That's my hale and hearty side."

"Okay, a gooey center. I got that. Is there anyone else either of you can think of?"

"Yes," Lou Lou said. "Let me just spit this out—Jeff Renfrew."

"Ms. Beverly mentioned him earlier. He plays Susan Cavendish's husband, right? Damian Sterling, the smooth sleaze who's after the Cavendish money?"

Lou Lou beamed at him. "Very good, Detective. You know more about the show than I thought."

Mary Lisa said, "Lou Lou thinks he's got a broken heart and that I'm the one who broke it. She thinks he doesn't show it because he's such a good actor. It's not true, Lou Lou, I keep telling you, he's not interested in me, at least not now."

Lou Lou reached over and patted Mary Lisa's knee. "Listen, sweetie, I've never told you this because I didn't think you needed to know, but I heard from a reliable source that Jeff hits his mother up for money to pay his gambling debts every six months or so, and she pays because she's afraid of him.

"There's something else. You wouldn't believe how long

he stares at himself in the mirror each morning. Someone like that can't stand being rejected. And when he's not admiring himself, he's staring at your boobs. Maybe he wouldn't hurt you, but with what I see every day, he's worth a look-see."

Detective Vasquez said, "So Jeff Renfrew gambles? And loses?"

Mary Lisa said, "I dated Jeff maybe three, four times—no, I didn't sleep with him—and he was always a nice guy. I never got a whiff of a gambling problem, if he has one, and I've never seen him violent." She shrugged. "Maybe he does like to look at himself in the mirror, that just makes him a narcissist. He's an actor, after all. And he's going to be leaving the show for a dramatic series pilot this fall, another *CSI* sort of thing—what's it called, Lou Lou?"

"Oh yeah, I forgot about that. It's called *Brain Fever*, I think. He's going to play a big-shot pathologist working with a special FBI profiling team."

"Right. So you see, Detective, there's no reason for him to try to run me down with fame and fortune on the horizon; it doesn't make sense."

"Hmmm," Lou Lou said. "Oh all right. But I personally think that Jeff would make a dandy mass murderer."

Mary Lisa rolled her eyes.

"You guys haven't agreed on much so far," Detective Vasquez said.

"I see the rust," Lou Lou said, "Mary Lisa always sees the shine."

Mary Lisa rolled her eyes again. "Yeah, that's me, gooey in the middle. I heard they're going to pretend to knock Damian off—on spec, you understand—in an ambiguous way. It's a favorite ploy when a popular actor decides to try his wings."

Detective Vasquez smiled. "If the pilot doesn't go well then he could turn up again, maybe with amnesia, lost in Africa?"

"Yeah, something like that," Lou Lou said.

Detective Vasquez saw that Mary Lisa suddenly didn't look too good. She was paler than she'd been a moment before, her eyes not quite focused. He rose and gently took her hand. "You need rest and a pain pill. I'll be getting back to you." He smiled at Lou Lou; again, Mary Lisa thought, definitely a guy smile.

After Detective Vasquez left with an autographed photo in his pocket for Detective Elena Farber, Mary Lisa called Bernie Barlow, listened to him shriek for five minutes, assured him a dozen times that she would be fine, that the cops were on top of things, then managed to lie prone on her sofa, an afghan over her, a pillow against her bruised hip, and another blessed pain pill swimming happily in her bloodstream.

Lou Lou called out as she stirred chicken noodle soup on the stove, "This has been quite a rough Saturday for you, Mary Lisa. I'm really thinking Paulie could have snapped, tried to drive you down. He simply can't let evil Sunday sleep with poor little Susan's husband."

"Paulie's not crazy, Lou Lou. He's pathetic more than anything. Can we talk about something else? My brain's starting to float on the ceiling. It's nice. Let me leave it up there. Would you like me to sing you a song?"

Lou Lou was treated to a full-bodied treatment of John Denver's "Rocky Mountain High" before she came back into the living room, carrying a tray.

"I can't believe you know all the words to that old song. Here, sit up a bit."

While Mary Lisa spooned the soup into her mouth, Lou Lou flopped down beside her, steepled her fingers. "Hey, sweetie, you're looking kind of vague. I'm going to stay with you tonight. Bernie will be all calmed down by Monday." Lou Lou took away the cell phone that was lying on Mary Lisa's chest. "You don't have to call Clyde, Bernie will do it. In fact, we should be hearing from Clyde any minute now."

Clyde called half an hour later. He nearly hyperventilated before she finally got him off the phone.

Lou Lou said, "Why didn't he call you sooner?"

Mary Lisa flopped back down. "He said he was afraid to, said Bernie finally managed to convince him that I was okay. You know Clyde's got spies everywhere. I'll lay you a five he's even got spies in the women's room at Taco Bell. I had to swear to him on the head of my father that I'd be okay to shoot on Monday. That gives me a day and a half to get myself back together."

"Yeah, you lucked out, it being a Saturday and all."

"That was sarcasm I heard, but I guess I am lucky. I don't have a day off until Thursday, but then it'll be a long weekend for me."

"Elizabeth and I will stick to you like gumballs until Thursday. Then why don't you get out of here? Like maybe home to Goddard Bay? You haven't seen your folks for a while, and maybe it's time, don't you think?"

"I miss my dad. Okay, I'll think about it."

At nine o'clock that evening, Elizabeth Fargas burst through the front door, a bottle of champagne under her arm, still wearing TV makeup, and a gorgeous pale yellow suit, and the three-inch heels she always wore even though she was seated behind the TV news desk. "Oh my, look at you, smiling and okay, right? I've been worried out of my mind. Goodness, do I ever need a drink!"

SIX

No way I can do this. No way. I'm an idiot.

There, good, he finally had a functioning brain again. He'd finally admitted it to himself. He didn't love her. Actually, now that he examined it, he really didn't like her all that much either.

He smiled as the crushing weight toppled right off his head. He was ready to yell with relief when, in the next instant, the weight jumped back on.

Wonderful, just wonderful. I've got to tell her before her mother books the Methodist church and it's all over town. He pulled the velvet box out of his inside jacket pocket, flipped it open, and looked with fear and loathing at the three-carat diamond winking up at him. It was the direct result of an early morning towering inferno of sex, a shake-the-rafters event that had cannonballed him onto his back when it was over, grinning like a loon, his brain waltzing in the ether. Surely, he thought, sex like that could get a man to do more than torture ever could. He'd have been willing to say anything, do anything for her after that brain-deadening, camel-humping sex, state secrets be damned.

And to prove it, by the time he'd finally talked his brain into crawling back inside his skull, he'd already bought the ring.

Thank God he had to focus on the mayor's daughter this morning—she'd been arrested for drunk driving the night before—so he hadn't been able to run right over to her house, a marriage proposal ready to pop out of his mouth.

But she was expecting him to propose, probably tonight when he took her to dinner at Le Fleur de Beijing. It was a new Asian/French restaurant in town that had the word *fusion* on every page of the menu, which meant, his father had told him, that you could get snails with sweet and sour sauce. It was expensive, though, and to quite a few folks in Goddard Bay and the environs, that meant it had class.

He'd been sleeping with her for close to four months now, at least four times a week. What *had* made that last time different? Didn't matter. He'd presented himself that morning at the jewelry store when the doors opened.

He happened to glance at himself in the mirror. He could still see the residue of wild fear in his eyes. He looked down again at the engagement ring, and thought he'd be better off without sex like that ever again in his life. It was too dangerous.

John McInnis Goddard, the great-great-great-grandson of Joshua Barrington Goddard, founder of Goddard Bay nearly a century and a half before, and a tough-as-nails district attorney referred to by local defense lawyers as a major shitkicker, was thinking he'd prefer a long winter's stay in a Siberian gulag or a campout in the Galápagos to a *fusion* dinner with Kelly Beverly.

John pulled out his cell phone. He had to talk Goon Leader into helping him.

But before he could punch in the numbers and grovel for the favor, his cell rang and Jack, the man himself, told him to get his butt over to the Jason Maynard house on Westview. His wife, Marci, had just found his body in the garage, lying in a pool of dried blood.

SEVEN

Before he was Spock, Leonard Nimoy played Bernie the
Pill Pusher on *General Hospital* in 1963.

BORN TO BE WILD
Adolphus Club, Founder's Day dance

Sunday Cavendish is slow dancing with Damian Sterling,
her half sister, Susan's, husband. She's wearing a long
black fitted gown with sheer black netting that begins
above her breasts all the way up to an inch-wide jet bead
collar around her neck. The net sleeves fit close to her
wrists. A slit in the netting gapes to show a very full cleavage. The back of the gown is cut nearly to the waist. Her
red hair is swept up on top of her head. Sparkling jet earrings dangle from her ears, winking in and out of the long
curls that fall nearly to her shoulders. Her mouth is crimson, her blue eyes brilliant with makeup. She knows she's
beautiful and the arrogance of that knowledge is clear in
her eyes, in her body language. She's the main attraction,
power and wealth in one beautiful, ruthless package, and
everyone in the big room knows it and accepts it.

Damian is in his late thirties, with light hair and contacts to give him pale green eyes. He looks elegant and
comfortable in a tux, like the smooth operator he is. He's
only a bit taller than Sunday, who's nearly six foot in her

stiletto heels. He looks about surreptitiously to make sure neither his wife nor her mother is around, then pulls Sunday very close, his mouth only an inch from her ear.

"You look incredible, Sunday."

She leans forward and lightly bites his earlobe. He goes stiff, looks surprised, then panicked. She smiles at him, only a flash of disgust shadowing her expression. "Don't worry, Romeo, your wife is in the women's room, probably whining about me to Mother." She laughs at the relief on his handsome face. "Since Mother's begun to have major problems with Bernard, she'll change the subject quickly enough."

"But Bernard loves her, seems to be interested in marrying her. What's the problem, Sunday?"

She gives him a lazy smile. "I told her to check out one of Bernard's offshore accounts, particularly the one in Bimini. I told her she might still find a lovely amount of newly transferred money there that just might have resided in her company vaults only last week. It could be gone by now, but the trail will still be there." Sunday shakes her head, looks sad. "Seems that her wonderful, grand self wasn't what was important to Bernard."

"You've got to be wrong. Surely she didn't believe you."

"She called me a liar, a troublemaker, oh my, any number of nice names, but I know she won't be able to help herself. She'll start stewing about it tomorrow or the next day. Then she'll have her investigator Toby the Leach check it out and Bernard will soon be history. So you see, she's mad and won't have the patience to listen to Susan complaining about us."

"You helped your mother. Why?"

Sunday shrugs, a gallic shrug she perfected when she studied at the Sorbonne in Paris. "Do you really think so?"

"Wait, you know the money's already gone, don't you? Or maybe Bernard never did anything wrong and you set him up."

"You think?"

"You still think Susan and your mother set that maniac on you, don't you?"

Sunday laughs, gives a little wave to a group of friends. "Let's just say it's time for a bit of *heart*burn for her. I would have made it all up, but the fact is, Bernard's a crook. I hate crooks."

"But you didn't warn her until he'd moved the money."

"Toby the Leach will find it, never fear." Sunday looks bored. "Enough of her problems, Damian. I know you're friends with Bernard. Could it be you had something more going on with him?"

"No!"

"Who cares? I don't. More power to you if you were working with Bernard trying to steal money from Mother's coffers. Now, I think it's best for you if you forget about this. Otherwise, Mother will be furious if she knows you've sniffed out her latest mistake."

"She spoke of marrying Bernard."

"Now she won't, will she?" She pauses a beat. "You look very fine in that tux."

He looks grim. "I've got to go, Sunday, I'll be back, give me five minutes—"

"To call Bernard, to warn him? Now, now, Damian, I would cut my losses if I were you."

He looks uncertain, knows the jig is up, and that he's been trapped. He pulls in a deep breath, manages a smile at the beautiful woman in his arms. "All right. Let Bernard roll around in his own swill. You know, Sunday, if Susan can't get your mother's sympathy, it means she'll be moaning to me about you later, accusing you of betraying her."

"Of course she will." Sunday shrugs her elegant shoulders, says flippantly, "So seduce her, then she'll believe anything you say. I don't suppose she'll ever consider that you're the one betraying her, not I."

His arms tighten around her, his voice lowers to a sexy whisper. "It doesn't matter. You know it's not her I want."

She looks at him, an arched eyebrow raised, a questioning look on her face that lasts and lasts until—

"Clear!"

Mary Lisa's hip throbbed. She slowly walked off the set and took a pain pill from Lou Lou's outstretched hand.

"Bad?"

"No, not really. It's just that Jeff was pushing hard on my hip there for a while."

"Detective Vasquez was back again this morning, talking to everyone in makeup and wardrobe. I think he's considering a stalker-gone-violent deal. It's happened before."

Mary Lisa sighed. "I guess I'd rather have a nutcase than someone I know who hates me and wants me gone, someone who's so clever I don't automatically suspect him or her. I'll bet Detective Vasquez doesn't find out anything if he hasn't by now. He did scare Paulie though. I told him again I didn't think Paulie has it in him to try to run someone down with a car. He hummed, you know the way he does, but wouldn't say what he thought."

"Hey, Mary Lisa, you hanging in there?"

As producer of *Born to Be Wild*, Clyde Dillard was responsible for monitoring the acting quality, while the four directors were responsible for the camera quality and the "look" of each scene, which sounded a bit strange to people not in the soap business, but worked very well. He lightly touched his fingers to her forearm.

She dredged up a smile and a nod.

"You really pulled off that scene with Damian. And the gown is perfect, not a bruise in sight. Good choice, Mavis." He nodded to the pixie-faced girl, who was actually pushing forty even though she looked more like fifteen, her eyes bright under a mop of red-streaked black hair. "If you're okay, Mary Lisa, we'll finish this scene in five minutes. Oh, yeah, about Paulie. His uncle Tom told me this job is very important to him, it's all he talks about, all he thinks about. He said to assure you that Paulie really likes you, Mary Lisa, that he wouldn't hurt a hair on your head—not even on Sunday's head. He told me Paulie's frightened of Detective Vasquez. You know as well as I do that Paulie can't throw a lobster into boiling water. He's certainly not stalking you, and no way would he run you down."

Mary Lisa didn't smile. "I don't think he is, either, but someone is, Clyde. Detective Vasquez will find out, I hope. As for Paulie, as long as he behaves himself, I've got no problem with him."

"Clyde is such a mushy worm," Lou Lou said a few moments later to Mary Lisa when Clyde turned to speak to Jeff about a camera angle the director wanted changed.

Not all that mushy. Mary Lisa said, an eyebrow cocked, "What kind of name is Paulie, anyway?"

Clyde turned back, looked thoughtfully at Mary Lisa. "I'd say it's the name of a kid who's never grown up. Hmm. Maybe it's time he did. You know, Mary Lisa, I wish that Detective Vasquez would finish up instead of disrupting everything and dizzying up everyone. It's playing havoc with the schedule." He realized then what he'd said, and coughed into his palm. "Of course he needs to find out who tried to hurt . . ."

He looked acutely uncomfortable and Mary Lisa, no fool, leaped at the opportunity to lobby him. "Hey, Clyde, please speak to Bernie about this plotline with Sunday sleeping with Damian. It's still not too late to come up with something else. He's such a sleaze, Clyde—Damian, not Bernie—and Sunday has too high an opinion of herself to sleep with him. She's not just any bitch, she's the goddess bitch who would never sleep with a weakling. She despises them. She could tease Damian, sure, make him twist for a while, but actually get naked with him? No way. I don't think even her desire for revenge against Susan would make her sink so low."

Clyde shrugged. "It's a solid story line, pet. Bernie told me sleeping with Damian is only phase one of Sunday's revenge. He said they're working on a twist that'll have everyone slack-jawed for Sweeps Week. The soap fanzines are already stirring things up with all their speculation."

"Sleeping with Damian will lessen Sunday, maybe forever."

Clyde's sparse gray eyebrows flew up. "Hmmm," he said, stroking the straggly Vandyke trying to cover his chin. "If I know Bernie, he's probably whipping lots of stuff into the pot to see what floats to the surface. Okay, okay, I'll mention it again. He's the final word, Mary Lisa, no one else, you know that. We've all got to trust his instincts. He got us here." He turned away when one of the actors wanted to ask him about something.

"Ha!" Lou Lou said under her breath next to Mary Lisa's ear. "You're the one who got us here."

"No, I just goosed things up. Come on, Lou Lou, what he means is that Bernie Barlow has been the soap's head writer, guru, and creative genius for well nigh seventeen years. Only the network people have the power to force him to change his mind."

"Yeah, yeah, and since they don't even agree on what constitutes casual Friday, Bernie always does what he pleases."

Mary Lisa nodded. Since the network lived and died by the weekly Nielsen ratings that still cranked syrup-slow out of the fax each Thursday, and *BTBW* had been at the top of the heap since shortly after Mary Lisa arrived, Bernie was golden. Not to mention that very recent Emmy for best soap. It didn't look good for Sunday's staying out of Damian's bed.

"Look at the bright side," Clyde continued, happy as a clam, turning back to her. "If they have Susan attempt suicide or something, it might even have viewers cheering for Susan and Lydia. And you'd be the most hated daytime star on TV for a while, until Sunday magicks the viewers again."

Jeff strolled over in his tux. "Not going to happen, Clyde. The viewers hate whomever Sunday hates, and that includes her half sister and mother."

"Whatever. Okay, kiddo, I'll pass this on to Bernie, give him a headache. Now, it's time for Sunday to make her assignation with Damian."

Lou Lou said, "Susan shouldn't only attempt suicide, she should succeed, that's what I say." She said it low enough for only Mary Lisa's ears so one could carry it back to Margie.

Three minutes later, Mary Lisa's hair was scrutinized, her dangling curls coaxed a bit lower, now nearly touching her shoulders, one of them twisting around a jet earring. She checked the monitor, and . . . Sunday resumes the same expression.

She smiles at Damian. The camera catches her full face, eyes slumberous as her hands lightly stroke up his arms. From the corner of her eye she sees her half sister, Susan, walking into the ballroom with their mother, Lydia, and she gives a small calculated smile. She stops stroking his arms even as she presses closer, her breasts against him, leans up, and whispers, "All you have to do is unfasten the collar around my neck and this gown drops."

Damian looks like he wants to leap on her. His eyes dilate a bit, he's breathing hard.

She laughs. "But not here. Here's your lovely wife, the old warship steaming along behind her. Why don't you call me after you've seduced your little woman and made her happy?"

Damian sees his wife from the corner of his eye, but he can't help himself. After a brief moment of uncertainty, he says, "Yes."

The camera moves to Susan's face. She's been crying but now she's wearing a brave look. "Damian," she says softly and lightly touches her fingertips to his forearm. "Take me home."

Damian looks down at her, his expression unreadable, holds it, holds it, until—

"Clear!"

In the dressing room, Mary Lisa heard Margie say angrily, "I heard about what you said, Lou Lou!"

"How is that possible? I barely heard myself."

"You said I should commit suicide, that I should succeed. Dammit, Susan isn't about to do that. Never."

"Hey, it's just another idea for Sweeps Week," Lou Lou said easily around a mouthful of eye shadow pencils.

"They could pretend you're in a coma, bring you back in a couple of months. Hey, it's no worse than poor Mary Lisa having to sleep with Susan's husband."

"It's not going to happen," Mary Lisa said. "Don't worry about it." She remembered what Detective Vasquez had said about a stranger listening in. Someone who didn't know would have no clue who was talking about whom. Mary Lisa smiled at Margie, who seemed mollified, and walked away, whistling, to have a bubble-gum-chewing Mavis help her out of the black gown.

It was Wednesday. It was Mary Lisa's last scene. She had four whole days off. Her hip didn't hurt.

EIGHT

Goddard Bay, Oregon

Chief of Police Jack Wolf looked down at the metal table where Jason Maynard's body lay, cold and gray, a green sheet pulled to his waist. His head no longer looked human from all the blows the killer had rained down on him.

The medical examiner, Dr. Washington Hughes, a big hulk of a man who'd played pro football defensive tackle for the Vikings in the '80s, stood next to him. "What you saw at the scene is what you get, Chief. Someone struck him hard enough on the back of the head with the golf club to kill him instantly. As you can see, the murderer didn't stop with the kill blow. So far, I've counted another half-dozen blows to the face. I've very seldom in my career seen a head and face this destroyed. The bloody golf club they found lying beside his body checks out as the murder weapon."

Jack stared down at the man he'd known only well enough to speak with about the coastal weather when they chanced to meet on the street. Jack bought his insurance from Jason's father-in-law.

He said, "It bespeaks a fine rage."

"Sure does. Out-of-control rage at work here, Chief."

It was impossible to tell now, but once Jason Maynard had been a handsome, fair-complexioned man with blondish hair and hazel eyes and a ready smile. "Okay, somehow, the murderer came up behind him, delivered the first blow to the back of his head. I'm thinking he bounced off the passenger side of the green Camry and fell onto his back on the garage floor. From the blood splatters, he didn't hit the Mercedes, but collapsed between the two cars. Then the murderer struck his face, half a dozen times you said? I'm inclined to believe the murderer knew he was already dead, but it didn't matter because he was in the red zone. And he struck only his face, to obliterate him? To make him disappear, no longer exist?"

"Did you ever see anything this bad in Chicago?"

"Yeah," Jack said, "I did, but I'll tell you, Doc, it's a shock to see it here in a quiet town like Goddard Bay. We may have someone walking around here who's deeply disturbed. Looking at all the blood splatters in that garage and on the two cars, I'd have to say he was even beyond the red zone, he was crazed, no brakes, no functioning brain at work. He was over the edge. But now I bet he's flying high because he thinks he's gotten away with it."

"A man did this, you think?"

Jack shrugged. "There isn't any particular heft to a golf club. Could just as easily be a woman." He looked down at Jason Maynard again. "Such a damned waste. It really pisses me off."

"Glad you're the one who has to nail him—or her—and not me."

Jack looked him up and down, snorted. "Whoever it is, you could twist off his neck with one hand."

Dr. Hughes grinned, flexed his hands. "Maybe, but I wouldn't enjoy it, and I wouldn't be any good at finding him."

"Can you give me an idea of when this happened?"

"I'd say he was killed between six and eight hours before the time Mrs. Maynard found him this morning, some-time in the early morning, maybe around one a.m."

"Anything from the tox screen on him yet? Alcohol levels? Drugs?"

"I'll get that all to you by tomorrow, noon." Dr. Hughes looked down at the wreck of a man he'd known only slightly, a good-looking young man of thirty-four, who, until early this morning, had a long life in front of him. "He was healthy as a horse until this. He was fit, took care of himself."

"No defensive wounds?"

"None. As I said, the first blow to the back of his head took him down, killed him instantly. It had to be a friend, family member, someone he trusted, right? Someone he would have let follow him into the garage?"

Jack nodded. "We'll find out who he'd been out with. We still don't know who that golf clubs belongs to. If it was Jason's, the club might have been right there when the murderer went over the edge and grabbed it. But there was no golf bag. Maybe the murderer grabbed the golf club out of his own bag and used it."

"That means it would have been where? In his backseat?"

"Someplace handy, that's for sure," Jack said. "We'll see. I'll bet my Beretta he knew his killer very well indeed. And he didn't think the person was a threat because he turned his back. I suppose someone could have been waiting for him, hiding in the garage without Jason Maynard seeing him, and come up behind him." Jack frowned. "But it would have been hard to surprise him like that. No place to hide." He sighed. "And that would mean premeditation. I can't buy that. The person found out something, and lost it. This was sudden, uncontrolled."

Jack picked up the golf club that was leaning beside the door in a plastic bag, already examined by the forensic people. "I don't golf. What can you tell me about this?"

"It's a Callaway, a Big Bertha Fusion FT-3 driver."

"Expensive?"

"Very, but about the same as some of the other big names. They're excellent."

"Would there be a whole lot of them out at the country club?"

"Sure. This is an affluent area."

"Okay, thanks. I'll be in touch." Jack left the morgue, actually a converted room in the basement of the Goddard Bay Community Hospital. At that moment, Jack was very glad he wasn't in Chicago with its chains of command and its protocols. He was free to do what he thought best. He punched up his friend John Goddard on his cell.

John answered, listened. When Jack finished, he said, "I thought I was going to throw up. I didn't know a human being had that much blood in him—and other stuff. It was everywhere. That was pretty ugly, Jack."

"Yeah, it was. Okay, I'm heading over to interview Marci Maynard. I'm betting she knows our murderer. You want to come?"

John thought about it. "No, I think it would be best if I stayed out of the investigation for now. This is a big case for us. I don't want to be accused of crossing any lines, of manufacturing evidence for an indictment."

"Okay, no problem. Hey, John, you don't golf much these days, do you?"

"No, not much. Jason was hit over the head with a driver, right?"

"Yeah, a Callaway."

"Good clubs, used by lots of pros, probably a lot of our locals as well. You might need some luck tracking that down. Oh yeah, Jack, something else. This isn't about the murder. This is about—well, it's a favor, a big one. I'm in a little trouble here." He told Jack about Kelly Beverly, the engagement ring, and the reservations at Le Fleur de Beijing that evening.

Jack laughed, couldn't help it. "She knocked you right out of your boots, did she?"

"She knocked them into the next town, Jack. I was a goner. You can take this to the bank: I swear on the grave of my crazy uncle Albert that I'm never going to do it again."

"Yeah, yeah, that's what you used to say when we were hanging our heads over the john the morning after one of those sorority parties."

"Okay, you're right. I don't want it again until I'm more mature, more able to control my brain afterward."

"Think a moment about a guy's hard wiring."

"Okay, maybe you're right. Will you help me out here?"

"So you want me to come fetch you at the Fleur de Beijing at exactly nine-thirty tonight, with something urgent about the case. That'll give you an hour—you're sure you'll have gotten yourself off the hook by then?"

"If I haven't, shoot me."

Jack grinned into his cell. He knew John didn't really need him to be there, only wanted some help to make a graceful exit after breaking up with Kelly. It had happened before. They'd met at Princeton, John a psychology major because he didn't know yet what he wanted to do with his life, and Jack in many of the same psych classes because he knew all along he wanted to be a cop. As it turned out John had gone to law school, while Jack went on for his master's degree in forensic science. The FBI had called, which was gratifying, but he'd wanted something local, and moved back to where his family lived, in Chicago. But now he was here, in Goddard Bay, largely because John Goddard, the newly elected district attorney, had called him at the perfect time. An eighteen-year-old boy, wasted on crack, had shot him in the side after missing him twice. Jack finally returned fire, killing him. Two months later, he was the newly elected chief of police in Goddard Bay. To his surprise, but not to John's, he really liked the job.

Jack said, "Okay, you got an hour to save your ass before I come and haul it out. I'll let you know what I find out from Marci Maynard. Wives, I've discovered over the years, always know something, if not everything."

NINE

Jack didn't drive back to the Maynard house on Westview but directly to Marci's parents' house. Milo and Olivia Hildebrand had come to get her not ten minutes after Jack had arrived at the crime scene that morning. Jason Maynard's parents lived across the country in Hartford, Connecticut, and Jack had hated to make that call. They'd be arriving tomorrow.

Milo Hildebrand, the owner of a local insurance company, savvy and well-off, seemingly sane and balanced, answered the door. "Hi, Jack, come on in. I think Marci's sleeping; our doctor gave her a sedative. Let me check."

"No problem, Milo. I need to speak to you and Mrs. Hildebrand in any case. Now is fine."

Olivia Hildebrand, looking thin and pale, sat on a high-backed chair in the antique-filled living room, her knees pressed together, her hands locked around them, wearing some sort of designer knit thing. She looked up when he came into the living room, then immediately back down again. He didn't know her well, only by sight, really. He knew Milo because he bought insurance from him.

"Mrs. Hildebrand," he said and walked to her, stretching out his hand to her. She was forced to let go of her knees. She shook his hand, her own hand limp, and said in a thread of a voice, "Please sit down, Chief. Would you like some coffee?"

Jack would very much have liked some coffee, but looking at those dull eyes and paper-white skin, he shook his head. "No, thank you, Mrs. Hildebrand, I'm fine. I'm very sorry to bother you but I need your help."

"Hello, Chief Wolf."

Jack looked up to see Patricia Bigelow walk into the living room.

"Patricia," he said, nodding. "What are you doing here?"

"She's our lawyer, Jack," Milo said. "I called her right after we brought Marci here. She will see to it that we're all legally protected."

"Your choice," Jack said, nodding to her, but he wasn't happy about this. He could only hope she wouldn't interfere with his questioning to impress her clients. Pat Bigelow had been in Goddard Bay a bit longer than he. She was a good criminal attorney, and according to John, a thorn in his side more than once. She was known to take no prisoners. She charged the moon, but her clients seemed to think she was worth it. She was able to hide all her toughness and her hard edges well. She was nice looking really, actually appeared more suited to hosting garden parties than defending crooks. She had soft blond hair, cut short, lovely sharp features, and long legs that she showed off, particularly in front of male-heavy juries.

"Don't worry, Chief, I have no intention of trying to hinder any legitimate fact-finding. I just don't want to see any sort of intimidation. Are we clear?"

Milo waved him to a chair, and said to his wife, his voice soft and easy, "He's here to speak to us, and to Marci, Livie. It's his job. He's got to find out who killed Jason."

"Well, he can't see Marci! She's ill, in shock, really—"

There was a flash of impatience in Milo's dark eyes, just as quickly gone, and he kept his voice soft. "Jack knows she's asleep. He also knows she's torn up about this mess. The chief isn't going to do anything to hurt her."

Olivia Hildebrand didn't move, nodded slightly, and turned her eyes to Jack's face. "It's not just a mess, Chief. Jason is dead. That's much more than a mess."

Jack nodded. "Yes, it is. Can you please tell me when you last saw Jason Maynard?"

Milo said, "As you know, Jack, Jason worked for me, so the last time I saw him was yesterday afternoon when he left the office for the day."

"And you, Mrs. Hildebrand?"

"At dinner last Tuesday night. They always come to dinner on Tuesday nights. I served spinach lasagna, Jason's favorite dish."

Milo Hildebrand took his wife's hand, gently squeezed it. "Yes, yes, Livie, Jack doesn't need the dinner menu. It was a pleasant evening, Jack, no surprises, no inkling of anything wrong with either Jason or Marci."

Jack continued smoothly, "Mrs. Hildebrand, how did Jason seem to you Tuesday night?"

"As Milo said—" She stopped and began shaking her head. He persevered. "Think back, Mrs. Hildebrand. Was he different in any way to you? Perhaps distracted? How did he and Marci deal with each other?"

Milo opened his mouth to speak, but Jack shook his head at him, never looking away from Mrs. Hildebrand. Next time, he would get her alone. He hadn't realized Milo was this dominant, but he wasn't surprised. Olivia Hildebrand had spent her whole married life inside this home, completely dependent on Milo. He looked around. She'd made it a beautiful home. He'd seen stunning antiques in another home in Goddard Bay, but he couldn't remember where at the moment.

Olivia said, tears thick in her voice, "Jason and Marci loved each other, Chief, very much. They've been married for nearly three years now, spoke about starting a family soon. Marci loves children, she's always wanted twins, you know. She was a twin, but her brother died when—"

Milo heaved out a sigh. "Livie, Jack doesn't need to know about Marci's dead twin. Try to focus on Jason."

She flinched as if she'd been struck, then put her head down again. She whispered, "Yes, Milo, I know. It's just that all this—" She looked up, waved her hand helplessly, then let it fall back onto her lap. She looked over at Pat, who'd remained standing, her arms folded, looking calm but concerned.

"There's no need to apologize, Mrs. Hildebrand," Patricia said easily. "We all understand what you're going through."

Jack said, "I didn't know Marci had a twin brother. I'm sorry to hear he died. But now I need you to come back to last Tuesday night." He looked over at Milo, then back at his wife. "It's not that I disbelieve Milo, it's simply that I've learned over the years that mothers can sometimes pick up on unspoken feelings in their families. So think back. Did Jason seem concerned about anything? Upset? Did he speak of anyone he was having a problem with? Did you feel anything at all that didn't seem quite right?"

"No, really, everything was fine. Even when he was quiet, he seemed content, not at all distracted or worried about anything. He laughed a lot, told several jokes—Jason could spin a joke out of every encounter he had—he was amazing, really. We had a nice visit." She shot her husband a look and lifted her chin. "Jason loved the German chocolate cake I made. It was another favorite of his."

Jack turned to Milo. "Jason worked for you, Milo. Did you notice anything in his behavior recently at the office?"

"Jason is—was—a good insurance agent. People liked him, trusted him. He made a good living. He seemed to get along with everyone. There are sometimes little tiffs between agents because of the competition, you understand, but nothing that could ever possibly lead to something like this." Milo had known what he was going to say, Jack thought, he'd obviously thought about it, rehearsed his answer. Was he hiding anything? Protecting someone? Maybe his daughter, afraid that somehow, she was involved. Jack understood that. His father, he knew, would probably have the same instincts toward him. But would he protect him if he feared Jack had murdered somebody?

"Jason came to work for you after his marriage to your daughter?"

"Yes. I offered him a job. He'd been working for the First Independent Bank and wasn't happy. We discussed it and he seemed pleased. He never complained. No reason to, since he made a very nice living. He was suited to it, a natural salesman. Livie's right about the jokes. I never could figure out where he got them all."

"Were there any problems between Marci and Jason?"

Milo said, "Certainly not! They were practically newly-weds."

Jack smiled at Milo, said he was parched, and asked him for some coffee. It was obvious to Jack that Milo didn't want to leave him alone with Mrs. Hildebrand, but he really had no choice. He raised an eyebrow to Pat Bigelow. She smiled at him, nodded, and he finally left the living room. She transferred her smile to Jack, to let him know he couldn't browbeat Mrs. Hildebrand. Jack motioned for Mrs. Hildebrand to keep seated. When Milo's footsteps receded down the hallway, he said, "I know this is very difficult, Mrs. Hildebrand, but I surely need your help." He studied her face a moment, then said straight out, "Now, why don't you tell me the truth. How were Marci and Jason really getting along?"

TEN

"Oh, I suppose you've heard some gossip, but you really shouldn't believe it."

"Tell me, Mrs. Hildebrand."

"No, there was nothing, really. They were having a rough patch, that's all. All couples have difficult times occasionally, and they were no exception. There wasn't anything they couldn't patch up."

And pigs fly. Jack made his choice and took his shot. "I know Jason was having an affair, Mrs. Hildebrand. It's easier if you just tell me about it."

He'd hit it on the mark. Not a flicker of surprise in her eyes. Her chin went up again, as if daring him to disagree. "They never spoke to me about it."

"What does Marci do outside the home, Mrs. Hildebrand?"

"She works at home. She's an artist. The Flynt Gallery in Portland sells her watercolors. The sailboats over there, those are some of hers."

Jack looked at the grouping of six rather small watercolors, beautifully framed, on the wall beside the fireplace. They seemed rather bland to him. On the other hand, he'd never cared much for watercolors.

"Was she financially independent?"

"Yes. No. Who can say? I don't know exactly how much she earns from her paintings. But I do know she's becoming quite popular. You'll have to ask her."

"Was Marci having an affair?"

"No! You mustn't speak like that, Chief. She's a good girl, she wanted children. Anything that's happened—it's not her fault."

So, had she found out her husband was betraying her and—what? Bashed him over the head and in the face?

Pat Bigelow said easily, "I think it's time you leave that subject, Chief."

Jack wanted to drop-kick Pat Bigelow out the front window, but he couldn't, and so he nodded. "Can you think of anyone who didn't like your son-in-law?"

Olivia Hildebrand looked down at the wedding ring on her finger. After a moment, she shook her head.

Milo Hildebrand came back into the living room, carrying two mugs. He held one out to Jack. Jack rose.

"Thanks, Milo. I think I'll see if Mrs. Maynard is up to seeing me for a few minutes."

Olivia jumped to her feet. "Let me go up, let me see if she's awake—"

She seemed frantic. Did she want to warn Marci that he knew about Jason's affair? He'd soon see. Jack said easily, "I'd appreciate that, Mrs. Hildebrand."

He heard her footfalls on the stairs, and turned back to Milo. He sipped at the coffee and nodded. It was rich and very hot. "I hear you're a pretty good golfer."

Pat Bigelow said, "Be careful here, Chief—"

Milo held up his hand. "Been golfing since my dad first took me out when I was nine years old. Olivia and I golf quite a bit."

"What brand of clubs do you use?"

"TaylorMade. Why?"

"Did Jason Maynard golf too?"

Milo nodded. "He really liked to play the club course. He wasn't all that good, but he was working at it. He and I went out once a week, usually on Saturday mornings."

"What was his brand of clubs?"

"Ping. Why?" Milo Hildebrand's eyes clouded. "Oh, damn. He was killed with a golf club, a Callaway?"

Jack nodded. "Yeah, a driver, specifically, a Big Bertha Fusion FT-3. Can you think offhand of anyone who uses Callaways at the club?"

Milo nodded. "I can think of a few people, but it's the caddies and the people at the pro shop you should talk to."

Mrs. Hildebrand was back more quickly than Jack had expected. "I don't understand her." She flapped her hands. "I thought she'd want to be alone, but no, Marci insists on speaking to you." She cut her eyes to Pat Bigelow, cleared her throat. "I told her you were here, Ms. Bigelow, that you would make sure the chief didn't bother her, but she said she wanted to see him alone."

And you don't want that, Jack thought.

Pat Bigelow said, "I don't think that's such a good idea, Mrs. Hildebrand." And she walked toward Jack. "Shall we, Chief?"

Jack saw no hope for it and nodded.

Mrs. Hildebrand trailed along behind them up the stairs. When they reached the bedroom door, Jack asked Mrs. Hildebrand to wait outside. Pat Bigelow nodded to her. He knocked lightly, then went into the bedroom. It must have been Marci Maynard's room for many years. It had stayed a teenager's room, very girlie-girl, with lots of pink and white and rock star posters from ten years ago. And watercolors, mostly sailboats, like her work on the walls downstairs.

Marci Maynard was propped up in bed, wearing a bathrobe, her hair pulled back in a ponytail. Her eyes were swollen from crying, and without makeup. She was as pale as the white bedroom walls. She was a big-boned woman, like her father, solid and fit, about thirty, with her mother's vague gray eyes. She looked ten years older than the last time he'd seen her, only this morning. But her gaze was focused, no drugs. Good.

Then she looked at Pat Bigelow. "I told my mother I wanted to see Chief Wolf alone."

Pat Bigelow's voice was gentle. "I'm here to make sure you're not harassed, Mrs. Maynard."

"Please leave. I don't need any protection."

"But—"

Marci Maynard stared her down. Pat Bigelow gave Jack a long look, shrugged, and said over her shoulder as she left, "I'll be downstairs with your parents."

"Good," Marci said when Jack closed the bedroom door. "I've never liked her."

Jack wanted to pursue that, but not now. He thanked her for seeing him and expressed his condolences. She was quiet, but alert.

He pulled up a chair beside the bed and straddled it, his arms over the back. "Tell me, Mrs. Maynard, do you know where your husband was all night?"

He saw her consider a lie, saw the instant she knew it wouldn't fly. She shrugged, looked him dead in the eye. "We had an argument. He slammed out of the house about nine o'clock. I went to bed at ten, after watching a rerun of *Alias*. When the alarm rang this morning, I saw that he hadn't come home. I was really mad, Chief Wolf, really mad. I made coffee, went out to get the newspaper, through the garage. I saw him lying on the garage floor, between the cars." She looked faintly disconnected. "There was blood splattered all over the Mercedes. It's white, you know. It looked sort of like a postmodern painting. I remember thinking it reminded me of Randolph Crier's work. I remember thinking Jason loves that car, he'll be—" Her eyes misted up again. "Then I realized he was dead and he won't care now, will he?"

Jack kept his voice low and calm. "No, he won't care now. You never awoke during the night?"

"No, I'm a sound sleeper."

"Tell me what you fought about, Mrs. Maynard."

Again, an instant when she considered a lie, and then she said, "Who cares who knows the truth now? The thing is, Jason had a girlfriend over in Cloverdale."

"And her name is . . . ?"

Marci Maynard shook her head. "I have no idea. I never wanted to know. I'll bet everyone knows her name but me."

"Including your parents?"

"My father, certainly. My father knows everything. When I was growing up, I could never get away with anything. He always found out. Always. My mother? If she knows, she'd force herself to lock it away, real deep."

"How do you know his girlfriend lives in Cloverdale?"

She frowned, looked down at her hands. "I suppose I must have heard someone say something about Jason going over to Cloverdale a lot these days. Yes, that's it."

"Who said that?"

"I don't remember. Ask my dad, he probably knows all about it, like I said."

"I'll ask him. How long was this affair going on?"

Marci pleated the white chenille bedspread. "Maybe three months, give or take."

"How did you find out about it?"

"A wife knows, Chief Wolf. A wife always knows. There doesn't have to be lipstick on a shirt collar. Jason was different, in bed, out of bed. I knew, and last night, he admitted it when I accused him."

"Had you spoken to him about this before your fight last night?"

"No."

"Why?"

"Last night was the very first time he wanted to leave during the evening. He even made up this stupid lie about seeing a client so he could get away. Like I said, he'd never done that before. I couldn't very well ignore it any longer, now could I? So I called him on it."

"He admitted to the affair but he didn't tell you her name."

"No, he didn't, and believe me, I asked him several times. But he did go on with the usual crap about how she was the one who really understood him, who gave him what he needed. I'll be honest here, Chief Wolf, if I'd had a gun I might have shot him, right there in the middle of the living room." She paused a moment, looking toward her white-lace-curtained window. She looked up at him again. "If I had, then at least at his funeral, we could still tell it was Jason."

That was surely the truth. "Were you ever tempted to get back at him, Mrs. Maynard? To have an affair yourself? Maybe a brief one? For revenge?"

She looked at him straight on. "Yes, I thought about it. In fact, I even cruised the Night Owl last week, half looking to see if there was a guy there for me, a guy bigger and better looking than Jason. I didn't see anyone who interested me. Then I realized how stupid it was."

"You play golf, Mrs. Maynard?"

She nodded. "Most everyone we know plays golf."

"Did either of you own Callaways?"

"My clubs are Titleist. Jason wouldn't ever let me touch his Pings."

"Where do you keep your golf clubs?"

"They're in the front hallway closet along with a pile of athletic junk Jason never used." She looked up at him blankly. "I wonder what the etiquette is about selling his sports stuff?"

Was she so bitter that not even his murder mattered? He asked her abruptly, "Mrs. Maynard, did you kill your husband?"

She flattened her back against the bed headboard. "No! Of course I didn't!"

"Who do you think killed him?"

"I don't know, Chief. I'd ask that Cloverdale bimbo, whoever she is."

"Why?"

Her eyes glittered. "Because the bottom line is, Chief, that there was no way Jason was going to divorce me. He wanted my father's company, and I came with it. After what happened between us last night, he probably told her that. She realized he would never marry her and followed him back to the house. She could have brought the club with her."

Somehow Jack couldn't imagine the planning had such cold logic, not with the crazy rage the killer had shown.

"Do you know anyone who owns Callaway clubs?"

She thought a moment, at least he thought she was considering it. "Sure, I've seen lots of them at the club, but I can't think of anyone in particular right off the top of my head."

Jack walked back downstairs and found Milo Hildebrand in his study, alone. He gently closed the door.

"Milo, I see your wife isn't here."

"No. I asked Pat to take her to her doctor. Olivia didn't want to see you again."

"So you decided you didn't need to have Ms. Bigelow here to protect you?"

Milo laughed. "Not likely, Chief. What can I do for you?"

"You can tell me about Jason's affair. You can tell me the woman's name."

Milo Hildebrand sat behind his desk. He said nothing for a moment, just tapped his pen lightly against the desk blotter, a handsome dark green wood-and-leather affair.

"I wondered if Marci would tell you. Well, now that she has I suppose there's nothing to protect her from." He shrugged. "I have no clue who she is. Maybe she's a golfer at the club since he was killed with a driver." He nodded. "Yes, I know it wasn't one of Jason's. I did ask Jason about it, but he told me he was faithful to my daughter, swore he'd never hurt Marci. So unless I found out for sure he was lying to me, there was nothing I could do."

"But you suspected him before Marci knew for sure?"

"Yeah, I suppose I did. It was clear something was wrong between them. The fact is since Jason was a salesman, he spent a good deal of time outside the office. He could have seen her as often as he liked."

"Did you notice if his work suffered recently? Fewer sales, say, for the past three months?"

"No, if anything, I'd have to say they went up." He shrugged. "In fact I'd say Jason didn't seem to be suffering in any way before he died."

ELEVEN

Late Thursday afternoon Mary Lisa Beverly left the terminal of the Goddard Bay Regional Airport outside the small town of Inverness. It was only a fifteen-minute boat ride to Goddard Bay, or an hour's drive on the coast road that wove south, then skimmed the southern end of the bay to downtown Goddard Bay.

Mary Lisa felt good to be home, and a state away from the person who'd tried to run her down. Before she'd left Los Angeles, Detective Vasquez had brought her a list of 111 names of people who owned a 2000 LeSabre but she hadn't recognized any of them.

Only Lou Lou and Elizabeth and her agent at Trident Media knew where she'd gone. It was a relief to leave L.A., what with the *National Enquirer* and the *Star* carrying the photos Puker had snapped of her laid out on a gurney looking pathetic and dazed. The captions beneath the photos ranged from "Drunk Soap Star Hit by Passing Car" to "Mary Lisa Beverly Run Down by Angry Lover." If she'd seen Puker she would have tried to rip his throat out.

At least the photos were inside and not staring at the world from the cover.

At least her hip no longer looked like Australia. The massive bruise had retreated to the size of Mississippi, and all the vivid shades had muted. She'd taken off the last Band-Aid this morning and found she'd not needed any more makeup to cover the healing cuts and scrapes.

She drove her rented red Cadillac convertible down the narrow two-lane coast road, crossed a small bridge over a bay inlet, and headed down to the tiny hamlet of Berrytown, the beginning of her favorite part of the trip, the southern stretch of the coastline toward Goddard Bay.

She hadn't been home in three years and had to admit she was worried about how it would go. Still, some primal part of her recognized the air, the way it smelled, the way it settled on her skin. She breathed in deeply, enjoyed the warmth of the sun on her face, and knew that from one minute to the next, the rain could pour down, not at all like Southern California.

She drove slowly, even stopping once to take in the sand dunes that glowed golden beneath the afternoon sun.

When she turned onto Central Boulevard and stopped for her first red light, the first person she saw was Chief of Police Jack Wolf, a big man with a hard face and intense blue eyes that were too smart and seemed to see too much. He was walking purposefully, dressed in dark gray slacks, white shirt, no tie, and a dark brown leather jacket. He appeared deep in thought. And then, for no good reason, he looked up at the convertible, and saw her. He did a little double take, as if he couldn't believe who it was. His hard face seemed to turn to stone. He did not look like a happy man, definitely not ready to do handsprings at the sight of her. Well, big surprise there, not after he'd tossed her in jail before she'd left three years before. She gave him a sweet smile and a jaunty little wave, but she wasn't about to stop and have a nice little tête-à-tête with him.

Some things never changed, she thought, as she continued down Central Boulevard, past a good dozen downtown stores she'd known since she was a child, having arrived in Goddard Bay with her family at the age of five. She breathed in the clear, sharp bay air, glad she'd rented a convertible, and made a note to check out the new boutiques. The town seemed to be thriving with the growing tourist trade.

She waved at Peter Perlman, owner of Pete's Paint Store, who yelled a greeting at her and grinned his head off. His place was gossip central in town, so by nightfall everyone in Goddard Bay would know Mary Lisa Beverly was back.

She wondered as she drove toward her parents' house on Riverview Drive how her mother and sisters would greet her.

MARY Lisa walked the neat flagstone path to the front door, looking around her as she walked, as if checking out a set for a shoot. Nothing had changed. Her mother had always loved flowers, and they were still everywhere, bursting with wild color in the late spring, the scents of the roses mixing with the scent of the jasmine on the light breeze. At the entry, beside the beautifully stenciled glass doors, Mary Lisa touched her finger to the doorbell and wondered what role she would be called upon to play in this upcoming scene with her mother. The return of the prodigal daughter? No, that would require her mother to show a bit of joy at the sight of her. Well, who knew? It had been three years. Her father had visited her perhaps a dozen times in L.A., even helped her through the experience of buying her first house, in Malibu. But her mother had never come, not that she'd wanted her to. And she hadn't asked her father. She hadn't wanted him to have to make excuses.

So why did I come back here? Fact is, New York's lovely this time of year. So is London. So is Grapevine, Texas. People don't change, they simply become more so. And the problem with being gone for three years is that you forget the bone-deep hurt waiting for you until it's too late.

It was too late. She rang the doorbell again, and heard soft footfalls approaching.

The door opened. Her mother saw her daughter standing there, her hair windblown, big sunglasses covering half her face, the handle of the wheeled carry-on in her hand. There was a moment of silence, of bland scrutiny, and then, "Well, it's nice that you've come back, dear."

Not promising. Mary Lisa made no move to embrace the elegant woman who stood in front of her, the woman who was her mother. She wasn't stupid. She took off her sunglasses and slipped them into the bulging side of her hobo bag, which weighed five pounds on a light day, and gave her mother a big smile. "Would you be interested in some Tupperware, ma'am?"

"Sorry, dear," her mother said without pause, "all our storage containers are glass."

"That was a good line, Mother."

"Where do you think you got that mouth of yours?"

Hey, maybe we've got some softening here. At least some recognition. "How are you doing?"

Her mother looked at Mary Lisa's single carry-on and stepped back. "Do come in, dear, we can't have you standing there." Her mother turned away from her and walked toward the living room. She called out from the doorway, "Betty, would you please bring some tea and two cups? We have an unexpected visitor with a carry-on."

Unexpected visitor? Well, that was better than an unwelcome visitor, or maybe it was a euphemism. The living room looked the same as it had three years ago, with one new addition, a side chair with dark green satin upholstery that looked vaguely Regency, another jewel set in her mother's beautiful living room with the rest of her nineteenth-century English antiques. Mary Lisa sat down in it across from her mother. For the first time she saw faint lines of dissatisfaction around her mouth. What did her mother have to be unhappy about?

In that moment, looking around at the magnificent, light-filled living room with its precious old furniture, Mary Lisa saw herself as a girl, carefully polishing all those chairs, the two sofas, the precious marquetry table. She remembered stained fingers and criticism.

Mary Lisa said, "It's been a long time, Mom, too long. I don't have to go back until Sunday. I thought I'd come for a visit, see how everyone was doing."

"Everyone is fine. But of course you saw your father two months ago." Her mother frowned when Betty walked into the living room, carrying a tray holding more than the tea and two cups she'd ordered.

Betty Harmon said, "Oh, Mary Lisa, hello! It is so good to see you again. Mrs. Abrams heard your voice, said you loved her spice cake, and she was so happy that she had a bit left, just for you."

Betty stood beaming at Mary Lisa in the face of her mother's silence.

Mary Lisa was on her feet in an instant. She hugged Betty and leaned back to look down at all five feet two inches of her. "How wonderful to see you. Those dimples, how I always envied you those dimples." Her mother was waiting to lambaste her; Mary Lisa knew the signs. Even after three years of not having an occasion to even think about it, she threw herself into the breach as if she'd never been gone. She continued talking, nonsense really, while Betty poured tea, smiling and laughing, never took a breath while Betty sliced her a piece of spice cake, and finally turned to ask her mother if she'd like a slice. Her mother said, "That's quite enough, Mary Lisa. Betty, no cake for me. Now, Mary Lisa will be staying until Sunday, so if you would make certain her room is ready . . ." She raised a brow to her daughter. "This means three nights?"

Mary Lisa nodded, wishing she could simply get up, grab her suitcase and her slice of spice cake, and march back out the front door.

"Yes, ma'am." Betty turned and left the living room, seemingly oblivious of the displeasure in Mrs. Beverly's voice, but Mary Lisa knew she wasn't. Deaf or blind, you could still feel the freeze.

"Mrs. Abrams insists on making the spice cake for your father. No one else eats it. No one else likes it."

"Good, that means I get to finish it off before Dad gets home."

Kathleen Beverly was as tall as her daughter, and her black hair was cut in a bob and untouched by gray due to her hairdresser's diligence. She looked her daughter up and down. "I'm surprised you're eating that. I understand the camera adds ten pounds."

"That's true. Aren't I lucky I have Dad's genes?" She knew that even with a good dose of his genes, she still had to watch what she ate, and exercise like mad, but she didn't feel like conceding the point. "He's eaten everything in sight for as long as I can remember and never gains an ounce."

Her mother nodded, not looking all that happy about it. Mary Lisa didn't blame her.

She gave her mother a sunny smile. "He told me once that he and I were aliens and that I'd surely bless him when I grew up. He was right, I do. Is Kelly engaged yet to her Prince Charming? She e-mailed me about him."

TWELVE

Her mother started to say something, but suddenly held it back, with an expression not unlike a soap actor's before a commercial break. What was this about? Mary Lisa prodded a bit. "She was excited, said he was rich and handsome, and not a sleaze like the guys down in L.A. She ended it with 'I might marry him, who knows?'"

Mary Lisa had said enough. She knew a minefield when she saw one. Had Prince Charming's crown lost its luster? Had he belched at dinner? Or worse, said something distressingly common in her mother's hearing?

Her mother sipped her tea, shrugged indifferently.

"Kelly called it off, two days ago."

"Goodness, why?"

"I believe she called him a controlling jerk."

"That's a surprise. She sure was high on him last week. What happened?"

"Who knows? Sometimes a girl's blinders come off before it's too late."

"Who is this jerk? Is he local? She never told me his name."

"John Goddard."

"John Goddard. Hmmm. I think I remember him, at least I remember his name. I was pretty young when he left to go back east to college, right?"

"That's right. It's a pity he turned out to be unsatisfactory since his family is one of *the* families in the area. They own a good deal of property and business interests in and around Goddard Bay. At first your father and I were very pleased, but apparently he didn't suit her." She looked toward the fireplace and frowned.

Mary Lisa wondered why Kelly had really changed her mind. Most girls, and especially Kelly, could tell whether a guy was a jerk pretty fast—it wasn't usually a sudden epiphany.

Maybe this John Goddard was a selfish lover, that would certainly be a deal breaker, even qualify him as a jerk.

She said, "Kelly's young and pretty, there'll be lots of men who come her way."

"Yes, of course. After Jared, we thought—well, never mind that. It's water under the bridge."

"What bridge? Who's Jared?"

Her mother flapped her hands. "Oh, all right. Jared Hennessey was a mistake, nothing more, over quickly. He's gone, moved out of town. She's quite over him. I think Kelly's grown to be as beautiful as Monica. Maybe even more so. She has her degree in communications from Oregon State University, an excellent field, and she could do anything she wants to do. She could be an actress like you if she wanted to, so many people have told her that after they've watched you on TV. But I don't think she would be happy in Los Angeles—it's so plastic and cheap and they expect the women to be whores to get anywhere."

Mary Lisa absorbed the multiple blows without a whimper. It had been three years and yet it seemed like yesterday.

Nothing ever changed—sad, but true. But the difference now was that she had thicker skin. She said easily, "I believe the whore part had some truth to it in the bad old days, for both men and women actually."

"How pathetic." Her mother picked up her teacup and looked over the rim at her middle daughter, one corner of her mouth curled up in a hint of a smile. "Aren't you going to ask about Monica?"

"How is Monica doing?"

"She getting ready to run for the Oregon House of Representatives."

I've fallen into the Twilight Zone. "Monica, a politician? Her degree is in art history. She's hardly even voted."

"So what? She's gorgeous, bright, and knows how to get what she wants. The incumbent's weak, too old for the energy it takes to get things done, and has broken his promises too many times now." That sounded memorized, like she was spouting the party line.

"There are—what, sixty state representatives, if I remember my civics class?"

Her mother nodded. "Yes, two-year terms. They meet on the second Monday in January in odd years. The sessions usually last about six months, but she'll be serving on interim committees after that to study issues scheduled to come up in the next legislative session. She wouldn't have to spend all her time in Salem."

Mary Lisa agreed with her mother. Monica would make an excellent politician. It wasn't any calling for public service, it was the draw of power and notoriety that would be attracting her sister. Monica had always wanted to be standing in the spotlight, center stage, more than Mary Lisa. Now that she considered it, Monica and politics were a perfect fit. "She'll be good. She's ambitious and focused and she's tough."

"The Board of County Commissioners certainly think she's a strong candidate. They're saying she could be a state senator by the time she's thirty-five. I'm glad to see you're over your snit with her, Mary Lisa."

Mary Lisa cocked her head slightly to one side and put on her best poker face. "What snit would that be, Mother?"

"Your resentment of your sister ever since she married Mark Bridges. It's time you got over it and moved on."

What was she to say to that? Of course there was some truth to it. She remembered what an infatuated twit she'd been, ready to leave L.A. and her brand-new role as Sunday Cavendish on *Born to Be Wild*, forget all about an acting career for the dubious privilege of becoming Mark Bridges's wife, move back to Goddard Bay and—what? Thank the good Lord that noodle-brained, rudderless Mary Lisa Beverly no longer existed. She seemed like a stranger from another lifetime. Mark Bridges was as handsome as Brad Pitt playing Achilles but without the rough edges. No, he was as smooth as a rock in a creek bed, and, unfortunately, faithless as a French ally. Had she really been that stupid, that recently? Yes, she had, but that was before she became a bonafide grown-up, even if she did have some goo left in her otherwise solid center. Mary Lisa smiled, a joyous, full-bodied smile, and sat forward a little. "Between us, Mother, let me tell you that I send endless thanks heavenward that Monica took Mark away from me. Imagine if I'd married him before he betrayed me." She actually shuddered.

Her mother's voice was sharp. "You make it sound inevitable, his betrayal."

"I think he's that kind of man."

"That's your bitterness talking, Mary Lisa, your envy. Mark would never betray Monica. He worships her. Nor was it really betrayal. After all, you weren't married, and that was the whole point. There were no vows to break. He married Monica; he would never look at another woman now."

Mary Lisa grinned. "If he did, Monica would cut off his b—ah, she'd make him sorry he was ever born."

Red stained her mother's cheeks. "Is that the way you talk down in Los Angeles?"

"Well, it seems to be the way everyone speaks most everywhere unless they're with their mothers and then they catch themselves. As I did."

Her mother swiftly got to her feet, smoothed down her lovely cream linen slacks. "We eat dinner at six. You'll need time to get yourself together, Mary Lisa. You can go up now." She nodded and left the living room. Mary Lisa slowly ate some more spice cake. *Welcome home, Mary Lisa.* She wondered yet again as she climbed the stairs what had brought her here from L.A. Maybe it was some vague sense she'd be safe at home. Well, perhaps her body might be safer here, but not her spirit.

THIRTEEN

"He's a bastard."

You said that already, Mary Lisa thought, but she nodded dutifully. She was beginning to wish John Goddard had never been born, much less swum into her sister's waters. She'd already listened to a five-minute harangue and it showed no signs of winding down. "He's a dreadful lover, selfish, rolls off and snores like a bull. And all he does is work, work, work. I never saw him and if I called him at his office, he was rude, or had his secretary kiss me off with some excuse about his being in court or meeting with investigators or a defense attorney or some scummy criminal. Always another criminal, no end to them. I heard Mr. Millsom—you remember, Mary Lisa, the lawyer—he said John Goddard didn't care about right or wrong anyway, just winning, about carving notches on his belt. Mr. Millsom said it's pure ambition and he'll do anything, including prosecuting innocent people, to get ahead."

"Hmm."

"I can't believe I ever saw anything in him."

"He sounds pretty bad, all right. Mother said he was crude and controlling, didn't like you being independent."

"Sure. That goes without saying. He works with lowlifes all day, naturally he'd become crude."

"You mean other lawyers?"

"Ha ha. Yes, His Highness expected me to be at his beck and call, as if he thought I'd stay in my apartment until he announced what he wanted to do."

"What apartment? I thought you were living here."

"Jared and I moved to an apartment. Then I kicked him out. I kept the apartment, but after I broke it off with John two days ago, I decided I'd stay here for a while."

"So tell me about Jared."

"Jared Hennessey. You never met him. He talked me into eloping with him, but he turned out to be a con who only wanted to get to Daddy's money. I just saw through him a little late. He's gone now and I really don't like to talk about him anymore."

"You were *married* to this guy? I mean, he was your husband?"

"Yeah, for all of two weeks, then *poof*, it was over."

And no one bothered to tell me, Mary Lisa thought, *not even Kelly.*

"He works out too much, Mary Lisa. I'd want to go to a movie or a restaurant, but no, he wanted to work out, or run, claimed it de-stressed him. He thought only about himself."

"Jared Hennessey?"

"No, John Goddard."

"Okay. Well, it's too bad you didn't notice all this bad stuff—about John Goddard—until after you'd slept with him."

To her surprise, Kelly looked down at her Ferragamo-clad feet, then shoved her hands into the pockets of her black slacks. "Yeah, well, I didn't get pregnant, no thanks to him."

Now this was serious. "You mean he refused to wear a condom?"

Kelly jumped to her feet. "I'm hungry. You sure are skinny, Mary Lisa. Oh yeah, did you know? Mom called Monica, asked her to dinner. With Mark of course. You're not going to make a scene, are you?"

Oh joy. Mary Lisa shook her head. "Nope. I left all my scenes in L.A." She shoved her sister out of her bedroom and shut the door.

Kelly had been very busy. But why had she moved back home? To lick her wounds? But wouldn't their mother be all over her? Well, maybe not. She'd see about that at dinner.

She hadn't brought any dress-up clothes with her. Her mother would notice. Did she care?

If Mary Lisa had harbored the notion she could make it unscathed through a meal with her entire family plus her ex-fiancé, Mark Bridges, she knew now she'd been as bright as a Russian lightbulb. Three years was a long time, but since it appeared that no one and nothing ever changed, it ended up being like yesterday. The pot was still bubbling gaily under the lid.

MARY Lisa chewed slowly and lovingly on a blackened shrimp so deliciously hot and spicy it set her mouth to smoking. Mrs. Abrams had studied Creole cooking under Paul Prudhomme himself. Mary Lisa couldn't imagine the great man preparing the shrimp any better.

She sipped a crisp dry Chardonnay, one of her father's favorites, as she listened to her sister Monica talk about a cocktail party in Salem that the party bigwigs were throwing in her honor in a couple of weeks to introduce her to the important political rollers. "But most of the money's in Portland," she said. "Mark knows enough of the big-money people there to give us a start." She gave him a tender look, lightly touched her fingertips to his cheek, and then she smiled across the table at Mary Lisa.

"She can charm lemon juice out of an onion," Mark said. He toasted his wife, taking her hand and kissing her palm.

You obnoxious snake, Mary Lisa thought, *you shed your skin so well, I'll bet no one ever notices all the rot you leave lying in your wake.*

She caught herself, surprised her feelings were still so strong. She'd perhaps expected some lingering rage, perhaps a dollop of remembered humiliation, but no, this was bone-deep disgust. How nice. She gave all her attention to her father, George Beverly. Ah, but he was handsome, tall, lean, auburn haired, with eyes so blue that some people who met him for the first time thought they might be colored contacts. She watched her father continue the conversation with his eldest daughter. "What do you think your opponent will do? Might he retire?"

Bless her father for giving her his wonderful voice— melodic, light and dark by turns, always compelling. She remembered how he could always talk her and her sisters out of teenage snits. As if he felt her staring at him, he looked up and smiled. She gave him a thumbs-up. He was dressed in black slacks, a fine white chambray shirt, and an Italian geometric tie. She'd always thought he was the finest-looking Beverly. To the best of her knowledge he'd never strayed from her mother, though he owned one of the largest construction companies in northwestern Oregon and had spent nearly all of his fifty-five years surrounded by women at home, where all her mother's friends congregated, playing bridge late, she knew, so they could see him when he got home from work. He'd been the only boy in a gaggle of five sisters, and then the father of three girls. His mother, Aurora, had given both her son and her granddaughter her red hair and blue eyes, and her height. And her acting ability as well had come through to Mary Lisa, thank the good Lord. Aurora had never been in a movie or on Broadway, but she'd always acted in local theater productions in Seattle. When Mary Lisa was five years old, her grandmother introduced her to the stage. It had been a love affair since that first magic moment when she'd looked at Bottom lying in mountains of soft greenery with beautiful Titania cooing over him, feeding him peeled grapes. Such a wonderful memory. Monica's voice brought her back as she answered her father, "Champ Kuldak ready to retire? I don't think so, Dad. I doubt he'd willingly retire until they bury his carcass. But you're right, he's old enough to retire and fish or putter in a garden, whatever old men do. And after all these years, he's finally vulnerable. I don't think he's going to do much. Rest on his record that's mediocre at best?"

Mary Lisa saw the brief ironic smile play over her father's face, but he said nothing, only nodded. He turned to look at Mary Lisa. "As you can see, we've got lots of excitement going on here. I'm very glad you're home, honey. It's been too long and my Porsche is running a bit rough. Would you take a look at it?"

"At least it's running," she said, and laughed. "I'll bet you it's the plugs again. You and plugs, you've never learned to rub along well together." She sat forward. "Do you guys know that when Dad visited me a couple of months ago, everyone wanted to know who the movie star was, and wanted to meet him?"

"How embarrassing for you, George," Kathleen said with a delicate shudder.

"Not at all. I basked in the attention from all of Mary Lisa's young friends. An old guy like me loves to have a couple of pretty girls smile at him."

Mary Lisa laughed. "More like a dozen pretty girls, Dad." She looked up at her sisters and Mark. "When I took him to the gym with me and my friends, I thought some of the women were going to jump him."

Monica and Kelly beamed, but Kathleen frowned. Her husband said in a light voice, smiling toward his wife, "I tried not to sweat too much."

Mary Lisa laughed again. "It's great to see you, too, Dad. Don't worry about your precious Porsche. I'll look at it before you go to the office tomorrow morning." She knew he was probably the only one in this elegant dining room who really loved her, and not only because she was the only one who was his female double in her coloring and body. They had spent so much time together when she was a girl that she could lay tile, set a window, fix a toilet, hang wallpaper with no visible seams, and coax his Porsche into running like it had when she was ten years old, the same year her grandmother had told her she was a born actress, shortly before she'd died of breast cancer.

It seemed the only thing her mother had given her was her supercilious eyebrows, which, as it turned out, Sunday Cavendish used often to excellent effect. Monica and Kelly, though, strongly resembled their mother—dark hair and eyes and willowy builds. Except Kelly was streaking her hair now. It was charming and sexy.

George Beverly said to Monica, "I hope you won't spoil it for us, Monica. I've found over the years I rather like seeing both our federal and state governments gridlocked. That way it's harder for the nincompoops to hurt us."

Kathleen said, voice sharp, "Your daughter is not a nincompoop."

Monica opened her mouth and shut it. Mary Lisa knew she wasn't about to argue with anything her father said because she wanted money from him. Monica wasn't stupid.

Mark laughed, his eyes on Mary Lisa. "True enough, sir, but at least if she does become a nincompoop, she'll be the most beautiful of all of them. And Monica is your daughter after all. Maybe she'll stay above the money-grubbing powermongers." He continued seamlessly. "Mary Lisa, I haven't congratulated you yet for all your success on *Born to Be Wild*. And you won another Emmy. Fabulous. I read in *Variety* you're considered something of a phenomenon—the bitchier they make you, the more over-the-top you are, the more popular you become."

Kathleen raised her now famous eyebrows in an incredulous and pitying look. "You actually read that sleaze, Mark dear?" Mary Lisa found herself studying her expression, and decided it was extraordinarily effective. Sunday should definitely take on that look.

Mark shrugged. "Naturally I'm interested in what Mary Lisa's doing. But I haven't quite stooped to buying the soap opera fanzines in the checkout line at the supermarket, except if Mary Lisa's on the cover."

Kelly said, "That's because you never go to the supermarket, Mark. Hey, Mary Lisa, even I didn't know you were on a cover of *Soap Opera Digest* last month until Heddy at the beauty shop mentioned it."

Mary Lisa smiled in acknowledgment, but said nothing. It had been a fun shoot. Nor was she going to tell them that she'd be on one of the weekly covers again this month since she'd won the Emmy—she shared the cover with Bernie. The shoot had been a hoot.

Monica seemed bored as she took a delicate bite of her Caesar salad, frowned at a crouton, and gently shoved it to the side of the salad bowl.

Kathleen said smoothly, "Of course we're all happy for your success, Mary Lisa. But a soap opera—for heaven's sake, where did that ridiculous name come from? A soap opera just fills up the day for bored housewives—well, I hope after leaving this part you'll find some more meaningful parts. Isn't it difficult to be prancing around like that, dressed like a tart, sleeping with every man in sight?"

Mary Lisa felt her stomach knot, but said easily, blessed humor coming from somewhere, "Goodness, Mother. Why don't you tell us how you really feel?"

Her father burst into laughter. "Bored housewives? You know, Kathy, in our main office, the TV goes on religiously every day at eleven o'clock with a viewership upwards of a dozen people. We call it our soap brunch hour. And everyone cheers when they see Mary Lisa. I love to watch you, sweetheart, and of course to try to figure out who will end up marrying whom with every new season."

Mary Lisa nodded. "Too true. An unwritten rule is that the writers give a newly married couple about six months of marital bliss before they start messing with them."

Kathleen was staring at her husband. "When did you start watching television at your office?"

Her father's eyebrows went up. "I thought I'd told you, Kathy. The TV arrived the day Mary Lisa first started on *Born to Be Wild*."

"A lovely big-screen, Dad?"

"It's a forty-five-inch," he said and laughed.

Kelly looked her sister in the eye. "And look what happened when you accepted that part, Mary Lisa. While you were down there, poor Mark was up here, all alone. Except for Monica. Was it six months before Monica messed you two up?"

FOURTEEN

"Is there ever anything you decide not to say, Kelly?" Monica asked.

Mary Lisa looked thoughtful. "How very odd. It *was* about six months, as I remember. Wasn't it, Mark?"

"Maybe," Mark said, unperturbed, a small smile playing around his mouth. "Six months, Monica?"

"This is ridiculous," Kathleen said. "Stop it, all of you. It is not funny."

George said, nodding, "I agree with your mother. Drop it. Now, sometimes I'm in a meeting or up to my ears in a project, and I can't watch with everyone else. I'll hear cheering or groans or boos from the outer office. Most clients who come in know exactly who you are and want to take a break, watch the show too. Rain or shine, I see you most every day, sweetheart."

"I just hope it doesn't reflect on us," Kathleen said with a shrug.

"Why, of course it does. Everyone greatly enjoys watching our daughter perform so splendidly."

Rarely in her nearly twenty-eight years had Mary Lisa heard that hard a voice out of her father. She'd heard it out of Sunday Cavendish, however, a goodly number of times. She cleared her throat. "The fact is, Mom, whether or not you like or even approve of soap operas, a whole lot of people do. Upwards of twenty actors and five different crews work very hard to produce about thirty-eight minutes of airtime for a one-hour show. They're incredible professionals and I'm still learning from them every day. Did you know we have four different directors?"

"Four directors?" Kelly said, sitting forward. "Why?"

"There's simply too much happening for any fewer than four. You could come down and visit the set—you're all officially invited—and see how everything works."

Monica nodded. "Thank you, Mary Lisa. I'll definitely come down if I can ever find the time. I really have been wondering about something, though—why do they do your makeup so heavy sometimes? You're a woman who's supposed to be heading up a big corporation, and sometimes they make you look like a high-priced hooker with those dresses you wear."

"Yep, too much cleavage for the boardroom, that's for sure. Fact is, it's part of Sunday Cavendish's persona. She's sophisticated and worldly, rich and ruthless as a snake. She does what she wants and that includes pushing the envelope with her clothes. I really like her, actually. She's got guts."

Mrs. Abrams said from the doorway, "I think you're the most beautiful girl on the show, Mary Lisa, nearly as beautiful as your daddy."

George Beverly choked, spewed wine out of his mouth.

"That's the truth," Kelly said. "Get over it, Dad."

Mrs. Abrams never looked away from Mary Lisa. "I love to guess what new trouble Sunday is going to stir up. But you know, I sure hope she doesn't sleep with her sister's husband. No matter what she thinks of her sister and her mother, she still wouldn't sleep with her sister's louse of a husband. Would she?"

That innocently dropped bomb rendered the table markedly silent for a moment until Mary Lisa laughed. "I happen to agree with you. Who knows what the writers will do, Mrs. Abrams? I'll be sure to pass along what you think."

She looked up to see Mark staring at her, and there was something in his expression that disturbed her to her toes, something like regret, maybe.

Monica said, "Kelly, I hear you broke up with John Goddard and moved back home. What happened?"

Kelly shrugged. "I decided I'd had enough of him. He was going to push marriage soon. No way, not after that fiasco with Jared."

Monica arched a perfect brow. "Oh? *You* had enough of *him*? That isn't what I heard. A friend of mine was having dinner at the Beijing a couple of nights ago, saw you there with John, heard a bit of a scene before Jack Wolf came in to rescue him."

Before Kelly leaped over the table to go for her sister's throat, George pinned her in place with a look, then turned to Mary Lisa. "Did your mother tell you about our local murder?"

Mary Lisa shook her head.

"Jason Maynard, Marci Hildebrand's husband, was beaten to death early this week, found by his wife in the garage."

Kathleen said, "It's awful. Marci's mother, as all of you know—Olivia Hildebrand—is one of my best friends. She's in awful shape, understandably torn up about it, and the police don't yet know who killed poor Jason. I know it was a burglar of some sort, had to be."

Mary Lisa said, "I'm very sorry, Mother. Mrs. Hildebrand always seemed like a nice person. A murder. It seems impossible, not here in Goddard Bay."

Her father grunted, but didn't look up from his wineglass, simply continued to roll the crystal in his palms. She saw her mother frown at him.

What was that about?

Her father looked up at his wife. "I'm sorry that Olivia is involved in this, Kathy. It's got to be difficult for you."

"More so for her. Jack Wolf won't let her alone. She said Marci told him Jason was having an affair, but he hasn't found out who the other woman is. Livie said it was probably some bimbo over in Cloverdale." Her mother shrugged. "I suppose it must be true."

Kelly said, "Of course it's true. Jason was a man, he was good looking, he dressed nice. He and Marci were married for nearly three years, and fact was, he was quite a bit more attractive than Marci. How long have you and Mark been married now, Monica?"

"Just because John Goddard kissed you off is no reason to be nasty," Monica said. "Mark, would you please pass the green beans? Mrs. Abrams does them so nicely, don't you agree, Mother?"

"Yes, she does," Kathleen said, ignoring Kelly. "Mary Lisa said she's staying until Sunday."

"Well, that'll be nice," Monica said. She looked thoughtful. "So maybe we can do something Saturday night." She didn't pursue it.

Mary Lisa sat back in her chair. Monica was running for office, Kelly had been dumped by John Goddard—not vice versa—and there had been a murder in Goddard Bay. Her mother was still a champ at slice and dice, and Mark was still—she didn't know what he was, only that she was now appalled that she'd ever believed herself in love with the man. And here she'd thought she'd be bored.

As Mary Lisa finally climbed into bed that night, Kelly opened the door and poked her head in. "Mark was giving you the eyeball. It's like you're no longer interested in him and he can't stand it. And you're a celebrity. Every man wants a girl who's a celebrity, it's like they think you put on your panty hose differently or something. I thought Monica was going to leap over the table and stick a knife in your heart."

"There was no eyeball, Kelly. And I'm such a minor celebrity that nobody thinks about my panty hose."

Kelly shrugged and looked down at her pretty pink toe-nails. "What Monica said, it really wasn't like that. John Goddard really is a bastard."

"I'll take your word for it. What you need to think about is what you want to do now. How long are you going to stay here?"

"Oh, I'll probably move back to my apartment next week sometime. Good night, Mary Lisa. By the way, Mark was definitely giving you the eyeball." She left, her laughter floating behind her.

FIFTEEN

The ocean breeze was fresh and sharp on Mary Lisa's face as she ran along the dirt path above the beach beside Cape Peeley Highway. The smell of surf and seaweed was strong in the air, and a light blanket of fog stretched over the water like a gray veil.

What she should do, Mary Lisa had thought grimly before she fell asleep last night, was fly back to L.A. this very afternoon and move in with Detective Vasquez until he found the loon who had clipped her with his LeSabre.

But that was last night, when everything seemed dark and more unpleasant than a dentist visit. But now she was smiling. It was a beautiful day, full of fresh possibilities.

She kept her breathing steady and deep. A light sheen of sweat covered her. She felt good. Running always made her feel good, and she knew she didn't have to worry about a big car coming out of the mist to run her down.

She'd fixed her father's Porsche. The plugs, it was always the plugs with her father, not the temperamental electrical system, as if he didn't know that.

Time to punch it up. She engaged her rockets and very nearly ran right into the man. It was the sudden pounding of his running shoes that made her swerve sharply at the last instant; she stopped and swung around to look at him.

The man had swerved as well. She bent over, her hands on her thighs, breathing hard.

"Hi," he said, not much out of breath.

She raised her head, smiled. "Hi, yourself. Sorry I nearly ran you down. My endorphins were screaming to be free. The thing is, though, you give them a mile and they want two."

"No problem. I wasn't paying any attention either. I was off in never-never land. Thing about endorphins, sometimes they don't kick in and you collapse in your tracks."

She cocked her head at him. He looked familiar, but she couldn't place him. She said, "That was pretty good. Odd that neither of us saw the other. My endorphins and I have been known to flatten people who get in our way."

He laughed. "Not this morning. Hey, we're the only two people up and virtuous. I'm usually running with a friend, but he had too much on his plate this morning. It's nice to have company." He stuck out his hand. "I'm John Goddard."

She stared at him, nonplussed. The controlling jerk? The founder's great-great whatever? She shook his hand, studied his face. "I remember you now. I was thirteen years old when you went back east to school."

He looked at the bright red hair pulled back in a ponytail, the face clean of makeup, and recognized the smile that lit up the daytime TV screen as much as it did a foggy beach. "You're Mary Lisa Beverly, George and Kathleen's daughter. You hadn't left for L.A. yet when I came back here, but we never ran into each other."

"No, a pity. Where'd you go to college?"

"Princeton." He grinned. "You?"

"I went down to UCLA. Even when I was eighteen, I wanted to act. What'd you do then?"

"You have seventeen questions left."

"Sorry, but I do have my reasons for being so nosy."

"Okay. I went to law school. And yes, you're right. I'm the John Goddard who was seeing your sister Kelly until very recently. Kelly told me about your other sister Monica's husband leaving you at the altar and you moving permanently to L.A. You were really quite lucky, you know? You want to run with me?"

"Whoa, that's quite a lot you said there, Mr. Goddard."

"John."

"Regardless, Mark didn't exactly leave me at the altar."

"Does it still sting? Kelly said it was close enough to altar-time that they could have penciled through your name on the wedding invitations and written in Monica's." He grinned down at her, but not all that far. He was maybe six-two, but with heels she'd be nearly nose to nose with him. To go with that nice height, he had a good strong body, muscular torso and legs.

She burst into laughter. "Now that makes for a visual."

"Oh yeah."

"Why do you think I'm lucky?"

"Run with me and I'll tell you."

She gave him a whimsical look and turned with him to run south, back along the highway toward the hamlet of Stoddart. Mary Lisa was soon running smoothly beside him.

"Kelly said you worked out and ran to de-stress."

"That, and I enjoy being outside, especially here by the ocean. You?"

"Actually, this is my first run in a week, since I—"

"Since you what?"

"Well, there was an incident of sorts where I live and I was out of exercise commission until today."

A dark eyebrow shot up as he glanced at her. "What kind of incident?"

"Just a minor injury. Why do you think I'm lucky Mark dumped me?"

He ran silently for a moment, his eyes fastened on the outjutting promontory a quarter of a mile ahead. He said finally, "I don't think Mark Bridges is the type of guy to stick."

"Ah," she said.

"Ah, what?"

"And you think you're the type of guy who sticks?"

He kept running, and she saw he was thinking about that, seriously. "I guess your sister wouldn't think so, but—"

"But what?"

"If I found the right person, I'd stick."

"Hmm. Maybe the same is true with Mark. I have to say you're not particularly acting like a controlling jerk so far."

"What was that? Oh—I guess I should have known Kelly wouldn't sing my praises to her sister. I'm trying to think of a single person I control—you can't count people who work for you, that's a job. I wish I could think of one, but I can't."

"Earth to Mr. Goddard. Listen up. Kelly told me she kind of left you at the altar because you're a controlling jerk. It gives us something in common. Both of us kissed off, I mean."

He opened his mouth, shut it, and kicked up his stride. It took her a moment to catch up to him.

"I'm sorry. That was insensitive of me. Since this just happened you might still be hurting."

"I might," he said, not turning.

"Okay, it's none of my business. Why did you come back to Goddard Bay?"

"I told you, I'm a lawyer."

"Accept my condolences."

"Actually, I came back to run for district attorney."

"Yes, I know about that. You got it on your first try?"

He nodded. "I've got a good name around here, the right name." He gave her a lopsided grin. "At least right enough to be elected the Goddard Bay County district attorney. I like putting bad guys away and I like living here."

"Aren't you awfully young to be a D.A.? Do you have any experience?"

"Sure. I was an assistant D.A. in Manhattan for four years, and before that I clerked with an appellate court judge, Judge David Reed, in the Ninth Circuit."

"Well, then, it sounds like you're qualified for the job to me."

He inclined his head. "Thank you."

"Are you having fun?"

"Fun? I never thought of it that way—well, okay, yeah, I really enjoy it, particularly most of the time I spend in the courtroom."

"Sounds like you're as much an actor as I am."

"Could be," he said after a moment." He stopped. "You want to take a rest before we turn around and run back?"

"Where?"

"Over here. See that twisted pine? I like that the sea's nearly bowled it over onto itself."

As she followed him to the bent pine, he said over his shoulder, "I'm not a controlling jerk."

"Maybe not." Mary Lisa leaned her back against the tree and he hunched down beside her. "I thought it was either that or maybe a dud in bed. That would be a sure deal breaker for Kelly."

He looked appalled. "Hmm," was all he said.

Mary Lisa thought of Mark Bridges, her ex-fiancé, and a couple of wannabe movie stars she'd dated pretty seriously over the past three years. "I've come to the conclusion that most good-looking men are so self-absorbed no one really exists for them outside themselves. Their pleasure's what's important, no one else's."

"I'd say the same about some good-looking women. Take you, for instance, Ms. Beverly. Are you a dud in bed because you're beautiful and self-absorbed?"

She laughed. "Yep, that's me, so beautiful, I'm self-absorbed. I'm going back now. Good-bye, Mr. Goddard."

She was off and running before he got to his feet. He didn't try to catch her, just stood for a while by that gnarly old tree and watched her until she disappeared in the distance.

Just his damned luck. The beauty queen was Kelly's sister.

SIXTEEN

"I wonder why the killer would leave a perfectly good driver there lying beside the body," Kelly said at dinner that night. "Surely he—or she—knew it would be a big clue for Jack Wolf."

George said, "I spoke with John today. His office is deeply involved now. He's got two very good investigators on his staff and Jack agreed to use them. You're right about that Callaway. I'm glad I don't own any."

"Are you still using Nikes, Dad?"

"I'm a Tiger fan—what else would I use?"

Kathleen said, "Olivia told me that Jack won't leave them alone. She says he's going to arrest one of them because he can't very well let this go unsolved. She doesn't know what to do."

"She needn't worry too much since Milo hired Patricia Bigelow," Kelly said. "The rumor is she was there for the very first interview with the Hildebrand family. She's a barracuda."

George nodded. "I hope if I'm ever sued, she's not the opposing counsel—she's very bright, committed, as intense as they come. I've sometimes thought it a pity that Horace is such a longtime friend and only a middling lawyer. I'd hire her in an instant."

Kelly said, "Detective Lambrowski, who's an investigator in the D.A.'s office, said she was hinting at a police conspiracy. That had him huffing around."

"What did John Goddard say?" Mary Lisa asked.

Kelly buttered a dinner roll and didn't answer her. Her mother said, "As I understand it, neither John nor Jack is saying much of anything. But I'm so very worried about Olivia. She's scared. How I wish Monica were here this evening, she'd know what to do."

"And what would Monica do, Mother?" Mary Lisa asked, and immediately wished she had stuck her knife through her tongue instead. Was she nuts?

"Your sister," Kathleen said slowly, staring Mary Lisa down, "is a very clearheaded, focused individual. I will have to phone her in the morning and ask her what she thinks. I've always wondered if there was graft involved in the police department since Jack Wolf came here three years ago. He's from Chicago, you know."

"Graft about what, Mom? With whom?"

"Well, Mary Lisa, you've been gone for a long time, haven't you? No one would expect you to know much of anything about what's happening in Goddard Bay."

"Okay," Mary Lisa said. "But it was just a question, really."

Kathleen said, "Patricia Bigelow is Milo Hildebrand's lawyer in a lawsuit he has pending against John Goddard's father, Thomas. Olivia says Thomas Goddard is going to lose. And now his son is persecuting Milo, on his father's account."

Mary Lisa rolled her eyes, she couldn't help it.

Her mother ignored her. "Why wouldn't John want to help his father? Or Chief Wolf, for that matter? He and John Goddard went to school together. It was the Goddard family, with John's recommendation, that asked Jack to come out here, and then helped him get elected chief of police. So there's some payback owed there. If they push Milo as a suspect, it could ruin him, and maybe the lawsuit goes away. John Goddard and Chief Wolf have a lot of lee-way to push the investigation in any direction they wish. Everyone knows that."

George said, "I'll tell you why that couldn't happen, Kathleen. Thomas Goddard is a businessman, did his share of wheeling and dealing in his younger days, but this law-suit with Milo Hildebrand, from what I've heard about it, is more of a nuisance than a threat to Thomas. As for John Goddard, he's so honest I worry for him because there's room for gray in the world and I'm not sure he knows it when he sees it. He wouldn't bring charges against Milo Hildebrand unless he was convinced he was guilty. Noth-ing less."

"I can't believe you're defending John, Dad," Kelly said. "Look what he did to me, your own daughter. He's ruthless, and he'd do anything to be governor, whatever, like Mom said."

Mary Lisa saw anger in her father's eyes—her eyes. It was so rare, she stared at him, mesmerized. But when he spoke finally, his voice was calm, with only a bit of sar-casm leaking through. "Oh? Did he tell you he wanted to be governor, Kelly?"

"Well, not in so many words, but I do know him well enough to know he can't be trusted. He didn't do well back east so he came back here where his family has influence. His father got him elected district attorney, and that's who he owes his allegiance to."

Her mother looked ready to jump into the fray again, so Mary Lisa quickly said to her sister, "I met John Goddard running on the beach this morning."

Her sister froze for a second, and when she spoke, venom was thick in her voice. "I'll bet he told you he dumped me, didn't he? He's a liar, Mary Lisa. Don't you believe anything he said."

"You don't believe he would say anything like that about you to me, your sister, do you?"

Kelly looked uncertain, but her anger flared again. "Yeah, he'd say anything about me to anyone. He's furious because I gave him the boot. Men like him can't deal with being rejected."

"That may be, Kelly, but for your information, he was quite reticent about it," Mary Lisa said, and smiled. She looked down at the shrimp huddled in the middle of her plate on a small pile of brown rice. She reminded herself she'd come back mostly to see her father, and perhaps to find some comfort in being home again. But what had she really expected? She'd walked onto the stage of another soap opera, this one with a nice juicy murder, only this wasn't a stage. This was her family and it was real, as real as that LeSabre that struck her in Malibu.

"You don't look well, Mary Lisa," Kathleen said.

"It's nothing, really, just a headache brewing."

"I thought your friend Judy Reinbold was coming over," her father said.

"Yeah, she is. I'll take some aspirin and lie down before she comes. I also need to call my friend Lou Lou in Malibu." She laughed. "Hey, that rhymes."

"It sounds like a stripper's name."

"No, actually, she's an excellent makeup artist for the show. And it's not her real name."

"What is her real name?" Kelly asked.

"She won't tell me, won't tell anyone."

Kelly asked, "Are you going clubbing with Judy?"

"Not that I know of. Is there a new place in Goddard Bay where one would do that?"

Kelly shot a look toward her father. "It isn't exactly one of those posh clubs you're used to down in L.A. but there's this okay place now over in Tumaluck with a mostly twenties crowd. I'd take you there, introduce you around, but Mick's coming over."

"Mick who? Do I know him?" Mary Lisa asked.

"Yeah, Mick Maynard. He's Jason Maynard's older brother."

The table was suddenly deathly still.

"Why is he coming over, Kelly?" her father asked.

"I don't want him here," her mother said.

"He didn't do anything," Kelly said as she speared a green bean on her fork. "He's cute and unattached. Hey, maybe he'll tell me stuff."

Mary Lisa said slowly, "I remember Mick Maynard. He went to school with Monica, right?"

Kelly nodded, didn't look at either her mother or her father.

"This isn't a good idea for you to see him, Kelly," her father said. "Not now, not three days after his brother was murdered, the murderer still out there."

"We're not, like, dating or anything, Dad. He told me he was lonely and confused. I offered to let him talk to me. We're going for coffee out at the Goddard Bay Inn."

Silence again.

"For heaven's sake, I'm not going to sleep with him! I'm only doing a good deed."

Kathleen turned to Mary Lisa. "I think it's rather rude of you to leave tonight, Mary Lisa."

George said, his eyes still on Kelly, "This is a no-guilt household, Kathy. This is Mary Lisa's vacation, she doesn't need to spend it in our pockets. As for you, Kelly, I rather wish you would."

Kelly said, "I'm twenty-five, Dad. I'm an adult. I'm moving back to my apartment after this weekend, so this is all rather silly, isn't it?" Her parents remained silent, and Kelly added, too brightly, "I thought you played bridge tonight, Mom. Isn't it your turn to have all the ladies here?"

"No, no bridge tonight. Oh, I forgot to tell you, Mary Lisa, your sister is throwing a party for you tomorrow night."

Mary Lisa's dinner roll fell off her plate. She said slowly, "Why would Monica throw a party for me?"

Her father burst out laughing. "Your sister isn't stupid, sweetie. You're important. You're a TV star. You're a celebrity, which means you can draw people to her. Politically, it's a smart thing to do. She's fast, I'll say that for her. And you know what? It'll be an excellent party, Monica's that good."

When Mary Lisa finally escaped to her room, she called Lou Lou, but Lou Lou wasn't home. Her machine's message said, *"Tonight I'm working off two pounds on the dance floor. Tomorrow's Saturday, don't call me too early. Bye."*

Twenty minutes later, Mary Lisa led her friend Judy Reinbold in only as far as the living room doorway, knowing to her toes that one more step into her mother's domain would be a mistake. She remembered her mother didn't like Judy's parents, and would find a way to show it to their daughter. "Say hi to everyone, Judy, then we're off."

Judy Reinbold had the biggest, whitest smile west of the Mississippi. "Hi, everyone!"

"Wait! Come in here, Mary Lisa, and bring Judy."

"Sorry, Mom, we've got to go. We're already late, right, Judy?"

"Whatever you say, Mary Lisa."

Mary Lisa laughed as she ran to Judy's car at the curb. "You wouldn't have wanted to take another step into the house, trust me on that."

SHE was not running on Saturday morning because she hoped to see John Goddard again. No, she always ran in the mornings, no matter where she was. Yet, if she was honest about it, she found herself looking around quite a bit, and she was wearing lipstick, a lowering realization.

She had pretty much given up on him when she saw a man running out of the low-lying fog toward her, his pace fast and smooth. She slowed up when she realized it really was John Goddard. He pulled up in front of her, panting.

"I can't come closer or you'll run in the opposite direction. I'm sweating like a stoat."

"Are you running off your anger about this conspiracy thing Patricia Bigelow is talking about?"

"Nah. Pat's good. She's a street fighter. You hear how she's implying I'm going after Milo because of my father's lawsuit with him?"

Mary Lisa nodded. "It was a major topic at my parents' dinner table last night."

"It's her job to try to head us away from Milo, but I really could do without all the innuendo."

"My dad was saying most everyone likes your dad, so my guess is it might backfire on her."

"From your lips to God's ear," he said.

"Are you going to Monica's party tonight?"

"I suppose so. She's sure put it together fast. You're the big guest of honor, right?"

Mary Lisa nodded. "My dad says that she's doing this because I'm a celebrity, and people will listen to what I say. It seems weird to me. Can you imagine caring what Barbra Streisand or Johnny Depp thinks about politics? Let them stick to acting, that I know they do well. Hey, I hope you can tell me where I can buy a dress for this shindig. Trust me when I say I didn't bring anything appropriate."

"Just a second." He pulled his cell phone out of his shirt pocket, punched in a single digit. "Hello, Mom? Question. Where can a girl get a party dress on really short notice?"

He listened, then handed the phone to Mary Lisa. "Mrs. Goddard?"

"Mary Lisa, how lovely to speak to you. We're talking about your sister's party tonight?"

"Yes, ma'am."

"What size are you?"

"Ah, it depends—a size two or four, I guess."

"Isn't that perfect? John's sister is that small, well, not now, she isn't, since she's six months pregnant. Have John take you to her house and you can dive into her closet.

I know she'll be thrilled. She's always telling everyone she wants to be Sunday Cavendish after the baby's born. She can do it now. I'll call her. Bye, dear."

Mary Lisa handed back the phone. "Well, I really don't know what to do now. Your mother wants me to borrow a dress from your pregnant sister."

"Good idea. Come along, we'll go see Ms. Granola Bar."

"What?"

He walked toward his silver BMW parked behind a couple of stunted trees on the highway. "Beth was always a health nut. I started calling her that when she was fourteen or thereabouts. She's always been skinny as a stick. As a matter of fact, right now she's beginning to look like a spider that's just eaten something big. The doctor says it's twins."

"Two inside her at the same time? Oh, my."

"I know, I can't imagine it either. It's odd, but you don't look skinny."

"Thank you. How tall is your sister?"

"She's not as tall as you. Your legs are longer."

"Why are you doing this for me?"

"I'm not, my sister is."

"Come on, don't be a bonehead."

"Truth is, I've always admired Sunday Cavendish too. I've wondered, though, if she could take it as well as dish it out."

"Trust me on this, she can take just about anything."

"I guess whoever plays Sunday Cavendish needs to."

"I'll tell you about it sometime."

SEVENTEEN

Mary Lisa had never seen the house Mark and Monica had bought from a divorcing Portland portrait gallery owner three years before. Set amid a small enclave of expensive homes, it was the jewel of the neighborhood with flowing lines, endless wooden floors, and ocean views from most every window. Because Monica had their mother's good taste, and Mark's money, English antiques coexisted happily beside chrome and glass and white plastic cubes and soaring metal sculptures in fantastic twisted shapes.

The evening was balmy and clear, a half-moon sparkling over the water, a fairy-tale night, Mary Lisa thought. But she wondered how she could ever have been so stupid as to believe she'd loved Mark Bridges, fantasized about him endlessly in her every waking moment, even lost her brain to the extent she'd gladly have given up acting for him. She shuddered, remembering the shock of pain at his betrayal. She saw him across the long living room, listening to Mr. Crammer, who owned the local First Regional Bank of Oregon. Mark laughed, and it was too big and too loud and there was nothing behind it she wanted to know about. Once again, she felt immensely grateful that he'd been faithless. Monica stood in the midst of another group of people, smiling and nodding, looking charming. She had the knack of looking with intense focus directly into a person's face when they spoke, making an instant intimate connection. It was a politician's skill. Mary Lisa wondered if Monica loved Mark Bridges as much as Mary Lisa had sworn she herself had three years ago, before she'd received their wedding invitation in her mailbox in L.A.

She glanced at Kelly, wondering how she would treat John Goddard, the man she said she'd booted out of her life, because John Goddard was most certainly coming to this party. Kelly wore a short pale green cocktail dress that wouldn't have covered Mary Lisa's butt since Kelly was so much shorter than she was. She'd curled her streaked hair so it fell in waves to her shoulders. She looked as lovely as their mother, who was dressed in a long black gown, diamonds at her ears and throat, as ultrastylish and self-assured as Sunday Cavendish's mother, Lydia. As for Mary Lisa's father, George Beverly was born to wear a tux; he was, without a single doubt in Mary Lisa's loving eye, the most handsome man in the crowd of a good hundred people who milled about in the large open rooms, helping themselves to Monica's endless supply of very good champagne.

When Monica, Mark at her side, came toward them, Mary Lisa thought *The Bold and the Beautiful*, and laughed at herself.

Monica air-kissed each relative, and paused when she got to Mary Lisa. She winged up a dark brow, and her expression tightened. It was *the look* Mary Lisa remembered from her earliest childhood, the one that promised violence, or at least bad karma. Why, for heaven's sake? The thing was, Mary Lisa hadn't been here long enough to earn *the look*. Monica was the queen of this kingdom. Mary Lisa was only a short-term semifamous interloper in her sister's realm. And wasn't she here precisely to let Monica exploit her?

She gave her sister a sunny smile. "You've a lovely home," she said, and nodded at Mark as she spoke. "The views are spectacular."

Mark stepped forward, looking ready to hug Mary Lisa, as he had her mother and Kelly, but the death ray in his wife's eyes stopped him in his tracks. He shook her outstretched hand instead, but he held it a bit too long, and so Mary Lisa backed up, forcing Mark to release hers or be pulled toward her.

"All the Beverly women are gorgeous," he said, and looked straight at his wife. It sounded fairly sincere, a good thing for Mark's sex life.

George Beverly laughed, nodded to his son-in-law, and said to Monica, "My dear, this looks like a splendid party. However did you get everything together on such short notice? And a ton of A-list people too. Well done."

"She's got pull, sir," Mark said, and hugged his wife. "She can do anything. Heading committees in the state house will be child's play for her."

"Since they behave like children in the state house, that's exactly what it will be," George said. He pecked his eldest daughter on her cheek, his smile robbing his words of insult.

"Nincompoops, Dad, that's what you called politicians," Kelly, the born pot stirrer, said. "Are they children now too?"

A waiter approached with a tray of champagne. Everyone latched on to a gleaming crystal flute. Monica said to Mary Lisa, "Since this party is in your honor, you need to come with me so I can introduce you to everyone." Her eyes surveyed her sister's borrowed little black dress before she turned on her strappy, three-inch slides and motioned everyone to follow her.

There were so many people to greet, people Mary Lisa hadn't seen in three years, and many new faces as well, but everyone seemed to recognize her. She wondered if they really believed Sunday Cavendish was simply a role she played or if they felt they were in the presence of the

Goddess Bitch herself. She smiled and spoke and nodded as Monica pulled her in her wake, taking time to express support and admiration for her sister to anyone who seemed to expect it. When they reached the front of the room, Monica gestured her up onto the small dais. She stepped toward Mary Lisa, close enough so no one else could hear her, and whispered pleasantly, still smiling, "By the way, Mary Lisa, I'd appreciate your keeping away from Mark. I won't have you looking at him like you want to tongue his tonsils."

Mary Lisa, nonplussed only briefly by what sounded like a script line to her, said after a little pause, "Hello, Earth to Monica, listen up—I don't want him. The truth is, I don't even like him anymore. I've been grateful for a very long time now that he married you. I hope you're happy with him, but let me make it official: Thank you." She leaned forward and kissed her sister's cheek. Monica froze, but she knew guests were watching the show of affection and briefly hugged Mary Lisa to her. She pulled away and tapped her French-manicured fingernail against her champagne flute to draw everyone's attention, and those few people who hadn't been watching them already turned to face them. She thanked everyone for coming on such short notice, then smiled at Mary Lisa and thanked her for coming to help kick off her sister's political campaign.

Mary Lisa didn't so much as flare a nostril at that fine lie. She glanced at her father, and smiled at the look of amused tolerance on his face.

Monica continued, "As most of you know, Mary Lisa left Goddard Bay three years ago to live full-time in Los Angeles where her television show is shot. I hope all of you will join me in welcoming her home to Goddard Bay for this lovely, but alas, too short visit."

The guests stared at her as if mesmerized. If wasn't as if she was wildly famous and beautiful like Sandra Bullock or Nicole Kidman, neither of whom, she was certain, had much of a clue who she was nor cared a whit that she was on the same planet with them. She'd run into them occa-

sionally in Malibu, but then again, you ran into everyone in
Malibu at one time or another. Mary Lisa was a comfort-
ably sized fish in a big pond in L.A., nothing more. But
here in Goddard Bay, she wasn't simply the homegrown
girl, she was the Big Kahuna.

Mary Lisa kept it short, very careful of what she said
since she knew some people here would dine out on her
every word, her every expression, as if they were niblets of
gossip gleaned from *People* magazine. She was relieved
that Beth Goddard Sumter's little black dress was glam-
orous enough so that people who expected her to look like
a movie star weren't disappointed. On occasions like this,
she willingly gave them the actress they wanted to see—
the big smile, the full makeup, the glittering personality.
Several men eyed her like she was a sex goddess, nearly
salivating in their canapés. She was used to that too.

How very odd it all was, like dredging up an ersatz
memory. She knew that most Hollywood celebrities felt
this crazy disconnect, unless they actually bought into the
glowing lie, and got lost in it.

She smiled, accepted compliments, and listened patiently when a wealthy older woman told her she'd always
wanted to act, that she thought she might have had it in her
to get her own star on Hollywood Boulevard if only she'd
made it to L.A. to be seen. Mary Lisa's smile never
slipped. She had a writer friend who'd told her that more
than one person she'd met had told her matter-of-factly
that they could write a bestseller if only they had a free
weekend or two.

And there were the inevitable slights about soap operas,
from "Of course, I'd never watch tripe like that," to "I've
got a life, I don't have time to waste on that stuff," to "It's
all so silly and so melodramatic. No one looks like real
people, they're all too beautiful." *Yeah, and your point
would be?* Her romance writer friend said that everyone,
when asked what they read, stated categorically that they
read only nonfiction and biographies, which made her wonder where all those lovely royalty checks came from.

It seemed to Mary Lisa that most people never had a single clue they'd been rude. But their obliviousness still astounded her, even though it was no longer a surprise.

"I've never seen your show, Ms. Beverly, too busy during the day, I'm afraid, but I've certainly heard of you since your family lives here. A small town, isn't it? Nothing much exciting to talk about."

Mary Lisa turned slowly to face a striking woman, with dark bobbed hair, blue eyes, and lovely skin. She was showing a mile of leg attached to feet balanced on four-inch heels. On those stilts, she was nearly Mary Lisa's height. Now, who was this?

EIGHTEEN

"Hello." She shook the woman's hand, a strong hand.

"I'm Patricia Bigelow, attorney at large here in Goddard Bay."

"I'm Mary Lisa Beverly. You've moved here since I left because I surely would have remembered you."

"That's right. It's been nearly two years since I set up shop here. You don't see many redheads without freckles."

"I've got my grandmother's coloring. She didn't have any freckles either."

"Anywhere?"

"Not even on the bottoms of my feet."

"I'm being pushy because my cousin is a redhead and she's loaded with freckles. She's always looking for ways to make them disappear. I thought maybe you'd found the answer."

"I heard about cucumbers once but I don't know if it's only an old husband's tale."

"I'll pass it along. Oh, look who's coming this way. Mr. Well-Dressed Stud of Goddard Bay himself."

Mary Lisa saw John Goddard weaving his way toward them, through groups of people he stopped to greet along the way.

Patricia continued her observations in an expressionless voice. "John is very popular. It'll take him another five minutes to get here. I'm sure everyone wants to ask him about Jason Maynard's murder. I doubt he'll tell them anything, it would be unprofessional and he knows I'd burn his feet to the ankles with it if he did. I'm sure it's not me he's coming to see, so it's got to be you, the guest of honor. I'll introduce you."

Mary Lisa saw Patricia Bigelow lightly run her tongue over her bottom lip, her eyes never leaving John Goddard's face. Now this was interesting. Was he dating her on the rebound from Kelly? No, it was too soon, that couldn't be right. She said easily, "You and Mr. Goddard are on opposite sides in this murder case, I understand."

"Not as yet. However, if he and Jack Wolf have their way, I might be facing John in court." She continued to smile as she spoke, and she never looked away from John Goddard. "It's my job to kick his fine butt every day to keep him and the chief above any temptation to overstep with my clients."

"I suppose he does have a nice butt," Mary Lisa agreed, nodding.

"One of the best I've seen, east or west coast." A dark eyebrow went up. "Have you already met Mr. Goddard?"

"Yes, John and I have met two mornings in a row, running on the beach."

"How nice. I used to run with him," Patricia said. "But his little macho ego couldn't take it. You see, I always had more endurance—the tortoise and the hare sort of thing—drove him nuts."

John knew he was meant to overhear and laughed. "If Mary Lisa believes that, I've got a nearly bankrupt regional airport to sell her. Come on, Pat, I got you into running shoes a total of three times, and you whined about how the shoes hurt your arches. Look at those ice picks you're wearing tonight and tell me how running shoes could possibly hurt any more than those things."

Mary Lisa said, "I nearly mowed John down the day we met. I haven't raced him yet. Hmm, we'll see. I'll report back to you, Ms. Bigelow."

That dark eyebrow shot up again. "You work fast, but I guess that's what the L.A. crowd does."

A lovely punch to the gut. "Actually," Mary Lisa said, "I'm not working at all, only trying to relax. John, Ms. Bigelow tells me she's enjoying kicking your very fine butt to protect her client. Or is it clients?"

His real feelings about Patricia Bigelow flashed across his face—he wanted to drop-kick her through the front window—but he said nothing.

"Actually, I'm representing both Mr. and Mrs. Hildebrand. Perhaps their daughter Marci as well."

John ignored that, and turned to Mary Lisa. "I like Bethy's dress—it fits well on you. I always thought Beth was a beanpole, so it's a surprise."

Mary Lisa said to Patricia, "I borrowed this beautiful dress from John's sister."

Pat said, "I hope Beth is doing all right, John?"

"She's healthier than any other member of the family and impatient to have the babies in her arms instead of her belly. That's what she says."

"Ah, Chief Wolf," Patricia said. "How lovely to see you."

Chief Jack Wolf's face seemed hard and remote as he eyed the three of them with what seemed like clinical detachment. He managed a nod, and said, "Ms. Bigelow." He turned to Mary Lisa, and if anything, his hard face turned even harder. You didn't need much of an IQ to guess that he didn't like her. "Ms. Beverly," was all he said. To John, he said in a low voice, "I need to speak to you, when you have a moment."

"Certainly."

Jack Wolf nodded to the women again, and turned away, John at his side. Patricia and Mary Lisa watched the two men walk to a quiet corner of the room—two big men, friends of about the same age, but Mary Lisa had never seen even a twinkle of amusement in the chief's dark eyes.

Mary Lisa said, "Whenever he looks at me it's like he wants to strangle me until my eyes bug out."

Pat said, her eyes still following them, "He doesn't like me either, particularly when I try to represent my clients properly. He thinks I'm interfering with his investigation. I do have to say, though, that there walk two of the very finest butts I've ever had the privilege of appreciating. So I assume you're going back to L.A. soon?"

Mary Lisa nodded. "Yep, back to work Monday morning."

Pat asked, "Don't you have lines to memorize by Monday morning?"

"Why yes, but it's a two-hour flight and I'm only in three scenes on Monday. I'll be able to learn most of my lines in the air. They'll e-mail me the final version of the script tomorrow morning. Funny thing is, I usually wake up about three a.m. the morning of a shoot and go over them again."

"An internal alarm clock?"

"Something like that."

"I'll bet your boyfriend doesn't like that," Pat said.

"No, none of them do," Mary Lisa agreed. "Whine, whine, whine, all of them, not a single stoic in the lot." She laughed.

When Mary Lisa left Patricia Bigelow and her double-edged sword, she made her way to the nearest waiter to get another glass of champagne.

"Wait up, Mary Lisa, this isn't a race."

She turned to see John Goddard closing on her. She studied his face a moment. "Patricia Bigelow says she admires your butt, even if she does have to kick it sometimes."

He shrugged, smiled charmingly, and lied cleanly. "Only business as usual, nothing more than that."

Yeah, right. "She's a beautiful woman, and she seems terrifyingly smart. But what's odd to me about all this is that she has a thing for you."

"What thing? A voodoo doll in her pocket, needles sticking out of its gullet?"

"Nah. I don't think she'd go the voodoo-doll route. Just the way she looked at you, and your fine butt."

"Pat treats every guy like that. I haven't heard her say she likes my butt, though. And you agreed? That's nice." He looked beyond her left shoulder, his attention taken by something.

"She seems to admire Jack Wolf's butt, as well, so I wouldn't crow too much about it."

"I'll wait to tell him when he's taking a drink off a beer, watch him spew it all over everything."

She followed his line of vision and saw her sister Kelly looking toward them, her face cold and set.

This wasn't good. She said quietly, "It's tough to be in a small town when there's a breakup. And now my sister sees me consorting with the enemy." She was reminded of *The Young and the Restless*, and laughed at herself.

"That's me, Kelly's enemy. Patricia Bigelow's enemy. I am very unpopular at the moment. By the way, you really don't look bad in Bethy's dress. But why does Jack look like he wants to throw you in his jail without a blanket?"

"You could say I got in a little trouble before I left three years ago, and as a matter of fact, I did spend some time in his jail. I don't remember if there was a blanket or not."

"What possible kind of trouble could you have gotten yourself into to warrant a jail cell? Parking on Lover's Lane up on Grayland's Point? Four-wheeling on the sand dunes?"

"I was too old even then to park on Lover's Lane. And no four-wheeling either, not on those fragile sand dunes." She smiled at him, but said nothing more.

He glanced quickly at Kelly again, gave Mary Lisa a small salute, and turned on his heel to walk through the crowd to where his mother and father were holding court. She saw Patricia Bigelow looking after him.

"Beth's dress makes your shoulders look all bony. It never looked good on her either."

Mary Lisa turned to face her sister, saw the bright eyes, the flushed face. She had obviously downed too much of Monica's excellent champagne and was in a mood to rock and roll, or kill. It hadn't taken her long to spot Mary Lisa finally alone on the living room balcony. She took her sister's hand and squeezed it, to get her attention. "Kelly, listen to me now. I'm your sister. You're supposed to be kind to me, perhaps even love me a little bit."

"Yeah, yada, yada, but I just saw my sister yucking it up with John. Did you mention me?"

"I'm very sorry to tell you this, Kelly, but the world isn't always focused on you. It's a bummer, but it's true."

Kelly drank half of her champagne, gave a dainty hiccup, and eyed her sister with glaze-eyed frustration. "Monica says you're after Mark again and you think you can get him back since you're a big star now. She says men are so brain-dead it might be true."

"Is that really what Monica says?"

"Stop making fun of me, Mary Lisa!"

Mary Lisa sighed. "Then why did Monica throw this party for me if she thinks I'm a home wrecker?"

"Are you stupid? You know very well it's for her political campaign. You could have run down her mother-in-law and you'd still be her guest of honor."

"I'm surprised she'd believe I could be that important to her."

"I don't want to talk about Monica, I want to talk about John. I want you to keep away from him, Mary Lisa. Don't run tomorrow morning. He'll want to meet you because he's using you to upset me, make me jealous."

"But why would it upset you or make you jealous when you were the one who kissed him off? Why would you care what he does or who he dates now?"

Kelly downed the rest of her champagne. She walked to the railing with the careful gait of a person who knows they're seriously impaired. She leaned on the railing, looked down into a mess of rosebushes, and, laughing, dropped her champagne glass. It disappeared into the thick leaves.

She turned, leaned her elbows on the railing. "You're right. He's not worth my time, never was. I've decided I want Jack. Did you get a good look at him tonight? In that tux he's wearing, he looks elegant, more classy than dear old John."

"Not as elegant or classy as Dad."

Kelly ignored her. "I know for a fact Jack hasn't dated for a long while. I know he was married before he came here, back in Chicago. So he must be ready by now. Don't you think?"

NINETEEN

Mary Lisa followed her sister's eyes. Jack did look fine in a tux, but then again, so did most men. Uniforms and tuxes were definitely dangerous. "Chief of Police Jack Wolf? John Goddard's best friend? You think maybe this has something to do with making someone jealous? You know he'd arrest you in a minute for drunk driving if you headed out of here right now."

Kelly's voice sounded dreamy from all the champagne. "His name—it sounds sexy, doesn't it? Jack Wolf, like one of those macho fake names down in Hollywood."

"Nah, I think Matt Damon has a sexier name."

Kelly ignored that. "When I decide I'm ready, I think I'll take Jack next. Sooner or later, he'll hop to. What's even better is he doesn't like you."

Mary Lisa was nearly twenty-eight and Kelly was twenty-five—her younger sister hadn't been this self-absorbed, this seemingly man-crazy when she'd last seen her three years ago. What had happened? Was she still stuck on John?

Mary Lisa sighed. She found herself repeating to Kelly

what she'd just said to Monica. "We're sisters, Kelly. I'm not on this earth to hurt you. I'm not here to steal guys away from you." Then she thought of the girl-fight she'd had with Lou Lou over a surfer dude who'd asked them both out. For a day or two it had been touch-and-go between them until they saw him flirting with another girl on the beach; they just looked at each other and laughed their heads off. Lou Lou, as usually happened, had the last word. "That girl shouldn't wear a thong."

Kelly said, "He's only thirty-two, you know, same age as John."

"But he seems a hard man, Kelly. Have you ever seen him smile?"

"Sure, all the time. It's only you he doesn't smile at. Of course he doesn't like Pat Bigelow either, but that makes sense, what with Pat hassling him about the Hildebrands. What'd you do to make him dislike you so much?"

"Are you about ready to go home, Kelly? It's late, I swear I've spoken to every person in Monica's living room and powder room, and—"

"There's Jack looming over Patricia Bigelow. He looks like he wants to smack her. Hey, wouldn't that make Monica's boring party memorable? Could you imagine if the Hildebrands were here? Of course Monica didn't invite them."

Mary Lisa knew it was way past time to take her sister home. But Kelly wasn't done yet. She leaned back, her elbows on the railing. "So, Mary Lisa, tell me, did Monica take Mark from you because he's such a stud in bed?"

No, I think I was too happy and she couldn't stand that. "Could be. I don't remember. Let's go home."

Kelly twisted about and looked down into the bushes where she'd tossed the champagne flute. "I wonder how much that glass cost. I hope it puts her back some."

"Yeah, she might have to move out of this beautiful house," Mary Lisa said as she took her sister's arm. She'd managed ten steps inside the door when Kelly pulled away and went like a homing pigeon to Chief Jack Wolf.

"Jack," she said, her smile dazzling, looking not at all drunk. "You look taller tonight. Are you wearing lifts?"

For an instant, Mary Lisa thought she saw a flash of humor in the chief's dark blue eyes, but his mask settled in again. "No, not tonight, Kelly," he said, "I must have forgotten them at home. If it's height you want, why not borrow a pair of your sister's shoes? A big Hollywood actress probably has dozens of pairs of pole-vault heels."

Kelly said, "I would hope so. I've never seen Mary Lisa's shoe collection. Rodeo Drive, can you imagine how great that would be? Pradas and Blahniks on every block. But it wouldn't matter, Mary Lisa's feet are bigger than mine."

"Let's go, Kelly," Mary Lisa said, her hand cupping her sister's elbow. "Dad's waving at us."

He wasn't, Chief Wolf knew he wasn't, but he didn't say anything. "I hope you're not driving, Kelly," he said finally. "I'd have to give you a ticket."

Again, that glittering smile. "One of your guys gave me a ticket in March for speeding, only I wasn't, at least that time. It was Officer Gruber and he wanted to go out with me."

"I hope you took pity on him and didn't."

Mary Lisa saw that her sister was too trashed to figure her way to the insult. Mary Lisa looked him straight in the eye. "My sister is beautiful, smart, and fun. Any man she'd accept would be lucky."

He nodded. "As you say, Ms. Beverly. Good night." He turned abruptly, only to say over his shoulder, "The name of your show is perfect for you."

Kelly got her brain to focus. "What's that? Oh, you mean *Born to Be Wild*? Mary Lisa, wild?" Kelly laughed. "Mary Lisa is about as wild as listening to teeth grind. I think you've got us confused."

Mary Lisa rolled her eyes, grinned at Chief Wolf, and shrugged. "Call me Steppenwolf."

As Jack Wolf walked away, Kelly looked after him, and hiccupped. "Isn't he funny?"

"Oh yeah. Maybe he was a stand-up comedian before he got into law enforcement."

"Look over at old Mark. He's eyeballing you again, Mary Lisa. You want me to tell him to stop before Monica sees him?"

"Yeah, you tell him that, Kelly, but first let's get ourselves home."

"A lovely party," Kathleen said while George was driving them back to the house. "Beautifully planned and executed. Monica was impressive, as usual."

George pulled at the neck of his collar. "Executed is about right."

"Don't whine, Dad, you look very handsome. Every woman there was envying Mother. You rule."

"Yeah, Dad, you're a tux stud," Kelly said and giggled.

He looked in the rearview mirror at Mary Lisa and winked at her. "You were certainly popular tonight, sweetheart."

"It's the power of TV, that's all. I call it TVness. People kind of lose it around TVness."

Kelly was frowning. George said quickly, "Talk about popular, Kelly, I don't think I ever saw you alone."

"I guess not," Kelly said, her head drooping now from the champagne. "I only felt that way."

TWENTY

Early the next morning Mary Lisa took one last run before she had to pack and drive to the airport for her ll:05 fight back to L.A.

She hoped she would see John Goddard one last time. She had to see him, really, this morning or soon. She had set herself straight last night. Now she had to set him straight as well.

I am not a small person, she thought as she took off down the long beach, through the long tongue of gray fog that rolled over the valley nearly to the line of low coastal hills a mile inland. *I was bordering on being small last night, but not now.* She'd made up her mind before she went to sleep, and she'd slept soundly until near morning, when Jack Wolf had poked his head into her dreams. Suddenly he'd been standing in front of her, towering over her, telling her she was a spoiled brat and a juvenile delinquent—and, at all of twenty-five, a little old to be acting like a half-brained teenager.

She could smile about it now. Sort of. It was something like what Jack had said to her three years ago when he'd hauled her off to jail.

She picked up her pace, but didn't see John. He didn't seem to be running this morning. She'd have to write him, which she hated to have to do. Well, it was Sunday and maybe he was at church. She decided to run all out, letting the sweat run down her face and the lipstick she'd applied fend for itself. She had just started to slow again when he suddenly burst out of the fog, looking fine indeed, his sleeveless T-shirt sweated to his chest, his face stubbled with his morning beard.

"I am not a small person," she said aloud without thinking.

"What? Oh. No, you're not. What are you, five foot ten? In those stilts you were wearing last night, we were eye to eye."

She wiped her forehead on the bottom of her sweatshirt, smiled at him. "Nah, I think I was up to your eyebrows. I wanted to speak to you before I left to go back south."

"That makes two of us. That's why I'm running on a Sunday morning instead of sleeping in. I wanted to speak to you too. What time are you taking off?"

"Not for a while yet. Oh yes, please thank your sister for the loan of her beautiful dress. My mom will have the cleaners deliver it to her."

"No problem. Let's run for a while." She nodded. They ran side by side for ten minutes, and walked back to her car. Mary Lisa leaned over and waited for her breathing to ease and her heart to slow. Oddly, she didn't want to come right out with it. What she said was, "You seem to have this unusual relationship with Pat Bigelow. She keeps talking about Jack Wolf harassing the Hildebrands, not looking at other suspects, like in the O.J. case."

He cocked an eyebrow at her, but said easily enough, "Unusual is one way of putting it. The truth is that in the O.J. case, there was so much evidence against him so quickly, there wasn't any reason to search elsewhere. Besides, can you begin to imagine any shop run by Jack Wolf doing anything but a solid investigation?"

"I don't know. Chief Wolf doesn't confide in me."

"Trust me on this. Jack Wolf knows his job, and he does it well. But enough about Pat Bigelow. I enjoyed watching you center stage at Monica's last night. You handled yourself very well."

"Like I told my dad last night, the whole Hollywood thing fascinates people. They think, wow, she's on TV and conjure up this naturally skinny woman who parties with Russell Crowe every day and drinks espresso at the Ivy."

He stared at her a moment, raised his towel and wiped the sweat from her left temple. "I don't understand. It isn't true?"

"Maybe on Thursdays." She laughed, and cleared her throat. It was time to get it all out, but he beat her to it. He said, "I watched you and your family last night at Monica's party. Let me be honest here, Mary Lisa. Your mother and your sisters—I couldn't see much affection or gentleness between them—hell, it isn't any of my business if your family doesn't get along. Well, except for your father. I know he visits you often down in L.A., but you've never come up here, not for three years. I couldn't help but wonder why you came back here now if things are unpleasant for you with your family."

"I love my father dearly."

"Yes, I can see that."

She hadn't expected to talk about that. She'd elected not to tell anyone here about what had happened in Malibu because she didn't want to have to deal with her father wanting to come down and move in with her to protect her. They would probably find out soon enough.

"A short vacation, nothing more."

She looked up at his face. His expression turned from concern to a rueful look that she imagined he'd perfected in the courtroom. She grinned and folded. "All right, I'll tell you why I came back here after three years. But I want you to keep it quiet, all right?"

When he nodded, she said slowly, "Fact is, my friend Lou Lou suggested it because she was afraid for me."

She'd caught him by surprise. "Afraid? Of what? What's going on with you?"

"You remember the incident I mentioned to you Friday morning? Well, it was more like a hit and run. What happened is—well, some guy may have been trying to kill me."

"You've got to be kidding me. What happened?"

"Well, I'd just bought some T-shirts in an army surplus shop. I'd ducked in there because I was trying to get away from Puker Hodges, a paparazzo who's decided I'm his ticket to fame, when a car tried to run me down."

That stopped him cold. "That's how you got hurt? Did he actually hit you?"

"I got banged up a little bit, but I'm okay now. The bruises are nearly gone. No major injuries to brag about. The cops are looking into it. I suppose it's possible it was an accident. You know, someone who was high or not paying attention hit me, and was so freaked out he drove off."

He waved that away. "L.A. is quite a place, isn't it? What's the name of the detective looking into this? What does he think?"

"Detective Daniel Vasquez is in charge. He's with the Lost Hills Station. They take care of Malibu. He seems sharp and thorough. Don't worry. Whoever did it—well, it seems to me now that I overreacted. I shouldn't have come up here. And I'm sorry I even mentioned it. I would appreciate it if you'd keep it to yourself."

"No, I promised I would. Maybe you should stay here for a while, Mary Lisa."

"Can't. I'm in three scenes on Monday."

He cupped her shoulders with his hands. "When will you come back?"

She looked out over the ocean. The fog hadn't lifted. If anything it lay more heavily, the air cold and wet. "I don't know. I need to speak to you, John."

An eyebrow went up. "Am I not going to like this?"

"I really don't know, I haven't known you long enough to know whether or not you feel—well, the thing is when I met you here on Friday morning, I liked you immediately. You seem like a great guy."

"That's a kiss-off line if I ever heard it."

"Yeah, I guess it is, but not for the reasons you'd think." She drew a deep breath. "I didn't realize until last night that Kelly still has feelings for you." She looked at him dead on now. "You know what happened three years ago, everyone in this town knows—Mark Bridges and I were to get married and I found him and my sister Monica together in bed. No, please don't interrupt. The thing is once I realized Kelly still cares about you, I knew I couldn't let this go any further, whatever this is, and it might be nothing, it might all be on my side."

He said quietly, "No, it's not all on your side."

"I'm sorry about that. The thing is, John, she's my sister, and I won't have any part of doing any such thing to my sister."

"I'm not all that sure Kelly cares about me anymore. Well, other than wanting to castrate me or something—"

"She cares. She was playing up to Jack Wolf last night, trying to make you jealous. The thing about feelings, John—she can't simply turn them on and off, even if she wanted to." She touched her fingertips to his forearm. He felt warm to the touch. "Please understand. I don't want to alienate Kelly any more than she already is. I don't want to hurt her."

John turned away, streaked his fingers through his hair. "Dammit, what Kelly needs is a job. She needs to focus on something outside herself. As for her playing up to Jack— well, she'll find Jack isn't seeing any women, not since Rikki left him torn and bleeding."

"She told me he'd been married."

"Yeah, for three years."

"What happened?"

John shrugged. "Who knows? Most of the relationships— and believe me, just saying the word raises the hair on the back of my neck—I've ever had have ended with some-one's fur flying, sometimes mine, sometimes hers."

Mary Lisa said, "My longest relationship ended with finding my fiancé in bed with my sister. But there wasn't any fur flying. I just slinked out."

"I do wish Kelly would do something with that communications degree of hers. She'll forget about me soon enough."

"I guess we'll see. The first thing she needs to do is to move out of our folks' house, get back to her own apartment."

"Mary Lisa."

"Yes?"

"I know you don't want me to, but I'd like to tell Jack about what's happening down in Malibu."

"Oh no, please don't, John. Jack doesn't like me, he really doesn't. He thinks I'm a—"

"A what?"

"Never mind. It isn't important. Detective Vasquez is handling everything." She stuck out her hand. "I really liked meeting you, John. Good luck with the murder case."

He shook her hand, brushed her cheek with his fingers, and turned away.

TWENTY-ONE

John's cell rang with the theme to *Titanic* at eight o'clock Sunday evening.

"John, it's Jack. You want to come with me to make an arrest?"

"Whoa—what, Jack? Who?"

Jack said, "Meet me at the Hildebrands' house right away," and he punched off his cell.

Jack arrived first, with two of his deputies close behind him, and found the Hildebrand house dark and quiet. Only one downstairs light was on, a dim shine through the living room draperies. He checked the garage, and was pleased to see both their cars inside.

He climbed back into his truck to wait for John, and soon saw lights in his rearview mirror. He unlocked the passenger door, and watched John pull his sleek BMW behind his truck and turn off the lights. When John tapped on the window, Jack leaned over and opened the door.

"Who?" was John's first word.

Jack looked toward the Hildebrand house as he said, "Milo. The day after it happened, I knew to my bones he killed Jason Maynard. It just took a little work getting the proof, and now we have it. I'll tell you all about it at the station, John, but right now we need to do this. Are you ready?"

He gave a small wave to the two police cars parked in each direction half a block away, and waited a moment until he saw the four deputies fanning out around the house.

Milo Hildebrand answered the door on Jack's third knock. He looked haggard and wary, but he was well-dressed, as if he planned to go out. He stood in the doorway, blocking them.

"I heard you were asking more questions out at the club, Jack. I called my lawyer this afternoon. Ms. Bigelow said if you came by again you were bordering on harassment and I should refuse to talk to you unless she's present."

Jack nodded. "Yes, I've been out to the club three times now, interviewing people. And yes, your lawyer is trying to have you declared a saint, Milo. But I'm not here to talk this time. I'm here to make an arrest."

Milo stepped back, shoulders slumped. "Olivia? She really couldn't have realized what she was doing, Jack, she must have been crazed, angry—"

Now that was amazing. Jack interrupted him. "No, it's not your wife I'm here for. It's you, Milo. But you might want to tell Mrs. Hildebrand that I'm arresting you for the murder of your son-in-law, Jason Maynard, that you'll be spending the night in my nice jail."

"I don't believe this! Are you nuts, Jack? I didn't—"

They heard a noise from behind him and all turned to see Mrs. Olivia Hildebrand standing at the bottom of the stairs, her hand fisted against her mouth. She looked pale as death. "I'm sorry, ma'am, but he killed Jason, you know."

Milo walked toward her, saying, "Olivia, it's not true," and then suddenly turned and ran through an open door down a short hallway past the stairs.

John shouted, "Damn, that's his office!"

"He's got guns in there," Jack said. "I should have

cuffed him the instant he answered the door. You stay put, Mrs. Hildebrand, stay here."

Jack was after him, John on his heels. The door slammed in his face before he reached it. Milo yelled from inside, "Go away, Jack, or I'll shoot you! I'm not going to jail!"

Jack said through the door, keeping his voice calm and slow, "Milo, don't make this any worse by resisting arrest. I've got deputies outside. There's no way out for you. Open the door, and we can talk this through."

"I didn't kill the thieving little bastard. I didn't kill him!"

Jack waved John behind him, then backed up and kicked his foot hard against the doorknob. The door shuddered and gave way, crashing in against the office wall.

Jack drew his Beretta. "You stay out here, John."

Milo had one leg out the open window that gave onto the backyard. He jerked around and fired wildly, two of the bullets striking the wall behind Jack, a third shattering a crystal brandy carafe on a drink trolley, spraying the air with the scent of liquor.

Jack and John had both dropped and rolled behind Milo's desk. "Enough, Milo!" Jack shouted. "I don't want to shoot you. Put down your weapon now."

Jack came up fast to see Milo drop through the open window. He heard a shout from outside as he ran across the room. He climbed out the window, rolled as he hit the ground, and came up fast to his feet. He saw Milo running as fast as he could toward the back fence of his yard, and two of his deputies coming around the side of the house, yelling at him to stop. As Milo climbed over the high back fence, Jack took careful aim and fired. Milo yelled in pain, grabbed his calf, his handgun falling to the ground. He dropped backward onto his side, screaming.

"Nice shot, Chief," said Deputy Ames as they restrained and cuffed him.

"Yeah," John said, coming up to him, "so long as you weren't aiming for his arm."

Deputy Ames said, "An arm, a leg—I can't see it matters much."

TWENTY-TWO

On the eve of World War II, there were sixty-four daytime
serials broadcast each week.

BORN TO BE WILD
Monday

"Clear! Candy, fix Mary Lisa's hair. Lou Lou, touch up her
lipstick. Jeff, Mr. Dillard wants to speak to you for a minute
in the booth."

Mary Lisa nodded automatically toward the stage manager, a new guy named Todd Bickly who'd been on *As the
World Turns* for ten years and had come over to *Born to Be
Wild* because he'd wanted to see some new faces. He was
fortyish, slim, and liked to smile a lot, showing a space between his front teeth that marked him as definitely not an
actor. She'd told Detective Vasquez about him, since he
was so new, to have him checked out. Mary Lisa really had
no clue what to look for, but she didn't think Todd fit the
bill of being some kind of obsessed maniac. He looked
more like a friendly computer geek, with his shoulders
hunched forward. Not someone you'd meet in a gym.

While Candy was fiddling with Mary Lisa's hair—it
was done up in a high knot on top of her head with a thick
rooster tail of hair fanning out of it—Todd said, "Mary
Lisa, Mr. Dillard asked me to suggest you try to lighten up

your reactions to Jeff in your scenes with him. He wants the audience to really wonder if Sunday is going to jump Damian's bones, and he'd prefer you not hit the audience over the head with how revolting you think this all is. He said everyone understands revenge, and the audience loves Sunday so much she could kill the entire cast off and they'd be content to watch you play monologues."

It was clever of Clyde to throw that in, but it didn't help. She said, "I'm sorry, Todd, that Clyde set you up to give that little speech. The thing is, they're not going to forgive me, but that isn't your problem. Tell Clyde I'll be talking this over with Bernie." Unless she managed to change it, Sunday was going to have to roll around in bed with Damian within a couple of weeks—probably beginning on a Thursday, the deed well under way by the end of the show on Friday.

Candy patted her shoulder and said, "Good to go again, Mary Lisa, the rooster tail is outrageous." With a polite nod, Mary Lisa said, "Thank you," and dashed off the floor over to Bernie Barlow, the head writer. She had to give it one more try.

Bernie looked up, saw her, and rolled his eyes. "I know, I know, you're here to beg and whine about Sunday not doing the foul deed with Susan's husband." He raised his hand. "Stop. You can save it all, Mary Lisa. We decided you're right. Yeah, we thought it over, but don't gloat and brag to everyone else, and don't think this sets some sort of precedent. You should assume it will never happen again on this planet. In fact, in a couple of days you won't even remember all your whining angst because we've come up with an idea so Titanic it turns the show on its head." He beamed at her. "You're going off the revenge/sex hook altogether."

The burst of excitement she felt quickly turned to suspicion. "Hold on here a second, my world is spinning. There's got to be a catch here. What's this all about, Bernie? What is this Titanic plan? Are you putting me in a *Survivor*-type show? Maybe set in Siberia? Having me seduce one of my mother's lovers instead? Or have you got my pool guy waiting in the wings? Hmm, well, at least he's cute and tells a good joke."

"There isn't a *Survivor* show. Forget the pool guy, it's been overdone."

"But Bernie—"

"Pay attention here, Mary Lisa. This is all on the up-and-up. And don't worry about Clyde. We're having a meeting over lunch, we'll tell him then. But it's a done deal." He waved a script in her face. "You'll know when it's your time to know. But I like it. Everyone likes it. Clyde will too although he was looking forward to showing off some of your nice skin. You'll have your script soon. We launch the Titanic on Thursday." He beamed at her, like Father Christmas taking lumps of coal out of her shoes. Mary Lisa felt the lead cloud flash bright silver over her head, and a grin split her face. She grabbed Bernie's hand and pumped it up and down, yelling "Yippee! Thank you, Bernie!" And she wasn't done. She leaped on him. Bernie was a big guy, a good six foot six, a former college basketball player, still pretty fast and agile at forty-five, but he dropped the script when she wrapped her legs around his waist and kissed him on both cheeks.

"You're the best, Bernie, the very best!"

"Yeah, yeah, that's what my wife told me before she dragged me into that pink chapel in Las Vegas." A camera flashed. "Hey, which one of you clowns took that photo?"

From the corner of her eye Mary Lisa saw a man moving fast toward the big red Exit sign. She recognized Puker Hodges as he slithered out the door. She leaped off Bernie, furious. "I'm going to kill that little worm. You watch me, I'm going to roast him over nice hot coals on my neighbor's barbeque grill."

"Was that the paparazzo who's been tailing you?"

"Yeah."

Bernie patted her arm, then screamed loud enough to set the chandelier jangling in Sunday Cavendish's living room set. "Where's security? Frank, go catch that creep and stomp his camera into the asphalt! Mother Mary and Father Joseph, is anybody minding the fricking store here?"

Mary Lisa said, "Give me Gloria's cell number. I'm going to call her so she won't cut your feet off."

"It wouldn't be my feet she'd go after," Bernie said, and sighed. "Well, at least it's never boring around here. Frank, you yahoo, where are you?"

LOU Lou came over a couple of hours later to fetch her for lunch. Lunch pickings were light in this section of Burbank so both of them usually brought sack lunches. Today Lou Lou had a cold, thick steak sandwich stuffed inside a baguette, smothered in mayonnaise, a super-sized bag of potato chips, and a big plastic bottle of Diet Dr Pepper on the side.

The truly nauseating thing was, Lou Lou wasn't even a single pound overweight. The good fairy had gifted her with a freak metabolism that burned food even faster than Mary Lisa's. Not satisfied with that, Lou Lou topped it off with a sincere enjoyment of aerobics, the sweatier the better. Mary Lisa was usually with her, watching Lou Lou smile her way through spin classes as her own eyebrows fell, hair by hair, into the sweat running down her face. On top of that, Mary Lisa had to stay ten pounds below weight, a must since the camera put it right back on. Why, she'd wondered, in this digital age, couldn't they come up with a camera that took off ten pounds instead of adding it on? It was a male conspiracy, she'd decided, to keep women impossibly skinny and therefore, since they were deprived of the pleasure of eating real live food, tempted to have sex with them instead. Sometimes, Mary Lisa rebelled and ate real food, like a super-sized bag of potato chips, knowing she'd have to run five miles and sweat guilt. She tried not to whine aloud as she opened her plastic carton of salad— half a dozen small beef cubes mixed with lettuce and tomatoes, a single whiff of fat-free Caesar dressing on top—and tried to ignore the delicious aroma wafting toward her from Lou Lou's baguette.

"Ah, come on, Mary Lisa, don't be pitiful. Here, take a bite—a small one. No, it's okay, I cleared it with the director-of-the-day, trust me. So splurge."

Mary Lisa wanted a whole lot more than a small bite of that cold, thick, medium-rare steak sandwich, but she suspected Lou Lou would cut her off at the knees if she took more than a nip, so she controlled herself. She chewed slowly and sat back against the park bench they were sharing in their favorite little green spot next to the studio, closed her eyes, and chewed some more. The sun was bright, as it was every day in Southern California, and blessed be, there was next to no smog today, and the air was soft and warm. Traffic was thick and horns were honking. Everything was as it should be.

She greatly preferred this spot to staying in the studio, though some people walking by, especially if they were tourists, would do a double take. Most wouldn't notice her, since this was L.A. and seeing a woman in full makeup was no big deal, but every once in a while, someone would stop and ask her who she was. Rarely, someone would recognize her as Sunday and ask for an autograph.

Lou Lou said, "Promise you won't leave the studio and come outside by yourself, Mary Lisa. Right now, you should plan to have someone with you at all times. I can't believe Puker actually broke into the studio. This time, they're going to nail his butt. Frank in security was all muzzy-headed. He thinks Puker may have put something in his coffee. Otherwise, he doesn't know how Puker could have slipped by him."

"You'd think Frank would know about the danger of gift horses."

"Well, not this time. Puker must think he's on a roll, after getting those pictures he took of you in the ambulance into the tabloids. The truth is, all the paparazzi are getting out of hand, not just Puker. First they started boxing celebrities into their cars so they can't escape, taking as many photos as they want, and now they're even causing traffic accidents—remember that Mercedes convertible they broadsided?—all to get pictures of the actors and their reactions. Things have shifted now, so like I said, I think the studio is going to go after him—they're going to start arresting these jerks, taking them and the magazines who publish their photos to court."

Mary Lisa said, "I hope so. Clyde's already filled out a police report and the police said they can get a warrant to arrest Puker—for breaking and entering on the set and taking my picture, and maybe assault for drugging Frank, who got a nice little nap out of it. They said that one could be hard to prove, though. Go figure."

"And don't forget he violated your restraining order again, even though you had it renewed last week and he knew it. Arresting him is just a start—I want them to fry the little creep. At the very least, this will cost him big lawyer fees. Oh, I called Danny. He said the Burbank cops are handling Puker's case but he knows the detective who drew the case and he'll keep in touch."

"Danny? You mean Detective Daniel Vasquez? Why did you call him Danny?"

TWENTY-THREE

In 1987 Brad Pitt appeared on *Another World* for one day.

"Yep, that's him."

"Hmm . . . so tell me when all this Danny business came about. Now, no evasions."

Lou Lou bit into three large chips, shrugged, and said in an offhand voice, "Well, we had dinner Saturday night over at Crockers on Ellis and Vine. Not bad. They're heavy on the hot peppers, which makes you drink tons and keeps the cash register cha-chinging all night. They charge a truckload for beers, not to mention the heavy stuff."

"I guess I just assumed Detective Vasquez was married."

"He's a widower; his wife died of breast cancer three years ago. He said no one expected the cancer would go so fast, said it was really tough for a while. He hasn't dated much since then."

Mary Lisa pictured the no-nonsense detective whose job it was to find the man who ran her down. Danny? It was a *Danny* handling her case? "It's the oddest thing," Mary Lisa said, staring down at the remaining three bites of salad, "but you never know anyone, do you? Here I was only thinking of Detective Vasquez as a cop trying to help me, but he's a person with a life of his own, and this tragedy to deal with."

Lou Lou slowly nodded. "I think he's doing okay now. But we've been talking about this guy who hit you. And I remembered the guy who was stalking you last year."

Mary Lisa shook her head before Lou Lou stopped speaking. "No, you're kidding, right? That guy seemed to be around every corner for maybe a week, but then he disappeared when the studio hired on a bodyguard for a few days. Everybody thought he got scared, probably left L.A."

"So, it's been—what, eight months since the creep went walkabout? He could be back, he could be pissed, he could have escalated. That's the word the shrinks use on the cop shows, isn't it?"

"What did Detective Vasquez think about it?"

"He wishes you'd told him earlier. I remembered you'd worked with a police artist so he dug out the sketch of the guy from the studio, brought it over to me yesterday since you weren't back in town yet. He wants me to show it to you again."

Mary Lisa raised an eyebrow. "You saw Detective Vasquez again yesterday?"

Lou Lou huffed into her Diet Dr Pepper. "Chrysler, Mary Lisa, I've got a life, he's got a life. I don't shut myself in a suitcase when you're not around."

"I didn't mean that, it's—"

"Yeah, I know. It sort of freaks me out a little bit too. Me, Lou Lou Bollinger—the five-earringed rebel—with a cop." Lou Lou picked up her small, expensive leather bag with its long shoulder strap and opened it up. "Here's the police sketch. Take a look."

Mary Lisa stared down at the face of the man she hadn't thought about for a good many months, not even in an occasional dream. She looked down at the fleshy face with wide-set dark eyes, the light brown hair covered by a baseball cap, remembered his belly hanging over the wide belt of his blue jeans, and slowly nodded. "As best as I can remember, that looks like him. I only saw him clearly that one time when I caught him off guard."

"I remember. You and I went into Barneys and you remembered you'd left the blouse you were returning in the car. You walked right out and there he was, lurking by your car."

"He took off when he saw me. You know, as I think back, he looked a bit older than he does here, maybe late forties. If I hadn't frozen, I probably could have caught up with him. He wasn't in good shape."

"I'm glad you froze. That would have been way too dangerous. Danny will deal with it now. And he'll make sure old Puker is put behind bars, all cozy with a new boyfriend, if we're lucky. I hope there's a big bubba in residence at the sheriff's lockup who can fill the role. Now, it's your turn. Tell me more about the guy you met in Goddard Bay this weekend."

"Guy? Why would you say that?"

"Give me a break, Mary Lisa. Look at you, you're smiling too much, you're bouncing around, you were chatty with Candy even after she rooster-tailed your hair this morning."

Mary Lisa touched her fingers to the fan of hair. "Hmm. It's not too bad, is it? I have no idea how she did it. Do you know what amazes me? Sunday's rich. She's got people cleaning her mansion, draining her swimming pool, mowing her grounds—not just a simple yard, but grounds—chauffeuring her around in her big cars. She's even got a sexy male secretary and an English houseman who's her confidant. But she doesn't seem to have a hair stylist or a manicurist or a personal shopper—yet every day she's dressed like a fashion plate and her hair looks like it's been styled by a magician."

Lou Lou patted her knee. "It's Hollywood, sweetie, magic land. As for your hair, it looks nice since you went into your dressing room and calmed it down. Don't worry, it's just fine, as usual."

Mary Lisa looked deep into the plastic container. One more beef cube. "Don't forget I hate you for eating like that, Lou Lou."

Lou Lou laughed at her around a big bite of steak sandwich. "Don't whine, Mary Lisa, you gotta suffer for the big bucks, it's only fair. Now, out with it. Tell me all the dirt in Goddard Bay. Tell me about this dishy guy. Does he have a great butt?"

"What is all this sudden interest on everyone's part about guys' butts?"

Lou Lou said, "Well, Danny has a great butt, I guess he got me focused on them again. It's been a long dry spell."

"Cops don't have butts, Lou Lou. They have guns and handcuffs. They're not supposed to be sex objects. They're supposed to be the neck-ripping rottweilers who are protecting me. How can I focus on Detective Vasquez catching this guy if you get me thinking about his butt?"

"Yeah, okay, leave that to me. Now, about this guy in Goddard Bay?"

"Well, there could have been a dishy guy up there but it isn't possible now."

"You going to tell me why?"

Mary Lisa shrugged. "His name's John Goddard—from the clan of the original Goddard who established the town back in the 1850s. He's the local district attorney. The thing is, though, he broke up with my younger sister, Kelly, early last week. She claims she kissed him off, but she didn't sound too convincing; in fact it was the other way around although John didn't say a word. So I called it off, told him we could only be friends. No way am I going to do to her what Monica did to me. No way."

Lou Lou grunted. "That's a bummer, but you know what? I guess I'd do the same thing. A sister is a sister, after all, even though you've told me all about Kelly. Another thing, that guy's a gentleman, and the good Lord knows they're as rare as the great auk. I'm impressed. Now, about Kelly—"

"I know, I know. It's complicated, Lou Lou. Do you know, I'm actually worried about Kelly. I think she might have really fallen for him. He's up to his eyeballs now in a local murder case, along with the local chief of police, an honest-to-God rottweiler whose name is Jack Wolf. John told me he was going to tell Jack Wolf about this stuff down here. I should probably call him, see how the murder case is going." Mary Lisa sighed, popped the last beef cube into her mouth, and leaned back against the park bench again.

"Which one? The rottweiler or the D.A.?"

"The D.A. Okay, Lou Lou, maybe I've said too much about Kelly, shot off my mouth. The thing is, she talks tough, but she's vulnerable right now, kind of young for her age, you know?"

"From what you've told me over the years, she sounds like she's a self-centered little goomba."

"Goomba? Well, maybe. I found out quite by accident she was married to this guy I hadn't even known about. Didn't last long. She moved back into my parents' house after the breakup with the D.A."

"She's twenty-five, right? Three years younger than you?"

Mary Lisa nodded.

"If you ask me, she and your mom deserve each other. We definitely need to talk more about this later, Mary Lisa, I think I'm beginning to change my mind. Hey, here comes Danny. I told him we'd be here for lunch. Don't forget to tell him about aging the nutcase from last year."

Mary Lisa looked at Detective Daniel Vasquez with new eyes. He wasn't all that tall, but he was slender, with dark hair and dark eyes older than his years, a swarthy complexion, and a kind smile, kicked up charmingly by a small dimple in his cheek.

"Ms. Beverly," he said. He studied her hair a moment, said "Nice 'do," then turned to Lou Lou.

"Sit down, Detective Vasquez," Lou Lou said, and scooted over. He planted himself between the two women. "Here, Danny, would you like a bite of my steak sandwich?"

He eyed the baguette with sudden interest. "It's like the one you made me yesterday?"

"Sure is, all the way to being smothered in mayo."

He ate the last bit of the sandwich, lightly touched a napkin to his mouth, and gave his full attention to Mary Lisa. Lou Lou looked very pleased with him.

Mary Lisa said, "Detective Vasquez, I looked at the sketch. As best I can remember, it looks like the guy except I think now that he was older, maybe in his late forties. I know I didn't mention him earlier, but I'm sure you know that just about everybody in the business has experienced something like that. Frankly I hardly remember him. It's been a long time."

"Stalkers and movie stars—it's sort of like the rumba and the mambo."

"They're both dances?"

"No, you rarely see one without the other. Of course you're right, Ms. Beverly—there's a lot of fascination with actors, but we rarely see any of them hurt. Still, I'm glad Lou Lou brought him to our attention. Older, huh? I'll have the police artist age the guy a few years. Then we may be able to put it to use, see if anyone recognizes him. By the way, the Burbank police have got Puker Hodges's apartment staked out. It was pretty stupid of him to commit at least a couple of crimes in public, particularly now, Ms. Beverly. I can't believe he actually thought he'd get away with it."

Lou Lou looked thoughtful. "You're right. He couldn't count on getting a good photo of Mary Lisa. I wonder why he took such a chance?"

Detective Vasquez said, "I look forward to asking him."

Mary Lisa snorted. "I hope they break the little weasel's camera finger." She glanced at her watch, jumped to her feet. "I'm sorry, Detective Vasquez, but I've got to go. Being late is a major crime. Lou Lou, don't forget, we're having drinks with Freddie Morgan tonight, at Gumbo's. Bye, Detective." And Mary Lisa was off, headed back toward the studio.

Detective Vasquez asked, as he watched her rooster tail flopping, "Who's Freddie Morgan?"

Lou Lou smiled as she wadded up her paper sack. "He's a friend of Mary Lisa's, a hotshot producer who's got a couple of long-running TV series on—I forgot to tell you about tonight. The thing is, Freddie might want to sign me on to do the makeup for some of his A-list events. That would be big time, big names, it would really put me out there. I've got to go."

"No problem, Lou Lou. I'll call when I have some news. Tell your friend to be careful. I have this twitching elbow that tells me things."

"I'll keep reminding her."

"Good girl." He touched his fingers to her nose and smiled.

TWENTY-FOUR

John Aniston, Jennifer Aniston's father, played Victor
Kiriakis on *Days of Our Lives*.

Malibu
Late Wednesday afternoon

Today Mary Lisa ignored all the advice. She was alone and
on a mission. She looked carefully both ways down PCH
before she crossed. There were no dark sedans, no suspicious men in backward baseball caps anywhere on the
highway. But even if someone was hidden close by, she
hoped he wouldn't recognize her—she had her big Audrey
Hepburn sunglasses firmly in place, and a 49ers cap pressed
down on her head, covering her red hair. She was wearing a
sloppy XL Colts sweatshirt over ratty jeans and high-top
sneakers.

And she didn't have to worry about Puker Hodges chasing her with his Kodak. Detective Malloy had called her
from the Burbank PD to tell her they'd picked him up at his
apartment Monday afternoon, not even bothering to hide
their grins when he got all irate as they cuffed him, yelling
his head off for a lawyer and claiming a violation of his
civil rights as a member of the press. He insisted on taking
a slice of pizza he was eating with him in one of his hand-
cuffed hands, and ended up dropping it on the sidewalk

since the cops wouldn't unfasten the cuffs so he could eat it. The security guard Frank Hallick said Puker had offered him a piping hot grande nonfat mocha latte, his favorite, and how did the little dork know that? Turned out what was left of the grande was laced with heavy-duty sleeping pills. Detective Malloy of the Burbank PD laughed when he told Mary Lisa not to worry, they had the little loudmouth dead to rights. He said the doping charge was a serious one, and there were others, including Puker's violating Mary Lisa's new restraining order. Detective Malloy was pleased—he said Puker might even do some jail time, depending on the plea bargaining.

The only unfortunate thing was that Puker had already sold the photo to the *National Enquirer.* One of the *Born to Be Wild* deliveryboys, an enterprising son of a soap writer, had called to warn her. "Wow, Mary Lisa, you made the front page!" And so she was on her mission to buy a copy, see how bad the photo was and what lewd nonsense they'd invented to caption it.

The head of the studio, the savvy, no-nonsense, nail-biting Irene Ludlow, had called Mary Lisa, royally displeased, assuring her that the studio would prosecute Puker to the full extent of the law. This was studio policy now—like not negotiating with terrorists. Puker had already spent a night in jail, and they would use him to send a message, whether or not he and his lawyer screamed in two-part harmony for the ACLU.

She slipped into Big Glow market. There, right at eye level in the checkout line, for all to see, were a dozen copies of the *National Enquirer* with a big color photo of her, front and center. She stared at the photo and wanted to pull a produce bag over her head. What had possessed her to jump on Bernie, wrap her legs around his waist and her arms around his neck, and throw her head back, with that thick fan of hair sticking out the back of her head like a Mohawk? She looked wildly happy, her mouth so wide with laughter you could nearly see her tonsils. They'd cut out all the other people standing around. It was only she and Bernie with his face nearly in her cleavage, her dress rucked up to mid thigh. Since he was so much taller, it looked like they could be having sex, her billowing skirt covering the act.

And the tagline beneath the lovely big color photo: *Emmy winner Mary Lisa Beverly and new beau—naughty naughty, Mary Lisa, this Emmy winner is married.*

She bought a copy along with, for camouflage, three oranges and a pocket Kleenex, and slunk back outside. She leaned against the glass window and read the article.

They identified Bernie as the head writer for *Born to Be Wild*, wondered if he was the new man in her life, speculated about what went on in her dressing room if—snicker—this was a sample of what she did in public.

Mary Lisa pulled out her cell and dialed Bernie's house, heard three rings and a throaty "Hello."

"Gloria, it's Mary Lisa. I just bought the *National Enquirer.* It's awful, I'm so sorry, I don't know what to say. If the boys were still young I'd offer to babysit for a year free."

To her astonishment, Gloria Barlow howled with laughter. "It's okay, pet. I'm sure Bernie is preening as we speak. His sons are calling him Mr. Stud, high-fiving him with 'Way to go, Dad!' He announced a half hour ago he wanted to go to the club to play golf, but what he really wanted was to be sure none of his buddies missed all this. I had Thad drive him, and got no argument since he wanted his dad to tell him everything. It sounded to me like all of Bernie's golf buddies will buy him so many free drinks to dish up the dirt, he'll need Thad to drive him home. Do you know, I think he bought about a dozen copies to hand out? One for his dad too."

Mary Lisa burst out laughing. "But what about your mom?"

"She just called, told me all her friends want to meet you, said you had to be a mensch to jump Bernie's bones like that. Everything's fine, Mary Lisa, stop your worrying. It's a hoot. Thanks for the offer of babysitting, even if it's a decade too late."

When Mary Lisa walked through her front door ten minutes later, her home phone was ringing. She ran to pick it up. "Hello?"

"Shame on you, sleeping with a married man. Maybe next time you won't be so lucky." And the whispery voice hung up.

Mary Lisa stood in the center of her living room, staring down at the phone in her hand, listening to the dial tone.

She hadn't quite closed the door and it burst open and Lou Lou dashed in, panting. "I was talking to Danny when Morrie Bernstein, who owns Big Glow market, called to tell him you'd waltzed into his store alone, and how could the cops let that happen? I came as quickly as I could. Danny said he'd break free soon to come over and smack you upside the head." She waved the *Enquirer* around. "These bastards. I say we drop-kick all of them right into a snow-filled crevasse in Patagonia. Mary Lisa? What's wrong? Look, the photo and article aren't all that bad, they do lots worse, you know? And it's really kind of cute and funny—you look happy and Bernie's grinning like a fool. I don't think people will believe this crazy caption about you and Bernie. Everyone knows he's the head writer, and there you are in full makeup. You'll see, this will blow right over. Mary Lisa?"

Mary Lisa raised frightened eyes. "It's not the photo or the caption, Lou Lou. I just got a phone call. He said I shouldn't be sleeping with a married guy and next time I wouldn't be so lucky."

For a moment Lou Lou couldn't seem to take it in, then, "Oh shit. There aren't many people who have this number." She grabbed Mary Lisa's phone, called the sheriff's department, and asked for Detective Daniel Vasquez.

Thirty minutes later, Daniel Vasquez walked into Mary Lisa's living room to see a dozen people—old, young, three teenagers—all hovering over her, one offering her tea or coffee, another holding out a glass that looked like it held either water or straight vodka, all of them talking at once. He recognized a couple of TV actors. Mary Lisa wasn't saying anything, only looking at the cup she was holding between her hands. He saw Carlo, who'd had his birthday blast on the beach recently. And he recognized MacKenzie Corman, the wannabe actress, mainly because he recognized Honey Boy, her white toy poodle, who was sitting in Mary Lisa's lap, one of his small paws on her forearm. She didn't live in the Colony. How had she managed to get past Chad at the kiosk? Then he looked at the bright pink tube top she was wearing, the wonderful cleavage on display, and shook his head at himself. The house was nearly full. Did the woman collect people?

Mary Lisa looked up at him, gave him a ghastly smile. "You made really good time. Thank you for coming."

Detective Vasquez cleared his throat. Everyone looked up, including Lou Lou, who said, "Dan—Detective Vasquez! Glad you're here. Come in. Okay, everybody, you've all got to go. Everything'll be okay now. He's the police. Thank you for coming over."

Once she'd herded everyone out of the house, she turned and said quickly, "Danny, this isn't good. Now some weirdo's calling her, maybe the same guy—we've got to get him."

The place cleared out amazingly fast, Detective Vasquez thought. He waited until it was blessedly quiet. He looked at Mary Lisa. She was pale and looked pinched, but he saw anger beneath the surface, bubbling hot. That was good. He sat beside her and said, "You draw quite a crowd."

"News travels fast in the Colony."

There was a knock on the door. Detective Vasquez raised his hand. "Let me get it, okay?"

They watched him walk to the front door and open it about six inches. They heard men's voices but couldn't make out their words.

Mary Lisa's jaw nearly hit the carpet when the chief of police of Goddard Bay, Jack Wolf, walked through the door.

TWENTY-FIVE

Before *Superman*, Christopher Reeve played Ben on
Love of Life.

Mary Lisa jumped to her feet. "Whatever are you doing
here? Is something wrong? Is my dad okay?"

"Your dad is fine. He sends his love and told me he was
going to pin your ears back for not telling him about this
mess."

"I didn't want to worry him, didn't want to worry anybody."

"Yeah? Well, you told John and he told me. I called
down here and spoke to Detective Vasquez."

He walked to her and stopped about six inches from her
nose. "You look pale enough to fade out. Something else
has happened, hasn't it?"

Lou Lou said, "The jerk called her a little while ago.
Who are you, again?"

"Oh, I'm sorry," said Mary Lisa. "This is Chief of Police Jack Wolf from Goddard Bay."

"You're the rottweiler?"

He grinned, a big one that changed his face entirely.

"Yes, it sounds like that would be me." He shook hands with Lou Lou.

"Sit down, Chief Wolf." Mary Lisa waved to one of the love seats. "Would you care for something to drink?"

Jack looked about her bright living room for a moment before he selected a green-and-white-striped love seat. "You don't have to be a hostess, Mary Lisa. Tell me what happened here."

"But how did you get past Chad?"

"I showed him my badge, gave him your name and a look that clearly translated as official business, and he let me through without a single question."

Mary Lisa gave him a long look, then turned to Lou Lou. "Lou Lou, would you please take Detective Vasquez out on the deck, point out Big Dume to him?"

"But—"

"Please, Detective. I need a moment with Chief Wolf."

Once they were out of hearing, Jack said, "Okay, now what would you like to say to me?"

"I'd like you to tell me why you came down here. You've never seemed to like me. I didn't imagine you'd care if some loon ran me down or not."

"Actually, I was tied up until this morning or I would have been here sooner. I called Lost Hills Station and spoke to Detective Vasquez, and he told me to come on down." He sat forward, clasping his hands between his knees. "Listen, you've got family and a lot of friends in Goddard Bay who care about you, John included, and that makes you my responsibility as well."

"Whether you like me or not?"

"Liking you has nothing to do with anything, Ms. Beverly. Besides, John couldn't stop singing your praises. He wasn't happy about your kissing him off, but he admired you for doing it. He kept going and going until I wanted to punch him out. Then I thought about it awhile and decided that maybe you've grown up, maybe you wouldn't be pouring sugar into anyone's gas tank anymore if they crossed you."

Her face turned red as a Malibu sunset, not due for another four hours. "Crossed me? Like that even comes close to what that moron did. Dammit, I found my supposed fiancé in bed with my sister, you jerk! He was engaged to me, and he betrayed me. Thinking back on it, I should have shoved a potato up his exhaust pipe, maybe it would have blown him up!"

Jack tapped his fingertips on his knees. "Okay, so there was provocation, but it was a new Beemer, Ms. Beverly, and you destroyed the engine on that fine machine."

She threw up her hands. "Men!"

Suddenly, he grinned. "Okay, so the night in jail was a little bit overboard. Let me tell you, your dad climbed my frame up one side and down the other. Does that make you feel better?"

"Was that supposed to be an apology?"

"It's close, isn't it?"

"No."

Jack's dark brow shot up.

Mary Lisa threw up her hands. "Men and your genetic bond to machines—none of you can get over what I did to his precious car, a stupid machine, dammit. Well, to be honest here, that's exactly why I did it." She drew a deep breath. "So did you arrest one of the Hildebrands for killing Jason Maynard?"

"Why do you think it was one of the Hildebrands?"

Mary Lisa said patiently, "The person who did it was obviously very angry. A stranger or a simple acquaintance wouldn't get that worked up, would they? Who was it?"

"His father-in-law, Milo Hildebrand."

She nodded. "Milo. What was the motive?"

"It was all about money, not about any cheating Jason was doing on his wife. Jason had embezzled over three hundred thousand dollars from his father-in-law's company, and Milo found out about it. Milo confronted him in a rage, then followed him back to his house with a golf driver sitting beside him on the front seat. Since Milo stole it the day before the murder, it shows premeditation— lucky for him we don't have the death penalty in Oregon."

"Where'd he steal it? How did you find out about it?"

Jack grinned. "In big cities most crimes are solved by informants. In small towns, it's a matter of talking to people. One of the attendants who works in the men's dressing room at the club saw Milo take a golf club from a locker that isn't his. He didn't really think about it at the time, thought he was simply borrowing it, but he did think about it hard after I interviewed him along with everyone else who worked at the club. He came to me Sunday morning, said he'd seen Mr. Hildebrand take a Callaway driver.

"We matched the murder weapon up to the clubs we found in the locker. Milo surprised me—he kept screaming that his wife did it and ran. I had to shoot him in the leg so we could take him into custody. Unfortunately, he hasn't confessed. He continues to blame his wife, keeps swearing he stole the club for her but had no idea what she wanted to do with it."

"That makes a whole lot of sense."

"Oh yeah. Milo claims his wife found out Jason was sleeping around on their daughter and that's why she killed him. He claims he kept quiet to protect her. He claims he didn't know about the embezzlement."

"You have proof he did know?"

"Oh yes."

"Poor Mrs. Hildebrand."

"That's the truth. From all I can find out, Milo's controlled her for all of the thirty-five years of their married life, told her what to spend, where to spend it, how to dress, how to behave. And now he's trying to implicate her in the murder."

She shook her head. "I can't imagine that. And it was all for money, only money."

Jack shrugged. "Everyone has a different breaking point, and for Milo, it was rank betrayal by his son-in-law, the ultimate sin. The fact remains that he did it. It's over."

"So you solved the first murder in Goddard Bay—in well under a week."

Jack shrugged again, but Mary Lisa could swear she saw a stain of red on his cheekbones. It humanized him.

He said abruptly, "If you'll let me, I'm here to help you now, Ms. Beverly."

"Since you're here to help me, why don't you call me Mary Lisa?"

He nodded. "Tell me about this phone call, Ms.—Mary Lisa—exactly what he said, what he sounded like to you. Was he excited? Enraged? Did you hear anything in the background?"

Mary Lisa held up her hand. "Okay, you're in cop mode."

He grinned, and again it surprised her. All she'd ever seen on him was a hard, detached face, as if he didn't want to be in the same room with her, or in the same room with most people. She wanted to smile back, but she thought of the man on the phone and simply couldn't. "He said, exactly, *'Shame on you, sleeping with a married man. Maybe next time you won't be so lucky.'* That was all. He hung up. His voice was whispery, sort of hoarse. I'm sure it was a guy, but he didn't sound familiar, and he didn't sound particularly angry, sort of world-weary, like he'd expected all this, which sounds odd, but it's true. I didn't hear anything in the background. I couldn't tell how old he was—not real young and not real old either, I guess. I might recognize his voice if I heard it again, though. The only thing I'm sure of is that he wasn't an orangutan."

"Okay, that's good. Do you have any ideas on what you might have done to draw a crazy like this to you?"

"What *I* might have done?"

"You're an actress, Ms.—Mary Lisa. A celebrity. Most young women can kiss off a guy at a party, or spend lots of cash shopping on Rodeo Drive, and no one notices. For you, it's different. Someone has been watching, and that someone went over the edge."

She shook her head, her lips tightly seamed, until she interrupted him, her voice as cold as her mom's. "You're right, Chief Wolf—"

"Since I'm trying to help you, I guess you'd better call me Jack."

She couldn't say why, but it simply stunned her. How could this man possibly be simply Jack to her? "Why are you acting like this?"

"Like what?"

She waved her hands in his face. "Like you're human, like you might consider me human too."

"All right, you're angry with me. Go on. I believe you were about to pin my ears back."

"Yes, I am. You're acting as if I'm a party girl, without any morals or sense. Most actresses, myself included, work hard, enjoy their friends, spend most of their time at home. None of my actor friends go boozing at wild parties and I think I've only been on Rodeo Drive one time—to buy myself a real pearl necklace for winning my second Emmy."

"So, cutting through all that, you mean to say you haven't a clue who's doing this and you can't think of any way you could have brought it on."

"Would you like a soda? Lower your blasted eyebrow, Chie—Jack. I'm thirsty."

Venting at him had helped her get her balance back, he thought as he watched her walk to her kitchen. He followed her, and stopped dead, blown away by the magnificent view. Her cottage sat right on the beach. Not fifty feet away the Pacific waves lapped gently onto the sand, and a brilliant sun shone through the few wispy clouds that dotted the sky. He saw a few teenagers, her neighbors, he supposed, since this was a gated community, mostly lolling about, some playing volleyball, others simply stretched out on towels, sunning, the girls dressed in little designer swimsuits.

He said, "I love the ocean, always have. Unfortunately, my house is a bit too far inland to hear the waves. I love that sound, don't you?"

Again, she stared at him.

"Mary Lisa, I'm just a guy, like any other guy, and I like the ocean. I'd like it if I could sit beside Daniel and Lou Lou, feet up on the deck railing, just basking like they are."

She didn't look happy and so he said simply, "I also happen to be a cop. It's my job, like yours is being an actress. We need to get past what happened in Goddard Bay—you did something stupid three years ago and I'll admit it, I got the wrong impression of you."

"You treated me like a juvenile delinquent, a stupid teenager."

"Yep, I did. Even your father couldn't make me see you were so hurt you'd lashed out. Okay, the truth here—I'd just come to Goddard Bay and been elected chief of police. Then this ditsy girl comes along who destroys a valuable vehicle, and isn't at all sorry about what she's done. It's no real excuse, but I was coming off a really miserable divorce." He looked like he wanted to shut up and not say another word.

"Go ahead, spit it out, Jack."

"I guess I put you in the same boat with my ex-wife. She burned me bad, Mary Lisa. No excuse for what I did to you, but there you have it. I'm sorry."

She gave him a brilliant smile. "Now that's an apology I can live with." She handed him a Diet Dr Pepper, opened one for herself. She clicked her can to his. "Thanks for coming down to help me, Jack."

"Yeah, you're welcome. You really did kiss off John because of Kelly, didn't you?"

"I wasn't about to hurt her like Monica had hurt me. No way."

He nodded, drank more of his soda.

"Ah, so John made you think I'm selfless? Noble?"

"Nah, but he made me see you're okay."

"Nice to hear that from a yahoo chief of police from the boondocks."

For the first time, they smiled at each other.

TWENTY-SIX

Ricky Martin played Miguel, a hunky, world-famous singer, on *General Hospital*.

BORN TO BE WILD
Thursday morning

Sunday looks up to see her mother, Lydia Cavendish, sweep into her office, while her secretary, Ellis, waves his hands ineffectively behind her. "It's all right, Ellis. No one can stop a moving train." She waits until he closes the door, rises slowly but doesn't come around her desk. She's wearing a black suit with an open white silk blouse, a black ribbon choker around her neck. Her skirt is short, her long legs ending in black stiletto heels. Her red hair is in her signature chignon, two curls dangling in front of her black earrings. She arches an eyebrow and looks impatient. She says sarcastically, "To what do I owe this pleasure, Mother? Last thing I knew, you weren't speaking to me. Are you planning to use sign language?"

Lydia Cavendish is wearing a white suit with a bright red silk camisole that shows a good deal of cleavage. She looks more flamboyant than elegant, on the voluptuous side, and as arrogant as her eldest daughter. She's wearing flashy diamonds at her ears, throat, and wrist. "You needn't be so snide, Sunday," she says and tosses her purse on a chair.

Sunday crosses her arms over her chest, remains behind her desk. "I'm very busy, Mother, though you hardly seem to have noticed I've even come back from that boarding school in Austria. At least you came yourself, rather than sending another of those little psychos you seem to collect. By the way, how is Bernard? In jail yet?"

Lydia walks to the sideboard, pours herself a big shot of brandy, gulps it down. "You were better off in Europe." She throws back her head, closes her eyes. "You needn't bother sleeping with Damian. He's not worth it." Sunday is shocked, opens her mouth, but says nothing as she realizes her mother is very upset, almost ready to break down.

Alarmed, Sunday walks around her desk, but no closer. "What's wrong, Mother? Has Susan done something? Damian? You needn't cry about Bernard, he's a dishonest creep and we all know that now. You're far better off without him."

"No, this has nothing to do with Susan or with Bernard." She's silent again, looks around Sunday's office, frowns a bit. "How I hate this, Sunday. I hoped you would never know. He swore he would never come back. But he's here."

Sunday looks down at her watch. "I'm very busy, Mother. Who's here?"

"I didn't have to think about him for a very long time, but lately I see his face all over the TV, he's gotten so popular, and then of course I have to think about him. And now he's in town. He's here. The bastard."

"Mother, who are you talking about? Stop being such a drama queen and tell me!"

Sunday stares at her mother, her head cocked a bit to the side. And stares, stares—

"Clear!"

Three minutes later, the women's makeup touched up again, Todd Bickly, the stage manager, called out from the wing, "Ready, continue the scene."

Sunday is staring at her mother. "What is this all about, Mother? Please tell me who it is you're talking about."

Lydia draws a big breath, fans her hands in front of her, her diamonds winking in the light. "Your father, Sunday. Your father is demanding to see you."

Sunday leans against her desk, her arms folded over her chest. She says slowly, eyeing her mother, "My father's dead. He died when I was only a year old. He was doing business in Cambodia, and he was kidnapped and killed."

"Yes, that's what I told you. He was with the Rand Corporation, and he was indeed in Cambodia, that was true. But he didn't get kidnapped nor did he die there, more's the pity." Lydia picks up a crystal glass and hurls it against the far wall. A painting tilts at the impact.

"Mother—"

"You look like him, do you know that? You look exactly like his daughter, and now that he's seen you, he wants to meet you."

Sunday is shocked, confused. She looks blindly around her office, walks out from behind her desk to her mother, grabs her shoulders and shakes her. "Are you telling me you've kept me from my father all my life? Why? What did he do to you?"

"Oh, stop it, you stupid girl. It was a long time ago, but he hasn't changed, his kind don't ever change."

"I can't believe this, I really can't."

"For heaven's sake, haven't you ever wondered where you got your silly name?"

Sunday slowly shakes her head, takes a step back. "I know it's unusual, but it's just my name. Everyone has a name and no matter how weird it is, it's yours. Are you saying my father named me? For some specific reason?"

"It was after he came home from Cambodia, he was a different man, hard and unreachable, and he no longer wanted me or you, but he insisted on having your name changed, forced me to do it or he wouldn't give me a divorce."

"You divorced him?"

"Yes. He didn't love me, wouldn't touch me, said he was meant for something else. He said he would give me a divorce and wouldn't make a grab for any of my father's money if I agreed to change your name to Sunday."

"What was my name?"

"It was Angela."

"Why did he pick Sunday?"

Lydia takes a big breath, stares at her lovely nails, then looks blindly toward the sideboard where there are bottles of liquor. You can tell she'd like a drink, badly.

"Mother, enough of this. Who is my father? What is his name?"

Lydia finally meets her daughter's eyes. "It's Phillip Galliard."

"Who—?"

"Reverend Phillip Galliard."

"You don't mean the TV evangelist?"

"Oh yes, that's exactly who I mean."

"But my name isn't Galliard—" She stares at her mother, eyebrows drawn together, confused.

"Clear!"

Todd stepped onto the floor, waving the script about, grinning from ear to ear. "That was excellent, just excellent. I'll bet pins are dropping in every living room in America and you can hear them hit the floor." He listened a moment, then tapped his earpiece. "Clyde's screaming upstairs. He loved it!"

TWENTY-SEVEN

Mary Lisa looked hard at her home phone when it rang that afternoon, afraid it might be the crazy. Most people called her on her cell, not her house phone. And the guy didn't have her cell phone number. But the police wanted him to call, now that they had her phone tapped. That had been one thing Jack and Detective Vasquez had set up before they'd left the day before. And Jack wanted her to improve upon her security system. Fat chance. She picked it up.

"Hello?"

"Mary Lisa."

"Yes, who is this?"

"Your favorite paparazzo."

"There's no such animal in the universe. Come on now, who is this?"

"Don't you recognize my voice? I'm the artist who got you on the cover of the *Enquirer* with your legs looking so fine all wrapped around Bernie Barlow's waist."

"Ah, Puker."

"Puker? You called me Puker." Outrage sounded in his voice. "You actually called me Puker?"

"If the name fits. Don't tell me I'm your one phone call from jail."

"No, no, I'm long out of jail, no thanks to your studio and that security guy, Frank whatever. Doesn't anybody have a sense of humor anymore?"

"I see. It was all our fault for misunderstanding you. You're a real jerk, Puker, and you shouldn't be calling me, there's a court order—"

"That's for my corporeal self, not my voice. Listen up, Mary Lisa, I saw a guy in a dark sedan who seemed to be casing you out. He was wearing dark glasses but then he pulled them off to rub his eyes and I saw his face. I didn't like the way he looked—real hard, you know? I snapped pics before he slid his sunglasses back on. I think he might be the guy you're looking for."

Her hand tightened on the phone. He was lying, he had to be, it was what he did. Of course he knew much of what happened—he was there that day, snapping pictures. He could have guessed the rest.

"Mary Lisa?"

"Okay, Puker. Let's say you saw someone. Where was this?"

"Near the studio, on Fourth and Pine. He was parked, engine idling, wearing a baseball cap. I took some shots of him, telephoto, up close."

"So you're calling to give me the pictures?"

"Well, now, that depends, doesn't it?"

"On what, you jerk?"

"He was a mean-looking guy, Mary Lisa, like he was on a mission—maybe you? Hey, it could be dangerous for me to cross someone like that by giving you these photographs. So I want something in return. All you gotta do is call off the studio, talk them into dropping the charges and forgetting about any lawsuit against me."

"It's their decision, Puker, not mine."

"Don't call me that!"

"Maybe you're right, maybe it doesn't fit you, maybe I've been wrong and you're a fine upstanding individual with ethics." She had to get a grip here. She wondered again if he really did have photos or if he was lying. Probably lying, but she couldn't take the chance. She drew a deep breath. "Okay, I want to see those photos first, see if they're any good or even for real, and not one of your schemes."

"Nah, this is no stunt. I developed the prints and I know what I've got. They're real sharp, Mary Lisa, all three of them. Real sharp. You want to see them, you call off the dogs."

"I want to see them before I—"

"Before what? Before he kills you?" The line went dead.

Mary Lisa slowly laid the phone back in its cradle, picked it up again, and called Detective Vasquez's cell phone number. He was tied up so she called his house, where Jack was staying.

Thirty-five minutes later, both Detective Vasquez and Jack Wolf were at her house listening to the recording.

"That's it," Detective Vasquez said, pressing the stop button. "It sure sounds like Puker Hodges to me. You have any doubts?"

She shook her head.

Jack stared at her. "There's got to be a reason why this guy picked you. There's always a reason, we just have to discover it."

Daniel said, "She's not Sandra Bullock, but she's big enough that people want to know all about her. Puker uses that to make a living." He drew in a deep breath. "Unfortunately, some of those people mix up the actor and the person, and they become one."

Jack asked, "How long has this Puker guy been after you, Mary Lisa?"

"Six months or so. I got a restraining order on him. It didn't restrain him much, but I got it reinstated last week. It seems to me that one day Puker wasn't on my radar and the next he was in my face."

Jack grinned at her, something she thought she'd get used to in a year or so. "Puker really didn't like the nickname you gave him."

"Nope, you could tell it enraged him. He says his real name is Poker, but that sounds made up too. It's what he calls himself. Maybe he had a casino dealer for a father, who knows?"

Detective Vasquez said, "We already have quite a file on him. Puker got a good start as a photographer in Wilmington, Delaware, where he got his training and worked freelance for the local newspapers. Then he came out here five years ago, right after he turned twenty-five, and seems to have decided making money beat out having morals any day. He's been shooting celebrities ever since. So far as we know, he's never been married, dates occasionally, and has never gotten into any real trouble before. Now he's in very deep water with this latest stunt at the studio."

"And now this," Mary Lisa said. She rose and began pacing her living room. "I want to see those photos. Can't you make him turn them over, Detective Vasquez?"

"Well, now, Mary Lisa," said Daniel, slowly rising, "I was thinking maybe Jack and I could pay him a visit and ask him nicely."

"I want to go."

"It's police business, Mary Lisa," Jack said. "Learn your lines for tomorrow, and we'll be back later." He stood there a moment, waiting, knowing she couldn't let that order simply slide. But she didn't say anything.

Thirty minutes later, Daniel pulled his Crown Vic out of godawful traffic and up against the curb of an apartment building a dozen blocks east of Santa Monica Pier, not ten miles from Malibu. It was a small, upscale, slightly dated complex, with lots of palm trees and blooming flowers and well-kept late-model cars parked everywhere.

"What do you think, Jack?"

"The guy's making money. This isn't low-rent, is it?"

"No. Detective Malloy from Burbank told me the guy's

a pig, lives in this beautiful apartment like it was a dorm, strews pizza boxes and his shorts all over the place."

Puker's apartment was on the second floor, on the end. Jack nodded at Daniel, and knocked.

"Yeah? Who is it?"

Daniel said, "It's the police, Hodges, open up now."

"Hey, dude, I don't have anything to say to you guys. Talk to my lawyer."

Jack said in a pleasant, upbeat voice that would make anyone think twice, "Open the door, Puker, or I'll make you regret it. I might make you clean your kitchen."

They heard chains slide off, and the door opened. Puker was wearing baggy low-riding shorts and a ratty dark blue T-shirt. "Yeah?"

"Kitchen's that bad, is it?" Jack said, stepping forward, forcing Puker back into his apartment. "We're here to see the photos you took of this guy you claim is Mary Lisa Beverly's stalker."

Puker opened his mouth, but closed it when he saw the look on the big man's face. Then he said, "Hey, dude, you can't threaten me. I'm a citizen of Los Angeles. Haven't you guys figured out you can't go attacking civilians?"

Jack wrapped his fist around the neck of Puker's T-shirt, raised him onto his toes. "Listen to me, you little puke, I want to see those photos this minute or we'll book you for extortion and interfering with a police investigation. We'll get the photos anyway, and you'll have no chance at all with the studio."

Puker looked at Detective Vasquez, who was studying his fingernails. He shrugged.

"The photos," Jack said, and shook him. "Now."

"I want to call my lawyer, he'll—"

Jack said in the same pleasant voice, "Last chance, Puker. Really, you don't want to mess with me or I just might stuff you in your fridge." And Jack smiled at him, released his shirt and smoothed it, tough since it was so wrinkled.

Puker jumped back, splayed his hands toward them. "Hey, my fridge isn't all that bad."

Daniel said, "If you don't suffocate in the fridge, then I'll take you down to my jail, let you think things over in a holding cell with a dozen or so other upstanding citizens. How's that?"

Puker looked undecided, then he belched, shrugged. "All right. Come back here. I made my second bedroom into a darkroom."

Daniel grinned at the back of Puker's head as they followed him to his makeshift darkroom.

Puker closed the door and flipped on an overhead red light. The room looked like any professional darkroom Jack had ever seen, everything neatly in its place and well cared for, quite unlike the mess in the rest of the apartment.

"The photos are here." Puker handed them three color prints, still a bit damp at the edges.

Daniel turned on a lamp back in the living room and studied the photos. "Well, I'll be," he said after only a moment. "How about that?"

"What?" Jack asked. "You know this guy?"

"Yeah, I think most everybody at my station knows him." He turned to Puker. "See how easy it is to be a fine upstanding citizen, Mr. Hodges? Thank you for your invaluable assistance in this case. It's very possible that Mary Lisa won't be inclined now to press any charges against you. But who knows? Keep your nose clean."

Neither man spoke until they were in Daniel's car, the air-conditioning turned on high.

"Well?"

"Jack, my man, this here is Stuart Clapper, been in and out of prison since the age of thirteen, not very bright, but street-smart. He does coke, sells on the side, sent up for assault a few years ago. I think he beat a rape charge once. There's a problem though."

Jack arched a black brow. "Yeah, what?"

"I've never heard of him having a thing for any female celebrities."

"Well, there's always a first time."

"Yeah, you're right. I'll track down an address for him.

We should have time to show his photo to Mary Lisa, see if she recognizes him. Lou Lou too. She's so sharp it's scary. She would remember him if he's been around Malibu."

"Where does Lou Lou live?"

"She doesn't make the big bucks Mary Lisa makes, so she lives inland, about four blocks. Not that it matters, she's at Mary Lisa's house—along with half of Malibu— most of the time."

Daniel opened his cell. After a couple of minutes, he said to Jack, "Clapper just finished up ten months of parole. His P.O. only had his last known address. It's real common, the day the parolees are through, they're gone. Still, we'll check."

They drove in silence, Daniel weaving southeast, through the bleakest parts of central L.A. that had Jack thinking of the fresh sea air in Goddard Bay.

Daniel asked, "What's with you and Mary Lisa?"

"Nothing," Jack said. "At least nothing anymore. We had what you might call a meeting of the minds."

"You groveled, huh?"

Jack laughed. "Yeah, right."

"Okay, here we are, Sixty-four Kemper Street." Daniel pulled to the curb, pointed up at a tired, peeling gray four-story building that looked like it was condemned, or should have been. There were air-conditioning units hanging out of a few of the windows, but no fire escapes that Jack could see. "It'll smell like cabbage in the hallways," Daniel said. "It always does. I don't know why that is."

Jack said, "It's true in Chicago too."

It took them thirty minutes to get past the sullen stares and mumbled responses of two of the neighbors and find out from the super that Stuart Clapper had been gone for three weeks as best he could figure, no forwarding address. He'd cleared parole three weeks and two days ago.

TWENTY-EIGHT

Before *Star Wars*, Mark Hamill played Nurse Jessie's
nephew on *General Hospital*.

"I've never seen this guy before. Lou Lou, have you?"

Lou Lou scrutinized the three photos and slowly, regretfully, shook her head. "This is the guy trying to whack
Mary Lisa?"

"That sure makes me feel warm and fuzzy, Lou Lou."

"Probably not," Daniel said.

Lou Lou said thoughtfully, "Do you know, he kind of
looks familiar. Maybe—"

Mary Lisa smacked her head with the heel of her palm,
and cut her off. "Big duh. Guys, I think Puker pulled a fast
one on you."

Jack frowned at her. "What makes you say that? What
do you mean?"

"Puker told me the photos showed a guy with a baseball
cap inside a car. This man's wearing a raincoat and walking in a park in these photos. He can't be the same guy, or
at least not the same photos. Puker fooled you both. We've
got to readjust our thinking here—I had no idea he was that
good." Mary Lisa grabbed her purse and headed for the

front door. "It's my turn to see that little schmuck now, talk this all over with him. You guys coming?"

She had her hand on the doorknob before Jack slammed his palm against the door above her head.

"You're not going anywhere near that rathole."

"Rathole? What's that supposed to mean? I thought you said he lives in a nice place."

"It's a cop term," Daniel said. "It simply means a place where rats live. It could be a mansion, doesn't matter."

Meanwhile, Lou Lou had dialed her cell phone. She spoke quietly into it, and punched off. "Okay, you can stop playing tough guy, Jack. Mary Lisa, Clyde is getting Puker's address for us, so we can go by ourselves if you like."

Jack planted himself in front of both of them. "I don't want either of you going near that guy."

Mary Lisa smiled at him. "You trying to lose ground here, Jack?"

"It's our job, not yours. Daniel and I will go see him again."

"You're not going to move, are you? You better lighten up, or I'll morph into Schwarzenegger and shred you."

"Yeah? Who says? He should be so lucky."

A hank of her red hair hung into her face, nearly covering her eyes, but she ignored it, so angry she was nearly foaming at the mouth at him. He looked down into her pale furious face and thought, *Yep, a really big step backward.* "All right, I don't want to turn into a toad again for you, Mary Lisa. We were doing so well. Daniel, if it's all right with you, why don't all of us go see Puker? That okay with you?"

"I don't think—"

Mary Lisa began humming. "Lou Lou, what are you doing tonight, around midnight?"

"Hmm, maybe driving to this address hoping to find a rathole?"

Mary Lisa nodded. "Sounds like a plan to me."

"Well, then." Lou Lou turned to Detective Vasquez. "What is your problem? You look like Moses ready to smite the Egyptians—nothing's going to happen to us."

Daniel looked like he wanted to handcuff both of them to the big sofa leg. "Puker isn't exactly dangerous," he muttered to Jack. "But they're still civilians, dammit."

Lou Lou patted Daniel's arm. "Sometimes you just gotta suck it up, Danny."

"I'd take you to jail if I knew you wouldn't retaliate, but you would, wouldn't you? You'd never make me another steak sandwich."

"It's your fault for fraternizing with her," Mary Lisa said.

They all piled into Daniel's four-door Crown Vic, none of them feeling much like conversation. Mary Lisa stared out the car window toward the Pacific. It was darker now, but you could see the fog reflected in the lights, hovering like a thick miasma over the water, and a half-moon trying to break out of slowly moving dark clouds. It was threatening to rain, though it hardly ever did. There was little traffic this time of night, and Daniel pulled to the curb in front of Puker Hodges's apartment complex sooner than she expected. He pointed to the corner apartment on the second floor. "It's up there."

"All lit up," Jack said. "Good, our boy is still there. That surprises me. He had to know Mary Lisa would see through those pictures he gave us, that we'd be back. Maybe he thought it would take us longer."

Lou Lou jumped out of the backseat. "I'm going to kick that little pissant's butt myself. Hey, Danny, why don't you take a photo, we can sell it to the *Enquirer*."

Jack said, "Leave your fantasies about Puker to us, Lou Lou. And stay behind me."

When they reached the second floor, Jack knocked firmly on the door, twice. There was no answer.

Daniel called out, "Mr. Hodges, police, open up. We want to speak to you." And he rapped hard on the door.

Suddenly, Jack knew something wasn't right. He grasped Mary Lisa's upper arms, lifted her, and set her down against the stucco wall beside the door. "I don't like this. Please, both of you stay right here, don't move from this spot."

"What's wrong?"

"Mary Lisa, trust me on this, okay?"

Daniel nodded to Jack, who tried the doorknob. It was locked. He took a step back and sent his foot into the door. It shuddered, but didn't give. He kicked it again, nearly on the doorknob this time, and the door crashed inward.

Both men had their guns in their hands when they ducked inside. They swept the foyer, and stepped into the living room. It was obvious there'd been a fight. The sofa was knocked caddywumpus, and a chair lay on its back, a lamp broken beside it. Magazines were strewn on the floor, along with some books from the two bookcases. It was a royal mess. "Puker put up a fight." Jack turned and shouted, "You guys stay out there until we check the rest of the apartment."

Daniel called for backup.

The kitchen, Puker's bedroom, and his darkroom looked okay; the fight hadn't gone in there. They didn't find Puker. In his darkroom, there were maybe half a dozen photos strewn around on the floor, as if someone had looked them over and tossed them aside after checking them, but otherwise the equipment was okay.

"I'd say the guy either found the photos and took Puker anyway or he didn't find the photos and took Puker to get information out of him. Either way, you need an APB on him, Daniel."

Mary Lisa and Lou Lou stood in the foyer, staring at the wrecked living room. A lone fern had been toppled onto the floor, soil scattered and crushed, as if someone had walked in it on purpose. They heard sirens in the distance. Daniel walked toward them, his gun holstered.

"Is Puker dead? Is his body in there?"

"No, Lou Lou, Puker isn't here."

"By the looks of the living room," Mary Lisa said, "the guy who's after me dragged Puker out of here."

"Looks like," Daniel agreed. "Okay, I've got to stay here, fill in the LAPD when they show up since we're in their jurisdiction now. Jack's going to take you guys home."

Lou Lou took one last look around. "He fought. I'm glad he wasn't a wuss."

"Yeah, he fought," Detective Vasquez said. "I'll bet the guy didn't find the photos and that's why he took Puker. He's going to pull Puker's toenails out if he doesn't tell him where they are. Either that or kill him. What I can't figure is how this guy even knew Puker had photos of him in the first place."

"Oh, that's easy," Mary Lisa said. "There's no doubt in my mind Puker found out who he was and decided to try a little blackmail. After all, he tried it with me, didn't he?"

Jack and Detective Vasquez both nodded, then herded them toward the car. "Puker will have to fend for himself until the cops find him."

By the time Jack got ready to leave Mary Lisa's house, Lou Lou was already in a pair of Mary Lisa's pajamas, standing in the bedroom doorway, yawning. Mary Lisa was still pacing her living room, looking down at her lovely French pedicure that needed a redo. Jack took her hand and pulled her to the front door, out of Lou Lou's hearing. Without thinking, he tucked a thick curly strand of red hair behind her ear. "I know you're scared. Your life feels like it's out of control. Hang in there, Mary Lisa, and don't ever be alone, okay?"

Mary Lisa grabbed up her mess of hair, pulled it in a ponytail, and looped a rubber band from her pocket efficiently around it. But she'd clammed up.

The house phone rang. He heard Lou Lou answer it. She called out, "It's okay, Mary Lisa. It's not the creep."

Jack said, "Good. Now, I've got to go. Keep your doors locked, all right? And turn on your security system. It'll be okay, Mary Lisa. We'll figure this out."

Lou Lou came up behind Mary Lisa. "Carlo's on his way over with some of his friends, said he and his surfboard were going to camp out here for a couple of nights."

"Good. Have a pajama party, the more the merrier." He nodded to both of them, and left.

Mary Lisa drank a cup of tea and went off to bed, not

wishing to see anyone that night. Almost immediately she was dreaming about John Lennon. They were dancing in the huge engine room of a submarine and he was twirling her around and around, and then he started ringing. He didn't look at all surprised, he just puffed out his chest and rang.

It was her cell phone and it was one o'clock in the morning.

TWENTY-NINE

Nicole Kidman played a glue-sniffing teen on the
Australian soap *A Country Practice*.

The phone rang again, then once more.

"Hello?"

"What have you gotten yourself into? What is going on
down there?"

It didn't sound at all like John Lennon. "Who is this?"

"John Goddard. What's happening?"

His voice was warm and deep and definitely pissed off,
and she smiled into the phone. "Oh, a John by another name.
It's good to hear from you, but how did you know anything
was happening? It's kind of late down here, you know."

"Yeah, yeah, I'm sorry to call you so late. What do you
mean a John by another name?"

"I was dreaming about John Lennon and he started ringing and it was you. So, what's going on?"

"Your dad called me, said Jack had called him, told him
it was getting really complicated down there and he was
going to stay to see if he could help resolve things."

"Complicated? Is that cop talk for understatement? Can
you sing, John?"

He laughed. "Lock me in a shower and you can't shut me up."

Right there in her mind's eye was the visual of him crooning while she looked at his lovely wet butt. He turned and smiled at her. But it wasn't John's face, it was Jack's, and she jerked the shower curtain closed real fast. "Okay, I'm awake now. Why did my dad call you?"

There was a slight pause before John the tough district attorney said, "Why shouldn't he call me? I asked him to, I was worried about you. He thinks I should come down there, said Jack was okay, but it's time for the big gun."

Big gun, huh? "My father called you the big gun?"

"Maybe not his exact words."

"John, it's a nice thought, but you're preparing evidence for Milo Hildebrand's trial, aren't you? Seems to me you're pretty busy right now. Isn't Patricia Bigelow all over you with motions for this and that?"

"Well, the thing is, we've got all the evidence we need locked down. Pat can shriek and pull her hair if she likes, make motions until all the cows migrate to California, there's nothing she can do but wait for a plea bargain offer that's probably not going to come. And we don't have to worry about Milo skipping the jurisdiction. With obvious premeditation, Judge Howe turned down bail in a minute. Milo's in jail for the long haul."

"John, listen to me. I'm working all day tomorrow. Besides the police department, we've got the big rottweiler here on the case. Jack's a pretty big gun, don't you think? There's simply no reason for you to disrupt your life to come down."

"If you have to know," he said, "your sister was pissed when Jack left town after she'd put some of her moves on him, so now she's decided to light up my life again. I'm scared."

"So you think Jack showed up down here just to escape my sister? And you want to do the same?" Mary Lisa forgot for a moment that she'd been afraid to poke her head out her own door that day, and laughed. "So Kelly's got both of you machos on the run?"

"Sometimes telling the truth really hurts."

She had no sooner punched off than it rang again. "Grand Central."

A short pause, a strained laugh, then, "Lots of people calling you at all hours, huh? Mary Lisa, Jack swore to me you were all right. But I've been lying here and I can't sleep. I'm coming down tomorrow."

"Dad, there's no reason, I promise. This is exactly why I didn't want to worry you with all this when I was up there. After work tomorrow, I've got an interview with *Soap Opera Digest* and then a birthday party for a friend to go to. You already sent Jack Wolf down here to run loose in Malibu. Believe me, no one in their right mind would try anything with the original bad-ass close by."

"But he's not your father."

"Dad, please. Stay in Goddard Bay. Truth is, I'd worry myself into a coma if you were here nosing around."

"But—"

She heard her mother's voice clearly in the background. "You can't go to Malibu, George. Monica needs us at her campaign fund-raiser Saturday night. Come back to bed."

Her father's voice, a bit muffled because he'd obviously put his hand over the receiver, said, "Mary Lisa is in danger, Kathleen. A fund-raiser is nothing."

Her mother's voice became indistinct. She realized her dad had pressed his palm down harder over the phone.

She waited briefly, and her dad said, "Mary Lisa, I'll call you tomorrow morning, see what's going on. Yes, yes, I'll check in with Jack too. When do you leave for the studio?"

When Mary Lisa punched off her cell, she lay back and stared up at the ceiling. She listened to the sound of the waves, a bit closer, a bit frothier since a light rain was falling and the wind had picked up. She got up, checked on Lou Lou, who was sprawled in the middle of the guest room bed on her back, arms and legs snow-angeled, deeply asleep. Her thick streaked hair frothed around her head and over her face, and she looked adorable in Mary Lisa's cat pajamas. If Elizabeth had been here, she knew the two of them would have been sprawled side by side, but Elizabeth was still back in Connecticut dealing with family problems of her own. Another asshole man, she had said—or was she being redundant? She'd have to run that by Jack, to see the look on his face. At least she'd be back in the next day or two. She'd called, but neither Mary Lisa nor Lou Lou had told her anything more about the trouble. Elizabeth had enough on her plate without adding this course.

Mary Lisa went out onto her covered back deck, leaned her elbows on the railing, and watched the rain sheet lightly down in front of her. Carlo said from the depths of his sleeping bag, "You okay, Mary Lisa?"

"Yep, I'm fine, Carlo. Sorry I woke you up. You're not cold, are you?"

"Nah, this thing was made for the Antarctic. Good thing for you it's cool tonight because I sleep in the nude."

Mary Lisa laughed, thanked him, and headed back to bed. She said one final prayer—she thanked God she wasn't at this very moment lying in her bed in her mother's house in Goddard Bay.

THIRTY

With cries of American soap imperialism in the 1980s, the French and Germans launched their own direct imitations. Neither country's soap attempt flew very high or very long.

Lou Lou came out to the front porch the next morning, still in Mary Lisa's cat pajamas, carrying mugs of coffee on a tray. "Here's some coffee, sweetie. It'll clear the cobwebs."

Mary Lisa was sitting on a deck chair in her front yard wearing rumpled shorts and her favorite pea green T-shirt. She smiled up at Lou Lou as she took the coffee. "You're a princess."

She looked over to see Carlo talking on his cell phone, the toes of his bare feet digging into the rain-soaked grass, wearing a black and silver Oakland Raiders T-shirt and loose black pajama bottoms. Mary Lisa wondered briefly if he'd lied to her about sleeping nude or if he carried this stuff around in case of emergencies, such as now.

Carlo trotted over when he saw the mugs of coffee and took a cup from Lou Lou. "Those kitty cats on your pajamas are a real turn-on, Lou Lou."

"Good to know. Hmm. I think if Daniel said that, I might jump his bones. It's too bad you don't wear a badge, Carlo."

Carlo, who had more money than God, looked thoughtful. "That," he said, "could be arranged."

Mary Lisa spurted coffee, coughed, then laughed. "What a lovely way to start Friday morning. It's going to be a long day, Lou Lou. When did everyone go home?"

"Not long after you went to bed. Hey, there's some good news."

Mary Lisa's eyebrow went up.

"I wish I could do that, but both eyebrows go straight up when I try."

"It's a gift, unfortunate that it's from my mother. What happened that's so good?"

"Jack has volunteered to take you to work, and stick. You've got to be at the studio in forty-five minutes. As for me, I'm out of here as soon as I change out of my hot jammies."

"The living room looked fine, no big mess."

"Nope," Carlo said, watching Lou Lou's pajama bottoms disappear into the house. "I set up a cleaning detail. One of Nicole's friends even fluffed up a sofa pillow."

Mary Lisa settled again in her chair to finish her coffee. She stretched out her legs and breathed in the glorious Malibu morning air.

"I wouldn't want to tangle with that guy." Carlo sipped his coffee and pointed with it. "He looks like he belongs in the Outback in Australia, like he camps out on top of Ayers Rock."

Mary Lisa followed his pointing mug to Jack Wolf, who was walking toward them in a black T-shirt, tight ratty jeans, and low black boots. "Really? To me, he's just a guy, kind of ordinary, really."

"Other than looking like he could pull up that palm tree and scratch his back with it. Hey, you're acting rather blasé about him, aren't you, honey?"

"Okay, you're right, I was. Fact is, he scares me. Thanks for coming, Carlo. You're a prince." Mary Lisa walked back into her house without greeting Jack. She heard him and Carlo talking. She stopped a moment to look around her living room. It was pristine. She remembered she'd heard conversations from the kitchen floating into her bedroom after she'd gone to bed, heard the refrigerator door open and close multiple times. Oh dear, she'd have to find time to go grocery shopping, since the local locusts had surely cleaned her out.

She went to her bedroom, shut the door, and reemerged eleven minutes later, dressed in a skirt and tube top. She was slinging her purse over her shoulder when a man's voice said from not more than two feet away, "That was fast. Ready to go?"

She nearly leaped out of her shoes. She clapped her palms over her heart. "Oh goodness, whatever are you doing in here?"

Jack stared at her. "I told you I don't want you to be alone. Lou Lou had to leave since she's the one who smears on the makeup this morning and Carlo had to go wax his surfboard. As for Daniel, he's got a real job to go to. That left me."

And like Lou Lou had said, Jack stayed on at the studio. In fact, Clyde was very pleased he was there, as was Betsy Monroe, who played Lydia Cavendish. She wondered aloud, in his hearing, if he was unattached. So he was a little on the young side for her, who cared? This was make-believe land, anything could happen. Jack looked alarmed, then saw she was kidding him and laughed, told her she was too hot for a small-town guy like him.

Mary Lisa shot three scenes, from eight-thirty until noon. Jack mostly sat on a folding chair near the set with his legs crossed, beside Candy, whose job it was to keep an eye on Mary Lisa's wardrobe and hair. When she was done with the third scene, Mary Lisa walked over to him. "Give me ten minutes to wipe the goop off my face."

Lou Lou had to stay on into the afternoon since she also had to deal with Margie McCormick's makeup on Fridays.

As Mary Lisa walked out of the studio, Jack was slightly in front of her, assessing everyone in sight, scanning the parked cars and a stand of trees beyond them. "So your father is a TV evangelist and that's why he insisted your name be changed to Sunday?"

The three scenes they'd shot had been intense, two of them repeated multiple times. She was exhausted. And Sunday had yet to see her long-lost father for the first time. The writers were stretching out the anticipation for as long as they could.

"Yep, isn't it cool what they've come up with? This means I don't have to sleep with my half sister, Susan's, husband, who's a sleaze."

He grunted, never stopped looking. "Yeah, a real sleaze."

So he knew all about that, did he? She grinned up at him, but couldn't make out his expression because he was wearing his dark opaque aviator sunglasses. She put on her own sunglasses. "I begged and whined and pleaded for them not to have Sunday sleep with Damian, and lo and behold, the consulting writer, Suzanne, came up with this. Sunday has never questioned her name. I don't think anyone did until Suzanne came up with my supposedly long-dead preacher dad. This is going to change the course of the show for a good long time. On Monday I'll meet Phillip Galliard for the first time."

He grabbed her arm, pulled her behind him as a green Chevy roared past.

Then he saw the three teenage boys waving madly at her, whistling, calling out lovely suggestions.

Mary Lisa pulled a 49ers cap out of her purse, stuffed her hair beneath it, and pulled it down low on her forehead. "It's my hair. That's what makes me recognizable, or maybe they think, given where we are, that I should be someone famous. You never know."

Jack shook his head as he checked the street again. "What a weird life you lead."

She looked surprised, then thoughtful. "Yeah, maybe you're right. But you know, after a while, it simply became the way I live—you know, getting dressed, going to work, hanging out with friends. Well, of course there's memorizing lines. It becomes ordinary."

"You really don't see yourself as different? As someone special? As someone others look up to?"

"This obsession with celebrities, it's a little scary, like it's a giant beast and there's simply not enough food to appease it. The fact is, I'm an actor, Jack, that's my job, like being the chief of police of Goddard Bay is yours. The real difference between us, I guess, is that for now, I make more money, which is very nice indeed. On the other hand I have to wear really big dark glasses and a baseball cap over my hair whenever I go out of the Colony."

"Yeah, you could buy and sell me."

She said matter-of-factly, "Who cares? Don't you think it's strange that some men still feel insecure if they're not making more money?" An eyebrow went up. "Not you, surely."

"Of course not, but it's not that at all," he said, but she heard the touch of defensiveness in his voice and had to smile. He continued, "The fact remains, though, that men are supposed to take care of their families, they're regarded as bums if they don't."

"That was certainly true of our parents, but now? Both husband and wife usually work, fact of life. And I always knew that I never wanted to be dependent, that I always wanted to earn my own way. That's a problem with you?"

"Dammit, no. If a guy had a problem with that today, he'd be spit upon."

"Yep, that's true. As for me, I'm trying to salt it away like a squirrel getting ready for a long winter."

She shrugged as she got into the driver's seat of her red Mustang convertible.

He raised an eyebrow at the car. "That's the new model. You salted a good amount on this baby."

THIRTY-ONE

She grinned over at him. "Making money is fun, it makes me feel worthwhile, but I know it can't last forever. If an actor gets caught up in thinking he's the greatest thing in the universe, he's in for trouble. And that's why I stay with my circle of friends and try not to get drawn into all the ridiculous hype."

He gave her a sideways glance. "So you think it won't last? Your extreme popularity in this soap?"

She patted the dashboard. "Who knows? Truth be told, I'd rather drive Buffy than buy a thousand Manolo Blahniks."

He raised an eyebrow as he climbed in and closed the door. She laughed. "Okay, Blahnik designs the coolest shoes in the universe. And hey, Buffy's bright red keeps me awake." Once both of them had fastened their seat belts, she turned the key. "I got her from Chris Rock after I met him in a greenroom for some show we were both on. He said his wife didn't like the red, and so he gave me a good price."

He'd heard of Chris Rock, naturally, and she'd spoken

about him so naturally. He said, shaking his head, "No, Mary Lisa, your life is very different from mine. The last time I saw Chris Rock, we did not interact. He was behind the TV screen."

She laughed. "The thing is, Chris agrees with me—if you count on anything in this town, you're setting yourself up for a big punch in the mouth."

"But you're in a lucky situation, aren't you? Some of the soap opera stars keep their roles for years and years."

"Yep, like Kay Chancellor and Victor Newman on *The Young and the Restless*. We'll see. Maybe something else will come along or maybe it won't. Right now, I'm having a ball. And I know I'm lucky. Hey, I'll take you to lunch at Alfredo's, over in Santa Monica."

"I like Italian."

"Hmm, well, it's not exactly Italian."

What it was, Jack discovered twenty minutes later, was a fish and chips dive right across the street from the ocean, at the base of the long pier. He looked out to see at least fifty half-naked girls sprawled out on the sand for as far as the eye could see, guys in low-slung shorts trailing about, trying not to look too obvious about eyeing all the beautiful young bodies.

"This is never-never land," he said as he added some more vinegar to his French fries.

"A guy's fantasy life can be in full bloom here, that's for sure." She was contemplating a French fry. "This is my caloric meal for the week, so excuse me a moment, I'm connecting to my fat content."

He watched her eat a moment, savoring each vinegar-drenched French fry, then locking in on the deep-fried haddock. "I tell myself it's okay because it's fish. What do you think?"

"Self-deception isn't always a bad thing."

She chewed for a long time, finally swallowed, and laughed. "Have you always wanted to be a cop? Are you having fun with your choice right now?"

He stared at her a moment. "Usually I don't think about

it, but yeah, I always wanted to be a cop. My grandfather was a Chicago detective. He was the finest man I ever knew. I wanted to be like him. And I wanted local, not FBI." He ate another French fry, then looked at her thoughtfully. "I think I'm well suited to what I do. Yeah, I enjoy it."

What about his father, she wondered. She said, smiling at him, "Good. That's the way it's supposed to be. Oh yes, I heard from John. I hope he's decided not to come down."

The current French fry stopped two inches from Jack's mouth. "John said he was coming down here? Why?"

"I believe he said something like it was time for the big gun to take over."

Jack laughed. "Pitty Pat does fine with crooks after they're all cleaned up, in shackles, and have a guard on either side."

"Pitty Pat?"

"Yeah."

"What does that mean?"

"You'll have to ask him."

"What does John call you?"

"Goon Leader."

"I thought you two got along really well."

"As a matter of fact he's my best friend, but he shouldn't be down here, it would just muddy the water."

"Seems to me there's plenty of mud already."

"Excuse me a second." Jack pushed away from the table, pulled out his cell phone, and walked away.

Mary Lisa pulled out her own cell phone. After two rings, a man answered. "Yeah, Chico here."

"Chico? It's Mary Lisa Beverly. Can I see you this afternoon, say in thirty minutes?"

Silence, then: "Make it an hour. Now listen to me. You're gonna be real sore tonight, so plan to take a long hot tub and early to bed."

"The hot tub's a go, bed has to wait."

"It's your ass." Chico hung up.

Jack walked back to the table. "When do you memorize your lines?"

"Usually when I'm in bed at night. And every morning I have at least two hours in makeup and wardrobe. I can memorize a whole scene in a pinch while Candy is doing my hair in the style du jour. I need to drop you off somewhere after lunch. I have an appointment."

"Where?"

"One of the safest places in the land. You'll know soon enough, but not now, so I need to drop you off. Where would you like to go?"

"I don't want you by yourself. So I'll take you to this appointment."

"I swear I'll be as safe as I was in the clink that night you locked me in. You didn't even give me a blanket."

"There weren't any," he said absently. "I'd ordered some, but they hadn't come yet." He didn't like it, she could tell he didn't, but she didn't want to tell him where she was going, what she was doing, he'd just yell at her. He'd find out in good time. She grinned down at the half dozen limp French fries soaking in vinegar at the bottom of the cardboard box. She looked up to see the ocean breeze blowing black hair in his eyes. An impatient hand swiped it back. Big hands, long fingers, short filed nails. She was admiring his damned hands. She didn't like this, she really didn't. And now certainly wasn't the time, not with fear curdling her belly whenever her mind snapped back to this crazy guy after her, which was about every five minutes. She cleared her throat. "I'm not being stupid here so no arguments. Lou Lou will catch a ride to where I am and go home with me. No, I'm not going to tell you where I'm going. Now then, where can I drop you?"

He didn't look happy. Then he shrugged, popped the last French fry into his mouth, and said, "Lost Hills Station in Calabasas is fine. There's some stuff I need to check out with Daniel. I called John. He was having a screaming match with Pat Bigelow in his office. Between that and my telling him I didn't have a perp yet so he'd be about as helpful as a gerbil on a wheel, I don't think he'll be coming any time soon."

"Why is lawyer Bigelow screaming at John?"

"Pat wants a new bail hearing. She's claiming Milo's health is suffering because of his leg wound. She wants him home. John handed her a photo of Milo doing his push-ups this morning."

Mary Lisa laughed, a joyous sound, he thought, and for a moment, stared at her. She looked carefree, beautiful, and happy. Anyone who saw her wouldn't believe she was dealing with fear every minute of her life. He admired her greatly in that moment. How very odd life was, he thought, and looked out at the ocean. How could anyone want to hurt her?

"What are you thinking? You look all sorts of serious."

He looked back at her. "Do I? Maybe it's because I was realizing that I really like your hair."

She touched a finger to her tangling hair. "My hair?"

"Your dad was raving about you once—not to me, since I firmly believed you were a one-strike felon—but I'll admit I was listening. He was talking about how you had the most beautiful hair he'd ever seen, his own mother's hair, he said, only yours was a deeper red, and it was fuller, richer. Your dad thinks you walk on water."

She paused a moment, rubbing her hands up and down the sides of her glass, and out of her mouth came, "If you take off those sunglasses of yours I'll take off mine."

He pulled off the aviator glasses.

She stared at him right in his dark blue eyes, narrowed against the bright sun. "Okay, tell me what you think, Jack."

He reached across the narrow, battered wooden table, pulled off her 49ers cap, ran his fingers through her hair, then wrapped a thick curl around his finger. He leaned up and brought the hair to his cheek and rubbed it. He sat back, crossed his arms over his chest.

"Well?"

"Nah, your grandmother had fuller, richer hair. Softer too."

"You can't possibly know that!"

"I'm deducing it."

She threw a French fry at him.

"I didn't like you either," she said. "I really didn't. I didn't think you ever smiled."

He became very still.

"Jack—"

"You're not going to let it go, are you?"

She shook her head.

"Truth is, maybe you were right. After I left Chicago, I guess I didn't smile much, and—" He shook his head and concentrated on the last piece of fried haddock in the cardboard carton.

"I knew you were divorced. Why did you break up?"

He didn't look like he was going to answer. She was on the point of retracting the question—impertinent, she knew, and really none of her business—when he said, "Rikki wanted kids and she wanted a father to be there for her kids. I wasn't ready."

"Why not?"

"I honestly didn't know then, only that I kept telling her I wasn't ready. I finally figured it out a while back. My dad wasn't what you'd call a very moral character. He was never home, slept around on my mom, and treated us kids like we were an—imposition, like he wished we weren't there, like we cramped his style. It drove my grandfather nuts but there was nothing he could do about it except try to be there when he could break free from his job.

"I guess I didn't want to be the same way and knew if Rikki got pregnant I wouldn't be there to be a father, and I'd see my grandfather's face, staring at me like I was a loser." He stopped suddenly, looked appalled at himself. Color stained his high cheekbones. "I can't believe I said that. Forget it. It's got to be the flaky air down here. Damn."

Mary Lisa said thoughtfully, "Do you think your dad could take on my mom and win?"

He jerked back, the embarrassment fell off his face, and he grinned at her. "It would be some battle."

She raised her soda glass and clicked it to his. "To parents. They never cease to amaze."

"Hear, hear."

She watched him take a bite of that last piece of haddock. "Did you love her?"

He wadded his paper napkin and threw it into the trash container. "That's it, Mary Lisa. No more of this personal stuff, this damned relationship stuff that makes a man's innards twist and bend. You women, what's with you and all this gut-spilling crap anyway?"

And he got up, shoved his sunglasses back on, walked to her bright red Mustang, climbed into the passenger seat, and settled his head against the seat.

"It's been three years, Jack, get over it." She climbed into Buffy beside him. "It's time you came back and enjoyed yourself a bit, don't you think?" *With me, maybe.*

"Yeah? You mean like with you?"

Oh boy.

He hadn't moved. She turned the key in the ignition, still didn't look at him.

"What about John?"

Still not looking at him, she said, "John was off the table the minute I found out about Kelly's feelings."

He said nothing.

When she pulled up in front of the Lost Hills Station, Jack got out, then turned to look at her. "You be careful, you hear me? You promised me you weren't stupid. I'm holding you to that. I'll see you later."

"At home," she said.

He gave her an odd look. "Yeah," he said, "at home. Along with half the population of Southern California. Why won't you tell me where you're off to?"

She shook her head, laughed, waved, and drove off.

She headed for Venice. She didn't want to be late for Chico.

THIRTY-TWO

In the 1930s the big corporate sponsors were Procter &
Gamble, Pillsbury, American Home Products, and General
Foods. Thus the name was coined—soaps.

At four o'clock Friday afternoon, Mary Lisa knew death
was near. There was no way she could move, not if someone yelled fire, not if Brad Pitt walked naked in front of
her, and it was that last thought that made her realize just
how pathetic a condition she was in. Sprawled on her back,
boneless, her arms and legs flung out, her sweaty hair mat-
ted to her head, all she could do was focus on breathing. It
was hard even to suck enough air into her lungs, but at least
she could manage that without whimpering. She stared up
at the gorgeous man who'd done his best to kill her.

"Not so perky now, are you?"

Perky? Why was he talking about her breasts at a time
like this? Breath, she needed more breath to tell him what
she thought of him, none of it good. He offered her a hand,
and she stared at it, praying for the strength to leap up and
bite it. She managed a whisper. "If I press charges, do you
think the cops will lock you up?"

"Nah, since you paid me for this, it shows you desire
abuse and torture and gets me off the hook. I know you

think I'm a sadist, you don't think I feel your pain. Hmm. Come to think of it, actually, I don't. But listen, you did really good for your first lesson. You're in good shape, you've got good balance, and you move well. But to be effective, you can't let your eyes tell your opponent every move you're going to make. I'll teach you to blank out that expression. Surprise is everything. Now, don't lie there like a pitiful log. I told you kicking with force would use your core muscles like nothing else. Get up, I want you to jog in place for three minutes, otherwise you'll be stiffer than my old rheumatoid dog, Bart, by tomorrow. Come on, Mary Lisa, get your butt off that mat."

As she jogged in place, she told Chico Rayburn he must be registered a double-O-something with the Brits, she'd swear to that. He laughed and slapped her on the back, nearly sending her to the floor.

"I like your spunk, Mary Lisa. At this rate I can teach you some useful skills in a few weeks' time. But I need commitment from you. I told you I don't work with anyone who isn't committed, it's a waste of my time. Can you swear to me right now you're going to stick with this? You're not going to wimp out?"

Words, how to get words out of her mouth? "Yeah, fool that I am." She'd managed five words, good.

He beamed at her. "You're no quitter, I knew that. And you've got motivation, what with that moron out there chasing you around. You don't want to have to depend on the cops or bodyguards to protect you the rest of your life. You're doing the right thing."

She could breathe again and, glory be, she could speak, barely. "Yeah, I'm doing the right thing. I was hoping I'd be able to take the jerk down in maybe two weeks. Now I'm thinking maybe two hundred years."

"You'll have some nice moves in two weeks. The rest, like any skill, takes practice and effort."

"I want him mangled and whimpering at my feet. To be on the safe side, I want to practice—beginning with you."

He didn't grin at that. He studied her a moment, then slowly nodded. "Okay, good enough. You've got a fire in your gut, you want to kill me—all very commendable. Now, don't underestimate what I told you. Despite all the cardio, that cute little kickboxing class, and all that girl crap on the spinner, your body hasn't been through this before. You'll still be sore Sunday morning. I'll see you Sunday afternoon, say at one o'clock." He gave her a list of resistance exercises and stretches, thankfully illustrated with drawings since the last thing her brain could do at the moment was concentrate.

Mary Lisa gave Chico a little wave as she walked out of the innocently bland building that housed his dojo, set between two upscale antique shops on Briar Street in the middle of Venice. She had called Lou Lou, who was waiting for her, arms crossed over her breasts, leaning against Buffy.

"Dear sweet baby Jesus, Mary Lisa, you look like you've dropped five pounds in body sweat. And Chico, that man looks like a fallen angel."

"Only five pounds you think? As for Chico, he's no fallen angel, he's the devil himself. I saw it in the mirror on the way out and it was a near-death experience. You want to drive, Lou Lou?"

"Oh yeah, me and the Buffster, we're the duo."

"Don't kill me."

Mary Lisa grunted as she eased her maimed body into the passenger side, leaned her head back against the seat, and closed her eyes. "My mom would laugh her head off if she could see me now. You know what, Lou Lou?"

"You're going to keel over without help from that loon out there?"

"Not me." Mary Lisa opened her eyes and grinned real big. "I see everything very clearly now. I was born to be a karate queen. Maybe it won't even take me two weeks before that creep is really sorry he ever came after me. Oh yeah, come to Mamma. I'm gonna kick your sorry butt."

Lou Lou rolled her eyes, honked at a skateboarder, who promptly flipped her a finger, and cut off a little Volkswagen Beetle.

Mary Lisa alternately groaned and sang along with the radio on PCH on the way back home. She didn't flinch when Lou Lou nearly rear-ended an SUV that was stopped on the highway for no apparent reason. She braked so fast Mary Lisa pictured her front end crumpling. Lou Lou was embarrassed, so stuck her head out the window and yelled, "You cheap putz! Put some ninety-two octane in that honker!"

The driver, a woman with carrot-red hair, yelled back some really inventive curses that had them thinking of horses and goats in a very different way. Mary Lisa shook her head. "I wonder what Elizabeth would say about this goat deal."

"You'll see her tomorrow, ask her. She's flying in at about five o'clock."

Mary Lisa sighed. "She's going to chew my ear. Truth is I didn't want to worry her, so I haven't been exactly forthcoming about all that's happened."

Lou Lou pressed her foot on the gas pedal and swerved around a big Pathfinder, whose driver looked ready to spit nails until he saw Lou Lou up close and waved madly at her. "That's okay, Mary Lisa, I told her everything."

THIRTY-THREE

Dallas and *Dynasty* were the first American serials to be
successfully marketed internationally.

On Saturday morning, a cup of high-octane Kona coffee in
one hand, Mary Lisa opened her front door to an unexpected visitor.

"Hello, Mary Lisa. I'm glad you're home, but hey, you
don't leave home alone anymore, do you? Is Lou Lou still
sleeping over, or is that tough-looking son of a bitch I saw
you with yesterday spending his nights here?"

"Tough-looking? Yes, okay, I'll give him that, though
Jack Wolf has more a brooding in-your-face bad-boy look
if you ask me."

"Jack Wolf? Come on, that's a stage name. I'll bet he's got
a real name like Benny Schwartz and no one would hire him."

"Hmmm. Never thought of that, I'll freely admit it. I'll
ask him." Mary Lisa smiled at Margie McCormick, who
played her half sister, Susan Cavendish, on *Born to Be
Wild*. Margie stood at her front door looking thin, blond,
and gorgeous, dressed in tight hip-bone jeans and a brief
stretch top. Mary Lisa had no trouble at all picturing
Margie talking her way past Chad at the Colony kiosk.

There was no smile on Margie's face. Oh dear. What was wrong with her? "Nice to see you, Margie. What can I do for you on this beautiful Saturday morning? Come in, come in." She stepped back.

Margie said, "I don't suppose the cops have found the guy who ran you over yet?"

"Nope, nothing yet."

They walked into Mary Lisa's house together, where Margie had visited many times before, right to her favorite chair, a high wingback covered in a bright multicolored South Seas print. She sat down, crossed her legs.

Margie said, "I don't suppose the cops have found Puker Hodges yet?"

"No, still no word, still no leads as to where he was taken or who nabbed him."

"Most people think old Puker's sold his last photo to the fanzines, that he's in a drainage ditch somewhere."

"As much as I've wanted to hit him in the chops over the past months, I hope he isn't dead. It's true there was a fight in his apartment, but maybe the guy scared him so much, Puker went into hiding—"

"Oh, get real, Mary Lisa. Where else could he be? In Rio doing a photo spread on beach thongs? Enjoying a taco in Cancun?"

Mary Lisa said slowly, "That would make the guy a real monster, not just a—"

"A what?"

"I don't know, maybe a minimonster. Margie, can I get you something to drink?"

"No, thank you. I see you're studying your lines for all your scenes on Monday." Margie pointed over at some script pages on the sofa.

All my scenes? "Are you unhappy about something, Margie?"

Margie jumped up, began pacing the living room. Then she whirled about and said, "I've always been honest with you, Mary Lisa, and I've come to say I can't believe you talked Bernie out of the revenge plot!"

Mary Lisa cocked her head to one side. "I don't understand. You agreed with me that Sunday wouldn't sleep with her half sister's husband, you rolled your eyes at where the writers were headed. Betsy agreed too. She said no matter what Sunday's mother and half sister had done, Sunday would never sleep with Damian."

"You're trying to pretend Sunday always has reasonable motives for her behavior? That we all think things through before we act? You know very well that we have to do things that most normal people would think insane. For God's sake, Mary Lisa, it's a soap opera! It doesn't have to make perfect sense as long as it's entertaining, you know that. If the writers have a bad day, so do we all. Sunday sleeping with Damian? Why not? It's a meaty plotline, and both Jeff and I would have been right up front, right in the thick of it in a major way for at least three months! The possibilities were endless, and the writers would have hit them all!

"But instead you bitched and moaned until you got your way and turned everything on its head. What did you do, Mary Lisa? Threaten to walk? To go over to *General Hospital*? And so Bernie had to come up with a long-missing TV evangelist father for his little princess? Now we're out of it, do you hear me? I'm out of it. You happy now?"

Mary Lisa slowly set down her coffee. "I see," she said quietly. "I thought we were friends, Margie, but I guess that's not true. All you just said, I hadn't realized how you felt, I really hadn't, but now I do. You thought I stabbed you in the back. On purpose. Jeff too, right?"

"Jeff hasn't said much, so who knows?"

Mary Lisa waved that away. "You're saying I did this because I wanted more face time? And on my terms? Fact is, if you'd think about it for a minute, you'd realize that I'd have been featured as much sleeping with Damian as I will be now dealing with my long-lost father."

"None of us is stupid, Mary Lisa. We all know you're the lead on *Born to Be Wild*, and we're all very lucky everyone loves you so much. Even my own real mother knows and accepts that; in fact, she loves you too. We all accept it.

"But the revenge plot was my chance to share some of that with you. I'd have been woven right in, right in the middle of it—the wife betrayed by both her husband and her half sister. I was so ready! But it won't happen now, not anymore. I'll be lucky to have three scenes a bloody week. You betrayed me, Mary Lisa, big time."

Margie McCormick jumped up and ran out of the house, slamming the door behind her. Mary Lisa stood stock-still, listening as Margie gunned her pretty white Boxster and roared out of the driveway.

"Well, hello, Hollywood."

She turned to see Jack Wolf walk into the living room from the kitchen.

She wasn't surprised he was here, in her house. She didn't think she could be surprised by anything now. "What a mess. Do you know I never even realized, never even considered Margie or Jeff when I bitched and whined about the plotline? I thought only of myself. Aren't I a fine human being?"

He picked up a bright red pillow from her sofa and threw it at her. He threw it hard enough that she almost stumbled back when it hit her in the face.

"That's my fast pillow, you twit. You should see my curve. You will if you keep playing the pitiful martyr. What I heard was all about her, didn't you see that? There's only one Sunday Cavendish, Mary Lisa. Everyone roots for her, they care about what happens to her, can't wait to see what she does next. And Sunday is you, not Margie. I noticed she's skinnier than you are. Don't any of you ever eat?"

"You saw me chow down the fish and chips."

"It was probably your first solid food in two weeks."

"This is ridiculous." She threw the pillow back at him, but he snagged it out of the air, tossed it back and forth from his left to his right.

Throwing the stupid pillow reminded her that her muscles still throbbed and ached despite an hour in the hot tub the previous night and as many stretches as she could tolerate. She was sure her bones had grown longer.

"Don't you dare throw your curve pillow at me."

"Oh yeah? What would you do if I knocked you right over?"

She gave him an evil smile. "I'll tell you what I'll do, you bully. I'll call my sister Kelly and invite her down to stay with me."

In a flash he had a hunted look. It was so unexpected she laughed and followed through. "Where's my cell phone? Oh yeah, there it is." She managed to grab it up off the coffee table.

He grabbed her, lifted her easily off her feet, and took her down on the sofa, sprawled on top of her. He wrestled the cell phone from her hand, tossed it across the living room. "That's a dirty threat, Mary Lisa."

He was heavy. She felt every single portion of him. His nose was two inches above hers. She felt his warm breath on her cheek. "Dammit, you are a complete pain in the ass." He dipped his face down, stared at her mouth, then jerked away from her as if he'd been shot.

He walked to the front door, stopped, turned back. "I can't leave. You're alone. With your oblivious brain, you'd probably take a long lonely walk on the beach. Or, hey, you feel so guilty about what that idiot woman said to you maybe you'd shoot yourself."

"Nah, this is what I'm going to do." She managed to heave herself up onto one elbow, then grabbed a pillow and threw it at him as hard as she could, but it wasn't much of a missile. He grabbed the pillow out of the air, tossed it from his left to his right, back and forth, grinning down at her. "That was paltry."

If her muscles were fit for anything more, she would have leaped to her feet and rammed him. Her arm that had made the paltry throw throbbed and knotted. All she had were words. "You can leave. I won't be alone for long. Lou Lou has asked some people over tonight. I think she's decided it would make me feel better. She asked me to invite you, but please feel free to back out. Please feel free to re-move your butt from the premises."

"No, not until other people come." But he was looking at that front door like he wanted to slam through it.

She managed to sit up on her sofa, swing her legs to the floor. "How long were you eavesdropping in my kitchen?"

That brought his head up. The jerk grinned at her. "Do you like the bad-boy look?"

"That's only on the surface. You're all huff and puff, afraid of my little sister."

"Any sane man would be afraid of Kelly, Pitty Pat included."

"Go away, Chief Wolf. Or is Margie right? Did you change your name so people would take you seriously and hire you as a cop?"

"You found me out."

"Go away."

"Believe me, I would certainly like to. The thought of hanging back with a beer, maybe watching a ball game on TV instead—"

"Or you could always go all the way back home."

The big clod stood in the middle of her living room and laughed at her. Then she knew he was looking at her mouth.

She grabbed her empty mug, intending to flatten him with it, but the sudden movement hurt everywhere. She felt a sudden spasm in her arm, dropped the mug, and let her-self fall back into a chair.

THIRTY-FOUR

Irna Phillips created and wrote some of the most successful radio soap operas in the 1930s and 1940s, including *The Guiding Light*, which premiered in 1937.

"What's wrong? What did you do?"

She rubbed the muscle frantically. He slapped her hand away and began massaging her arm, deep and hard. She moaned, rocked back and forth on the chair.

"What did you do to your arm?"

"Just a cramp."

"I can see that. It's your biceps." He continued massaging, lightening up a bit. "Make a muscle for me."

"Are you nuts? No, no way. It's all right."

"Make a freaking muscle, would you?"

She made a freaking muscle, held the whimpers in her throat as he massaged. To her surprise, it helped.

"Okay, now loosen. That's it—flex, loosen, flex, like that. It's hard to tell which you're doing, you've got such skinny little arms."

"My arms are fine, you macho jerk."

He stared down as she held her arm. "Did you overdo it with weights at the gym?"

"No, I wasn't at the gym."

"Then what did you do? It had to be over the top to make your biceps cramp up like that."

Mary Lisa pictured herself in a graceful profile, sending her leg out smoothly at Chico to land her foot solidly in his gut. She pictured him grabbing his belly and keeling over onto the ground. Two weeks. Two more weeks and she could do that. "Too much shopping. Trying on all those shoes is tough on the arms."

"It's interesting," Jack said slowly, watching her stand up, still cradling her arm, "you're a good actress, I'll give you that, but still you're not convincing playing the spoiled prima donna."

She didn't know what else to say, and it was infuriating. She stomped off toward her bedroom, still holding her arm.

"Where are you going?"

"I think I'll go surfing with Carlo. If he's not around, there are usually lots of cute young guys to help me out."

She slammed the door.

"Yeah, right, give it a try, see how many of those horny teenage boys even know what a massage is."

She growled through the door. He heard it. He was pissed and horny, a miserable combination, and he guessed she knew it. He'd almost kissed her when he'd flattened her on the sofa. Almost. He'd managed to stop himself in time. He thanked the Lord he had gotten ahold of himself. He was here to help find out who was terrorizing her, not—well, he didn't want to think about that. He walked to the kitchen, got himself a bottled water from the fridge, rubbed it over his forehead. He sat down on the sofa, saw the soap script, and picked it up.

He was still reading it ten minutes later when Mary Lisa, wearing a cover-up over a swimsuit, paused a moment when she saw him. "The mail is due soon. Perhaps you'd like to read that too."

"Nah. You've seen one electric bill you've seen them all. Hey, this is pretty cool. I like this scene between Sunday and her father. Except—"

"Yeah, except . . . ?"

"It seems to me that you could make the announcement only once—you know, call a meeting of everyone involved. That makes more sense than having each person find out one at a time, drawing it out like that. I guess this way each character gets a chance to dramatize it?" He tossed the script back on the sofa. "Telling one character at a time about the evangelist father could go on for weeks."

"It will go on for at least a week, maybe two, before it's done. Welcome to the wonderful world of daytime entertainment." But she couldn't leave it alone, she had to justify it. "The viewers want to know how each character will react, or at least their favorite character. And every character will react differently to the news, depending on who they are, what's happened between them and Sunday or her mother, Lydia. Now, please feel free to take yourself home, Chief. I'm going out to the beach."

"I was lying on top of you, Mary Lisa. I very nearly kissed you and you know I probably wouldn't have stopped, and you wouldn't have stopped me—"

She started humming, very loudly. She grabbed up the script and went out back through the kitchen. Five minutes later, Jack was leaning on the deck railing, his opaque sunglasses in place, looking for Mary Lisa. He spotted her sitting in a deck chair some twenty yards down the beach, reading her script. Four surfers, all of them male, all of them below the legal drinking age, were clustered near her, occasionally eyeing her like she was an extra-crispy chicken breast.

They were playing around, strutting the way teenage boys do, poking each other, trying to impress her. It was almost enough to make a grown man wish he were back in Goddard Bay. Three girls in bathing suits walked up and joined them.

He pulled up a deck chair and sat down, his feet up on the deck railing, ankles crossed. He leaned back his head and closed his eyes. The midmorning sun was soft and warm against his face.

He must have dozed off because he only thought he heard a gunshot. There was a yell, then screams. He leaped over the deck railing, landed light, and ran toward Mary Lisa.

To his utter surprise, none of the kids had scattered. They'd shoved Mary Lisa down, covering her with their bodies. Her beach chair was overturned, and Mary Lisa lay on the sand, her script pages fluttering in the afternoon ocean breeze. He came to a halt over the pile of bodies. "I'm a cop. Is anyone hurt?"

A chorus of voices sang out, "We're okay. Mary Lisa's okay."

"Does anybody know where the shot came from?"

One of the boys—no, not a boy, this one hadn't been a teenager in at least five years—raised his head to look down the beach. "A guy fired at Mary Lisa from over there, from beside the Sanderson's house, the second to the end. I saw the bullet kick up sand a few feet from Mary Lisa's chair. We all dove on her."

"You all did good. Now it might be better if you let her breathe." Jack ran along the row of houses that backed up to the beach. He saw about a dozen beachgoers wondering what was going on, but no one suspicious looking. He noticed the young man was running beside him.

"I only heard one shot. Did you hear any more?"

"Nope, only one. The guy couldn't have driven in, that's for sure. He'd have had to run Chad down first. That's a public beach not fifteen feet away. He could have come under the fence, fired at her, crouched next to the Sanderson house, then run out again."

They made their way through scattered groups of people who rose to watch them. "Right about here, I'd say. By the way, my name's Mark Nickels. I'm a senior at USC, in film."

Jack nodded. "Chief of Police Jack Wolf."

"Wow, man, you're the chief of police of L.A.?"

"No, Goddard Bay, Oregon. To be the Big Dog here, you've got to know where all the bodies are buried. You think he was standing—where, right there?"

"Yeah, that seems right. It's nice and sheltered. I doubt anyone got a good look at him before he went back under the fence."

Jack knew he was right. He called Daniel to send in anyone close by, which would help only in case the shooter was dumb enough to draw attention to himself. He cupped his hand over his mouth. "Listen up, everyone! I'm Chief Jack Wolf. If any of you saw anything having to do with this shooting, come over and tell me."

Mark Nickels yelled, "The guy tried to shoot Mary Lisa, so if you're worried about the hassle or about missing a wave, forget it. Tell the chief what he needs to know."

A few people detached themselves from some of the groups and headed toward them.

Jack flipped out his badge, showed it around. "Chief Wolf."

The first kid who stepped up was so tanned and loaded down with tanning lotion, he looked like polished leather. "Dude, this sucks. Someone shooting up our own beach. I hope you guys catch this creep."

It was the third person to step up, a girl no older than sixteen, California tan and California beautiful, who had actually seen anything useful. "I know I saw him, Chief, a brief flash, like a speeded-up scene in a movie, but it was him—he wasn't all that tall, but tall enough, about like Dougie here, only skinnier. He was wearing a ball cap, backwards, you know? White T-shirt loose over baggy jeans, real dark lens sunglasses."

"Could you tell his age?"

"Well, I turned when I heard the shot and he moved fast, like he was young."

Jack called Daniel again with the description, but beyond that, the well was dry.

Jack thanked all of them, took the girl's name and cell phone number, and walked back to Mary Lisa.

Mark said, "Do you think this is a good description?"

"Maybe. If they spot him right away. Thanks for your help, Mark."

"That paparazzo guy still missing?"

Jack nodded.

It took Jack a few minutes to detach Mary Lisa from all the teenagers, but finally he walked her back to her house, staying on the beach side of her. She was still rubbing sand off herself where all the bodies had pressed down on her.

"Are you all right, Mary Lisa?"

If he expected her to be terrorized, she surprised him. "I have only a couple of hours to get myself together and cleaned up."

"You mean for the party? Why don't you cancel it?"

She shook her head. "No. After what happened, I want to be with some of my friends and neighbors. They deserve to know what's going on here in the Colony. They all live here too."

"Did John call you back?"

"Not yet. I called him but got his answering machine."

"You want to go back home?"

That stopped her in her tracks. "Back home," she repeated, and she frowned.

"Goddard Bay."

"Yeah, that's what you meant. Funny thing is, that isn't home any longer. I can't leave anyway. I'm solid on the soap for the next week. You know, we're taping the reunion of Sunday and her father. And I'm not going to let this . . . monster make me run and hide."

They had reached the house, and she turned to face him. "Thank you for being here. I'm not sorry I threw the pillow at you, but I'm glad you stayed."

"You're welcome."

"You know what? I'm thinking I'd feel a whole lot better if I took a hand in this."

He opened the deck gate for her. "What does that mean?"

"I'm not going to sit back any longer like a helpless ninny. I'm going to make a pretty good investigator, with me as my first client."

THIRTY-FIVE

Dallas was broadcast in fifty-seven countries and seen by 300 million viewers.

On Sunday morning, shortly after eight-thirty, Mary Lisa made her way through her trashed living room to the front door.

The doorbell sounded again and a big fist pounded on it three times.

She threw it open to see Jack Wolf and Detective Vasquez standing side by side in front of her. The morning sun blasted her in the face.

"I can't believe you two are here at this hour. You were the last to leave the party. Go away. It's early, my house is wrecked, and I want to go back to bed."

"We'll help you clean up," Jack said and simply pushed past her. "This is important, Mary Lisa. We need to talk."

She turned around and left them standing in her front door. Jack yelled, "I'm making coffee. Get your butt back out here in ten minutes or I'm coming in after you."

Her bedroom door slammed.

Daniel looked after her, then back at Jack, a dark brow raised. "What's with you two?"

"I told you what she let drop yesterday, about wanting to become her own investigator. I tried to pin her about it last night, but she wouldn't talk about it. This is something we've got to nip in the bud, Daniel."

"Yeah, well, on the other hand, it got a little wild here in the house last night—outside too—so I can understand her wishing we weren't here on Sunday morning." Daniel looked down at his watch. "I go to ten o'clock Mass. I got maybe thirty minutes with her, tops."

"Good morning, boys. How's things?"

Lou Lou walked into the living room, her hair tousled about her head, wearing a man's short-sleeved black T-shirt that came to the top of her thighs and nothing else. Well, maybe bikini panties, but Jack didn't want to think about that. She yawned hugely.

They heard another yawn and another woman appeared, this one wearing pale pink pajama bottoms that came to mid stomach and a dark blue short-cropped top. She looked over at the two men, nodded. "Good morning, Detective Vasquez. Chief Wolf. I forgot to ask last night—chief of what?"

Lou Lou laughed. "Don't shred his manhood this early, Elizabeth. He's the chief of police from Goddard Bay, Mary Lisa's hometown. He's here to assist Danny."

"That's me, Danny's assistant."

Elizabeth rubbed a hand over her very firm, tanned belly, both men's eyes on those moving fingers of hers. She yawned, streaked her fingers through her hair. "Good to see both of you again. But it's very early, you know."

Daniel said, "Lou Lou said you were flying home yesterday, but you didn't get here until about one o'clock in the morning. What happened?"

"Lucky me, the plane was delayed." She gave another huge yawn.

Jack was studying her, a slight frown on his face. "I thought this last night—you look familiar."

Lou Lou laughed. "She's Elizabeth Verras. She's one of our local TV newscasters."

Daniel Vasquez was walking toward the kitchen. "You want coffee, Lou Lou? Elizabeth?"

"That'd be nice, Danny. What are you two doing here? It's barely dawn."

"I know you didn't expect us, but why don't you go cover yourself up a bit, Lou Lou, Ms. Verras? Detective Vasquez here was just planning to go to church."

Lou Lou yawned again. She grinned now at Detective Vasquez. "Don't be a prude, Jack. Come on to the kitchen, I'll make the coffee. Elizabeth, you want tea?" Jack pictured her stretching up to reach the coffee or some mugs and made no move to join her.

"Jack makes great coffee," Daniel said. "Why don't you let him do it this time?"

Lou Lou shook her head. "Nope, I don't think that's such a good idea. See, Danny, he knows all the voices are going to bring Mary out of her bedroom in a few minutes, and he'd better have a plan when he sees her. Jack's a guy, he can't multitask, so I'll make the coffee."

Elizabeth gave them all a sleepy smile. "I'll go fetch Mary Lisa right now. If we're up it's only fair that she be up too."

Jack waited for Elizabeth to leave the kitchen. "I was wondering why Mary Lisa wears what she wears to bed and you wear this."

"Well, the thing is, we had a sort of slumber party last night after everyone left—what, around two a.m.? Thanks for shooing everyone out. Big problem though—a few people drifted back after you left, so we brought out the tarot cards and did readings until around four. Mary Lisa likes to sit cross-legged when she reads the tarot cards, and you can't wear a T-shirt and sit cross-legged. So she put on her pj's and that man's extra-large sweatshirt you saw her in. Maybe that's why she disappeared back to her bedroom. Anyway, some people crashed out on Mary Lisa's back deck. Mary Lisa bought a whole bunch of aerobeds last year, so the deck was covered with bodies. I heard them talking about an hour ago. Carlo suggested the Belgian coffee shop, so off they went, after they made sure I was sleeping with Mary Lisa. You know, so she wouldn't be alone and unprotected." She scratched her elbow. "So was Elizabeth, once we managed to haul her off to bed. See, she was reading a Major Arcana and just fell over."

The living room was a mess but the kitchen was spotless. "That's the deal," Lou Lou said. "Mary Lisa cleans up everything else if guests scrub down the kitchen."

"Well, we don't need any Belgian coffee shop." Daniel whipped a bag from behind his back. "I brought donuts."

Mary Lisa eyed that bag. "Mary Lisa can smell a donut from fifty feet."

They heard Mary Lisa's voice from the hallway. "Any glazed?"

The five of them were settling into the kitchen when Daniel got a call from the station. "I hate to spoil such a perfect breakfast, but I'm outta here. Puker Hodges just staggered in to the station. They took him to the hospital."

"HE was a skinny guy, slouchy jeans and T-shirt, dark sunglasses, a baseball cap turned backwards. He hit me and that's the last thing I saw." Puker's hand was shaking as he picked up a Styrofoam cup of hot black coffee and drank it.

Puker was going to be all right, a couple of bruises and a lump on the side of his head, and he was dehydrated. The hospital staff had cleaned him up, bagged his filthy clothes, and were currently dripping a liquid into his IV. Daniel sat on one side of his hospital bed, while Jack stood at the door, his arms crossed over his chest.

Daniel asked him, "It's been three days, Mr. Hodges. Where did he take you?"

"Okay, move aside, you guys, I want to see the lamebrain here." Mary Lisa slithered past Jack, who made a grab for her arm and missed. She stormed up to the bed, stared down at Puker, hands on her hips. "Well, you moron, I guess it's lucky you're still alive."

"Mary Lisa! What—hey, I'm not a moron! I was developing some photos, minding my own business, in my own apartment—I called you, didn't I?"

"Yeah, to extort something from me. Then you tried him. Did you find out who he was? Try a little blackmail?"

"I didn't try to blackmail anyone—"

Daniel rose. "You found out the guy's name and you called him, demanded money, didn't you, Puker?"

"My name's Poker! Don't call me Puker! You started it, Mary Lisa. Even the emergency room nurse called me Puker!"

"—So you made demands. Only the guy came to your apartment, clobbered you, only not quite hard enough, and got his hands on the photos, right, and hauled you out? He could have killed you, you idiot."

Puker's voice caught on a sob. "I thought he was going to kill me. He beat me up. It was awful!"

Jack said, "So why didn't he? Kill you, that is?"

Puker shot a quick look at the big man. "I don't know why he didn't kill me. He hauled me out of my apartment and kept me tied up in some old, empty store. He hardly fed me anything, only let me loose when I had to pee. He hardly even talked to me, even when I tried to get him to talk about Mary Lisa."

Mary Lisa nearly threw herself on him, but Jack caught her in time. "Let me go, Jack, I want to beat the stuffing out of this jackass. Oh dear, I just insulted an innocent animal. Look at you, Puker, you look more like a reject from Jurassic Park. Don't you realize what a stupid thing you did?"

Puker was cowering, his head pressed back against the thin pillow. "It was only business, Mary Lisa, only business. I didn't think he'd mind giving me a few bucks. Then I would have sent the photos to the cops and everyone would have been happy. I never dreamed he'd come to my apartment—"

"What's his name, Puker? Do you know his name?"

"It's Jamie Ramos. He drives a van with his damned name on the right side so that's how I knew what it was. His phone number was on the side of the van too."

"What was he advertising, this Jamie Ramos?" Daniel asked, leaning closer.

"He fixes motorcycles. There was a picture of a bike on the van."

"And how did you know he was the one trying to hurt Mary Lisa?"

Puker waved his hand for the nurse to come in when she appeared in the doorway. She shot a disgusted look at Puker, passed over the cops and Mary Lisa, then did a double take. She stared and began to smile. "I know who you are. Goodness gracious, you're Sunday Cavendish! I tape you every day and now your long-lost father is in town and—oh my, can I have your autograph?"

Puker whimpered. Daniel laughed, shook his head. "Mary Lisa, why don't you go outside for a moment and give Nurse Ffalkes your autograph. We'll keep Mr. Hodges company."

"Would that be all right, Nurse Ffalkes?" Mary Lisa asked as she walked out the door beside her.

Nurse Ffalkes sent a short look back toward Puker. "Well, it's not as if he's going to die or anything. What did he do?"

"He's a paparazzo who almost got me killed."

A brief silence, then Nurse Ffalkes, her face flushed, said, "Hammer the putz."

THIRTY-SIX

"I'm going to record this, Mr. Hodges," Daniel said. "Is that all right with you?"

Puker continued to look pitiful and stare down at his clasped hands. He shuddered a sigh, and nodded.

Mary Lisa wanted to kick him out the hospital window, the drama queen.

"When did you realize this man, Jamie Ramos, was the one who was trying to kill Mary Lisa Beverly?"

"When I happened to be near Mary Lisa—not too close, of course, because of that restraining order—I noticed he was following her. I knew he wasn't another freelance photographer—"

"*Excuse* me? Freelance what?"

Daniel frowned toward Mary Lisa, shook his head. "Yes, Mr. Hodges, please continue."

"Yeah, well, that's what I am. A freelance photographer. Anyway, I thought he was acting kind of weird, so I stayed with him. I figured he might be the guy who'd tried to run her down."

"What do you mean he was acting weird?"

"He had this notebook and every time he stopped the van for a red light, he wrote in the notebook."

"Did you ever see him make a move toward her?"

"No, but it was obvious to me he was pissed because he couldn't get near her. She always had people around her. I saw him bang his fists on the steering wheel, and then he wrote something really fast in his notebook."

"So you took his picture?"

"Yes, I took three snapshots."

"Describe the man to me again, Mr. Hodges, in more detail this time."

"He's about five foot ten inches, maybe thirty, a little older, hard to tell. He always wore really dark sunglasses. I think he might be Hispanic, because he was all dark skinned, or maybe he had a really good tan. I never really saw his hair because he always wore a baseball cap, backward, you know?"

"Okay, he's got short hair since the cap covered it. When he spoke to you, did he have an accent?"

"Yeah, but I couldn't place it. It wasn't real thick, like he came to the U.S. when he was young."

"All right, so you snapped his picture. You said you wrote down his name and phone number off the side of the van. You said there was a motorcycle on the side of the van. Any more writing?"

"Yeah, block printing, all black. 'Motorcycle Repair.' There was a drawing of a Harley underneath it."

"You took a picture of the side of the van?"

"Yes, but he destroyed it, along with everything else, the bastard."

"Stay with me here, Mr. Hodges. What make was the van? Describe it."

"An old Dodge van, I think, white but dirty, with windows only in the back."

"Did you get the license plate?"

"No, I didn't see it."

"Okay, then you went back to your apartment, processed the film, and called Mary Lisa, right?"

"Yes, that's right."

"How long after you spoke to Mary Lisa did you call Jamie Ramos?"

Puker pleated the thin hospital blanket. "Well, ah, I wouldn't have called the guy, but I was thinking I wasn't really sure he was the right guy—you know, the one who tried to run Mary Lisa down. I only wanted to talk to him, make sure before I got him in trouble. I didn't call him to blackmail him, I didn't. I wanted to do the right thing. I didn't want to accuse the wrong guy."

He looked up for a response from Detective Vasquez, but an arched brow was all he got. "Please continue, Mr. Hodges. You called the phone number on the side of the van?"

"Yes, I'm guessing it was a cell phone. He answered it right away."

"Do you have that number, Mr. Hodges?"

"It was on the photograph. I'm not sure. Maybe it'll be on my phone record?"

"What did you say to him, Mr. Hodges?"

"I told him I'd seen him following Mary Lisa Beverly and I wondered if he was the guy who's trying to kill her. He was silent for at least ten seconds, then he offered to pay me five thousand dollars for the pictures and the film."

"How'd he know you had pictures and film, Mr. Hodges?"

"Well, I guess I must have told him, you know, in the course of our conversation."

Mary Lisa snarled.

"So before he went silent for ten seconds, you not only asked him if he was the guy but you told him you took photos of him and his van."

"Yeah, I guess I did. But I didn't mean anything by it. I was nervous. I guess I blabbed it out."

"Then what happened?"

"Well, I told him that wasn't going to happen, that I didn't want to see Mary Lisa hurt and I was going to take the photos to the police."

"Weren't you afraid of retribution?"

"I didn't really think about it. Besides, how could the guy know who I was?"

"You think he could have known you've been taking pictures of Mary Lisa for the tabloids? Or maybe caller ID?"

Puker looked down at his hands. "Oh shit."

"And what did he say?"

"He hung up on me."

"But you didn't call the police, Mr. Hodges."

"No, not right away, but it isn't why you think, Detective Vasquez. I was just taking a little time to think it over, you know? All right, I thought making a few extra prints might be useful, you know, when I took the prints to the police, so I was in the darkroom when the doorbell rang. I thought it was Mary Lisa, only it wasn't. It was Ramos, and he hit me hard, knocked me down, then he kicked me, knocked me into the living room. I fought back, and we wrecked some of my furniture, but then he hit me with something hard in his hand—a sap, or something—and I was out."

Jack stood beside Mary Lisa, his hand around her forearm. She sucked in her breath, pulsing with anger, but she managed to be still. He grinned at her and began to lightly rub her elbow.

Daniel sighed. "What happened then?"

"Like I said, when he hit me with that sap, I was out. When I woke up, I was in this empty room staring at a blank wall, tied to a chair."

"Where did he take you, Mr. Hodges?"

"I didn't know then and I still don't know. Like I said, when I woke up I was there, tied up."

"What color are his eyes, Mr. Hodges?"

"I told you, Detective Vasquez, he always wore sunglasses, never took them off, but like I said, maybe he was Hispanic, on the dark side, you know? He didn't look all that strong—kind of skinny, loose clothes, and his white T-shirt wasn't clean."

It sounded like the description the California girl had given Jack on the beach yesterday afternoon.

"Was he there when you woke up?"

"No. I was alone, facing that wall. I don't know for how long, but it seemed like a long time before I heard him come in behind me. He hit me first thing, in the stomach, then in my face—see, I still have bruises on my cheek. He told me I shouldn't have gotten in the way, that he was going to make me pay for that. That's when I knew he was going to kill me."

Puker began to cry.

THIRTY-SEVEN

Mary Lisa looked away from him. It wasn't Puker's sniveling she couldn't stand, it was her own vision of this faceless madman she had dreamed about that Puker had brought to life. She felt her fear digging deep and tried to make it stop, tried to get hold of herself.

Jack whispered close to her ear, "This yahoo isn't going to hurt you, Mary Lisa. I'll kill him first. Trust me on this, all right?"

Mary Lisa's fear, dark and endless as a corridor in a dream, dropped away at the sound of his voice. She looked up at him, saw the utter certainty in his eyes, and slowly nodded. And then it hit her, deep and fierce. "You won't have to kill him, Jack, I will."

"Good girl."

Daniel looked at them a moment, jerked around, as if asking them for silence, and continued quietly, "Did Jamie Ramos tell you what Mary Lisa had done to him to make him stalk her, try to hurt her?"

"No, he hardly talked to me, wouldn't answer my questions. If I talked too much, he'd hit me. He acted kind of crazy, like he'd walk around hitting his fist against his palm. It was creepy. I was real scared."

"Did he say if he'd asked her out? That that was why he was angry, because she'd turned him down?"

"He didn't say. Like I told you, I was scared, you know? I thought he was going to kill me so I kept real quiet. He came and went, tied me up and gagged me when he wanted to. One time he ate a large pepperoni pizza in front of me, drank a giant-sized cola, slurped it right down, didn't offer me anything. When he was done, he belched and laughed. I asked him what he was going to do to me."

"And what did he say?"

"He grinned at me—he was always grinning, even when he hit me, and he had crooked teeth, the front two over-lapped, you know? I wouldn't grin so much if my teeth looked like that—and well, he shook his head. He let me go to the bathroom a few times, gave me some slices of cold pizza and let me drink from the tap. Then he'd tie me to the chair again and hit me, cursing her while he did it." Puker burst into tears again.

Mary Lisa growled deep in her throat, tried to pull away from Jack. "This time he's faking it, Daniel. The little weasel."

Jack placed his palm over her mouth. She tried to bite him. He whispered, "You're being recorded, Mary Lisa. Can we let Detective Vasquez do his job?"

She nodded finally, reluctantly, relaxed her hands.

Daniel asked, "Mr. Hodges, he kept you tied up in that room for three days. Are you saying you didn't talk about anything?"

"He wasn't there that much. I figured he was out following Mary Lisa around, maybe at the studio in Burbank, whatever. Maybe he was fixing a hog or two. I always hated it when he came back because he always came back mad and he'd hit me again, and he'd curse her while he hit me. I hadn't done anything to him, it wasn't fair! All I did was take his photo and try to help Mary Lisa."

"How did you get away, Mr. Hodges?"

"I'm sitting there, real hungry, when he comes in, hits me, leans against the wall, and crosses his arms over his chest. He says some other people saw him at the beach, tells me he's heading out of town, that the bitch can die of old age for all he cares. He hits me again, and I start praying because I think he's going to kill me right there. But then he says he's going to blindfold me and drop me off in the van.

"I thank him. You know what he does? He looks at me and laughs and says something like, 'They're never going to find me, anyway. And you're just a stupid paparazzo who can't prove a thing. They might not even believe you. Nah, you're not worth Murder One.' He gives me this cocky salute and then swaggers out."

"That's it? He let you go?"

Puker nodded. "I was so grateful I would have puckered up and kissed the bastard, if he'd wanted me to. Anyway, he threw me out of the van in a parking lot and when I got my eyes free I realized I was in Santa Monica, off Delbert Avenue. I found an open coffee shop, got myself some bacon and eggs, then called 911. You know the rest."

Detective Vasquez nodded. "You'll find this interesting, Mr. Hodges. There are a lot of people named Ramos, but there's no record of any Jamie Ramos, there is no van registered in that name, and there is no such business."

"Well, what about my apartment? His damned fingerprints ought to be all over it. And all over me! Dust me down!"

"Actually, Mr. Hodges, your apartment was treated as a crime scene. We haven't found any fingerprints that match our computer database. Except yours, of course."

Puker raised his tearstained face to Daniel. "I guess he's a criminal and he made up his name. That makes sense, doesn't it? I don't know, it's what he told me. That was the name on the van."

"Puker."

His head snapped up and he looked over into the shadows on the far side of the hospital room. "Mary Lisa?"

"Why does he want to hurt me?"

"I told you, Mary Lisa, I don't know. I don't think his bulbs were all screwed in, you know what I mean? Most of the time I saw him, he was just pacing or eating pepperoni pizza." He tapped the side of his head. "But he left, Mary Lisa. He said he was out of there. I think it's over, for all of us." He sent her a big toothy smile.

Daniel slowly nodded. He rose, looked over at Jack, eyebrow raised, but Jack shook his head. Daniel turned back to Puker. "We'll keep someone outside your door, Mr. Hodges, in case Jamie Ramos decides to come pay you a visit. We'll be inviting you down to the station when you're discharged for a more formal interview. The doctor said you'll be going home tomorrow. You're going to be fine, Mr. Hodges."

"Thank God. It was agony, believe me."

"More like divine justice, you little whiner," Mary Lisa said over her shoulder as Jack crowded her out the door. "And don't think for a minute I believe that twaddle you made up."

"It's the truth, I swear it's the truth! Oh, sweet Jesus, I hurt."

Mary Lisa sent him a disgusted look. "I'd like to bean him with the bedpan," Daniel heard her say before Jack closed the door behind them.

"Twaddle?" Jack cocked an eyebrow at her.

Mary Lisa opened her mouth, but Daniel came out of the room at that moment, his eyes on her face. "You're right that it's a just-so story. At the very least he's holding back something." Detective Vasquez paused a moment, streaked his fingers through his hair. "At least this Jamie Ramos isn't a killer. And that's a very good thing."

"If there is a Jamie Ramos," Mary Lisa said. "All right, if there was a guy, do you think he could have stolen the van and put some kind of logo on it? Then driven around in it?"

"Maybe, but it sounds stupid on his part, doesn't it? Driving around something that identifiable doesn't seem too bright, unless he only used the van a couple of times. And that starts adding up to a lot of coincidences."

Mary Lisa suddenly smiled. "Well, finally. I've got a way I can help." She turned and walked away, pulling out her cell phone as she walked.

"Where are you going?"

She said over her shoulder, "I've got an appointment in a few minutes, Jack. You heard Puker. It's safe for me now."

"Right. And I'm the Sheik of Aran."

She gave him a cocky grin, tilted her head to the side, and said, "Hmmm. I thought that was a group of islands off the coast of Ireland." She stepped onto the elevator, and closed the doors before Jack could get there.

Jack slammed his fists against the elevator doors. "Come back here, you twit!"

He heard whistling, growing faint.

Daniel said behind him, "I wonder who she's calling."

"It ain't Ireland, that's for sure."

THIRTY-EIGHT

By 1940, soap operas represented 90 percent of all commercially sponsored daytime broadcast hours.

Daniel and Jack arrived at Mary Lisa's house at exactly a quarter to six that evening, the exact time Lou Lou had made Daniel promise to be there when she'd called him two hours earlier. Jack had complained, and hadn't stopped complaining when he stepped out of Daniel's car.

"Why does she want us here at exactly"—he looked down at his watch—"five forty-five?"

"You heard me, ask Lou Lou. She said don't bother trying to grill her like a cop and she started singing 'Kiss My Earrings,' that new funky song by some idiot I've never heard of that drives me nuts. I tried threatening her with handcuffs—"

"Yeah, yeah, I'll bet that really scared her. Knowing Lou Lou, I'll bet she told you to bring them on."

"Hmm, she did mention something about soft fur lining being nice. It's their show tonight, Jack, so it's their rules—at least this time."

There were no parking places in the driveway so they'd had to park half a block away. They walked in through the open door to see a dozen people sprawled in Mary Lisa's living room, all of them busy talking, eating Wheat Thins, cheese cubes, and deli food off huge trays, and drinking beers and soda. Jack carefully stepped over some remains of salsa and tortilla chips. Mary Lisa looked up, grinned, and waved them in. She looked so utterly pleased with herself, that Jack felt his blood run cold.

Daniel watched Lou Lou dive for the last cheddar cheese cube, beating a tall, lanky guy he'd never seen before. He didn't look like a movie star or a producer. Maybe he was just a regular guy, who knew?

Someone put a beer in their hands, offered them some guacamole dip and a bowl of thick greasy tortilla chips.

Lou Lou clapped her hands. "Showtime!" It was almost six o'clock on the dot. Everyone quieted, and the chewing noises grew faint as Mary Lisa clicked the remote to the local news.

The camera panned over to anchorwoman Elizabeth Verras and for the first time Jack saw her on full display. She looked buff and gorgeous, her teeth so white they nearly glared on the TV screen. The first item out of her mouth, after her greeting, was Ramos's name and a description of the white van, with an artist's mock-up of what the van must have looked like with the letters and the motorcycle on its side. "If anyone knows the whereabouts of this van please contact Channel 6. The owner is considered dangerous and is wanted for questioning in connection with a kidnapping." The station phone number scrolled across the bottom of the screen. Then Elizabeth read it aloud twice. She never mentioned Puker or Mary Lisa, but she presented the piece cleverly, acknowledging it was rare for the station to make such an announcement, but with an unspoken glimmer that promised all would be revealed if the right person called in to help.

Mary Lisa clicked off the TV and gave everyone a big fat smile and a bow. "Well, what do you think? It's gonna get called in, you know it will."

There was clapping and a chorus of cheers, with shouts of *"Way to go, Mary Lisa,"* and *"Well done!"*

"I wonder if the guy really fixes hogs."

"Or if he brings home the bacon."

There were boos and laughter, and some high-fives for Mary Lisa.

Jack dipped a thick chip into the guacamole, furiously chewed, and swallowed it. "So that's who you called from the hospital."

She nodded, looking all superior, and studied her fingernails, lightly buffed them against her sleeve, knowing he was not taking this well and enjoying herself.

"Yep, it's my first foray into investigatorhood. Not bad, huh? You know, I should add a bit more lemon juice to the guacamole, it's turning."

"Forget the frigging guacamole. How'd you get the station to do it?"

"Well, not the station, really. It was Elizabeth. She did brilliantly, didn't she?" She frowned down at the guacamole. "Fact is, she owed me one."

"What?"

"Sorry, you're the wrong chromosome."

Daniel shook his head at her and grinned when Lou Lou turned to smack him on the shoulder. "Is she smart, or what? Both she and Elizabeth."

Jack chewed on another chip. "She's an idiot. If she had a brain, she'd probably loan it out to one of her friends."

Mary Lisa rounded on him. "Oh yeah? I'll bet your brain is so primitive it takes you hours of excruciating concentration to achieve a synapse. Let's see what happens, all right? What would you have done?"

He counted off on his fingers. "We put an APB on the damned van, we're checking state and federal databases for a James or Jamie Ramos or his aliases, we put in a call to Immigration, and we have detectives out checking the motorcycle repair and parts shops."

"Right, Jack, we've done all that, but with no results yet—"

"—So far." Jack pointed a finger at Mary Lisa, ignoring all the interested onlookers, some of whose autographs he was sure he could sell back in Goddard Bay. "You are not an investigator, Mary Lisa, you're a soap opera star with an alter ego who's even nuttier than you are."

Mary Lisa was sore from her afternoon with Chico, but she managed to throw a pillow at him, and got him square in the face. "That was my fast pillow. You want to see my curve?"

The place fell apart. Jack was sure the howls of laughter could be heard all over the street, that is, if any of her neighbors weren't already there with them. He looked over at Daniel, who was trying not to laugh. He bent down and dove at Mary Lisa's waist, caught her as she whirled around to run.

"Police brutality!"

"Hit him with your curve, Mary Lisa!"

Jack carried her outside over his shoulder, climbed down her back deck stairs, and walked through the sand toward the ocean.

She was laughing too hard to really hurt him, but she still pounded his back for show. He considered walking to the water with her and throwing her out as far as he could, but the fact was, he was wearing his new low black Italian leather boots.

He set her down, still holding her arms. "You stole that line from me."

She laughed. When she was down to hiccups, she said, "When we get back, I'll give you credit, okay? 'Hey, guys, it was Jack's line about the curve pillow!' Talk about a pitiful ego. Poor baby, I didn't—"

Jack growled, pulled her hard against him, and kissed her. "You damned witch—" And he kept kissing her.

Mary Lisa froze, shocked to her toes. What was happening here? It was lust, incredible lust, and it was ripping through her, and she thought she was going to simply lift off the beach and float, or maybe become one with the beach sand, maybe rip off his clothes so she could kiss every inch of him. Boy, would that ever be nice and—*what was she doing?* This was Jack Wolf who was kissing her, the guy who'd tossed her butt in jail three years ago and would have tossed the key into the ocean if he could have gotten away with it. He was also the guy who'd come down here because she was in trouble, to help her. It didn't matter. What she was feeling, she didn't want it to stop. She thought about how nice it would be to trip him backward and fall on top of him. *Maybe I can get Daniel's cuffs, lock his hands over his head, and kiss him and keep kissing him—*

He let her arms go and pulled her so tight against him the people on her deck couldn't see even a sliver of light from the half-moon between them.

Jack was locked and loaded and crazed. His only thought was to take her down to the sand and rip her clothes off, his Italian leather boots be damned. He wanted to do the beach scene from that old movie *From Here to Eternity* right here on this mostly dry sand. He became aware of noise, too much noise. *No, block it out, it's not important. Who cares?*

But he raised his head to see every single person who'd been in her living room standing on the back deck, watching and laughing at them.

He cursed, jerked her arms from around his neck, and managed to pull away from her. He was in sorry shape, actually in pain. He stepped back and took a breath, his heart kettledrumming the 1812 Overture. "I didn't mean to do that. I'm sorry." And he turned on his beautiful booted heel and strode back up the beach toward her house.

Mary Lisa felt like he'd smacked her silly. Her wonderful lust mixed with rage. She yelled after him, "Just what did you mean, you 'didn't mean to do that,' you jerk?"

He didn't turn, kept walking. He felt a wet clot of sand hit him square in the back.

"You coward! You tease! You should be shot!"

He was a man in pain, a man on the edge. He'd done the

right thing, only to have the object of his lust scream at him, throw dirt on him. So he was a coward and a tease, was he?

He jerked off his beautiful boots, shrugged off his jacket, threw his wallet and gun down on top of the pile, and strode toward her.

Mary Lisa recognized a man who'd slipped his tether. She took off. She couldn't hear him but she knew he was after her. He heard the shouts.

"She's fast, five bucks says she'll beat him!"

"Nah, he's in real good shape. Ten bucks says he'll bring her down in the next ten yards."

"What's he gonna do, anyway?"

"Does she really want to get away from him? I don't think so."

There were hoots of laughter, and then Lou Lou yelled, "He's a serious man, Mary Lisa. Run! Well, if you really want to, that is."

Jack never saw the piece of driftwood until he tripped over it and went airborne.

THIRTY-NINE

Jack twisted in the air to land on his side and rolled. He lay on his back and mentally checked his parts. Fine, he was fine, nothing broken or maimed. But still, it was probably wise to lie here for a little while, breathe in the nice ocean air, clear his head, like that was possible, curse her. He cocked an eye open to see Mary Lisa standing over him, hands on her hips. "Are you all right?" She smacked her palm to her forehead. "Of course you are, you're indestructible. If a missile brought you down, you'd chew on it like a cigar, and jump up again. Isn't that right?" She kicked a clot of sand on him. "Don't you pay attention to where you're running?"

He didn't say anything, just lay on his back watching the moonlight play over her face and streak through her red hair, most of it free of her ponytail, curling wildly around her face. Then he closed his eyes.

"You aren't hurt, are you?" She fell on her knees beside him and slapped his face, not all that lightly. "Come on, stop faking. You're as bad as Puker. Open your eyes. Tell me I'm an idiot again. Give me more orders, you do that so well. Open your eyes, or at least wiggle a finger."

He opened his eyes again and grinned up at her. Then he started laughing, so hard he nearly choked himself. "I can't believe you came dancing back to the big bad man. Not smart, but then you've loaned your brain out, haven't you?" Fast as a snake, he grabbed her arms and pulled her down on top of him.

He was aware in a sliver of his brain that there wasn't any more laughter or hoots or advice coming from the back deck of Mary Lisa's house. There was nothing but silence, the sound of the waves breaking gently onto the sand maybe three feet from his head, and the moonlight splashing down, haloing Mary Lisa's head.

She pushed up on her elbows and stared down at him. "When you first came to Goddard Bay, we used to call you the Big Bad Wolf. You were always strutting around, looking all sorts of tough and hard, a real chick magnet, the Big Bad Chief of Police. I know, it's not very original, but there you have it."

"Strutting around?" He grabbed her hair and pulled her face down to his. She stretched out on top of him and felt her nerve endings hum, knew her blood was flowing through her thick, heavy and sweet. She felt wonderful and wanted more.

Suddenly, she jerked back. "Good grief, this is nuts. What are we doing? You've come to L.A. and, look at me—lying on top of you and I'm not all that eager to move and that really should bother me, on some level."

He laughed. "What level is that?" He lightly chopped her elbows to land her back on top of him. He put his hands in her hair, pulling her down, and it wasn't much of a pull because she wanted it too, wanted to feel him against her again, maybe even wanted the waves to flow gently over her toes, make them sizzle, she was that hot.

She pulled away again, and said close to his face, "You know this is crazy. You don't even like me. And you know what else? I haven't decided if I really like you either."

"Now, that's good to hear." And he began kissing her again, and his hands molded on her hips and he was moving her against him, slow, then faster. He pulled forward, then back, and Mary Lisa couldn't believe the wild urgency roaring through her. She pressed down against him as much as he let her, felt the hard slide through his jeans, felt his hands raising her away, driving her mad, then pushing her hard against him again.

She came, fast and hard and loud. He grabbed the back of her head with one hand and kissed her hard, taking her hoarse cries into his mouth. He was so close himself, he was heaving with it, nearly bursting, but—

"Oh my," she whispered into his mouth, beyond herself. "Oh my."

"Yes," he said, and he kept kissing her, both hands molding her hips now, pressing her against him, for him this time, not her. But he had to stop, knew it, or he'd come too, and that wouldn't be smart—

They both froze at the voice filled with irony, a familiar voice, way too familiar. Mary Lisa twisted to look up into John Goddard's face. She felt dazed, limp, incredibly energized, all at the same time, and she felt every hard square inch of Jack's body beneath her and never wanted to move.

"Well, John," she said, pleased she could talk, quite relieved that she sounded all sorts of normal, "if this doesn't beat all."

And he knew, of course, from those vague eyes of hers, the flush that he could see in the moonlight, the pain on Jack's face, knew exactly what had happened. "I was thinking along similar lines myself."

Jack let her go. He wanted to curse and weep with the loss of her against him, the deep ache in his groin. She climbed to her feet, straightened her clothes, slapping off the sand, and grinned at him. "Well, hello, John. Long time no see. You know this big guy sprawled down there, grinning like a fool? Well, he's not really grinning, is he?"

"Hi, Mary Lisa. Yeah, I know this guy. My question is what are you doing lying on top of him on the beach?"

"I was running away from him, and he caught me. He was pissed because I did something useful."

Jack shook himself, got slowly to his feet, tested out that all his moving parts were, thankfully, in good working order. "Actually I was pissed because she stole my line." He managed to grin now, and buffeted John Goddard's shoulder with a good deal of strength, a guy greeting, which, in Mary Lisa's study of life and men, could mean best friends or worst enemies—but guys. "Hey, Pitty Pat, what brings you down to this neck of the woods?"

"As in here on the beach, watching you trying to get your tongue down Mary Lisa's throat?"

Jack thought about how very fine it had felt, how incredible it had felt when she came and shuddered and quaked and he'd felt every quiver, tasted every moan out of her beautiful mouth, and slowly he nodded. "Yeah, I guess that's about right."

Mary Lisa smacked Jack's arm. "Talk about unprofessional. Well, you hardly did anything that I noticed all that much. Well, maybe some things, but—so, what are you doing here, Pitty—John?"

"So he told you he calls me Pitty Pat?"

"Yeah, I did. I also told her you call me the Goon Leader."

"I want to know what Pitty Pat means."

John shook his head. "Not in this lifetime. I flew down here this afternoon for an overnighter, to see how you are, see what Jack here has accomplished. Apart from getting you on top of him on the beach, of course, and—well, never mind that. Your father sends his love, practically ordered me down here since you won't let him come down himself."

"That was very nice of you, John. I really should call my father. We have some good news for him. The guy's gone, left L.A."

Jack looked at her like she'd lost her mind.

"What?" Mary Lisa turned on him, hands on her hips. "Why are you looking at me like I'm the village idiot?"

Jack loooked her straight in the eye. "Stop trying to pretend everything's okay now. You don't really believe that guy's gone any more than I do, any more than Daniel does. The tide's coming in. I need to get my stuff before the water does. Then let's go back to the house. John needs to hear what's going on."

John looked more bemused than pissed, Mary Lisa thought as they walked back to the house, which relieved her greatly. John said, "I've heard bits and pieces from Lou Lou and Daniel already, and this old guy, Carlo, offered to give me surfing lessons."

Mary Lisa rolled her eyes. "You already met Lou Lou and Daniel? And made friends with Carlo? How long have you been here, John?"

"Not that long. I was watching with the rest of your friends from your back deck when Goon Leader here tried to catch you. You looked really graceful, Jack, going airborne like that. Like a ballerina, and you landed soft and rolled. That was well done. Oh, by the way, there are a lot of gorgeous women in your house, Mary Lisa."

"All Jack lacked was a tutu when he did his grand jeté. Yeah, this place is loaded with both gorgeous guys and girls."

Jack grinned at her as he rubbed his left shoulder, rotated it a bit. "Did you see Little Miss Ego come flitting back because she thought I was mortally wounded?"

"Little Miss what? Ego? You call *me* Little Miss Ego?" She'd watched Chico do it a dozen times, and she'd tried it twice as often herself that afternoon. She presented her side, rose onto her toes, and lashed out at his side with her left leg. It wasn't badly done, but she held back a bit because, she supposed, her insides still felt so gooey and fluid, and Jack grabbed her ankle before it landed in his belly and flipped her. She went down, and he snagged her wrist to pull her up again. He stared down at her. "So that's why you had such bad muscle cramps on Friday. Some martial arts instructor has been beating the crap out of you."

She'd lost her kicking shoe. She jerked away from him, picked it up and shook it at him. "Next time I won't hold back, Jack Wolf. Next time I might get you but good."

"Why were you holding back?"

His voice was sexy and deep and she wanted to jump on him and kiss his face off and kick him at the same time, the jerk, but all she could do was stand there, without a word to say, because John was standing only two feet away, watching them.

John said, his head cocked to one side, understanding in his eyes, "Er, can we go back to your house now, Mary Lisa? Jack, you'd best move fast and rescue your boots before the waves drown them. You need any help, old man?"

Jack laughed at that.

"What's this? That wasn't all that funny, Jack. Why are you encouraging him?"

"An old joke," Jack said.

"I'm one month older than Goon Leader," John said.

"It still wasn't very funny," Mary Lisa said; she turned and began to walk back up the beach and paused to pick up Jack's boots. He saw them in her hand as she began trotting toward the surf, whistling.

"No!" He stopped between her and the water, panting, his arms out, like a basketball guard. "No, not my boots. Please, Mary Lisa, they're new."

"They're beautiful. I wouldn't hurt them. You, however, are another matter entirely, but I guess that will have to be later." She laughed, dropped his boots on dry sand, and ran back to her house, up the deck steps to her friends.

FORTY

Demi Moore spent some of her early acting days on
General Hospital.

BORN TO BE WILD

Sunday Cavendish faces the man who's her father. She
studies him, says slowly, "You're even more impressive in
person than on TV."

Phillip Galliard, in his fifties, tall, with silver wings in
his dark hair and Sunday's blue eyes, is immaculately
dressed in a gray suit, white shirt, and black shoes. He in-
clines his head toward her. "Thank you."

Sunday looks around his lavish office. "You're certainly
not a monk, are you?"

"No, not in any sense. This, though," he says, waving
his arms around the office, "is for show. People expect it.
Years ago, my office, my home, my car reflected my own
tastes—functional and spare are good words, I suppose.
I never had a thought for anything outside of God's works.
I was what I was and I didn't think it could matter. But it
did. My staid surroundings did not go over well. People who
wanted to believe what I preached also wanted me to be different from them somehow. They wanted to see me as special and so my surroundings had to be special—I suppose

few in the modern world want to follow a man who looks
like a beggar. I learned that the TV people, all the sponsors
who make my work possible, wanted the trappings even
more than my followers did. They wanted glamour and obvious signs of wealth. I think they were right—my audience grew, and it helped people to believe me, entrust their
money to me."

She wants to smile, but holds it in. He's charming, she
recognizes it, but she's not about to let him see that. "You
know my mother never told me about you."

"I'm not surprised. She told me she wouldn't."

"Look, I don't know you. Why, all of a sudden, do you
want to know me?"

"Well, now, that's a long story . . ."

He looks at her, his expression troubled—

"Clear!"

The shine was off Norman's face three minutes later
when Todd Bickly, the stage manager, shouted, "Okay, go!"

Sunday gives her father a sneer. "A long story? As in
complicated? It seems simple enough to me. You decide
you don't want me and Mom, and you leave. She never
wants to see you again, understandable after you cut out on
us. You never contact us. She remarries and I have a step-
father, not much of one, but at least he was there, at least
until we got rid of him."

"You mean after he tried to molest your half sister."

"All he did was try." She waves her hand at him. "Now
that I'm grown, I'm successful, I've got money, you suddenly pop into Los Angeles, announce to my mother that
you're back, and you want to see me. I've been thinking
about why you'd do that, Mr. Galliard. I've decided all this
display of wealth is a sham. You need money, don't you?"

Her father walks behind his desk, picks up a glass, and
pours water into it from a crystal carafe. He drinks deeply,
sets down the glass. He turns to face her. "You look like
me. I've watched you over the years, Sunday, seen your
photos in European magazines, read in the business sec-
tions of newspapers about how you're running a huge

corporation. You fascinate people, you know—you're so very young, and yet you've managed to squeeze both your mother and your half sister off the board, you even landed one of your mother's lovers in jail when he tried to hurt her. You're on top now. You're so very young and yet you're on top of everything."

Sunday laughs. "I guess my mother didn't tell you about her latest attempt to ruin me, to climb back to control the board with my half sister at her side, did she?"

"No, she'd hardly tell me that, would she? What did she do?"

"She bribed one of my staff to drug me, and had me carried to a sleazy motel where she arranged for some mob guy to be staying. When the press got there, it looked like I was shacking up with a lowlife right out of *Pulp Fiction*. She wanted the board of directors to turn leadership back over to her. Susan would have been her CEO."

"That couldn't have been pleasant for you."

"I won't forget that headache for a long time, that's for sure. As for the rest—" Sunday shrugs and gives him a cold smile. "It's the cost of doing business with the likes of my mother."

"You're making light of it, but it was an evil thing for her to do."

Sunday shrugs again, looks bored. "You married her. You must have guessed what she was capable of."

He shakes his head. "Not really. She was young then, so full of possibilities."

"Maybe she wouldn't have become what she is if you hadn't run out on us. Maybe if you'd stayed married, I wouldn't have a half sister who'd shoot me if she had the guts."

He looks like he wants to say something, but he doesn't, only shakes his head.

"And you want to know what else, *Reverend* Galliard? For revenge against my half sister, I was thinking about sleeping with her husband, a real winner, that guy. Would that have sent me right to hell?" She gives him a patently false smile. "I was going to cut him off at the knees, of course, once I was done with him. But then you came along. You saved me from wasting my time on him."

She stops, stares at him. "I can't believe what just came out of my mouth. You're good, you know that? You're really good. A preacher, a shrink—you're good at both."

He looks at her steadily. "Maybe you feel on a gut level that you can trust me. No, don't say you'd rather trust the devil. I hope to show you it's true."

"Don't be ridiculous. I don't even know you."

"I never wanted to leave you, Sunday, never, but—"

"Yes, there's always a 'but,' isn't there? You know what, Reverend Galliard? I don't want to hear it, although I'm willing to bet your delivery would be worthy of you." She waves her hand around his office. "I bet you've come to love your trappings and your Italian loafers. I'll bet you'd do anything before you gave them up. Good luck saving all those souls in exchange for their worldly goods."

She flicks a finger at his suit. "Versace, right?" She turns on her three-inch black heels and walks out.

He doesn't move, stands staring after her—

"Clear! Good scene, Norman, Mary Lisa. Just great. You're on again right after lunch, Norman."

Clyde came bounding onto the set. "Not bad, guys. We're off to a good start. I gotta tell you I wasn't sure when Bernie sold me this story line. But it's going to grab our viewers. And it's completely fresh, we'll be working it for months."

Mary Lisa patted his arm. "I'm glad you're pleased, Clyde. So am I."

Clyde was already trotting back to the booth where the director stood watching them, toasting them with his cup of black coffee.

"The powers that be are happy. Good for us." Mary Lisa smiled at Norman Gellis, newly arrived to play her father from *ATWT—As the World Turns*—and patted his arm. "Welcome aboard." What an incestuous business the soaps were. Norman had run out of enthusiasm for his character on *ATWT* and so they'd killed him off, shot by his jealous wife when he'd come home from a hunting trip late at night. Mary Lisa thought Norman Gellis was perfect for the role of Reverend Phillip Galliard, Sunday's long-absent father. He was an experienced, accomplished actor, and he'd played off her very well in their initial scene. Amazingly, his eyes were nearly the same color as hers, and she actually resembled him quite a bit. Was it all a co-incidence, or had the producers planned to bring him over all along?

FORTY-ONE

Lou Lou caught up with her as she walked toward the front door of the studio. "Your father here yet?"

"Which father?" Mary Lisa grinned. "Everyone's talking about how much Norman and I look alike. My real father—I hope I talked him out of coming. I heard Jack promise he'd call Dad if they needed him. Then he backed me up and lied, said everything was under control."

Lou Lou began humming.

"Spit it out, Lou Lou."

"I just wondered when you were going to tell me what's happening between you and Jack."

"Of course, Lou Lou, what are lunches for? But if you have another steak sandwich the size of Chicago in that lunch bag of yours I'm going to hit you with my sneaker."

"Nah, it's fish and chips today. They're probably a little limp, but nothing that mayo relish won't perk up. Come on, let's sit down."

Lou Lou had at least a pound of fish and chips, along with her favorite sweet-and-sour green relish for the chips.

Mary Lisa looked down at her own lunch, two small tubs of strawberry yogurt, with real strawberries mixed in. They were nice and cold. She'd sprinkled some pecans on top. Mary Lisa dug in, determined not to whine.

"Jack Wolf," Lou Lou said, waving a French fry at her. "That was some show you guys put on last night until I managed to get everyone back inside."

"Thank you." Mary Lisa savored the yogurt. It was hard, but she did it. It was cold, wasn't it, and that was nice. "I had an orgasm," she said.

"What?"

"You saw me lying on top of him, you must have seen his hands on my butt. Well, he did all the right things and I'll tell you, Lou Lou, I zoomed right into outer space. I've never felt like that before in my life. And it was unstoppable; it was on me and I flew out of control." She grinned. "He's something else."

"Yeah, he is, as a matter of fact. I've felt the tension between the two of you, but I didn't think—well, never mind that."

"You didn't think it was mutual? That we wanted to jump each other? Fact is, I didn't realize it either. That, or it was simmering inside me and it all burst out last night. You know something else, Lou Lou? I really like him. He makes me laugh as much as he makes me want to punch him out." She paused, grinning off at nothing at all. "Fact is, I can't wait to do it again, only this time I'll get him out of his jeans and—"

It was then she saw a black Italian boot appear on the bench beside her. She heard Lou Lou snicker as she followed that lovely boot upward and into Jack Wolf's face. He was grinning at her and it was clear what he was thinking. The curse of all redheads—she turned as red as the strawberries in her yogurt.

"Hi, Goon Leader. Where's Pitty Pat?"

"He's parking the car. He'll be here in a minute." He paused a moment, and Mary Lisa knew, she just knew, he was going to innuendo her into the ground, but what he said was, "What in the name of heaven are you eating?"

"Yogurt. Strawberry. Pecan halves. Umm umm good."

Jack looked revolted and picked up a French fry from Lou Lou's pile, frowned at the relish, but dipped and ate it. As he chewed he closed his eyes in bliss.

Mary Lisa eyed him, waiting for him to say something sweet perhaps, or maybe finally dredge out some sly innuendo, but he kept on chewing, happy as a clam. "You want to try my yogurt?"

He gave her a slow smile. "Not in this lifetime."

"Nice boots, Jack." Lou Lou offered him a chunk of fried whitefish. "Good shine. We were all glad Mary Lisa didn't toss them into the Pacific last night."

"If she had, there would have been hell to pay."

"Hell to pay," Mary Lisa repeated slowly. "I wonder where that phrase comes from."

He looked momentarily flummoxed. "Well, I could have thrown you in jail again."

Mary Lisa nodded to Lou Lou. "See, he's careful to make a believable threat since he's already plunked me down in jail once, no reason to believe he wouldn't do it again."

"Are you ever going to tell us what Mary Lisa did in Goddard Bay, Jack? Graffiti the gas station? Steal a wrench from Goose's Hardware?"

"How do you know about Goose's Hardware?" John asked as he walked up.

"Mary Lisa's a great storyteller, when she wants to be. I thought I knew all about Goddard Bay, but she never told us about the jail part, until Jack showed up."

"I'll tell you what, John. I'll tell Lou Lou all about my night in jail if you tell me where Pitty Pat comes from."

John grinned. "Actually, I'll get that out of Jack sooner or later. Given what a straight arrow he is, Lou Lou, I'm sure you know she deserved it. You got a juvie record now, Mary Lisa?"

"No thanks to him that I don't."

John snagged a French fry from Lou Lou's dwindling pile and ate it. "Thanks, Lou Lou. Great relish."

"Yeah, I finally taught the guy down at the fish 'n' chips

place how to do it right." She laughed. "He's got a great place, old and decrepit. It's called Vinegar by the Sea. On Moravia Street."

"It's delicious. We knew you'd be out here, and didn't want to miss mooching some lunch. And Daniel wants to see you, bring you up to date about Jamie Ramos's van. Turns out Elizabeth called him."

Mary Lisa jumped to her feet. "I told you people would respond to Elizabeth's appeal last night on the news. Let's go see now—rats, I've got another couple hours' shooting. Hey, I can call Elizabeth, she'll tell me since the calls went to the station."

"Don't bother. Daniel said they haven't found anything yet, but they're following up leads. Why don't all of us come by your house after work?"

"That'd be great, John. Elizabeth too."

John took one last French fry. "Hey, Jack, you think we can find this vinegar place on Moravia?"

"It might be fun to try."

"Your local tax dollar in action," Mary Lisa said. Before Jack walked away, he leaned down next to Mary Lisa's ear. "I make you laugh, huh?"

She couldn't help it. She turned and said, not an inch from his mouth, "Since I'm thinking about other things right now, I'm not really thinking about laughing."

Mary Lisa thought he was going to grab her, but he didn't. He straightened like a shot. "I'll see you later."

She and Lou Lou watched Jack and John walk away, their heads together.

Lou Lou said thoughtfully, "At least John doesn't act like his heart's broken."

"No," Mary Lisa said, "he doesn't. It would have been nice of him to appear a little hurt though, don't you think?"

Lou Lou laughed and ate her final French fry.

"I hate yogurt," Mary Lisa said.

She felt Lou Lou's hand on her arm. "Laughter is good. It holds the crap at bay. And I know you use it to keep people from seeing that you're scared. Talk to me, Mary Lisa. How are you holding up, sweetie?"

Mary Lisa came crashing back to earth. She swallowed. "I'm holding up. Don't worry, Lou Lou, I'm dealing with it."

"I know you are. You also know I'll worry. You want to talk about this Jamie Ramos guy?"

Mary Lisa's voice shook only a little bit. "I really don't like to talk about him, it's just too scary. But I know he's out there, Lou Lou. I know it, you know it, everyone knows it. No way did he leave, Jack's right about that."

FORTY-TWO

"Sixteen calls about the Harley van," Elizabeth panted as she hunched down into her stationary bike. The Mad Bitch leading the spin class was shouting instructions again— *"Pedal faster, you girlie girls—get those quads burning— this is where we chase Lance Armstrong. Go!"* The sound of thirty bikes spinning on a manic high over the dance music was deafening. Headbands were soaked, legs pumped, and muscles screamed.

It was impossible to talk now. For three minutes they chased Lance. Then the Mad Bitch shouted out, *"Lance is going up the Matterhorn! No way you'll catch him now! Back off, slow down. Cool off. Not great but not too bad. Maybe you can ask him for an autograph."*

After the five-minute cooldown, Lou Lou crawled off her stationary bike, wiped her face with her towel. "Thank God Lance went up the Matterhorn—I was ready to pull out a gun and shoot him. Is my face still above my neck or has it sweated off?"

Mary Lisa laughed. "Only the eyebrows. They're down by your mouth, kinda like cute mustachios."

"Har har." But Lou Lou's fingers traced over her eyebrows. "I'm pitiful, you get me every time."

Elizabeth tucked a long damp hank of hair behind Lou Lou's ear. "That's only because your brain is too tired to care. I feel so limp you could pour Bolognese sauce on me, with a sprinkle of Parmesan. Hey, maybe I should call my boyfriend, see if that gives him any ideas. Wait a second—I don't have a boyfriend. Well, damn, so much for a spaghetti fantasy."

Mary Lisa, whose water bottle was tipped up to her mouth, spewed water. Lou Lou smacked her back.

The three women walked out of the World Gym in the shopping center off Webb Road a few minutes later, bedraggled and sweat-soaked, all their pre-spin-class makeup sweated off. They hadn't showered, since they were close to Mary Lisa's house, but they looked buff, their muscles warm and glistening, virtue oozing out of every pore. Their first stop was the Subway on the corner for some diet sodas, and of course some bags of potato chips: barbecue for Mary Lisa, onion and cheddar for Lou Lou, original for Elizabeth.

They waved to Chad in the kiosk at the gate and walked past him toward Mary Lisa's house. Deciding on the beach rather than the shower, they grabbed some towels and sat down on the soft sand.

"So as I was saying before I had to catch Lance," Elizabeth said, "I told Daniel there was one call that sounded interesting, from a guy named Scooter who lives here in Malibu. He said he'd get back to me. Actually, I think it's the only one with possibilities. Anyway, Scooter claims he saw that van yesterday, heading down PCH past Santa Monica. He was riding his Harley, passing the van, and waved to the driver, said the driver gave him a thumbs-up."

"He was on the driver's side? They were both driving south?" Mary Lisa asked.

"Yeah."

"What's wrong, Mary Lisa? What are you thinking?" Mary Lisa couldn't answer because she'd stuffed a barbecue potato chip in her mouth. She automatically chewed, swallowed. "Well, the thing is, I thought Puker said the motorcycle and the sign were on the right side of the van."

Elizabeth slugged down a big drink of Diet Seven-Up. She wiped her hand over her mouth. "So if they were going south, Scooter would have been passing on his hog on the driver's side—the left side, not the ocean side where the logo was. No road there to ride on."

"So it sounds like this Scooter guy was putting you on," Lou Lou said. She wadded up her empty bag of potato chips and tossed it hard toward a trash can Mary Lisa had put on the beach. The bag banked off the back side and plopped right in.

"You never miss," Mary Lisa said, waving at her very nice trash can, painted a bright blue with a yellow happy face on it. The teenagers who lived in the Colony used it for target practice.

Elizabeth shook her head at herself, and dug into the sand with her toes. "How slow can I get? The lying little jerk. I'll never live this down. However am I going to get out of this with Detective Vasquez? Good shot, Lou Lou."

"Thanks," Lou Lou said, and turned her attention back to Elizabeth. "Hey, you're a great liar, maybe you can tell him you checked out Scooter and it didn't pan out. Don't worry. You're right, this bozo is a lying little jerk."

Elizabeth said, "Hey, look who's here." The women looked up to see Detective Vasquez, John Goddard, and Jack Wolf walking toward them, all three of them in slacks and loafers, looking like they owned the earth.

"Is that a macho strut or what?" Elizabeth said.

Lou Lou batted her eyes, patted her heart. "Oh wow, do you think these guys are movie stars? Maybe we could barter our bodies for their autographs!"

Mary Lisa looked them up and down. "Nah, they look more like strolling mariachis who couldn't find the cantina. You look on the warm side, Detective Vasquez."

Daniel was the only one wearing a jacket because he had a holster with a Beretta in it fastened with a clip to his belt. "Yeah, I suffer for my job."

Mary Lisa laughed, and introduced John to Elizabeth. They eyed each other and Mary Lisa found that immensely interesting. She smiled up at Jack, found herself wanting to jump up, no makeup, ratty ponytail, dried sweat and all, and take him down.

John nodded down to Elizabeth. "Jack and Daniel told me about your segment on TV last evening. So who's the lying little jerk you guys were talking about?"

"Big ears," Elizabeth said and scuffed her bare toes in the sand.

Mary Lisa looked at Detective Vasquez and gave him a smile that many *BTBW* viewers knew to distrust on sight. "This creep at Turley & Tom's who lied to Elizabeth, told her he wasn't married."

Elizabeth nodded. "The idiot was so clueless he didn't even know he had a tan line from his wedding ring."

Jack looked down at the sand. Mary Lisa knew he was debating whether or not to sit down in his dress slacks.

She patted the ground beside her, and gave him a shameless grin. "Well, pretty boy?"

He shook his head after giving her the once-over. "Unlike you, I'm clean and working. I just got these pants back from the cleaners. They ain't going back for two more wearings."

"Unless a catsup bottle gets you," Lou Lou said.

Mary Lisa rolled her eyes. "I can't believe we're discussing Jack's dry cleaning."

Elizabeth eyed John Goddard. "Shall we discuss yours, instead, John?" she asked while she gave his ring finger a blatant look and grinned at him.

John looked down at her—hair sweated down to her head, not a dollop of lipstick on her smart mouth, and the whitest teeth he'd ever seen. "Hard to believe you're really a TV newscaster."

Elizabeth gave him a sweet smile.

Mary Lisa shook her head at him. "What? You don't believe this scrap heap of a gym bunny you don't want to sit too close to before she showers is a TV goddess?"

John waved his hand at her. "Actually, I was just thinking goddess myself."

Jack said, "And she was willing to read your lame script about the van."

Elizabeth's white teeth gritted. "Mary Lisa didn't write that lame script, I did. And it's netted—what—"

Daniel said, "You told me sixteen calls so far. And this Scooter guy. You've got to tell me more about him so I can try to locate him."

Elizabeth cursed under her breath.

Daniel gave her a perplexed look, saw she wasn't going to say any more about it, and made a big deal of sniffing the air. "So this is why you guys are sitting close to the water? To dissipate the gym smells?"

Mary Lisa patted Elizabeth's knee, said up to him, "We sure hope so. Nothing but salt air and potato chips. You want some?" She stuck the nearly empty bag at Jack.

He took the bag, looked in it, and shook his head. "You offer me crumbs? After last night?"

He tossed the bag back at her and watched her funnel it, expertly settle the edge of the bag on her lower lip, and slide the rest of the crumbs into her mouth. He also saw the flush on her cheeks. He grinned. He'd never before seen a girl do the funneling thing, well, except for his sister Connie. Mary Lisa tossed it to Lou Lou who threw it cleanly into the trash can.

Daniel said, "So first you guys work your butts off then you sit out here on the beach and chow down on potato chips? What's wrong with this picture?"

Mary Lisa grinned up at him. "I would have thought you understood the art of exercise. A full hour at the gym spinning with the Mad Bitch and you're hurled into the Negative Calorie Zone—"

Elizabeth leaped in. "A wondrous place where calories are guilt-free. Who could ask for more?"

There was some laughter, but it quickly dwindled into silence. The jokes were good, Lou Lou was thinking, wishing for something else clever to say. At least they'd kept Mary Lisa's mind off what was happening, actually all their minds, for a little while. John cleared his throat. "I told you guys last night it was only an overnighter for me. I came to say good-bye. I've got to head back home."

Elizabeth's head quickly came up.

"A late afternoon flight," John said, his eyes on Elizabeth. "But I'll be back when I can break free again." He said to Mary Lisa, "I'm leaving you in good hands. You take care, all right?"

She swallowed. "Yes, all right. Have a safe trip, John. Thanks for coming down."

He looked from her to Jack, smiled reluctantly. "It was an enlightening trip."

FORTY-THREE

In 1951, on *Love of Life*, there were only two commercials, one at the beginning, one at the end. Today, actual soap time runs about thirty-eight minutes out of an hour.

BORN TO BE WILD

Susan slams out. You can hear the front door hitting hard from the living room. Not three minutes later, the doorbell rings and Draper, Sunday's butler, bodyguard, and confidant, answers it. She hears low voices, then her father walks into the living room. To Sunday's surprise he's in casual dress, an open-collared shirt and slacks. He looks very handsome.

She's surprised to see him, but she is over it quickly. "Since you've come, Mr. Galliard, you might as well tell me why you and Mom split up. Why you left and let me believe I didn't have a father."

"Good morning to you too, Sunday. Do you mind if I call you Sunday? After all, it's the name I gave you when you were born."

"You can call me Ducky, I don't care. It's time for some answers. If you're not ready to give me any, you can leave."

He looks at her, studies her.

Sunday calls out, "Draper—"

Draper appears in the doorway.

Her father slowly nods, says, "Very well, I'll answer your questions."

Sunday nods to Draper. He disappears.

"Let's get to it then. I have a great deal to do today and you weren't on the schedule. Why did you leave Mom?"

He spots a coffee carafe on the sideboard and walks over to it, pours himself a cup, raises it slowly to his mouth. He sets the cup back down on the sideboard.

She taps her watch face. "I'm waiting."

He draws a deep breath, as if steadying himself. "Your mother didn't want to be a preacher's wife. It's as simple as that."

"No, nothing's that simple."

"All right. Don't forget, Sunday, the Cavendish family is old-time wealth, on the social A-list for too many years to count. They run foundations, control large charities. They own more commercial and private real estate than anyone in the state. You know that very well, since you run the Cavendish empire. They were at least as dominant when your grandfather ran the show.

"Lydia was young, fresh, spirited, and bright. She expected to shop in Paris, ski at St. Moritz—to live the life her wealth could give her. When I told her I planned to enroll in the seminary, she thought about it, and told me it was over, with her family's backing."

Sunday says meditatively, "My mother always thinks of herself, I'll grant you that. And it's true she was spoiled all her life, given anything she wanted, she had only to ask. When she was only thirty, Grandfather had a heart attack and she took over. She ran everything until she tried to grind me under—" Sunday shrugs. "In any case, she is, regardless of her machinations, the head of the Cavendish family." Sunday suddenly smiles. "One thing I'll say for her—she never gives up. When she wants something, she goes after it."

"You paint an estimable woman, Sunday."

"I've wondered if her dislike of me all these years was because of you, because I'm your daughter. You walked out and she was stuck with your offspring at a young age, a child of a man she felt—what did she feel about you?" She nails him, her eyes hard on his face. "There must have been more between you than you've told me."

"Of course there was more, there's always more when human beings try to relate to each other, but in essence, what I said is the truth. Why don't you ask her?"

"She'd never tell me the truth unless she knew it would hurt me. Would it?"

"You were barely on this earth when we went our separate ways. We wanted different things from life."

Sunday mimics him. " 'We wanted different things from life.' Now that's a despicable old chestnut."

He shrugs. "It's the truth. I don't know how better to say it. We both moved on."

Sunday rubs her hands over her arms as if she's cold. "All right, I'll believe you for now. I suppose I'd hoped it was something deeper, more intriguing, not simple selfishness, on both your parts."

"But I—"

"Yeah, I know, you were a budding saint. The fact is, you married her under false pretenses. How did you present yourself to her in the first place? Not as a future preacher, I'll bet."

Phillip Galliard shrugs again. "No. I'd graduated from Boston College. I wasn't sure what I wanted to do. I was looking, searching within myself."

"And? Where did Mom fit in? Are you saying you came to Los Angeles to find yourself?"

"No, my aunt and uncle lived here. I decided on graduate school in philosophy at UCLA. I lived with them."

"How did you meet Mother?"

"She'd just graduated from Vassar. She was flitting all over L.A. in those days, partying, shopping, drinking too much. I met her when I was working in a small pipe boutique on Rodeo Drive. It was fast. We married three weeks later."

"And I was born right away?"

He nods. "I was thrilled, Sunday. You were gorgeous, and you had my eyes. Your grandparents decided to name you Angela. I wanted Sunday because it was the miracle of your birth that made me decide what I was meant to do with my life. I cannot tell you what it felt like to hold you in my arms that first time."

Sunday looks at him, says finally, with a nice big sneer, "So I come along and you get carried away with the miracle of life and want to go preach in Timbuktu. You held me in your arms and couldn't wait to get out of there. What a wholesome image that is."

They stare at each other, antipathy alive in the air. Stare, stare—

"Clear!"

"Good, excellent," Bernie said. "We'll look at it, but it's probably finished." He gave Mary Lisa a big hug, and bounded off to speak to the director.

Norman said, "I'm not on with you tomorrow. I've got a heavy-duty scene with Betsy. I think she's going to hit me."

Mary Lisa patted his arm. "Hopefully she won't send a psychopath after you like she did me once. See you tomorrow, Norman."

FORTY-FOUR

The doorbell rang at seven-thirty the following morning. Mary Lisa, with Elizabeth behind her, didn't open it immediately.

"Who is it?"

"Jack, Mary Lisa."

She threw the door open, a smile on her face that quickly fell away. She grabbed his arm and pulled him inside. "What is it? What's wrong? Come in, come in. We were just about ready to leave for work."

Elizabeth was standing back, watching. She said, "Jack, what's the matter?"

He said, "I'm glad you're here, Elizabeth, glad Mary Lisa isn't alone. I've got to fly home."

"But, why?"

He lightly laid his palm against Mary Lisa's cheek. "Milo Hildebrand—my deputies found him dead in his cell an hour ago." He added to Elizabeth, "He was a murderer, in jail awaiting trial. I'm waiting for a call from the M.E. to tell me what caused his death. My deputy thinks he was poisoned."

"Sit down," Mary Lisa said. "I'm getting you some coffee."

He sat. When she handed him the last cup of coffee from her coffeemaker, she said, "It'll grow hair where you don't want it, it'll be so strong, but I think you need it." She said nothing more until he'd taken a couple of drinks. He closed his eyes a moment, then set the cup down on the side table. "My flight leaves at ten o'clock."

"I'm really sorry about this, Jack," Mary Lisa said as she eased down beside him. "Do the deputies know who did it? Who visited him? Anything?"

He shook his head. His cell phone rang. "I hope it's the M.E. Chief Wolf here."

When he hung up nearly five minutes later, he said, "My deputy was right, Milo Hildebrand was poisoned. My deputy had told me there was blood coming out of his mouth and nose. The M.E. said his pupils were dilated—he said they were blown—and that means a part of his brain was compressed, probably by internal bleeding. He thought it was the work of an anticoagulant, like coumarin, the rat poison. He said he's checking the blood work now, and they're looking for his meal trays in the garbage, since that's how it had to have been done. Dr. Hughes says he can't speculate about whether Milo cooperated, that is, whether or not he committed assisted suicide, or was murdered. I knew Milo. I would swear he was one person who would never take his own life. It was cold-blooded murder, no doubt in my mind, and it was done on my watch, in my jail. I can't believe this, dammit."

"Where did he get his meals?" Elizabeth asked.

"From the Goddard Bay Inn, and my people are already over there checking the kitchen and talking to the staff, to guests, to anyone they can find who might have seen someone local in the kitchen or nearby. I've trained them well, but I've got to be there." He slammed his fist on his leg. "It smacks me in the face that this was either a revenge killing or Milo was going to implicate somebody else in the crime. I know he was guilty, the evidence was so strong." He jumped to his feet. "I've got to go," he said. He grabbed Mary Lisa and pulled her close. "Do you want me to hire a bodyguard or a private investigator to stick to you like glue?"

"No, I've always got people with me. You know that. I'll be okay. Don't worry."

"Yeah, right." He didn't want to let her go, he was afraid for her, but both of them knew he had to go back to Goddard Bay. She pulled away from him, touched her fingertips to his cheek. "I'll be fine."

"Lou Lou and I will be Krazy Glue, Jack."

He gave her a long look, slowly nodded.

Mary Lisa said, "Call me when you find out what exactly is going on, all right?"

He kissed her hard, nodded to Elizabeth, and was gone.

Set of BORN TO BE WILD

It was ten o'clock in the morning, and actors were lolling about the set, sprawled in chairs, reading their scripts, drinking coffee. Betsy Monroe had brought in two dozen of what she claimed were low-fat donuts stuffed with sugar-free raspberry filling, a few of which the crew hadn't yet devoured. Only the light guys and the sound guys were busy, making adjustments for the next set. She heard the director-of-the-day, Tom O'Hurley, Paulie Thomas's uncle, speaking to Bernie Barlow about a reaction Susan had had in her last scene he hadn't liked. She heard one of the wardrobe people griping about how late she would have to work. Though she made an effort to keep up a conversation with Betsy, Mary Lisa felt apart from the people around her. Truth was, she was exhausted. She had had a lot of trouble sleeping the previous night, and now Jack was gone.

Lou Lou was already in Mary Lisa's dressing room to meet her. "What's up, Mary Lisa?"

Once the door was closed Lou Lou patted the chair. Mary Lisa sat down and closed her eyes while Lou Lou freshened her makeup. "Okay, what's wrong?"

The eyebrow brush dug into Mary Lisa's left eyebrow. "Oops, let me Q-tip this off. Okay, that's good to go again. You tell me about it, honey."

"I'm just starting to feel exhausted, Lou Lou. I'm frightened. And I miss Jack. Is that sad or what? He only just left."

Lou Lou looked down at Mary Lisa, picked up her hands and rubbed them. "Listen to me, it's going to be all right. This idiot's not going to get to you. Think of me as your own personal spandex. Are you okay with your lines? Okay to go back on?"

Mary Lisa nodded. She felt numb to her feet. Saying it out loud had made it real again.

"Danny will come over this evening. Then we'll talk about it. Jack'll call tonight, tell us what's going on up in Goddard Bay."

Mary Lisa nodded. She looked at herself in the mirror, saw Sunday Cavendish, smart, beautiful, took crap from no one. What would she do about this? More than martial arts classes and having a friend make an announcement on the six o'clock news, that's for sure. The last thing Sunday would do was leave everything up to the men. She wouldn't be pitiful.

Mary Lisa straightened her shoulders and walked, chin high, back onto the set. She wasn't going to let this creep paralyze her. She had two minutes before she had to be in the club dining room to see her mother.

She called Chico, then Elizabeth.

BORN TO BE WILD

Sunday walks into the club dining room, by herself, sees her mother sitting alone, drinking coffee, a sweet roll at her elbow, untouched. Sunday pauses, then slowly walks to her table, stands over her, stares down at her. She despises this woman in her bright red power suit, the red lipstick and the red fingernails that are surely too young for her. She despises her for casting her aside when her half sister, Susan, came along, for continually trying to sabotage her, and yet—she looks so alone, so vulnerable, so infinitely sad—and this is reflected on Sunday's face.

"Mother."

Lydia jerks, looks up at Sunday with naked pain on her face, then her mask slips smoothly back into place. An elegant eyebrow goes up, and there's a slight sneer on the lips.

"May I join you?"

A look of surprise, or wariness, but Lydia doesn't say anything, merely sweeps her hand toward the empty chair opposite her.

Sunday sits down, sets her purse and briefcase on the floor beside her.

"When I saw your red fingernails I thought they looked like blood."

Lydia looks at her fingernails, then shrugs, says, "You saw your father again. That would make me think of blood too."

Sunday nods slowly. "Why? Did he abuse you? Hit you?"

"No."

A moment of uncomfortable silence, then, "He came to my house on Saturday. So did Susan, only apparently she didn't leave when my father showed up. Draper told me later she was lurking about, probably eavesdropped outside the living room window, and she heard my conversation with him."

Lydia flushes, shrugs, finally picks up a white linen napkin and begins to rub her hands with it. Sunday looks at her mother's hands, then says, "Ah, so she told you about it. Did she give you all the juicy details?"

"Yes."

"Well, that simplifies things, doesn't it? I don't have to do a he said/she said and have you accuse me of lying or accuse him of lying. Of course, Susan would lie in a flash to get something she wanted, but you've never questioned her, have you? You buy everything that comes out of her mouth."

"Your sister doesn't lie."

"She's my half sister. So what do you think? Why is Phillip Galliard here in Los Angeles now, after twenty-seven years?"

"He wants something, but not money. Phillip doesn't need money, he's never been about that. He's always wanted power."

"Money is power, you know that. But I tend to agree with you. I get the impression that money, in and of itself, doesn't motivate him. Do you know why he's here then?"

Lydia folds the napkin, lays it beside her plate with its untouched roll. "How would you expect me to know? I haven't seen him in twenty-seven years."

"All right. Then maybe you'd like to tell me why you two broke up all those years ago."

A waiter appears at Sunday's elbow. Not just any waiter, but the majordomo, Jacques Trudeau. "Mademoiselle Cavendish? Can I bring you some tea? Earl Grey?"

"That would be wonderful, Jacques, thank you."

"Madame? May I freshen your coffee? Perhaps bring you something else?"

Lydia doesn't look at him, merely shakes her head. He leaves.

Sunday looks at her mother straight on—her face shows sadness. Her mother sees this, sees her daughter's pain and weariness, and presses back against her chair.

But Sunday doesn't look away. "Did you ever love him?"

Lydia tries to evade her, but can't, not with her daughter looking at her like that. She draws a deep breath. Her hand trembles a bit as she reaches for her water glass, then drops away. She flattens her hands on the white tablecloth, then slowly clutches them. Lydia finally whispers, "I loved him more than I loved myself. I would have given my life for him."

"Then why did you let him leave us?" The pain on

Sunday's face, the pain in her voice, is palpable, thick between the two women.

Lydia's face is pale. She slowly moves her fisted hands to her lap.

Sunday's eyes sheen over. She says slowly, "I have never loved a man like that. But I know if I did, I would never let him go. Never. Mother, if you ever loved me, tell me what happened."

Lydia shudders, then looks her daughter straight in the face. "The truth—dear God, Sunday, it's been such a long time. Memories blur."

"That's a lie and you know it. Memories of the man you say you loved more than your own life would never blur. Tell me."

"All right. All right! My father—your grandfather—believed Phillip was not right for me, not right for you—or for the family."

"A man of God—not right? Now that makes a whole lot of sense. Why?"

"I—I never knew, Sunday. Phillip refused to discuss it with me, he never told me."

"Mother, please—" Sunday reaches out, grasps her mother's hand. Lydia looks down at that lovely white hand clasping hers. There's shock on her face, but she doesn't move her hand. "You have his hands. Odd how I never before noticed that."

"Please, Mother, tell me the truth."

Her eyes still on Sunday's hand, Lydia says, "I can't swear this is true, but my mother told me she overheard them talking the day Phillip left. She said Phillip told my father he'd found out he'd used extortion, manipulated stock, ruined lives and reputations to get what he wanted. He said my father was responsible for a friend's suicide. Can you begin to imagine anyone saying such things to your grandfather? He was enraged, beside himself with fury—"

"My grandmother told you this?"

Lydia nods. "She said that he—oh God, Sunday, she

claimed my father almost killed Phillip. She said he was panting he was so furious, that he pulled a revolver out of his desk drawer and started screaming at Phillip—that he was a sheep, he was weak, he'd never amount to anything. And that he'd see him dead before he allowed him to stay in the family.

"My mother said there was a shot. She rushed in to see that Phillip had taken the revolver from my father and he was white as death, but unhurt. Then he threw the revolver in the fireplace and walked out. He didn't say anything to either of them, simply walked out. I never saw him again."

"But you don't know if this really happened."

"Unless my mother dreamed it up to protect me. I know you always believed your grandmother was weak because she never stood up for herself, pathetic because your grandfather controlled her completely. Well, after your father left, I was a wreck. I was told that he'd simply said he was sick of me and sick of the baby. I locked myself in my bedroom and wouldn't leave it, wouldn't eat. Until one day she came into my room, sat down beside me, took my hand, and told me this is what happened."

"My father never talked to you about any of this?"

Lydia shakes her head. "I told you, I never saw or heard from him again. There were divorce papers with his signature at the bottom, that was it."

"So many lies. All lies, from you, from my father, from my grandparents." Suddenly Sunday freezes. She whispers, "Grandfather has never said my name. Never."

Lydia looks startled, then nods. "No, he hasn't. He hated Phillip so much that from that day on he refused to see you, to admit you carried his precious blood, my blood, as well as Phillip's. He certainly didn't want to call you by that name your father gave you. It was he who insisted on sending you to boarding school in Europe—"

Lydia's face contorts as she places her palm over her own mouth, as if to hold the words in. She leaps to her feet, knocks the chair over, grabs her purse, and runs from the club dining room.

Jacques Trudeau rushes after her, then stops. He turns and looks at Sunday, starts toward her, and stops again.

The camera rests on Sunday's face. Tears sheen her eyes, slowly begin to slide down her cheeks. She doesn't move, then her lips form the word *Father*.

"Clear!"

There was silence on the set, and then, something that rarely happened, there was applause.

It took Mary Lisa a good minute to bring herself back. She blinked, but the tears continued to fall.

She heard Bernie yell, "You just won the Emmy for next year, sweetheart!"

Betsy walked up to her, marveled at the tears on her face, and grabbed her hand. "You were incredible, Mary Lisa, and you know what? You made me better. You drew me right into it. Well done, well done. Hey, sweetie, maybe we'll both get Emmys next year. Hey, are you all right, Mary Lisa?"

"Huh? Oh, I'm fine, Betsy. I've got stuff on my mind, I guess. I've got to get changed now."

Betsy, besides being a good actor, was also a shrewd woman. She lightly touched her fingertips to Mary Lisa's arm. "It's amazing you can function at all, with all you've been through, Mary Lisa. You keep your chin up. I want you to know that all of us are on the alert. Come along now, let's walk to the dressing room together. Hey, Lou Lou, are you free to touch up Mary Lisa's makeup?"

FORTY-FIVE

Chico held a kick pad in front of him as he yelled at Mary Lisa that she wasn't kicking hard enough. When she yelled and went at him, Chico turned, feinted, and leaped backward, all the while yelling at her—"Keep your knee straight!"—"Stay balanced!"—"More energy!"

After five straight minutes, she was panting so hard, she collapsed where she stood. He tossed the kick pad onto a mat, leaned down and patted her shoulder. "Not bad for your third lesson. Next time wear a band around your forehead, it'll keep the sweat from dribbling into your eyes. I know that stings."

No kidding, Chico de Sade. She kept her head down, still trying to simply draw breath into her lungs.

"Mary Lisa, you've got some talent, you're tough. Come on, now, get yourself together. Here's a Coke, loaded with sugar. Catch your breath, and then we're going to do it again at"—he consulted the big clock on the wall—"a quarter after, okay?"

Three minutes from now? You're giving me three lousy

minutes to come back to life? She raised her head as she drank down the Coke. "I want to kill you. Promise you'll let me take you down, and I'll do it."

"You can try, Mary Lisa, you can try." He patted her sweaty shoulder again and walked away, whistling. She watched him pull out his cell, punch in numbers, then talk. Here she was dying and he was calling his girlfriend?

Three minutes later, with the help of a full can of Coke racing through her system and lots of deep breathing, she knew she was going to live. She splashed cold water on her face, slipped one of Chico's sweatbands over her forehead, and got to her feet again. She focused all her strength, all her energy, all her fury and fear, on him. Her first kick was so hard he stumbled backward. He gave her a huge grin, waved his fingers at her. "Is that a onetime deal or do you think you can do that again?"

When she was hovering at the edge of collapse again, unable to give Chico even a hate-filled look, he called a halt and told her not to forget the aspirin and hot tub.

Mary Lisa wanted to get going so she didn't take time to shower in Chico's minimalist unisex locker room. As she walked barefoot across the mats, she noticed the bright red polish on three toenails of her right foot was badly chipped. She grinned at Chico, pointed to her toes. "One of the hazards of the sport, Chico?"

"As long as none of those cute little toes are broken, they'll just serve as a reminder you're in training," Chico said.

She gave him a fist to his perfectly polished bicep on her way out. "I'm going to clean the floor with you next time, Chico."

"Yeah, I'll count on it. Don't forget the exercises, Mary Lisa."

Mary Lisa rolled her eyes. She had forty-eight hours to convince her muscles they wouldn't implode. And she was actually paying for this?

She was surprised to notice this time, though, that she was actually walking out of the dojo without all her muscles screaming at her. Only her foot was sore. When she climbed into her Mustang, she pulled out her cell, noticed a message from Jack. She hit the Call Number button.

Jack answered his cell on the third ring. "Yeah?"

"Hey. It's Mary Lisa. I gather since you called you're in need of some of my insights into that mess you've got in Goddard Bay?"

"Right. But first, Mary Lisa, how are you? You're taking care, right? Still the most popular girl in the Colony?"

"I'll tell you, I don't feel very popular right now. I haven't felt this unpopular since I called Robbie James impotent in the eighth grade."

He laughed. She smiled listening to that wonderful laugh. He'd sounded tired, but now that was all forgotten, at least for a minute.

"How did you know he was impotent?"

"I heard my father mention the word to my mother, about a friend of theirs. I asked her what it meant and I thought she'd faint. She told me to forget it—"

"So of course you used it the first chance you got."

"Robbie was being a real jerk, talking about how a friend of mine didn't have any boobs when he knew both of us could hear him, along with a dozen other kids, so I called him an impotent jerk, told him I'd read it in the girls' bathroom."

"What did Robbie do?"

"His face turned as red as the trim on our neighbor's house and his friends started hooting, poking him, you know the teenage boy drill."

"You think maybe he's the one down there trying to do you in?"

"Nah. Last I heard, Robbie was living in Moscow, Idaho, teaching history at the local high school." She laughed. "That's enough about me, big boy. Tell me what you've found out about Milo Hildebrand's murder."

Jack was in his office. He took a sip of his cold, dead coffee, put his feet up, and tilted his head back. "The M.E. has confirmed Milo died of poisoning with coumarin—you remember I told you it's a kind of rodent poison. It's only loosely regulated, fairly easy to get. We found traces of it in what was left of the mashed potatoes on Milo's dinner tray. So it looks like someone did slip into the kitchen at the Goddard Bay Inn, or got to the tray after it left there. We've shown photos of everyone close to the case—the Hildebrand family and Mick Maynard, Jason's brother—to everyone at the inn and to our own staff. No one recalls seeing any of them around the time Milo's dinner was prepared in the kitchen." He sighed. "It turns out Marci Hildebrand worked in the inn five years ago, long before she married Jason Maynard, but so have lots of people in Goddard Bay over the years."

"No one from the kitchen staff remembered anything unusual?"

"Yeah, an old bum who came by for a handout, real unusual for Goddard Bay. He caused a bit of a ruckus, tried to pee in the drinking fountain in the kitchen. That disrupted everything for a while."

"There you go. Your poisoner could have slipped in while he was causing mayhem. Do you think the killer maybe bribed the old guy?"

"That's what I'm thinking. However, the old guy disappeared. But where would he go? Everyone agreed he looked homeless, ill-kempt, bad teeth, layered dirty clothes."

"A disguise, you think?"

"Yeah, that's possible too."

"A woman?"

"Could be. I don't know. I've got all my deputies out near the inn looking for him, or for his clothes."

"What has John been up to?"

"Among other things, he's been dealing with Patricia Bigelow. She been all over city hall, threatening to wipe out the town's coffers with a lawsuit on Olivia and Marci's behalf. She says Milo was innocent and in our custody, and we're liable for his death. She seems really excited about the possibility of a large contingency fee."

"So she's rubbing your noses in it. You don't think it's possible, do you, that Milo was innocent?"

"Truth is, you always feel better if the perp confesses. Milo didn't. But the evidence, Mary Lisa. There was simply too much evidence against him. And he tried to run."

"But say he didn't do it, say he made himself look guilty because he was protecting someone. There are only two people he'd protect, right? Olivia, his wife, and Marci, his daughter. Maybe something happened to make him turn on the guilty one."

"When I arrested Milo, he was trying to blame his wife, so go figure. There's Marci, of course, the apple of her daddy's eyes. I can't think of another person in the world Milo might protect."

Mary Lisa said, "I never did like Marci in school. She was always gossiping, bad stuff that hurt people."

"I'll keep that in mind."

She heard the fatigue in his voice again. "Hey, Jack, if I think of anything else you can do, I'll be sure to call you."

He was silent for a moment. She was hanging in there, trying to keep his spirits up, her own as well, he supposed. He admired her in that moment. He was proud of her. The fact was he missed her—missed her smile, her ready laugh, her smart mouth, all of her, not to mention that orgasm she'd had lying on top of him. That made him hard just remembering the movement of her against him, remembering those screams of hers in his mouth. He wanted to do that again, like right now. He wanted her powerful bad. He hoped she couldn't hear his shudder through the phone. "You do that," he said. "Oh yes, listen to what Daniel tells you. Ah, Mary Lisa? Keep that blanket of friends wrapped around you. Take care of yourself, no rides with strange men." He paused. "I miss you, kiddo. I really do."

She closed her eyes, felt her heart beat slow heavy beats. "I miss you too."

He wanted to keep talking to her, but his office phone buzzed. "I've got to go. Please, sweetheart, you take care of yourself. We'll get through this, I promise."

"Okay."

As soon as he'd punched off, he barked into the phone, "Yeah?"

His secretary, Mulhouse, just Mulhouse, thank you, said in her scratchy smoker's voice, "The D.A.'s on the line, Chief. He wants to meet you at Marci Maynard's house."

"Got it."

When Jack pulled into the Maynard driveway ten minutes later, John Goddard waved him over to the living room window.

FORTY-SIX

Malibu

At Monte's, just off PCH, Elizabeth and Lou Lou waved Mary Lisa to their favorite back booth. They were talking to a couple of people, who greeted Mary Lisa when she came in. It was ten minutes before they were finally alone with three Diet Dr Peppers on their table.

Elizabeth said, "Okay, Mary Lisa, what is this about?"

Mary Lisa raised her soda and clicked it to Elizabeth's glass, then to Lou Lou's. "It's something I mentioned before, but I didn't act on it because everything happened all at once." She sucked in a deep breath. "But I'd like to now, and I need your help."

Elizabeth gave her a reporter's stare. "Help with what, exactly?"

Mary Lisa sat forward, lowered her voice. "You were an investigative reporter, Elizabeth. You know all about how to run an investigation, how to dissect evidence, how to break a story. You're really smart. Lou Lou and I are smart too, but we don't have your experience, your way of looking at things. I hate to admit this, but Detective Vasquez isn't getting anywhere. He can't find Jamie Ramos and there isn't anything more for him to do unless this crazy tries to kill me again. I'm going to get an ulcer if I just wait around for him to try again because next time he could succeed. I'm tired of being paralyzed with fear, Elizabeth. I want you to help me find him, not wait around like a help-less wuss and hope I survive next time."

Both Lou Lou and Mary Lisa looked at Elizabeth while she tapped her fingernails on the tabletop. She said slowly, "You've held up remarkably well so far, but I can see you're near the edge, and you have a right to be. We could hire a private investigator, Mary Lisa. I'll bet the studio would instantly provide you with private security guards. All you'd have to do is ask. Or you could take a leave of absence. Understand, it's not that I don't want to help you, it's just that directly involving ourselves could be danger-ous, more dangerous than it is now."

"I can't think of a single way it could be any more dan-gerous. Look, I'm already doing something to protect myself—I'm taking karate lessons. Elizabeth, you went on TV about the van and Jamie Ramos. But it's not enough. Would you at least help me do something else to protect myself?" Mary Lisa cut her eyes to Lou Lou. "Are you in this with me, Lou Lou?"

Lou Lou never hesitated. She covered Mary Lisa's hand with hers. "All the way."

"Okay, would you teach us how to shoot, how to use a handgun?"

Elizabeth looked closely again at the women she'd con-sidered her best friends for some time now. Every day that passed without someone on the radar was a danger for Mary Lisa. Lou Lou knew that too and it was driving her nuts. "Okay, you guys, I'm in. We're all in this together?" At their nods, she raised her glass, clicked it to Mary Lisa's and then to Lou Lou's. The three of them drank silently.

Elizabeth continued. "Teaching you to shoot is no prob-lem. We can get you started right away. Do either of you know anything about guns?"

"Nope, not a blessed thing," Lou Lou said and Mary Lisa nodded.

"Okay, you know I have a permit to carry a handgun, but I'm not about to pull it out of my purse and freak everyone out. It's not easy to get a permit in L.A., but you're a celebrity, Mary Lisa, and there have been attempts on your life. I'm sure you could get one, and with Daniel's help, maybe quickly. The first thing we need to do is get you to a gun shop."

Mary Lisa asked, "Can Lou Lou and I buy a gun right away?"

"By law you'll need to take a handgun safety course first. Takes about an hour, and I can ask Frank Reynolds, an old friend who owns the gun shop I use in Calabasas, to make time to give you guys one. We might be able to head over there now and get you some practice on the firing range."

Mary Lisa said, "Perfect. What kind of gun should we get?"

"I carry a nine-millimeter SIG Sauer P239 semiautomatic. The P stands for personal, which means it's small and light, and there's not much recoil. The clip or magazine holds seven bullets."

"What does nine-millimeter mean?" Lou Lou asked.

"Nine millimeters refers to the caliber—the size of the bullet. About a third of an inch. There are more powerful rounds, but if you aim it right, it's enough to stop anyone.

"We'll get you started at the firing range with the basics, like aiming at the largest part of an assailant who's coming at you. Almost all shooting with a handgun is very close up. Of course a live person is more difficult than a target because live targets move around and they can shoot back."

Mary Lisa said, "Yes, I understand that."

"And respect, guys. You've got to respect your gun and you've got to respect what it can do." Elizabeth searched both their faces, then nodded. She made a call on her cell, closed it, and tossed a ten on the table. "Okay, Frank says we're on. Let's head over to the range in Calabasas. You're going to feel like Bruce Willis by tonight."

FORTY-SEVEN

At midnight, after she'd gone over her lines for the next day so many times Mary Lisa figured she'd recite them in her dreams, she snuggled down, exhausted and mellow after an hour in the immense hot tub at Carlo's house six doors down the street. Elizabeh had called her a natural at the firing range and surely that had to count for something. Though she felt tired, she found she couldn't sleep—her mind kept churning, wouldn't quiet down. And Jack was there, always there, and she marveled that he'd come into her life at such a time. Well, if she couldn't sleep, it only seemed right the sexy bozo in Goddard Bay shouldn't either. She dialed Jack's cell number.

He answered on the fourth ring, his voice low and irritated. "If this isn't an emergency, I'm going to bust your ass."

"What if this were your mother?"

Silence, then, "You're right. Not cool. What's up, kiddo?"

"Has Detective Vasquez called you?"

"No. What happened?" His voice was alert now. She suddenly saw him sitting up in bed, chest bare, a sheet pulled up to his waist, or maybe it was real warm tonight in Goddard Bay, and he didn't need a sheet. Maybe he was lying there, all sprawled out, every lovely inch of him nice and bare.

"Mary Lisa, you there?"

The picture tube in her brain went blank. "No, nothing's happened. I thought Detective Vasquez might have told you something. You know, cop to cop. I know it's late, but I couldn't sleep. Another thing, I called you earlier this evening only you didn't answer. What's up? Where were you?"

His voice changed subtly. It was lighter, with a hint of amusement she immediately distrusted. "I was busy tonight and turned my phone off." She could see that sexy grin of his, see it clear as day. "Now don't think I didn't check my messages, I did. I mean if someone had capped you, Daniel would have called a dozen times and I'd have called him back. Is that okay with you, Mom?"

"No, not okay, you jerk. Where were you?"

"Speaking of moms, did you know I ran into your mom this afternoon near the station? She actually stopped me in my car to tell me to keep away from Kelly, that her little darling was fragile and didn't need me messing with her. Isn't that a corker?"

So he wasn't going to tell her what he was doing this evening. Maybe she could take him down on the beach again, and after she kicked him a couple of times, she could cover him like a spandex wet suit. "Why would Mom do that? I mean, why would she have to?"

"Well, Mary Lisa, I think Kelly may have told her she was going to come over to my office. I'd just gotten back from the D.A.'s office, tired and hungry, and she was waiting there to tell me she was making spaghetti and meatballs with garlic toast and spinach salad, and I should come over for dinner."

Deep, dead silence.

He had the nerve to laugh.

"I hope you enjoyed the meal." You jerk. She disconnected.

Her phone rang three seconds later.

"Ouch. Don't hang up again, Mary Lisa. Okay, the truth is I didn't go to dinner with her, but I'll tell you, it was tough to turn down. I was really hungry."

"You're a sorry excuse for a man."

"Yes, well, uh, tell me, is it a beautiful night down there?"

"Oh, yes, it's calm and warm. The moonlight is making the ocean glitter like there are diamonds strewn on top of it. Is it warm in Goddard Bay?"

"Nah, cold as January and fog thick enough to keep you indoors with some good home-cooked chili, wishing for someone to huddle up with for warmth."

Cold as January? That meant pajamas or a blanket to his neck. That was a pity. "Well, don't drive off a cliff in the fog," she said, in a voice that sounded like she was going to hang up again.

"Wait a second, Mary Lisa, let me tell you what happened up here this afternoon."

"Okay, what happened? You solve the case?"

"Not quite yet. Pitty Pat called me, said to come over to the Maynard house—that's where the murdered son-in-law lived with his wife, Marci."

"She's living there by herself?"

"Yep. You're not going to believe this."

"Okay, hotshot, I'm all atwitter. What happened?"

Jack yawned really big, and Mary Lisa could swear he was scratching his belly. Her heart did a mad leap. "I pull in the driveway right behind John's Beemer. He's standing next to the living room window. He hears me, waves me over. He whispers, 'Your timing's perfect. Take a look.'"

He paused again—this time on purpose, for effect. "Have you ever thought of being an actor, Jack? That's some timing shtick you've got there. Okay, what did you see?"

"The murdered husband's widow—Marci—she was on her knees doing a Paris Hilton on her dead husband's older brother, Mick."

"What?"

"You remember Mick Maynard, don't you? He owns a local auto repair shop on Indiana Avenue. He's been divorced about three years now, his ex took the kids to live in Salem."

"But that's nuts!"

"Yeah, well, I'll tell you John was so shocked he could hardly get enough spit in his mouth to say anything."

"But why would Marci do that? I know I told you I didn't like her in high school, but I wasn't really all that serious. But this? I mean, her husband's murdered, her father's now murdered too—"

"Agreed."

"Well, whatever the reason, you're a couple of Peeping Toms, pretending it's okay because you're a cop. You're disgusting, Jack Wolf."

"Well, not really. It's an investigation. Well, okay, maybe it wasn't necessary to look."

She couldn't help herself. "Okay, what happened?"

He had the gall to laugh at her.

"Come on, Jack, tell me you and John left immediately, tell me you didn't keep looking."

"Actually, we did stop looking. It felt too weird. We gave them another ten minutes since neither of us knew what—well, never mind that. Then we went to the door."

"Wait a minute here." Mary Lisa sputtered into the phone. "You said John called you to come over. Are you telling me she was on her knees for more than ten minutes?"

Jack grinned. "I wondered the same thing. John said there were lots of preliminaries. The main feature started a couple of minutes before I drove up." He paused. "Do you want me to go on?"

She cleared her throat. "Please do."

"Like I said, after ten minutes we knocked on the front door. Mick answered. He had a beer in his hand and he had this complacent smirk on his face—every guy in the universe knows that look."

"So does every woman, you jackass."

"Maybe, but like I said, a guy always knows. So Mick gives us both this look like *I ain't feeling no pain and you schmucks are* and offers us a beer. Then Marci comes out and she's all chirpy, got this flush on her cheeks. John tells Marci he'd like to speak to her and you know what? She looks at Mick, silently asking him what to do. He gives her a little nod, hands her his beer can, stretches, and tells us he'll be leaving us to it and out the door he goes."

"Don't tell me he was whistling."

"Could have been. So John asks Marci how long she's been seeing Mick, you know, he's trying to ease into it, but she sings right out that it's been a week now and he's made her feel so much better about things. How after Jason's murder he was such a comfort to her, but now—she stops talking and stands there and glows. And John and I are thinking about how she's certainly made old Mick feel better."

"I'm sorry, Jack, but I have to say it. That's incredibly tacky. Her husband was murdered such a short time ago."

"Not to mention her dad. We asked her about who could have killed her father, asked her whether she or her mother had visited the Goddard Bay Inn. She claimed she didn't know a thing, that her mother adored her father and wouldn't ever have hurt him, that she was devastated. Meanwhile, she's still glowing. Then a yapping dog comes racing into the living room and she gets all kissy-face with it. She says she's devastated too and she's so grateful to Mick for helping her get through this nightmare. When I ask her how long Mick's been on the scene, she loses her glow and gets all huffy. She claims she was never unfaithful to Jason— what a horrible thing that would be for us to think— particularly since Jason was Mick's younger brother. Anyway, that's all that's happened up here. I know you want more details, Mary Lisa, but I'm a cop and all those little details are privileged info. Hey, I'm glad you called. Do you think you can go to sleep now?"

"I sure hope so. Hey, I'm nearly nodding off into the phone."

He laughed. "Sure you are."

"Thanks for getting my mind off my own troubles. Did I ever tell you I think you're a good man? Good night, Jack." She disconnected, pleased she'd managed not to ask him if he was wearing pajamas.

FORTY-EIGHT

Chris Noth played Lucky on *As the World Turns* before his role on *Law & Order*.

BORN TO BE WILD

Sunday Cavendish walks into her grandfather's library, past paneled bookshelves filled with books, dark leather furniture, and thick draperies. It's old-money rich, understated and elegant.

"Hello, Grandfather."

Nelson Blakeney Cavendish II, eighty-one years old, looking frail but with a lovely head of white hair, is sitting in a big leather chair reading the newspaper. He looks up, nods.

She walks to the leather chair opposite him and sits down. "My father is in town."

She watches him closely as she says it. Slowly, he folds the newspaper and lays it on his lap. "Your mother told me." He shrugs. "What does he want?"

"I don't know, he hasn't told me. I understand that Grandmother eavesdropped on your conversation with him twenty-seven years ago, that you tried to kill him with a gun but he took it away from you."

The old man doesn't hesitate, shrugs. "I'm glad he did. It would have been difficult to keep his death by gunshot out of the papers and behind the doors in the D.A.'s office."

"Difficult even for you?"

"Yes, even for me. Not impossible, I would probably have managed it, since I was the one who put the D.A. in office in the first place and the last thing he'd ever want to do is embarrass me."

"Grandmother said my father accused you of breaking the law—extortion, stock manipulations—business as usual?"

"Your grandmother was always a fanciful woman."

"Then why is it you never call me by my name?"

He stares at her a long moment. Finally he says, "It's a ridiculous name given to you by a pompous, hypocritical charlatan who has done nothing in his life but swindle people out of their money with the idiotic promise of setting them on the path to eternal life. It makes me sick, always has."

"Me as well," Sunday says.

He looks surprised.

"The thing is, I'm not at all sure my father is a charlatan. Have you ever watched him on TV?"

Her grandfather looks disgusted. "Oh, he's a good actor, I know that. He has an oily charm that appeals to gullible people. Don't let him draw you in because that's why he's come back—to draw you in, to make you believe all of us were wrong about him."

"That's certainly possible," Sunday says. "Was it true? Did you cheat people? Break laws? Ruin lives?"

He gives a scratchy laugh. "You, of all people, ask me that? You know as well as I do that power, no matter how wisely used, can have bad consequences, for some. When elephants fight, the grass suffers, as they say. You do it yourself every day. Have you done a head count of the people you've hurt with your company policies? Your buyouts? You don't think much about who gets hurt, do you? Of course not. Your mother never did either. She enjoyed having power, until you managed to take it from her. Are you honest enough to admit it? Tough enough?"

She looks at him steadily. "You wanted to kill your own son-in-law because he stood up to you?"

She waits a moment, but he doesn't answer her.

"Why did you react so violently to what he said to you?"

"You're like a damned lawyer. You don't answer a question, you ask another one. Your mother trained you well."

"My mother never trained me at all. What she did was send me out of the country. Or was it you who did that? You who saw to it that I, the hypocrite's seed, was removed from your sight?"

He sips a glass of water from the carafe at his side. He sets the glass down, looks at her thoughtfully. "Self-pity doesn't suit you, it hangs better on Susan. Maybe it was good for your character that your mother cut you loose— very well, that *we* cut you loose. Yes, I was the one who insisted I wanted you gone." He snaps his fingers in her face. "Gone."

She is stiff with pain, but she tries not to show it. She's known how he felt, but hasn't ever admitted it, never asked him or her mother. She stares at him. She smiles. "Why then, thank you, Grandfather."

"You're good. Very good. You would have made an excellent lawyer."

She draws a breath, shrugs. "Think of it as part of your heritage, Grandfather—and his."

Her grandfather looks at her broodingly—

"Clear!"

The last scene. A relief. Once out of her makeup, back into jeans and a T-shirt, Mary Lisa walked out of the studio into the bright late afternoon sunlight. She rummaged in her purse for her sunglasses. There were people from the studio scattered around her. She raised her face to the sun, smiled. She'd wait for Lou Lou right there.

But then she heard Lou Lou yelling her name. She heard a scream, and then the rumble of a motorcycle. It was close, coming closer. It was jumping the curb, roaring louder than a rocket now, coming straight at her.

FORTY-NINE

The last network radio soap opera went off the air in
November 1960.

It happened in an instant. Jeff Renfrew shoved her back
against the door, and the bike skidded sharply away, tires
screeching, engine revving. Jeff leaped forward, and threw
a hard punch, hitting the rider against his shoulder. The
bike jerked and skidded some more, but the man in the
black helmet managed to stay on and keep the bike upright.
He turned on a dime and took off, bounced over the curb
and wove back between two cars, horns honking all around
him, curses filling the air. Jeff raced after him and cut him
off before he could pick up speed. He kicked the back tire,
but the guy managed to pull in front of a car, blocking him
off. Jeff stepped back, watched the bike speed up, and
knew he couldn't catch the guy now. He trotted back to
Mary Lisa.

"You okay, Mary Lisa?" Her face was perfectly white,
people were hovering around her, all talking at once. She
blinked, then to his surprise, she smiled at him. "Thank
you, Jeff. You saved my neck."

Suddenly they heard a horrendous screech of brakes, a

car horn sounding, and the sickening sound of a loud thud.

They ran back out on the sidewalk, toward the sound of the crash. Cars were stopped, drivers leaping out, trying to find out what had happened. They ran around the side of a white Pathfinder and saw the driver leap from the cab and run toward the front of the SUV. Traffic was gridlocked now, nobody was going anywhere.

A man was lying on his side in front of the SUV, unmoving, his Honda motorcycle beside him, one of its wheels bent nearly in two.

"It's him," Mary Lisa said. "The man who tried to run me down."

Someone yelled that he'd called 911.

The driver of the SUV was on his knees beside the man and felt for his pulse, all the while saying the motorcycle had jumped right in front of him. He took off his light jacket and laid it over the man. His helmet was still on his head.

People from surrounding cars converged, elbowed their way through to see the man.

"The guy jumped right in front of him! I couldn't believe what that bike was doing!"

"Is he dead?"

"You're Mary Lisa Beverly?"

"You're on Born to Be Wild, *right? You play Damian Sterling, don't you?"*

Mary Lisa started to go down to her hands and knees next to the man, but Lou Lou grabbed her. "No, stand back now, okay? The ambulance will be here soon. There's nothing you can do."

"Do you think he's dead, Lou Lou?"

Mary Lisa sounded perfectly calm and that worried Lou Lou. "It doesn't matter. Now, you come back with me." As she spoke, she called Daniel on her cell.

They soon heard sirens in the distance, then the paramedics' voices.

"Let us through! Come on, folks, move aside."

They saw the paramedics, and then a police officer, striding through the crowd, telling people to step back.

Mary Lisa stepped up to him and said, "Excuse me, but the biker, he tried to kill me."

The officer's head whipped around. "What did you say? Who are you?"

"I'm Mary Lisa Beverly. We've called Detective Daniel Vasquez at the Lost Hills Station. He's on his way."

"Who is the guy?"

"I don't know. He's got a helmet on."

"They'll leave it on too. The doctors will take it off. So you don't know who he is?"

"No."

The officer was trying to understand what had happened when Daniel ran up. People hovered around her, nothing new in that. She sat on a bench in front of the studio, sunglasses perched on her nose, a bottle of water in her hand. She was speaking alternately to a Burbank police officer and to Jeff Renfrew. He heard her say, "I can't believe it's over. Officer, this is Jeff Renfrew, he saw the guy coming toward me and shoved me out of the way. Then he kicked his back tire, messed him up. We still don't know who he is. Detective Vasquez, thank heaven you're here." She gave him a huge grin. "It's over."

"I'll want to hear everything, Mary Lisa, everything, but first things first."

"I don't know if he's dead. They left his helmet on. I don't know who he is."

"That, Mary Lisa, we'll find out fast enough." He nodded to Lou Lou. "Okay, you guys want to come with me?"

He led them to the cordon the police were setting up around the site. Daniel had to show three different cops ID before they were let through.

When they reached the ambulance crew, the paramedics were lifting the man on a board onto a stretcher. His helmet was dented and scuffed, and there was a restraint around his neck. The man wasn't moving, no, wait, his left leg twitched. They'd cut off some of his clothes, pulled a sheet to his waist. They saw blood.

Daniel spoke briefly to one of them and looked down into the man's face under the helmet's opaque visor, which the paramedics had lifted.

"Mary Lisa, come up here."

Daniel pulled her beside him so she could see the man's face. He said nothing, waited.

Even though the man's face was covered with blood, she knew who he was. She was surprised even though she supposed she shouldn't be.

She said, "It's Paulie Thomas. He's Tom O'Hurley's nephew. Tom's one of the directors for *Born to Be Wild*. But you already know that, Detective Vasquez. Paulie was here at the studio today, I saw him. Is he going to be all right?" This to one of the paramedics.

"I don't know. Sorry. Okay, we're out of here now. Step back, please."

Daniel pulled her away. They watched in silence as the ambulance wove its way through the crowds of people and cars and, siren on, began to pick up speed.

Daniel took both her hands in his. "Listen to me now, Mary Lisa. It's over." He saw Lou Lou muscling her way through to them. "There's my tough girl. Okay, I want the two of you to go home now. There's nothing more you can do here. You drive, okay, Lou Lou?"

"I can drive, Detective Vasquez," Mary Lisa said, her voice surprisingly firm. "I'm dandy now."

He nodded slowly. "All right. I'll call you when I know more about this."

FIFTY

**The head writer makes all decisions. Script writers are
called dialoguers.**

Mary Lisa's house didn't stay empty for very long. Within
the hour, there was a cacophony of voices pouring out the
open front door and the open windows. A half dozen people had gathered out on her deck, patting her, handing her
sodas, beers, a straight shot of vodka.

"It's over," Mary Lisa heard them say over and over,
"thank God it's finally over and you're okay."

Mary Lisa stood in the middle of all the well-wishers,
wondering why she didn't feel much of anything at all.
What about relief? Surely she should be feeling immense
relief, but she wasn't. There was nothing, simply nothing.

She knew if she fell to her knees and thanked God for
getting her through this, she wouldn't mean it, she wouldn't
mean anything. She sat on one of her deck chairs, a soda in
one hand and a beer in the other, staring at the kitchen
glass that held straight vodka beside her elbow on a side
table and wondering who would drink this deadly stuff.
She hadn't known there was any in the house.

Paulie Thomas. She said his name a couple of times in her mind. He'd been the one to hit her with the car, the one to shoot at her on the beach, the one who'd called her. He was Jamie Ramos? He'd kidnapped Puker?

Her questions fell into a black hole. She got up and wandered into her kitchen. She saw Buzz Snyder laying out a half-dozen pizzas on her kitchen counter. For the first time, she smiled. Snyder was as skinny as the mirror above Mary Lisa's bathroom sink, though he personally made about two hundred pizzas a day at Reality Pizza, a place he owned on PCH in Malibu. How could he not pop a dozen or two slices into his mouth every single day?

A dog barked, a little-dog bark even though it was loud. It was Honey Boy, only five pounds on a rainy day, which meant that MacKenzie Corman, his doting mama, wannabe actress, and Mary Lisa's newest friend, had arrived as well.

Mary Lisa heard Breaker Barney's scratchy laugh. He called himself the local "gangsta" because he made his living running gambling sites—some on the Internet and at least half a dozen for private clients in posh card rooms. He lived ten doors down in the Colony, and try as he might to slick his hair back and look tough and sexy, he looked like a preacher. She'd met him at Monte's the first month she'd been in L.A., and had a standing Thursday morning date for espresso. His grin was so big she saw the gold filling in one of his molars.

Mary Lisa looked out over the back deck, her kitchen and living room filled with people, and in that moment, she did feel something—immense gratitude for all of her friends. She didn't think; she threw back her head and drank down the straight vodka.

When everyone had a slice of pizza and had congregated on the back deck, she joined them, smiling widely now because someone, she didn't know who, had poured another half glass of vodka for her, and she'd drunk it right down. She called out, "Hey, dudes, I'm heading over to the dojo tomorrow, working on my black belt. Any of you losers want to come with me and try to take me on?"

There was laughter, some hoots, some voices yelling out.

"Must be more like a pretty pink belt."

"You can't stand peace and quiet, is that it?"

"You couldn't take on Honey Boy."

Woof, woof, yip, yip.

"Come to Mama, Honey Boy, I don't want Mary Lisa to try to beat you up."

Of all things, that second vodka brought her right back, planted her feet firmly on her wooden deck. She heard seagulls overhead, saw a pelican wing its way ponderously down the beach, right at the edge of the foaming waves.

She listened to Carlo tell about a surfing lesson with Millie Cartwright, a young actress just breaking in, and how she'd fallen right on her head on the board and still came up smiling. She didn't hear her cell phone over the din of voices, but she felt it vibrate in her jeans pocket.

It was Tom O'Hurley.

The first words out of his mouth were, "Paulie lost control of his bike, he wouldn't do anything like this on purpose. He's shy, Mary Lisa, you know that, but the thing is he's always gotten these ideas into his head, but—" He paused, got ahold of himself, and sucked in a deep breath.

"Tom, I—"

"No, no, I'm sorry. You've been under a great deal of stress, everyone knows it. I'm very sorry for all of it. But Paulie—no, Mary Lisa, he really liked you, he wanted to ask you out, he told me that once, but I discouraged him."

Mary Lisa wasn't deaf. She heard the pain and fear in his voice. She wanted to tell him Paulie badly needed professional help, that he'd obviously lost it today, but she didn't. She said, "Tom, listen to me now. It wasn't me Paulie was interested in, it was Margie. He didn't like me, Tom, truly—"

"Yes, he did like you but that doesn't matter now. Listen, Mary Lisa, I'm so sorry about all this—this accident.

It's such a relief you weren't hurt, even though Paulie was. And you know it was an accident, it had to be."

What to say now? Tom wasn't thinking logically and who could blame him? "Perhaps it was an accident, Tom. How is he doing?"

"They said he's had a lot of bleeding into and around his brain. They've taken him to the operating room." There was a hitch in his voice. "His mother is frantic. The doctors are closemouthed, but I could tell they think he could die. Everyone keeps repeating we have to be patient."

"I'm very sorry, Tom."

Silence a moment, then, "I heard there was some talk that he didn't climb the curb on his bike accidentally, that he was trying to hit you, that it was Jeff Renfrew who shoved you away and kicked his bike."

"Yes, Paulie did jump the curb, Tom. I'm sorry, but he did it on purpose, he wanted to run me down. A half dozen people saw the whole thing. I know this is difficult, but it's what happened. When Paulie gets out of the hospital, he'll need professional help, Tom, lots of it." She prayed he was hearing her, not only hearing, but taking it in, understanding and accepting it.

His breathing hitched again, he moaned. "If I'd had the slightest idea Paulie was capable of such a thing, he wouldn't have been anywhere near you, or the studio. He so loved the show, loved being near the actors. He's never been violent, Mary Lisa, I swear it to you."

"Like I said, Tom, it was Margie he loved, or maybe obsessed is the right word, Tom, not me."

Silence, then, "I'll offer my resignation to the studio in the morning."

So now he'd decided to take the blame for all this. She wasn't about to let him. He was a good director, the show needed him. "Tom, I don't blame you for what happened, no one does. I want you to forget about the studio for a while, okay? Now isn't the time for a big decision like that."

"But I—" She heard someone speaking and he hung up. Slowly, Mary Lisa disconnected, and stood staring at the portrait of a colorful sailboat on the far wall of her living room.

She was still staring at the oil when Irene called from the studio. She supposed she'd been expecting this. The brass must be scared out of their minds and Irene was, currently, the biggest brass.

"No injuries, Mary Lisa?"

"No, Irene, I'm fine. Paulie is in the O.R. Tom told me they don't know anything yet."

Irene made a rude noise. "Well, at least it's over. Now, you've been through the wringer, Mary Lisa. I asked Bernie to spread out the scenes you've already shot. You're now officially off duty. Rest, Mary Lisa, get your bearings back. Take it easy. You need anything at all, you call me, all right?"

Mary Lisa smiled at her cell phone. She had nearly been run down on studio property by an employee. They must be terrified it would get out and she would sue them, and whatever— She said, "Irene, thank you for giving me some time off. I rather need it, you know?"

"I know. Is there anything I can do, Mary Lisa?"

"No, I'm fine. Thank you for calling, Irene." She disconnected, and looked up to see Lou Lou standing close, a slice of veggie pizza in her hand. "They're as concerned for their own skins as they are for mine," she said, and laughed. She actually laughed.

"I don't blame them. That was Irene, right?"

"Yeah. I'll bet she's chewed her nails down to her knuckles. Hey, Lou Lou, can I have a bit of that cold pizza?"

Snyder, who'd worshipped Lou Lou from afar for as long as Mary Lisa could remember, ran up with a slice of hot pizza on a napkin and reverently placed it in her hand.

Mary Lisa chewed on the cold pizza—no fresh hot slice for her—and made her way back out onto her deck. She heard the doorbell ring, but didn't turn. She was listening to everyone's advice, like, "You should fly over to Honolulu, catch some waves at Diamond Head"—that from Carlo. "You need a nice spa experience. They give the cutest pedicures at the Golden Door, like a golden door painted on your big toe"—this from MacKenzie, Honey Boy barking his agreement.

Mary Lisa turned slowly to see Lou Lou leading Detective Vasquez through the mess of people, a slice of artichoke pizza in his hand.

FIFTY-ONE

"Daniel," Breaker Barney shouted out, "any good news for us? You find any bodies in Paulie Thomas's closet? You've been to where he lives, right?"

Here he was, Daniel thought, fraternizing with a small-time hood. At least this one was smart enough to stay away from petty crimes. "Sorry, guys, I didn't find a single finger," Daniel said easily, and took another big bite of pizza.

"No dinner, Daniel?" Lou Lou asked him.

He shook his head and smiled at Lou Lou as he chewed. Someone stuck a beer in his hand, which he regretfully handed back. When he finished his pizza slice, he raised his hand. "Here's the deal, people. I'm still working right now, and I need to speak to Mary Lisa alone."

There was no empty spot in the house except in Mary Lisa's bedroom. Still, they had to wait for a teenage girl to leave the bathroom, pausing to hug Mary Lisa on her way out. When Mary Lisa pulled the door shut, she saw that Daniel was looking very serious. She flipped the lock on the door. Her heart speeded up. She grabbed his arm, shook it. "What's wrong, Daniel?"

"Paulie Thomas just died. I wanted to tell you privately."

She stumbled back, fell onto her bed. He sat down beside her. "He never woke up, Mary Lisa, barely got through surgery. They said his heart stopped, simply stopped. They managed to revive him once, but when his heart stopped again, they couldn't bring him back."

She stared at him, still unable to take it in. Paulie Thomas, dead. He'd been alive this afternoon, and now he was dead. She felt numb. "How old was he?"

"Thirty-two."

"That's around Jack Wolf's age. How old are you, Daniel?"

He smiled. "That's the first time you've called me by my first name. I'm thirty-one."

"He was thirty-two and everyone still called him Paulie, not Paul. That isn't right, Daniel. That means everyone knew he wasn't right."

"Yes, I know. Can I get you something, Mary Lisa?"

She shook her head. "No, just give me a moment to take this all in. How is Paulie's mother? His uncle?"

"They're both very upset."

She nodded. "Did his mother have any explanation for why he tried to kill me?"

"She was too upset for me to get much out of her. She said only that Paulie seemed pretty hyper yesterday. He kept going on about seeing Margie McCormick crying on the set—something about her character, Susan Cavendish, having less of a role to play on *Born to Be Wild*. Paulie's uncle Tom finally said Paulie told him that Margie blamed you because of the new plotline you'd worked out with Bernie."

"There is some truth to that, you know."

"Don't be a fool. It doesn't matter. From what I could glean, Paulie had never managed a relationship, he was a loner, but he was very attached to Ms. McCormick. His mother hadn't made much of it until this happened.

"The thing is, Mary Lisa, when we got to his apartment with a search warrant, we didn't know what we'd find." He sighed. "Fact is, we found a huge motive—his bedroom was filled with press clippings about Margie McCormick, and photos of her plastered on all the walls. On the wall facing his bed was a huge poster-sized photo of her in a bikini."

"So you think Paulie was trying to kill me because of Margie? He thought I was hurting her?"

Daniel drew a deep breath, took both her hands in his. "Mary Lisa, whatever drove him to do this, he snapped and acted. I think this was a onetime thing for Paulie. Your stalker is someone else."

She stared at him, suddenly so cold she felt frozen. "Not the stalker?"

He shook his head.

"But Paulie tried to run me down on his motorcycle. A gazillion people saw him try."

Daniel nodded. "Yes, I know. But stay with me a moment, okay? The decision about the plotline—and Ms. Mc-Cormick being unhappy about it and complaining aloud—I realized that didn't happen until after that car hit you here in Malibu. More importantly, you had already mentioned Paulie to us, and we checked out where he was both on the day of the auto accident and at the time of the shooting on the beach. He had strong alibis on both days—he was with family and friends, and this afternoon we checked them again, got independent verification. It couldn't have been Paulie, either time.

"And finally, Mary Lisa, we found Puker Hodges a couple of hours ago, claimed he'd been on assignment in Santa Barbara and just gotten back. We took him over to the hospital." Daniel sighed. "Puker said Paulie Thomas wasn't Jamie Ramos, the man we've been looking for. He said he'd seen Paulie Thomas only once before and that was when he broke onto the set of *Born to Be Wild* and took that photo of you and Bernie."

Mary Lisa couldn't believe this. She didn't want to believe it, much less hear it. She turned on him, angry now because he'd told her the truth and she couldn't bear it.

Daniel handed her a glass of water from the table beside her bed.

She drank it down, clutched the glass between her hands, and said slowly, "Then—what? You think Paulie did this as a copycat?"

"Maybe."

"Then Jamie Ramos is still out there?"

He said nothing, he didn't need to.

She looked at him for a very long time, looked down at her bare feet, at the three chipped French toenails, and whispered, "Well, shit."

IT was midnight. Jack was angry and scared for her, pissed that he hadn't been there, even more pissed that he couldn't come down. She made him swear he wouldn't tell her father, at least not yet.

When Mary Lisa disconnected, she was exhausted, but her brain was squirreling around so madly she began to pace her living room, unable to keep still. Only Elizabeth and Lou Lou were here now, Lou Lou sprawled on one of the living room rugs, her legs up on a chair, bare toes in the air. Elizabeth, elegant in her TV clothes, sat on a love seat, a cup of coffee in her hand.

"We will get through this," she said to Mary Lisa. "We will."

Mary Lisa was wearing her favorite pea green T-shirt she'd bought that fateful Saturday and a pair of banged-up low-cut jeans. She nodded toward Elizabeth, and went out to her back deck to look up at the star-strewn heavens. "So many interesting shapes up there. I don't see a single motorcycle."

Lou Lou walked out behind her, yawning. "No, I don't either. Now, Daniel is as upset as we are, mostly with himself because everything is dead-ended again. When he's upset, he paces around like you, he's not focusing on anything but you. Do you know I've even told him the name of your third-grade teacher?"

"You don't know the name of my third-grade teacher." Mary Lisa paused, turned to rest her elbows on the deck railing. "Do you know I don't remember it either?"

"Yeah, well, I didn't want to disappoint him so I told him her name was Mrs. Pilsner, how's that? I think I was drinking a beer at the time. Damn, Mary Lisa, this is getting old. I'm ready for an ending, you know? A happy ending."

Mary Lisa watched Elizabeth stroll out on the deck. She'd taken off her stilt heels and came to stand at the railing beside Mary Lisa, dangling her shoes by their straps over the side. She'd taken off her panty hose and her bright crimson–painted toes sparkled in the dim light.

Mary Lisa said, "I'm going to spend six hours with Chico tomorrow, then I'm going to the firing range for another six hours. Then I'm going to call Irene at the studio and tell her I want the studio to hire me around-the-clock bodyguards, about a dozen of them."

"And the studio'll do it in a flash," Elizabeth said. "They're not stupid."

"About that six hours with Chico . . ." Lou Lou began.

Mary Lisa held up her hand, eyes narrowed. "What? You think that's not enough?"

"Maybe I'm thinking it's too much the other way."

"Elizabeth, you agree with Lou Lou?"

"Six straight sessions with Chico and you'd be a cripple, if not dead. Yeah, cut that down to three sessions."

Mary Lisa sighed. "Okay, I need you guys to tell me if I've gone over the edge."

"You have," Lou Lou said. "A long time ago. It's okay."

The three women stood side by side beneath the beautiful black sky, a quarter moon bright above their heads, a warm breeze against their faces, hearing conversations from people walking on the beach. None of them said anything.

Finally, Mary Lisa whispered, "Okay, three straight lessons. I can do that."

FIFTY-TWO

Goddard Bay

It was midmorning on a sunny Friday. Jack sat at his desk studying the transcripts of all the interviews conducted since Milo's death two days before. Only two days? It seemed like beyond forever. He hadn't gone home the night before, stayed here at the office and thought and reread all the reports until he was nearly blind. He'd gotten only a couple of hours' sleep. He was vaguely aware of voices outside his office door, but he blocked them out and tried to focus. The words blurred in his head. He knew he was tired, too tired, really, to see something he'd missed. He swigged down some coffee so thick it could make its own Rorschach if he spilled it.

He was trying to concentrate on proving it was Olivia Hildebrand who had killed her husband. He had little doubt about that by now. But the problem was, Mary Lisa kept coming front and center into his mind. She'd called him last night, not five minutes after he'd spoken to Daniel, and he'd listened to her tell him about Paulie Thomas's mad motorcycle attack and all that happened afterward. He was so scared for her as those words had rained on him that he'd felt paralyzed with it. He'd heard the fear in her voice as well, she was unable to hide it from him, actress or no. He'd known her such a short time, he thought, but he was coming to know her well. She had tried to present a picture of control for him, and he admired her greatly for it. Mary Lisa was solid, and what was cool, in that moment he thought of his mother and how she'd say Mary Lisa was solid as well. He smiled at that. She'd erased the lingering stain left from his failed marriage, the memories of distrust and dread that had haunted his mind, and betrayal, the final nail Rikki had banged in his coffin. He tapped his pen on his desktop, wondering if Mary Lisa was feeling something like what he felt, if in the short time he'd known her, he'd helped to rub out that jerk Mark Bridges from her mind. It was still awfully soon, dammit, maybe he was expecting too much.

He wanted to be in Malibu, he wanted to find the creep who was terrorizing her, which meant, bottom line, that he had to get Olivia Hildebrand into his jail, and her signed confession into his pocket. So he forced his mind back to Milo's murder yet again. He simply had to. How had Olivia managed to get the poison into Milo's food tray? They'd found rat poison at her home, but that wasn't nearly enough, as Pat Bigelow had acidly pointed out to him. Rats were common enough in Goddard Bay.

He wanted to find that bum who'd been around the Goddard Bay Inn kitchen. He was the key, Jack knew it.

He underlined something Mrs. Hildebrand had said— "I've loved my husband for thirty-five years, only him." And he'd asked, "And did your husband love your daughter, Mrs. Hildebrand?"

"Ah, Marci—such a talented, beautiful child."

He drummed his fingertips on the transcripts.

"Hey."

That soft voice sounded sharp in his mind. No, the voice wasn't in his mind, and it was supposed to be down in Malibu. He jerked up.

Mary Lisa stood in the doorway, grinning at him.

He stared at her, her windblown hair, the big sunglasses she wore dangling in her fingers. She was wearing baize slacks and a fitted top beneath a navy blazer.

He nearly knocked his chair over as he went to her. He hauled her up against him, buried his face in her hair, breathed in the lemony smell, and reveled in the softness against his skin. He felt his fatigue fall away from him, forgotten.

He hugged her for what seemed like a long time, feeling her heart beating against his, and finally whispered against her ear, "I can't believe you're here. I was just thinking about you and hating that I couldn't be down in Malibu with you. Sweet Jesus, Mary Lisa, this is a wonderful surprise." He eased her back, looked down at the face he'd once seen on the other side of bars in his jail, grinned and kissed her. He said into her mouth, "If I'd have managed to get to bed since Milo's murder, I'd have dreamed about this."

She laughed into his mouth, felt the hard length of him that fit against her so perfectly, so naturally, and knew what coming home really felt like, for the first time in her life.

She squeezed him hard, went up on her tiptoes and kissed him. He tasted like heat and man and really strong coffee.

He was hard against her belly and shaking and she loved it. "I'm here to see you, Jack. With just a little nudge from the mad stalker."

"When you called me last night, I'll tell you, Mary Lisa, I wanted to fly down there, tuck you into my duffel bag, and take you to Australia. Scared me spitless."

"I was pretty near the edge myself there for a while. But now"—she paused, kissed his mouth again, hugged him tightly—"but now I'm with you and the world is right for at least awhile. Did I manage to surprise you?"

"Nah, you just gave me the excuse to leap on you and kiss you stupid."

She grinned, touched her fingertips to his face, studying him, seeing the bone-deep weariness, the frustration, and joy, the joy he felt because she was here. She glowed, couldn't help it. She sobered quickly. "I know you're up to your ears in this mess. I won't be a bother, it's just that I missed you and, yeah, I was afraid down there—"

"Having you here is what I needed. It's true things aren't settled here yet, and I don't know when I'll get things cleaned up. It's all a matter of finding enough proof." He paused, looked into her vibrant blue eyes, and said, "I'm quite sure it was Milo's wife, Olivia Hildebrand."

"Oh dear. This is going to hit my mom pretty hard. You know she and my mother are close friends."

He frowned down at her. "Yes, of course. Your mom hasn't missed a chance to bust my chops about harassing Olivia. But tell me what's going on with you."

"Well, Lou Lou and Elizabeth came up here with me, and we're all staying at the Goddard Bay Inn—no way would I have them at my mother's mercy at the house. They groused and complained when I dropped them off, but I told them I wanted to surprise you—alone. They got the picture. You don't mind, do you, Jack? That I didn't tell you I was coming up here?"

"Doesn't matter now." He started to kiss her again.

"Jack, wait, I've got things to tell you."

"I know, but not now, Mary Lisa. Not now. There's a time for words but now's the time for this." He cupped her in his hands and pulled her hard against him. It was amazing, almost as amazing as when he lay on his back on the beach, with her on top of him. "I want to take you back to the beach again."

"That was"—she gulped, kissing his cheek, his chin, his mouth—"an experience I want again, real soon."

There was a knock on his office door, but he was grinning like a madman, and paid it no attention.

"Chief."

Chief?

It was Mary Lisa who pulled away, only about two inches, and turned back to see one of his deputies standing in the doorway, face crimson, looking so miserable Mary

Lisa would have laughed if she wasn't thinking so much about pushing Jack back onto his desktop. She sucked in a deep breath and whispered, "Jack."

"Go away, Ames."

"I'm very sorry, Chief, but Mr. Beverly is here wanting to see Mary Lisa. He's, ah, fact is, Chief, he's right here, as in right behind me."

"What?"

"I called Dad," Mary Lisa said, "got his voice mail. I told him I was coming to see you, and I'd go over to his office later. I guess he had another idea."

She turned to see her father behind the deputy, staring at her and Jack. "So," George Beverly said, "I hope I'm not interrupting you, Jack."

You sure as hell are. But those were not words to be spoken aloud. Jack touched his forehead for a moment to Mary Lisa's, kissed the tip of her nose, and raised his head to look at the man he was now seeing for the first time as his future father-in-law. Whoa, wait a minute, that wasn't possible, was it? He stared blankly at George Beverly, relieved he was focused on his daughter.

"Hi, sweetheart." He gently shoved the deputy out of Jack's office and closed the door.

She didn't want to leave Jack, really didn't, but this was her father and she loved him. She pulled out of Jack's arms and turned to grin at him. "Hi, Dad. I suppose I surprised Jack as much as you."

"It looks to me like he got over the surprise part real fast."

Mary Lisa nodded, looking all sorts of pleased with herself. "Yes, amazing, isn't he?"

George Beverly struck a pose, fingers stroking his chin. "I seem to recall that Chief Wolf wasn't at all amazing two weeks ago. I hadn't realized that you were interested in each other. Indeed, there seemed to be a goodly amount of dislike on both your parts."

She thought about that, and slowly shook her head. "Mr. Macho and his jail cell—ancient history, Dad. Isn't life strange?"

Her father hugged her close. "I gave up long ago trying to figure out what life is," he said, "I just try to live it." She breathed in his familiar scent, rested her head on his shoulder for a moment.

She heard him say, "You look dead tired, Jack."

"Not now, sir. Your daughter could rejuvenate a dead plant."

Jack felt like he could run a marathon at that moment, that or have about six hours of sex with Mary Lisa, enough to last him for a little while. He remembered how he felt at the beach again, relived that endless moment when she'd climaxed and nearly rocketed him right over the edge, and tried not to shudder in his Italian boots in front of her father.

Mary Lisa looked at Jack, and the look in their eyes told George Beverly everything he needed to know, and a lot he didn't want to know about. "You should rest, anyway, Jack," he said. "Okay, sweetheart, you need to tell me everything that's going on down south."

"Detective Vasquez is still on it, Dad. The studio insisted I take off for a while, and the truth is, I really needed to get away. I thought about spending every day with Chico at his dojo and realized I needed to come up here to see Jack and you."

Her father waved away her words as he looked from her to Jack standing behind her. "Definitely in that order, I see."

She took Jack's hand. "Well, there's no denying this guy's mojo. And he's got all this stuff he's got to deal with and I thought he could use my help up here."

"No way," Jack said.

"Well, I guess we'll see—"

"There could be a jail cell with your name on it if you give me any grief, Mary Lisa."

"Would I get a blanket this time?"

Her father, eyebrow arched, said, "I'm glad you're home and safe, Mary Lisa. Can I take you along to the house?"

"Well, the thing is, Dad, both Elizabeth and Lou Lou are with me. I stashed them at the Goddard Bay Inn, told them I had to see Jack. They wanted to come but I begged them to order the blueberry pancakes from room service instead. It worked since Lou Lou's a sucker for pancakes."

"Why don't all of you come stay at the house? Kelly moved back to her apartment two days ago."

"I don't think Mom would like three women invading her space. Not enough bathrooms, you know? Why don't we all come for dinner this evening?"

He nodded slowly. "Yes, I can see why you'd say that. Truth is, your mother is more than a little strung out, what with all that's happened to Olivia. When Olivia isn't at our house, Kathleen is at her house. It'll be a pleasure to see Elizabeth and Lou Lou again, Mary Lisa. They're both fine women, and good friends. You know anything more about Milo's murder, Jack?"

Jack shook his head. "I really can't discuss it, sir, I'm sorry."

"When was the last time you had any sleep?"

"I look that bad?"

"Yeah, pretty much."

Jack thought about it, slowly shook his head. He took Mary Lisa's hand. He hadn't thought about it before, but he saw she wore only one ring, a ruby set up high amid some small diamonds. It looked like an antique.

Mary Lisa hugged her father again. "I'll be okay, Dad. We can hope Detective Vasquez turns up something while I'm out of town."

George nodded, smiled at Jack. "You come to dinner as well, all right, Jack?"

FIFTY-THREE

Jack was surprised at John's reaction when he heard Elizabeth, Lou Lou, and Mary Lisa were all at the Goddard Bay Inn. He insisted on calling them and inviting them all to lunch.

"Elizabeth is something, isn't she, Jack?" John asked as Jack pulled his truck into traffic.

Now this was interesting. Had he been blind down in Malibu? He looked at the contented look on his friend's face, and smiled. "She is."

"She told me they'd stop eating breakfast right away." And he gave Jack a fatuous grin. Jack nearly jerked the wheel into an old Pontiac parked on the side of the street.

"Hey, careful, Jack. You really needed a break, I can see that, and so do I. So let's try not to talk about business for a couple of hours, *capisce*?"

"Since when did you get a transfusion of Italian blood?"

John merely shook his head and looked happy.

A few minutes later, Jack pulled up in front of the circular entrance of the old gray stone edifice built long before either of them was born.

John said as he got out of the truck, "I've always been grateful this place is nearly completely hidden behind all these oak trees. You only have to see those seedy old chimneys poking up through the tops of the trees. They look like smudge pots, all sixteen of them."

Jack waved one of the parking attendants over. "Keep an eye on this state-of-the-art machine."

"Yes, sir, dude—Chief, sir."

They walked across the formal lobby with its overstuffed dark furniture and huge palm trees, whose sweeping fronds looked big enough to swallow them, to the creaky elevator that belonged in a scary movie. They got off on the third and top floor, took a right down a long, dismal hallway with an ancient cabbage rose runner, and knocked on 333B.

Lou Lou answered the door. "Hi, guys. Have you figured out why room 333B is on the third floor?"

John said, "Hi, Lou Lou. Old Man Willis built this place and died two years ago when he was nearly ninety. They say he chose all the room numbers at random."

"Oh, I see, the 'consistency is the hobgoblin' theory?"

"I'm not so sure about that," John said. "Mr. Willis was, to put it kindly, the local eccentric who did as he pleased."

"You mean he was crazy."

"Nope, he was too rich to be crazy. Definitely eccentric." Jack kissed Lou Lou's cheek.

"Come on in, guys," she said. "Hey, Elizabeth, Mary Lisa, we got both the big guns here."

Mary Lisa contented herself with a smile and said, "Hello, Jack."

"Mary Lisa."

Lou Lou looked from one to the other and knew the air was cracking hot between them. A chief of police—who knew? And, Lou Lou suspected, he would be good for her, maybe a husband kind of good. She smiled, waved the men to sit down on the big eggplant sofa, the cracks in the leather as old as they were.

Jack sniffed. "The room smells like vanilla."

Mary Lisa laughed. "Yep, I stopped at Ernie's little rip-off 24/7 and bought some on the way over. I hope it helps. Smelled musty before."

John said, his voice all awkward angles, which made Jack jerk his head around and stare at him, "Elizabeth, it's really good to see you again. I'm glad you came up with Mary Lisa and Lou Lou. Ah, I'm surprised you could get away."

"It required lots of shuffling, begging, calling in markers, promising favors, but Mary Lisa said she needed me."

Lou Lou said slowly, eyebrow arched at Elizabeth, "I think one of the reasons you wanted to come up was to see this district attorney here."

Elizabeth met John's eyes, smiled. "Maybe so."

"Good," John said.

"And how is the investigation going, John?" Elizabeth asked, more naturally now. "We decided we might as well give you a hand. Anything you need done, we're available. I was born for excitement."

"Where were you born?" John asked.

"Millicent, Texas, population six hundred and twenty-one. But in the past five years we've had a population explosion."

"Oh yeah?"

She nodded. "We're up to six hundred and forty-seven. A local—Neddy Opper—opened a new rib house off the highway, all down-home with long wood tables and lots of paper towels. I hear that people drive from miles around."

Mary Lisa took Jack's hand in hers. "Listen, Elizabeth is right. We're here, let us help."

"Why not?" John said. "It's a deal. We don't have to pay them, Jack."

Jack closed his hand tightly around Mary Lisa's. "John's talking out of both sides of his mouth. He made me promise not to talk about any business here today. Besides, there's nothing to be done. After lunch, why don't you all go sightsee?"

"It's the same ocean, Jack," Lou Lou said. "When you've seen one wave, you've seen them all."

"Are you going to arrest Olivia Hildebrand?" Elizabeth asked.

"As in take her to jail? No, but she's at home, and I've posted two female deputies there to keep an eye on her. Her lawyer didn't have a problem with that, thank heaven. Her doctor's got her sedated so I don't have to worry about her trying to take off. So is everyone ready for lunch?"

"Where are we going?" Elizabeth asked.

"Le Fleur de Beijing," John said, "featuring real cloth napkins. And they've got mysterious foreign names for the food so you have to ask the waiter, giving him a chance to look at you like you're an illiterate varmint and don't belong in such a classy establishment. They're the big deal here in Goddard Bay right now."

"Now that's what I'm looking for," Lou Lou said. "Stuff like Japanese soba noodles in creamy mushroom sauce. Some people might blanche at that, but not me."

Jack didn't like French food, since it was usually big on presentation and microscopic on serving size. "I think I counted a total of eleven noodles on my plate the last time I was there," he said.

"So get the octopus," Lou Lou said. "That way you'll be guaranteed eight legs."

Ten minutes later, Lou Lou locked the suite door with a key the size of Burbank and hummed as they walked down the long hall toward the creaky elevator. As it lurched downward, Lou Lou patted the mirrored walls. "I love this thing."

Elizabeth's eyes were tightly closed. "Next time I'm taking the stairs."

"The inspector said the stairs weren't too bad," John told her. "But that was last year."

Halfway across the lobby, their path was blocked by the manager, Mr. Clement Rogers, who'd known Mary Lisa since her family had moved here over twenty years before.

He spoke directly to Jack. "Chief, Mrs. Willis saw you and District Attorney Goddard go up to the *ladies'* suite a while ago. She instructed me to ask if there was any reason for concern."

Mary Lisa lightly touched her fingers to Mr. Rogers's arm. "It's okay, Mr. Rogers. Please tell Mrs. Willis that I am personally keeping an eye on these two very respectable gentlemen. Assure her that I will not give them any beer."

"We will drink the beer ourselves, Mr. Rogers, tonight," Elizabeth said. "It was too early this morning for the gentlemen to imbibe anything more than your excellent coffee."

"Besides, there are only three bottles in the bar," Lou Lou said. "We want them ourselves."

Mr. Rogers said, softening under Lou Lou's brilliant smile, as did most people, "It's Mrs. Willis's favorite, miss, not that heavy hops-happy German stuff, so I'm sure you'll enjoy it." He shot a look at Jack and John.

"The gentlemen will not be returning with us, Mr. Rogers. Assure Mrs. Willis of that. We need our afternoon naps."

"Thank you, Mary Lisa. Mrs. Willis loves your show, watches it every day, talks about what a believable bad girl your character is. She says you do 'bad' with a real flair."

Two hours later, Jack and John followed the women back to the inn. Jack didn't kiss Mary Lisa, not that he didn't want to, but there were eyes everywhere, so he merely took her arm, leaned down, and whispered against her ear, "Believe me, there's nothing you can do to help. I want you to keep out of trouble."

Mary Lisa patted his cheek. "You heard Lou Lou—it's nap time." John and Jack left under the suspicious eye of

Mr. Rogers, who actually followed them out of the inn and watched Jack's truck until they were out of sight.

"Does he think we're going to circle back, sneak in for an afternoon orgy?"

"Nah," John said. "Not Mr. Rogers. But that old bat Mrs. Willis is another thing."

FIFTY-FOUR

Mary Lisa took a bite of Mrs. Abrams's pot roast and chewed slowly, savoring the taste of the spices Mrs. Abrams kept secret.

"Have you ever tasted anything more delicious in your lives?" she asked. Lou Lou and Elizabeth were seated on either side of Kelly, opposite Mary Lisa and Jack. Mary Lisa's parents sat at the ends of the formal dining room table. The women wore dresses and heels, and the men were in suits, except for Kelly, who had on tight jeans and an oversized sweater. She was looking from Mary Lisa to Jack, but there wasn't a laser death ray in her eyes, which greatly relieved Mary Lisa. John, when told about dinner, readily excused himself from attending. He was a smart man.

"Even better than the blueberry pancakes this morning," Elizabeth said, "and that's saying something."

"It's great, Mrs. Beverly," Lou Lou said, nodding toward Kathleen.

Mary Lisa was glad she didn't have to deal with Monica and Mark being there as well. Both of them were in Salem overnight for one of Monica's campaign rallies, a blessed relief.

"Elizabeth is an anchorwoman on a local L.A. TV station," Mary Lisa said.

"Oh?"

Her mother's voice sounded only mildly disapproving, Mary Lisa thought, and plowed onward. "She was a crime reporter with the *L.A. Times* until about a year ago when the TV station producer spotted her at a party."

Elizabeth said, "Serendipity or happenstance, whatever you wish to call it, it's a wonderful thing. Nearly the same thing happened to Mary Lisa."

Jack asked, "How did you get started, Mary Lisa?"

"My agent called me one morning, said he'd gotten me an audition on *Born to Be Wild*. He said it was a lead role, sighed, and added that the audition would be good experience for me. Yep, he had no hope that I'd land it. Anyway, everything worked out very nicely."

Lou Lou said, "Mary Lisa, sometimes I want to smack you, you're so bloody modest. Mrs. Beverly, your daughter is the biggest soap actress in history. Her very first year, she won the Emmy for the best lead actress. It's never been done before, and now she's won it a second and third time."

"And the rest is history," Elizabeth said. "Hey, here's to Mary Lisa."

"Hear, hear," Lou Lou said. Everyone clicked glasses together. Kathleen Beverly slowly raised her glass.

"And Lou Lou is about the greatest makeup artist in La-La Land," Elizabeth said.

Mary Lisa waited, tense and wary, but again, her mother merely looked at Lou Lou, nodding.

George Beverly said, "Hey, Lou Lou, Mary Lisa told me you landed that primo makeup contract with the big producer."

Lou Lou nodded. "Yep, that worked out well."

Kathleen set her wineglass back on the table and said to Lou Lou, "You appear to know my husband well."

"Well, ma'am, he's very popular with all of Mary Lisa's friends."

"Are you responsible for Mary Lisa's makeup on the soap?"

"Most of the time."

"You sure like to paint her up sometimes," Kelly said.

"Yeah," Lou Lou said easily. "That's for sure. Hey, it's Hollywood."

Social time over, Mary Lisa thought, as a blanket of silence fell over the table. She tried to think of something innocent and light to say, but her mother leaned forward slightly and said to Jack, "Before we came in to dinner, Chief Wolf, you mentioned that you wished to speak to me about Olivia Hildebrand."

"Yes, ma'am. I understand you are best friends. I hadn't realized how very close you were to her."

"Yes, well, I would like to speak to you about her as well. I've told you once already that she's been through quite enough. She's sedated at home, as you know, under a doctor's care, with two of your deputies hanging around her house. And she's a wreck. Please have the decency to leave her alone. She did not kill Milo."

George said slowly, his eyes on his wife's face, "You don't know that, Kathy. I've been thinking about telling you this all week, Jack. The fact is, Milo beat her their entire married life as best I can tell. I think she might have snapped. Maybe Milo's killing Jason and hurting Marci drove her over the edge."

There was silence at the table. Only Kelly continued to eat, stabbing a small baked potato off the edge of the beautifully arranged oval platter with the pot roast at its center.

Jack carefully set down his fork. "Milo beat his wife? I noticed when I was with them right after Jason's murder that he appeared rather controlling with her, but—you're certain? He beat her? I didn't know this, Mr. Beverly. No one's said a single word to me about that."

Kathleen said, "That doesn't matter. You don't understand. Olivia isn't a murderess, she isn't!"

"Perhaps," George said, eyeing his wife from the other end of the dining table, "we'd best leave this for a while."

"No!" Kathleen nearly came up out of her chair. "You're the one who started it, telling Chief Wolf that Milo hit her sometimes, giving her a motive in his mind to suppose my best friend killed her husband. Well, she didn't."

"Why not, Mrs. Beverly?" Jack asked calmly.

"You want the truth, Chief? All right, here it is. She's a wuss, no spine at all. She couldn't even discipline that loose daughter of hers."

All the ugliness splatted in the open by the beautiful pot roast. Jack saw Mary Lisa open her mouth, then close it. He squeezed her hand beneath the table.

George Beverly said, "Kathy's right about Olivia being weak. Once, a long time ago, Olivia came here, all bent over like an old woman, clutching her ribs, crying and moaning. She said Milo had kicked her when she was crawling away from him. I was so mad, I went to see Milo." He stopped, and stared around at the people at his dining room table. "Now isn't the time," he said. "It really isn't."

"Yes, Dad, Jack needs to hear this, please," Mary Lisa said.

"Please, sir, she's right," Jack said.

"All right. As I said, I went over there, confronted Milo. He was swaggering around, told me to mind my own business. Then he lost control and actually hit me. I hit him back, in the ribs, and he went down. Turns out Olivia followed me there. She came running in, screaming at me to leave him alone. When I managed to get her off me, I stood there, so shocked and appalled I couldn't think straight, watched her crouch over him, cooing and rubbing him where I'd hit him. Old Milo moaned and she looked up at me and threatened to have the police throw me in jail."

"You never told us that, Dad," Kelly said.

He shrugged. "Why should I? It had nothing to do with you girls. Besides, after that night, Olivia never dragged herself over here again to your mother after he'd beaten her. Maybe she didn't because she was afraid of what I'd do. I don't know." He looked down the table at his wife. "What did she do from then on, Kathy? Call you? Beg you to meet her somewhere?"

"That's cruel, George. But it makes my point. Olivia would never have hurt Milo. She adored him, even though he was a monster. She would have done anything he told her to, anything."

Jack said, "You and Olivia Hildebrand seem like very different people, Mrs. Beverly. How is it you're such good friends?"

She looked at Jack, locked her eyes on his face. "When we first arrived in Goddard Bay nearly twenty-five years ago, Olivia went out of her way to make me feel welcome." The words seemed to catch in her throat. She downed some wine, swallowed. "No one else did. But Olivia came over to see me and we talked and talked. She became my best friend. That's all." *And even you need a friend, don't you, Mom?* Mary Lisa thought.

Good enough, Jack thought. "Thank you, Mrs. Beverly, Mr. Beverly, for telling me about this."

"You still think she's guilty, don't you?"

Jack looked at the beautiful woman who seemed better suited to a life in Manhattan, with doormen and limos and charity balls, than to a small town like Goddard Bay. He said, "It's my job to find out, Mrs. Beverly. This has got to come to an end somehow. Thank you for helping me."

Kelly said suddenly, "I remember hearing Marci yelling at her mother once, called her a boring old rug. It was something about her father not letting her go somewhere and her mother not doing anything about it." Kelly shrugged. "All the usual teenage angst, I suppose. But the rug bit fits, doesn't it?"

George Beverly cleared his throat. "I suppose we've let this dinner take a very unorthodox path. For that I apologize."

Lou Lou smiled, raised her glass. "I would like to thank Mrs. Beverly for having us all over with almost no advance notice at all." Lou Lou clicked her glass to Kathleen's, and glasses were raised all around.

Kelly, bless her heart, began speaking about Monica's run for state office. Then she eyed Mary Lisa and remarked, "Monica's husband nearly married Mary Lisa. But that didn't work out."

"No," Mary Lisa said, grinning hugely, "it didn't. Thank you, God."

Jack's cell phone vibrated. He looked at Kathleen as he pulled his cell out of his jacket. "Excuse me, ma'am." He nodded to Mrs. Beverly and walked out of the dining room.

He heard Mary Lisa say, "Kelly, what are you up to?"

He went outside. It was chilly tonight, and damp, the clouds covering the stars and the sickle moon. "Chief Wolf."

FIFTY-FIVE

Mary Lisa yawned as she walked back toward the elevators, Lou Lou's morning paper in her hand.

From the corner of her eye she saw a tired-looking businessman follow the bellboy out the front doors. Nearly there, she thought, and reached her hand out to press the elevator button when the old scratchy voice nailed her to the spot.

"Will you be checking out today, Mary Lisa?"

She turned to see Mrs. Willis, her old bird eyes bright with interest and cunning, standing beside the reception counter, her arms crossed over her bright-pink-wool-sweatered chest. There was a strong smell of lavender wafting off her. "Good morning, Mrs. Willis."

"What have you got there, Mary Lisa?"

"One of my friends wanted her morning paper. I guess you don't provide them on Saturday mornings?"

"Nope, costs too much to throw in Saturday too," said Mrs. Willis. "You sure that's all you've got there?"

"Yes, ma'am. We won't be checking out today, perhaps

tomorrow."

"That'll be fine, Mary Lisa. I hope you and your girl-friends will stay for a while, maybe help us find this person who poisoned our food. You know, I was thinking Mr. Rogers has sure gotten crotchety over the years—do you know he chews nearly two packs of tobacco every day even though he can't keep his blood pressure down? I'm thinking maybe he's our man."

"I suppose anything's possible, Mrs. Willis. But my problem is I don't see a motive for him to kill anyone."

The old woman cackled. "You're not looking hard enough. It's morning and here you are wide awake. Where were you and your girlfriends last night, young lady?"

She sighed. "We were all here, Mrs. Willis, happily sleeping in your comfortable beds." And Mary Lisa smiled, gave the old woman a little wave, and stepped into the elevator.

Lou Lou walked out of one of the bedrooms when Mary Lisa came into the suite, scratching her head and yawning.

"You look all perky this morning. Oh good, you got me a paper. You're a princess, Mary Lisa."

"Elizabeth still asleep?"

"I heard her in the shower already. I'm going to order room service. Dry toast for you, coffee?"

Mary Lisa nodded and wandered off into the bedroom to call Jack.

When she came out of the bedroom, she saw Lou Lou taking her first sip of coffee. Her friend sat back in her chair and said, "Okay, I know you called Jack. Why did he dash out of your folks' house last night? Who called him?"

"A Sheriff Davis called him from Pomack, that's a small town about thirty minutes south of Goddard Bay. He nabbed a homeless Vietnam vet who's been on a walka-bout. He thinks he might be the man Jack's been looking for. Jack drove down there last night." She chewed on her toast. "He's still tied up."

Elizabeth said, "I was thinking in the shower. Here we are, a trio of slugs up here, not being helpful at all. How about we pay Marci Maynard a visit? Her mother and yours are best friends, after all. No one could object, I mean, our offering condolences for her loss."

Mary Lisa quirked an eyebrow at her. "What about John?"

Elizabeth laughed. "That obvious, huh? Okay, I called him this morning. He was on his way over to see Jack." She threw out her arms. "I'm free, fortunately. Lou Lou, what do you think?"

"Let me finish the sports section and I'm with you."

Mary Lisa said, "Well, why not? Jack won't like it, but it's better than sitting around waiting for him or watching the sailboats." *Or visiting my mother,* she thought.

Elizabeth rose and stretched. She'd put her sleep shirt back on after her shower. It said in blazing pink across the chest, *Politicians Spin in Their Graves.* She looked at Mary Lisa thoughtfully. "I know you had high hopes for a lovely night at Jack's house, babe, but things don't always work out."

Lou Lou said, eyeing Elizabeth over the top of the newspaper, "As if you weren't crying in your pillow because John wasn't around."

Elizabeth nodded. "I don't know about the crying part, but I'll admit seeing him again didn't set him back any."

And why should it? Mary Lisa thought. "Okay, you guys, you've got ten minutes to get dressed, then we're out of here."

THE three women arrived at Marci Maynard's house as the sun was burning away the lacy gray morning fog. Mary Lisa rang the doorbell.

They heard a dog barking, but no one appeared at the door.

After several more fruitless tries, Elizabeth said, "Any ideas, Mary Lisa?"

"Why, yes. We can go see Mick."

He wasn't in his shop, not a surprise since it was Saturday morning, but his assistant manager, Hop Clooney, was there, looking older than the antique Corvette hubcaps displayed on the walls. "Well, now, it seems Mick caught a tetch of something, sounded pretty putrid when he called me a couple hours ago. Maybe he'll be back tomorrow. Better be—I need him to work on that big Caddy back there." He shrugged. "I see you're driving a rental from the airport. What's the problem with it?"

"Not a thing, Hop, we're trying to locate Mick. Thanks for the info."

"So we can go to his house," Mary Lisa said as they walked out of the shop. She went into Buckman's Pharmacy, borrowed Mr. Clive's phone book, and looked up Mick Maynard's address.

Mick Maynard's repair shop might have appealed to car aficionados, but his home looked like all it needed was a banged-up car set on bricks to finish off the ratty front yard. It sat at the end of a cul-de-sac, Martindale Lane, backed up against a hillock, hidden by pine and hemlock trees. The nearest neighbor was a good block away.

Elizabeth looked at the rusted machinery parts strewn around the car, unable to identify them, and said, "If I were a guy and I managed to snag a woman for some hanky-panky, I'd for sure go to her house, not here. I wouldn't think seeing this dump site would be a positive first step toward a meaningful relationship."

Lou Lou and Mary Lisa laughed. Mary Lisa said, "It is pretty bad, isn't it? One thing you gotta say about it, though—lots of privacy."

"Yeah," Elizabeth said slowly, "this guy could do about anything he wanted to out here."

There was an old banged-up Chevy truck sitting next to a well-kept Camry in the driveway, a clean, bright blue. Marci's car? Very likely. "I guess Marci doesn't mind the hoedown front yard since she's here. I wonder if she spent the night."

Lou Lou said, "That's why Mick called in with the putrid throat. Morning sex."

"That seems pretty cold," Elizabeth said, "what with her mother sedated in bed, suspected of murdering her father."

They walked up the weed-infested path to the front of the 1940s bungalow. It was a single story with a small footprint, probably considered quaint and charming thirty years ago, but tired and run-down now, in need of fresh flowers and paint. The draperies were drawn over the wide front window and the two narrow windows beside it. Mary Lisa marched up to the front door and banged loudly.

She banged again, at least half a dozen times.

Finally they heard a shout. "Hey, what do you want? Go away!"

Lou Lou murmured, "He sounds a bit testy."

Mary Lisa pounded some more. "Let him."

The door flew back. Mick Maynard stood in the doorway, his jeans looking like he'd just pulled them on, the zipper halfway up, the button at the waist unfastened. He wasn't wearing jockeys or anything else under the jeans, just his muscular body, a bit of black chest hair, and a thick morning beard. He scratched his belly, drawing their eyes down to his fingers, and slowly, let a grin—no, a smirk—replace his pissed-off look. "Well, ladies, to what do I owe this pleasure? Are you from the PTA, here for a contribution? Or maybe you're a very late welcome wagon?"

"I'm Mary Lisa Beverly. Hop said you called in sounding all putrid. You're some fast healer."

The smirk was in full bloom. "To get better, all one needs is proper motivation."

"Well, yes, I suppose that's true. We're here to see Marci. Is she here?"

"Oh yeah, I know who you are—Little Miss Soap Opera Star. Why do you want to speak to her? What the hell do you have to do with anything? Where's the police chief?" He stepped out on the front porch and glanced around, stepped back. "Just you three little piggies here to see the big bad wolf?" He laughed. "No, I guess that's Jack, isn't it?" He turned, shouted, "Marci, we've got some ladies from the Junior League here who want to interrogate you." Then, suddenly, he twisted back to them, and without another word, he slammed the door in their faces. They heard it lock. Mary Lisa would swear she heard him laugh.

"Well," Lou Lou said to the dump of a yard, "at least he has very nice abs, don't you think?"

Mary Lisa kicked at a hubcap next to the overgrown path. "This doesn't happen in the movies."

Elizabeth said, "It's too bad we're civilians, so we can't exactly cuff him or force our way in. What do we do now, Mary Lisa?"

"Well, there's still Olivia Hildebrand. I really do want to talk to her about my mother."

"I was hoping you'd say that," Elizabeth said.

The Hildebrand house was a pale yellow gem set in an upper-middle-class neighborhood with wide yards, well maintained and lovingly tended. Deputy Susan Randall opened the door on the first knock. "Mary Lisa! What are you doing here?" She stared around Mary Lisa at Elizabeth and Lou Lou.

"Hi, Susan." Mary Lisa quickly introduced Susan to Lou Lou and Elizabeth. "Do you think it's possible for us to speak to Mrs. Hildebrand for a couple of minutes?"

"Well, I don't know, Mary Lisa. I mean, the chief didn't say anything about your coming—"

"She and my mom are so very close, Susan, you know that. I mean, my mom visited her last night, right? I wanted to check on her, you know, see how she's feeling."

Elizabeth gently and slowly pushed forward, making Deputy Randall back up. "I know it's a huge favor, but Mary Lisa really is worried about her mother. She's been going through all this with her, as you know."

"Well, yeah, I guess it'd be all right. But not long, okay? She still might be asleep. She hasn't come down yet."

Mary Lisa realized she'd never before been in the Hildebrand house. Through all the years, Olivia had always been the one to visit her mother. They stopped in the middle of the large entryway with a skylight two stories overhead.

Mary Lisa supposed she was upstairs in the master bedroom. Without asking, they all headed for the main staircase and took them up two at a time.

She looked down at Deputy Randall, who was standing next to another female deputy Mary Lisa recognized but didn't know. She smiled at both of them, gave a little wave. Then she knocked lightly on the door, and opened it.

She wished she hadn't.

FIFTY-SIX

No one screamed. They stood in the doorway, staring at Olivia Hildebrand hanging from one of the beautifully painted oak ceiling beams, a vanity chair on its side beneath her.

Mary Lisa ran to her and lifted her by her thighs as best she could to relieve the awful pressure twisting her neck. She wasn't going to let her die. She heaved the woman up, felt the taut rope ease. "Lou Lou, Elizabeth, quick, help me get her down. Hurry!"

Elizabeth turned over the chair Mrs. Hildebrand had stood on and then had kicked away, and climbed up on it. "No, I still can't reach the knot." She felt for a pulse in Mrs. Hildebrand's throat, knowing there wouldn't be one. Elizabeth hadn't seen violent death since she'd covered a bank robbery in Venice Beach nearly a year before, but she knew that, now as then, this human being was dead and there was nothing to do for her except to help protect her dignity. Her throat felt dry and cool, too cool. She looked at Mary Lisa's set face, her arms still around Mrs. Hildebrand's legs, and back at Lou Lou, who seemed frozen, her eyes filled with horror. "I'm sorry, guys, she's dead. Her skin's chilled. She's been dead a long time." She climbed back down, laid her hand lightly on Mary Lisa's shoulder, but Mary Lisa was shaking her head.

"No, she can't be dead. Cut her down, Elizabeth, please cut her down. She's hurt bad, I know she's hurt real bad. Hurry, please, hurry, she's heavy and I don't know how much longer Lou Lou and I can hold her up. Lou Lou, help me."

"No, Mary Lisa, Lou Lou," Elizabeth said, her hand on their shoulders, "we can't touch her. Even if I could cut her down, I know that it's the wrong thing to do. This is a crime scene now and we don't want to touch anything. I'm sorry, but you have to let her go. That's right, Lou Lou, call Jack, then call 911. And get the deputies downstairs."

Lou Lou raced out of the bedroom, her cell in her hand.

Mary Lisa still held Mrs. Hildebrand. Tears were streaming down her face. "I can't let her go, Elizabeth. Don't you see? The pain would be so bad if I let her loose. I can't."

They heard Lou Lou yelling for the deputies outside, and then they heard her on her cell phone.

"Please, Elizabeth, cut her down. She's heavy. I don't know how much longer I can hold her up. I can't let go, Elizabeth, she'll break her neck if I let go. Please, Elizabeth."

"I'm sorry, sweetheart, but I can't. The forensic team needs to study everything so they can figure out exactly what happened. If we move her, then they can't figure things out. Do you understand?"

Mary Lisa nodded, her forehead against Mrs. Hildebrand's leg. "But—"

"I know, Mary Lisa, I know. I'll tell you what, we'll both hold her up until help arrives."

Jack got there incredibly fast, a bit ahead of the paramedics. They heard him running flat out up the stairs. When he hit the bedroom doorway, he saw Elizabeth and Mary Lisa holding Mrs. Hildebrand's body up, Lou Lou and his two deputies standing beside them. Why were they holding her up? It was clear Mrs. Hildebrand's neck was broken, she was dead. He started to say something, but Elizabeth caught his eye and shook her head. He took in what was happening, that it was Mary Lisa who couldn't deal with the reality that Mrs. Hildebrand was violently, horribly dead, couldn't accept that she was helpless to change it. Jack had seen perhaps half a dozen people hanged over the years, most of them suicides, and not all of them well done. It was a violent, ugly death—the bulging, reddened eyes, the tongue thick and swollen, thrust partially out of her half-open mouth. Dear God, and it was Mary Lisa holding up that body.

The paramedics crowded behind him. He shook his head at them and walked to Mary Lisa and Elizabeth. He said, "Mary Lisa, you and Elizabeth have done a very good job. Now it's time for you to come away. It's time for you to let me take care of Mrs. Hildebrand. All right?"

Mary Lisa stared up at him. "But Jack, I can't let her down. If I do—"

Elizabeth closed her eyes a moment. "Jack's here now, Mary Lisa, and the paramedics. They can cut her down. Come along now, sweetheart, we have to let them do their job."

Jack nodded three paramedics over. "I want you to hold up Mrs. Hildebrand, all right?"

They realized what was happening and silently nodded. When the three of them had taken over, Jack took Mary Lisa's hand and led her to the bedroom door. Lou Lou stood with them in the doorway, her eyes on Mary Lisa. He said to Elizabeth, "Please take Mary Lisa and Lou Lou downstairs to the living room. Wait there for me, all right? I'll call John. He needs to get over here as well."

His words gave Elizabeth the focus she needed. She nodded. "Yes, don't worry about us, Jack. We'll take care of Mary Lisa. We'll wait for you." She led Lou Lou and Mary Lisa down the wide staircase toward the open front door, where paramedics and policemen were still streaming in.

Elizabeth kept Mary Lisa and Lou Lou headed directly for the living room. "That's it, we'll go in here. This isn't the time to talk to these people. They're here to take care of Mrs. Hildebrand." They sat down on the sofa and huddled together, content to say nothing. Elizabeth hoped John would arrive soon.

Upstairs, Jack motioned Deputy Randall out of the bedroom. She didn't look well and he couldn't blame her.

"This can't be happening, Chief. It can't—" Her face grew pale, and she swallowed hard, turned, and raced down the hall toward the bathroom. Jack hoped she made it in time.

He and the forensic team went about their business. They started with dozens of photos. The M.E., Dr. Washington Hughes, arrived and spent about ten minutes examining the body in situ. He bagged Mrs. Hildebrand's hands to preserve any traces of rope fibers on her palms or beneath her fingernails. Finally, they cut the body down. Soon after John arrived, the paramedics wheeled her out of the house to the morgue.

Dr. Hughes held up the rope. "Okay, Chief, as a preliminary, the body showed all the stigmata of hanging, you know that. Death occurred about six hours ago, give or take. It looks like a classic suicide. She got ahold of this rope, climbed up on this chair, flipped the rope over the beam, then tied it around her neck, and kicked away the chair."

"Yes, that's how it looks."

"I'll get started on the autopsy right away."

Jack nodded. "It seems she got up sometime during the night, went out to the garage where she had this handy rope lying around, or she planned it and had the rope in here beforehand."

"I don't keep heavy-duty rope like that in my garage," one of the techs said.

"It could be that she planned it long ago," said John. "Rope's not hard to find."

Jack asked John to see to Mary Lisa, and tried to stay focused on his job. He watched his team dust the surfaces in the bedroom for fingerprints. He himself examined the window, the sill. He climbed out the window, saw it was an easy step up onto the roof and over to the edge where there was an emergency ladder to the ground. No problem at all for anyone to go up or down, Mrs. Hildebrand included. The garage was tucked around in the back, not a dozen feet from the ladder.

Back in the hallway, he ran into Deputy Randall again, looking surprisingly calm. He smiled down at her. "You're doing very well, Deputy. Can you tell me who came to see Mrs. Hildebrand last night?"

Her hands shaking, which she hated, Deputy Susan Randall opened her notebook and read aloud, pleased her voice didn't shake. "Mrs. Beverly came by last evening at eight o'clock. Mrs. Hildebrand's daughter, Marci, came at nine-thirty, right after Mrs. Beverly left, and stayed an hour." Deputy Randall cleared her throat. "I didn't hear any arguing, no raised voices." She shut her notebook. "No one else came by, Chief. I personally spoke to Mrs. Hildebrand at about ten o'clock, asked her if I could get her anything. She said no, she was tired and she wanted to sleep. She asked not to be disturbed, said she was going to take another sleeping pill, maybe sleep late. So I said good night and closed her bedroom door. Then Lucy and I shut up the house, set the alarm at about midnight. I went upstairs to check on Mrs. Hildebrand and she was sleeping soundly, at least it looked that way.

"When Lucy and I knocked on her door about eight o'clock this morning and there was no answer, we didn't go in. We decided to leave her alone, let the poor woman sleep." She paused, ran her tongue over her dry mouth. "Only she wasn't asleep."

Jack laid his hand on her shoulder, to comfort her a bit, he hoped. "I know this is tough, Deputy. Was there anything else?"

"No, we didn't check on her again. When Mary Lisa and her friends arrived, we waved them up. I wasn't worried, I really wasn't. Why not let Mary Lisa speak to her? And they found her. Oh dear God, I'll never forget Mary

Lisa trying to get Mrs. Hildebrand to wake up, trying to convince everyone that she'd be all right."

She looked ready to crumble again, and Jack now took her hands and squeezed them between his. "You're doing great. So there was nothing at all to alert you or Lucy during the night?"

She screwed up her face in concentration, but in the end she had to shake her head. "No, we didn't hear any unusual noises during the night. The house creaks, but all older houses do."

"You got no impression when you spoke to her last evening that Mrs. Hildebrand was unusually depressed or worried, pick up on anything unusual that could explain her suicide?"

"She had a great deal to be very sad about, we all know that. But I didn't expect this of her, Chief."

He arched an eyebrow at her.

"My grandfather killed himself. With him I knew something was terribly wrong, it was like he was waving a red flag for several days before he stuck a gun in his mouth. I didn't sense that from Mrs. Hildebrand." She drew in a deep breath. "I can't believe she managed to do this, Chief."

He patted her arm. "Thank you, Susan. Take Lucy back to the station. I'll speak to her later. Keep a lid on this, all right?"

Jack stepped back into the bedroom and looked around one last time. He'd learned long ago never to jump to a conclusion until all the facts were in. He would have to wait until the autopsy was done. But he wondered. Had Mrs. Hildebrand been overcome with remorse for poisoning her husband, and opted to kill herself? *Unless,* a voice said in his head, *unless she thought her suicide would mean I'd close the case, and she was trying to protect her daughter.* But he shook his head. If that was the case, where was the suicide note? And if it was a murder, it was extremely well done. Dammit, why hadn't this case come together for him before this happened? Why did everything still seem scrambled behind a veil?

It was close to an hour before Jack opened the living room door. The three friends sat side by side on a lovely overstuffed cream sofa, speaking quietly. He wanted to go to Mary Lisa, try to tell her everything was going to be all right, but it wasn't the time. "I'm sorry this is taking so long," he said.

"No problem, Jack," Elizabeth said, with remarkable calm. "Do what you have to do. We'll be here." He saw she was holding both Lou Lou's and Mary Lisa's hands. Mary Lisa didn't look up at him. She was looking inward, probably still seeing Mrs. Hildebrand, still unable to accept it. Lou Lou looked up at him, no, beyond him. He wondered when he'd see the vivacious smart-mouthed women he'd come to like so much.

He said, "I'm sorry the three of you had to find her. That had to be very tough."

Mary Lisa raised her eyes to his, back for the moment to the world of the present.

John Goddard appeared in the living room doorway beside him. "I've been on the phone to Dr. Hughes, Jack." At Jack's nod, he turned to the three women. "You guys all right?" But his eyes were on Elizabeth, and he walked to her like a homing pigeon. She smiled up at him. "Yes, John, we're fine."

"We should get you all out of here," John said. "There might be media, especially if they find out Mary Lisa is here."

"You're right," Jack said. He cursed under his breath, streaked his fingers through his hair, making it stick straight up. He looked out the wide front window. Neighbors were standing in their yards, a clump of them directly across the street huddled together. At least a dozen cars were still in the Hildebrand driveway, some climbed onto the curb in front of the house, one even parked on the grass. He couldn't, at that moment, think of anything that could possibly be worse.

He walked over to Mary Lisa and held his hand out to her. She took it and stood up, and he pulled her into his arms. "I'm sorry, really sorry you had to find her."

She pressed her cheek against his neck. "It was pretty bad." She swallowed down a sob. No more falling apart. It wouldn't help anything.

"I want you to go back to the inn, okay? Please, stay there until I can get back to you."

She leaned back in his arms, studied his face. "All right," she said finally, "but I need to go see my parents soon."

FIFTY-SEVEN

Mary Lisa stepped quietly into the living room. Her father was holding her mother, her head on his shoulder, and he was rocking her. He looked up, gave her a strained smile. Slowly, he eased her mother back.

"Mary Lisa is here, Kathy."

Kathleen Beverly looked worn, somehow hollowed out, her makeup smudged, her eyes red-rimmed and vague. She looked toward her daughter and said, "I don't think there's enough luncheon meat for you, Mary Lisa, since you didn't give us any warning you were coming to lunch."

"I'm not here for lunch, Mom. I came to tell you how very sorry I am about Mrs. Hildebrand."

Kathleen said, not looking at her, "How very nice of you." She cleared her throat. "I understand you were the one who found her."

Mary Lisa nodded. "Yes, Lou Lou and Elizabeth and I. It was—very bad."

"You saw her hanging there?"

Mary Lisa nodded, mute for a moment. "One of the deputies said you went to visit her last night."

George Beverly waved his daughter to a chair, but he didn't look away from his wife's face. "I wondered where you'd gone last evening. So, you went to see Olivia?"

"What is this? Are the two of you ganging up on me? I find it interesting you are questioning me, Mary Lisa, as if you cared about what's been happening with us in Goddard Bay all these years."

George Beverly cut in, his voice sharp. "Kathleen, I know this has been a terrible time for you, but please watch how you speak to Mary Lisa. She is your daughter, and you will strive for a little kindness, a hint of civility at least, if kindness isn't in your repertoire."

"I'm sorry if I've let the cat out of the bag, Mother. I was hoping I could learn something about what happened. Olivia Hildebrand was your best friend. Did you have any hint she'd do this?"

George Beverly looked up to see Jack Wolf standing in the living room doorway. How long had he been there? Probably long enough, George thought. He waved him in. "Please come in, Jack. We were just waiting for my wife to answer that question you heard. Do be seated, have some tea."

He soon had Jack sitting opposite his wife, the steam from the hot tea wafting up beside his hand. "Mrs. Beverly, I'm very sorry for your loss. But please go ahead. Did Olivia Hildebrand give you any warning about this?"

Kathleen Beverly shook her head, all the while seeming to study a painting on the wall, a Dutch countryside scene with its requisite cows and shepherd and hazy light. "How very wise the lot of you think you are. Olivia was my first close friend, my only close friend, really. Of course I was worried for her. The fact is, she didn't kill anyone. I think that breakdown she had this week was staged, because she was trying to protect her daughter. Why don't you arrest Marci, Jack, instead of sniffing around Mary Lisa?"

They all looked at her, astonished.

Then Kathleen shrugged, impatiently wiped the back of her hand over her eyes. Her mascara was badly smeared. "She's gone. It doesn't matter now."

"I'm very sorry, Mom. I know she meant a great deal to you."

Kathleen raised her head, stared at Mary Lisa, through her really. She slowly stood up. She was wearing a light cream V-necked sweater with a cream silk blouse and a pair of darker linen trousers. But today, when she stood, she didn't look beautiful and rich, in control of her world. She looked at each of them. "Marci killed both her husband and her father and her mother. You need only find the proof."

"Actually, Mrs. Beverly, one of the reasons I came over was that Dr. Hughes, the medical examiner, just called me," Jack said. "The rope she used was quite thick and heavy, and I really couldn't see how she managed to fashion a noose and, well, to pull it tightly enough. I doubted she had the strength to do it. But the fact is, she somehow managed it. Dr. Hughes said there were rope burns on her palms where she'd yanked on the rope, and hemp fibers beneath her fingernails. He said she worked really hard but she handled it. She killed herself, Mrs. Beverly. I'm very sorry."

Kathleen's harsh choppy breath was the loudest sound in the living room. She looked at each of them, her face utterly without expression, and said, "I don't believe that," and she left the living room.

George Beverly sighed, looked down at his clenched hands. He unclenched them, splayed his palms on his thighs. "Until a month ago, our lives were quite pleasant really, never too much excitement, but enough to stave off boredom. Now, I seem to be standing in the midst of a shambles." He rose, walked to his daughter, kissed her brow. "I'm sorry, sweetheart, but you're used to her ways, aren't you?"

She hugged her father close. She really didn't want to let him go. He had been her support for so long. He whispered against her ear, "You did well with her. You're a brave, good girl."

"Yeah," she said, nodding, "that's me, brave and good. I'm so sorry about all this, Dad. I probably shouldn't have come, but I had to. She's so terribly hurt." She paused a moment. "Do you know I've never before seen her makeup smeared?"

"And you're always trying to fix things. Maybe your mother will learn to expand her borders a bit at long last. There are very nice people in Goddard Bay. Who knows, maybe she'll let herself get close to some of them now that Olivia's gone." He saw the pain in his daughter's eyes—his eyes—and couldn't help but add, "Dearest, dredging up the past would cause too much pain for everyone, myself included, and it would be for your mother to do, in any case. But know this. None of what your mother feels is your fault. You are a very fine woman, and you are the child of my heart." He nodded to Jack, and followed his wife from the living room.

Mary Lisa looked over at Jack. Her frown smoothed out. "Jack, I don't know if I can do as my father says, stop banging my head against this particular wall, stop trying to understand my mother. I've always trusted him, and I know I should try to let it all go, but how can I? What did he mean, it would bring them too much pain? What happened?

"Oh, all right, so be it. At least I know it's not about me, me as a person. You know something else? I am a good person and I will be the child of my father's heart until I die."

And the woman of my heart, he thought. She didn't respond and he realized the words were only in his mind.

She was shaking her head. "Do you know I actually had the half-baked idea that I could find out something important, not just about Mrs. Hildebrand, but maybe about my mother? I didn't find out anything, not really."

"It seems to me you got a whole lot out of coming here, Mary Lisa. You got a little understanding, and maybe a little peace. And now, maybe, you'll get more." He pulled her against him. "Mary Lisa, there's something else. I came here to show it to your mother privately, but now I want to show it to you first. There was a note, Olivia left it for her. She left it in the garage for some reason, probably where that thick rope was lying. I don't know why."

"A note? For my mother?"

He took an unsealed white envelope from his jacket pocket. It had her mother's name on it. She looked down at it, realized she was afraid to read it. Slowly, she let Jack place the envelope in her hand, and saw him turn away from her to give her privacy.

She pulled the single piece of folded stationery out of the envelope and opened it.

My dearest Kathy,

I know you're in great pain at this moment and very angry with me as well. I take solace only in knowing that the pain of my death will ease, and perhaps the anger as well. It's time for honesty between us, too rare a commodity in both of our lives, I think.

You are the only person, besides Marci, who has mattered to me, Kathy, and though I have prized you both, isn't that a shattering indictment of me? After you left last night, Marci came to see me, but only to tell me she would never see me again. I had told her the truth, you see, that it was I who poisoned Milo, her precious father, that I couldn't stand to see him alive anymore after he killed Jason for nothing more than money, just stupid money, the only important thing in his life. Marci's feelings never even entered his mind. I thought she would understand it, Kathy. She says she hates me now, hates me. At least the monster is dead. And now I will die too. I am not sorry for what I did.

Forgive me, Kathy, I admire you and I love you. But listen to me now. I'm dying with Marci's hate tearing my heart. I want you to make peace with Mary Lisa. You told me you simply can't help yourself, but Kathy, you have to let the past go. Let your beautiful daughter into your heart. The affair George had so many years ago while you were pregnant with her, even that terrible time you spent in a psychiatric hospital where you gave birth to her, surely it has lost its importance. You cannot let it tear at your life forever. He came back to you and his family and you recovered. Forgive him. Forgive her. Forgive yourself. Let it go, dearest, let it go.

Your dearest friend,
Olivia

Mary Lisa had a sheen of tears in her eyes as she folded the letter into the envelope and handed it back to Jack.

"Shall I tell her you read it?" he asked her.

"No, Jack, let it be up to my mother. Olivia's letter has already made a difference, at least to one of us. Who knows what else it will accomplish?"

And this time, he said it aloud, "You are the woman of my heart, Mary Lisa Beverly."

FIFTY-EIGHT

There are approximately fifty hours of soap operas each week on the three major networks.

BORN TO BE WILD

Sunday Cavendish is staring out the window of her office, her arms crossed over her chest. She's wearing a black suit with a white silk blouse beneath, and three-inch black heels. Her red hair is piled atop her head, tendrils lazily curling down in front of her ears. She's thinking about the scene with her mother at her club when she'd bared her soul.

They roll the club dining room footage, gauzy and vague as Sunday's memory, then clear. She sees her mother's pain, the sheen of tears in her eyes—it left her with no doubt that her mother loved her father dearly, and perhaps she still does. Sunday knows it wasn't an act, but real as it gets. And now he is back.

She shakes herself, pours a glass of water from the crystal carafe, sips slowly. She thinks about her father the last time she saw him, three days before.

They roll the footage of father and daughter in her living room, fading it in again as her remembered thoughts strengthen. Looking somehow diffident, his voice soft, nearly pleading, he told her how much he's missed her, the awful hollowing pain he's felt all these years without her. Her uncertainty, her desire to believe him, the tug she's feeling toward him, are all clear on her face.

She says aloud, barely above a whisper, "Who are you? Who are you both?"

There's a knock on her office door, pulling her back to the present.

"Enter."

Her father walks in. "Sunday," he says, then crosses the distance between them and bends to clasp her hands and kiss them. He straightens and she pulls her hands away. "I wanted to see you. I couldn't wait. Your secretary said you don't have an appointment for ten more minutes."

"I thought you were taping a sermon this morning."

"It's done. I came directly here."

She lightly touches her fingers to his cheek. "Don't you wear makeup? Or did you wash it off?"

He shakes his head. "The TV people are talking about it, but I'm hanging tough. I've always thought it ridiculous for a grown man to have his face powdered up."

She grins back at him, and nods.

He looks at her intently. "I know you, Sunday. What's wrong? Something's bothering you."

"You've known me for two weeks, Father," says Sunday, her voice light, dismissive. "You can't begin to tell if there's anything wrong with me."

He pauses a moment. "I'll admit I had some help."

An eyebrow goes up.

"I saw your mother last night."

She looks astonished, holds it, holds it—

"Clear! Mary Lisa, you need to have your nose powdered, it's shining like a beacon under the lights. You too Norman."

Mary Lisa grinned at Norman. "The TV people are talking about makeup again."

Norman got his own nose powdered while Lou Lou dusted away the shine on Mary Lisa's nose. A couple of minutes later, they picked up the scene again.

Sunday looks astonished. "You saw Mom? Goodness, that must have been an adventure. I don't see any wounds. Was there lots of blood?"

He laughs. "Not really. It seems to me that your mother has mellowed a bit over the years."

"Surely you jest. It proves you don't know any of us. It's been too long, far too long."

He says slowly, thoughtfully, "Is she really the monster you've painted, Sunday?"

She looks at him. "I'm still wondering if you're the monster she's painted. The monster my grandfather painted as well."

"Does the old fraud still have his brain?"

"Oh yes. He can still shoot down anything that walks on two legs."

"I want to see you this evening, Sunday. Perhaps we can meet for dinner. You can select the restaurant."

She stares at him a moment, studies his face, then slowly nods. "All right," she says. "*Dino's*, at seven o'clock."

MARY Lisa was glad to see the end of an incredibly difficult day on the set, ruled by Murphy's Law. The dialogue of a scene between her half sister, Susan, and Susan's husband, Damian, had misfired so badly the actors were making gagging noises, and then to make matters worse, Betsy Monroe, her TV mom, had her hair dyed and it turned a virulent Halloween orange. Out of sheer frustration, Mary Lisa had eaten a bacon cheeseburger for lunch with Lou Lou staring at her, disbelieving, while Jack, grinning, offered her catsup. She felt the curse of guilt until she promised herself she'd drink a diet soda for dinner, nothing else, or she'd roast in hell.

But Jack seemed to have enjoyed the day. He was treated royally on the set of *Born to Be Wild*, since he was guarding the Golden Goose and the studio didn't have to pay for it. He rarely left her side, eyes always on alert, watching her and those around her hour after hour, absorbing the bustling activity, the turnarounds sometimes frenetic enough to stress out a doped-up elephant. He thought the acting was decent, and sometimes very good, and he especially enjoyed watching Mary Lisa, particularly when Sunday Cavendish put her outstanding cleavage on display.

Mary Lisa was happy as a clam when she was finally able to put her Mustang in park, turn off the ignition, and forget all about it. They were home, tucked away in the Colony, together and alone. What she had in mind at that moment was to haul Jack into her house, lock the door, take him down to the floor, and kiss every gorgeous inch of him. And so she said, "Listen up, Chief. You're mine as soon as I can get your splendid self on the other side of that door."

He immediately launched himself out of the Mustang and stood against her front door, his arms crossed over his chest, his foot tapping, those aviator glasses of his hiding his eyes, his windblown dark hair falling over his forehead, the whole package making him look like a Top Gun.

Mary Lisa, eyes on him, lust heating up her innards, managed to get out of the car, but that was as far as she got. Six-year-old Alice Neuerberg, with her beautiful board-straight dark hair that had never been cut, was on her, dancing and prancing all around her, showing off her new black patent leather shoes.

Murphy's Law had followed her home.

Alice's shoes were for her grandmother's wedding, she told Mary Lisa, and her mom had paid sixty-nine dollars for them and told her she needed to stop growing. She never once stopped talking, showed her shoes to Mary Lisa from every angle, until she saw another neighbor two doors down drive into her driveway, and skipped off to nab a new audience.

Jack was sitting on her front porch by this time, his long legs stretched out, ankles crossed, grinning toward her. He'd taken off his sunglasses. He looked tired, she thought, maybe a hint of strain around his beautiful eyes from worry, but mostly, he looked happy to be right where he was. Well, she felt all of those things too.

"Great shoes," he said, waving toward Alice.

"Oh yeah. Everyone who's home in the Colony is in for a treat. Her mom will hunt her down in about a half hour."

"Her grandmother's wedding?"

"Yeah, Millicent's an actress, popular everywhere she goes, and the guy she's marrying is an accountant for one of the studios, real sharp, just graduated from Harvard. Come on in and I'll get us something to drink."

"Sounds nice." He followed her into her house, habitually checking for anything out of place, listening for any noise that shouldn't be there. "I talked to Danny during that last scene," he said, catching a can of Diet Dr Pepper Mary Lisa tossed to him from the fridge. "He doesn't know where to go from here."

"I know."

"There are always so many other things happening, things that pull him this way and that. Not that he'll stop trying to find out who's doing this—you're Lou Lou's friend, after all, and trust me, she's got lots of pull with Danny. It doesn't hurt that he likes you, and you're famous. He won't let them put you on the back burner. But he just pulled a homicide in Calabasas, a particularly nasty one."

Mary Lisa touched her can of soda to his. "I know Detective Vasquez wouldn't let them forget about me. And unlike you, Chief, he doesn't keep threatening to throw my ass in jail to keep me safe. In fact, he's never even mentioned my ass and jail in the same breath."

He spewed soda all over himself he laughed so hard, and coughed a couple of times. She pounded his back. He set his can on the counter next to hers and hauled her against him. He buried his face in her hair. "Don't you understand I talk like that because I want you safe? I don't want anything to happen to you. It would kill me if something happened to you, don't you get that?"

"Yes," she said, "I get that." She kissed him, ran her hands up and down his back. She loved the feel of him, the long sleek length of him. She whispered in his mouth, "No one's supposed to come by for at least an hour. Hey, sailor, you want to come check out the battle charts I keep over my bunk? Play some war games?"

Jack looked down at her mouth, only a touch of peachy lipstick left on her lips. "Battle stations, as in battleships and subs and periscopes?"

She nearly ran to her bedroom, Jack right behind her. The room was cool because she always kept the air-conditioning on. She looked at her watch. "Yep, we've got at least an hour."

He laughed as she pushed him backward onto her bed. She fell down over him, pulling up at his light sweater until she got it over his head, and threw it on a chair, then leaned back on her heels, astride him. "Oh my. My own private treat."

She splayed her palms on his chest, moved them lower to his belly. She looked utterly absorbed. Jack found himself both horny and amused, and grinned up at her like a loon. "You look like you're ready to unwrap your favorite candy."

She hummed deep in her throat as she carefully unzipped his jeans. "Don't distract me. I'm busy here, okay?"

She was still dressed when she got his clothes off him and settled astride him again. She leaned forward and cupped his face between her palms. "I wanted you the moment I saw you, Jack, but you didn't like me. And then I saw you at Monica's party, and there you were looking all tough and gorgeous in that tux and I think you even smiled at me. I was a goner, I just didn't realize it yet."

"That's okay. Some of us are a little slow." He chuckled, jerked her down to his chest, and kissed her.

When she was naked and panting, and she couldn't think of another thing to say, he whispered against her cheek, "Do you have any clue how good you feel to me?"

She moved over him, felt him shudder, heard him suck in his breath, and knew that when he came inside her she would go over the edge with him. "You were worth the wait," she said. She arched up, and he came into her, slowly, touching his fingers to her as he moved deeper and deeper, and she wondered if her brain would explode along with her body. Then he touched her womb as his warm fingers moved over her, and she screamed.

He flipped her onto her back, and whispered into her mouth, "I love you, Mary Lisa."

To her surprise, she said against his neck with absolutely no hesitation at all, "I love you, too, Jack. I love you more." He started moving again, and she said, "Oh yes, I want more of that too."

When he was lying sated and stupid, nearly asleep on top of her, he kissed her again, then his mouth slid off her face, and he nestled his head beside hers on the pillow.

FIFTY-NINE

Before *When Harry Met Sally*, Meg Ryan played Betsy Andropoulos on *As the World Turns*.

Mary Lisa woke up half an hour later feeling loose and ready to take on the world. Jack was spooning her, his steady breath warm against the back of her neck, the weight of his arm around her waist. She turned, kissed him lightly on the tip of his nose, admired his thick long eyelashes and that stubborn jaw of his. She eased back a bit, took in the whole long length of him. Beautiful, just beautiful. And he was all hers.

She wriggled out of bed without waking him, threw on a T-shirt and shorts, and was whistling when she walked into the kitchen. She took a bottled water from the fridge. She hadn't taken two drinks from the bottle when she sensed him more than heard him. She turned, smiling, handed him the bottle, and marched out the back door, saying over her shoulder, "Hey, how many calories do you think I burned up playing war with you?"

He considered this. "Enough for a couple of carrots at least."

"That sounds great if they were on top of a pizza. Maybe a thin-crust pizza would be okay."

"Another war game and you can have a thick crust."

Her eyes on his mouth, she said, "I'll see what we can come up with."

He sat down on a deck chair, took a swig of water, then sat forward, rolling the cold bottle between his hands. He watched her lean against the railing, taking in the glorious late afternoon sun, the light afternoon breeze ruffling her hair.

He got to his feet, walked to the railing, and stood next to her. She looked thoughtful, so he kept his hands to himself for the moment. He looked out at the half dozen teenagers playing volleyball on the beach, yelling and laughing, and listened to the soft hiss of the breaking waves, foaming onto shore like fine lace. He said, not turning, "Living here on the beach there's always the echo of the waves and laughter and muted conversation." He paused a moment. "It's nice."

"Yes, it is. When it's overcast and dismal, though, it gets pretty quiet, just the sound of the waves. I like that too, though I like it with people more."

He turned to face her, pulled her up against him, and carried her to the chaise. He stretched her on her back and watched her turn boneless as a kid, her eyes closed as she leaned her head back against the cushion rest. He looked down at her a moment, and lightly traced his fingertips over her eyebrows. Slowly, she opened her eyes and looked up at him.

"Nice eyebrows."

"Do you know I'm told that all the time? Evidently the eyebrows are one of my best selling points."

"I love your smart mouth."

She gave him a sunny smile and sat up. She looked beyond him to wave back at a teenage boy who was clowning around to get her attention while another kid tried to stick a volleyball down his trunks. The girls hooted.

She said, "Did I tell you? Tomorrow I'll have my very own SIG P232. The P stands for personal, you know. They've issued me a concealed weapons permit and I'll be able to carry it in my purse."

He leaned down, his hands on the arms of her deck chair, his face close to hers. He could see a light sheen of perspiration on her cheeks from the warm afternoon sun. "You don't need a gun."

She tapped her fingertips on the arms of her deck chair, kept looking out at the teenagers. "I bought the black hard-anodized aluminum alloy. It makes the SIG even lighter. Elizabeth has already taken me and Lou Lou to her shooting range three times now. She says I'm a natural, that I could compete if I worked at it. You should come with us, set your mind at rest."

He actually hissed, and she looked him straight in the eye, her voice as serious as a claims adjuster's. "I've got to be able to protect myself, Jack, okay? And there's Chico—"

He gave it up. "Yeah, okay, Chico—Danny told me he's well regarded. You're in good hands with him. But I hate this." He streaked his fingers through his dark hair, making it stand upright.

She gave him a huge grin. "Glory be, so karate is all right with you, even if I end up better than you in a couple of weeks? Don't you sneer at me, I'm getting good. Oh, by the way, thank you for hiring Sergeant McClusky. Did you know the poor man has the beginnings of prostate problems and was using the bushes? Mrs. Deffenbach nearly caught him in the act last night. I offered him a bathroom, which he gratefully accepted."

Jack stared at her, nonplussed. "The man's a professional, he was a cop for thirty-five years. Are you saying you made him?"

"I'm afraid so. I know every car that belongs in the Colony, everyone does. He told me he's using his son's clever new hybrid, a Prius, and moves it around often. There are a couple of the hybrids in the Colony, which is the only reason I didn't tune into him right away."

"So he told you all about keeping an eye on your house at night?"

"Yep, he did. Sergeant Ed's a very nice man, Jack. Even with you inside, I kind of like the idea that he's outside."

"Even with the extra protection, I'm thinking I could do more, like kidnap you, take you to Budapest. It's a beautiful place."

"I'd like to go, but I don't have a vacation until the second week in September."

He pictured them there, strolling hand in hand along the Danube, walking over one of the many bridges to the Pest side. He'd show her the bullet holes he'd seen gouged in some of the buildings by Russian guns in the long-ago revolution.

Mary Lisa roused herself, went to the railing, and called out, "Hey, anyone want some nonfat milk with some Oreos?"

There were yells and cheers, and the herd of teenagers stampeded toward them.

She said over her shoulder as she went into the kitchen, "It'll cut down on their beer consumption, always a good thing. And who in the world doesn't like Oreos?"

He marveled at her as she emptied a brand-new half-gallon carton of milk into a dozen glasses and handed out Oreos to the oil-coated, windblown, starving teenagers, all of whom appeared to know Mary Lisa, her kitchen, her bathroom, and her two televisions very well.

"Hey, you're Mary Lisa's cop, aren't you?"

It was the teenage girl who'd helped him that day Mary Lisa was shot at on the beach. "Yeah, that's me."

A little milk mustache adorned her upper lip and she looked adorable with Oreo crumbs on her chin. She was also lovely enough to make a young man's teeth ache to look at her, with her long streaked blond hair tousled and windblown, and an almost-but-not-quite thong covering a tad of her perfectly tanned butt. She said in a serious voice, her hand on his forearm, "My name's Holly and I live four doors down. We all live around here. And I want you to know we're keeping an eye on Mary Lisa. Nobody is going to shoot at her here again, that's for sure."

Jack put his hand on hers and said, "Thank you. I really appreciate that, Holly."

He heard Mary Lisa laugh, let the sound settle deep into him, and knew he was right where he wanted to be. He supposed he might be living down here, maybe joining up with local law enforcement.

One of the teenagers turned on the TV and Jack wandered into the living room. He wanted to watch Elizabeth broadcast the news.

He heard a cell phone, heard Mary Lisa's voice, then dead silence.

He couldn't help it, he was on his feet and turning toward the kitchen when she walked out, still holding her cell phone open in her hand. If he didn't know better he would have thought someone had whacked her on the head.

He was at her side in a moment, his hands on her shoulders, shaking her. "What's wrong? What's happened?"

"Weirdest thing," Mary Lisa said after a blank moment, looking up at him, "that was my mother."

SIXTY

Soap operas are the most popular genre of television drama in the world today. No other form of television fiction has attracted more viewers in more countries over a longer period of time.

Mary Lisa was breathing in the wonderful aroma of her beef taco, loaded with the hottest sauce Tia's Tacos served, waiting as long as possible to sink her teeth into that crunchy shell so she could make the whole experience last. She was also trying to wait until Jack got here with his own lunch, a Machu Picchu burrito that required more prep time. Last she saw him, he was hanging by the counter turned away from everyone, speaking on his cell phone, probably to Detective Vasquez. She closed her eyes a moment, hoping if she didn't look at her very favorite food, all hot and crispy and not two feet from her mouth, she wouldn't have it all chowed down by the time Jack got back to the car.

"You're finally alone."

A familiar voice. Mary Lisa opened her eyes and said, "Go away, Puker. Don't forget the restraining order. I'll call the cops, don't think I won't."

"No reason for that," he said as he opened the passenger door of the Mustang and slid into the seat beside her.

"I saw your big bad cop inside, tied up on his cell phone looking real serious, and figured this was my chance. Let's go, Mary Lisa. We haven't got much time."

She opened her eyes to see a nasty little pistol aimed at her, two inches from her chest. He saw the instant she realized what was happening, and chuckled.

"Yep, it's me. Yours truly. Let's go. You and I have lots of stuff to do and I don't want your cop to see you leave."

He shoved the pistol against her ribs. "Now, Mary Lisa, or I'll have to shoot you right here, and all we'll have are death photos of you I'm sure will move the world to tears."

Her gun was in her purse lying by her left foot on the floor. She knew she couldn't get it out of the purse fast enough. She considered laying on the horn. That would bring Jack running.

"No more stalling. Now, dammit, or you're roadkill, Mary Lisa!"

He sounded like he meant it. She tossed her taco out the window, turned the key in the ignition, and backed out of the parking lot.

"Go right on PCH."

She heard him draw a relieved breath when she turned onto the highway. It was unfortunate, but there weren't any cars coming so she wasn't able to delay for even an instant.

He'd been in her life for so long as a nuisance, as a two-faced weasel, nothing more than that. But now, he had a gun and things were different. He was different. He was deadly, and she knew that all the way to her soul. She realized something was very wrong with him, even more wrong than she'd imagined. And now he was planning to kill her. But why? "You gonna kill me, Puker?" she asked.

He smiled, looking happy as a clam, the wind blowing through his hair. "You'll just have to sweat this one out, won't you?"

"Where are we going, Puker?"

"Dammit, don't call me that! I'm tired of your disrespecting me like that, Mary Lisa." He shoved the gun hard against her arm. "It's really not the time for it."

It hurt, but she didn't flinch or groan. She glanced over at him. "Give me one reason why I should respect you. For heaven's sake, Puker, you're holding a gun on me. You've shot at me, you tried to run me down!"

"It wasn't anything personal, Mary Lisa," he said. "I got some really nice photos from that car hit, made five grand on them. See, it was just business. Now, shut up and keep driving."

"Where are we going?"

"Go past Pepperdine."

Should she floor it? Crash her car, maybe draw a cop? Not here, not yet.

Pepperdine University stretched across the hill to her right. The beautiful Pacific and Amarillo Beach sprawled out to her left. They passed Puerco Beach.

"Hey, Mary Lisa, look here!"

She jerked her head toward him, fear and fury in her eyes, and she knew he saw it. He was grinning wildly as his camera clicked rapidly in burst mode, then quickly dropped it to his lap and brought his gun back up, this time shoving it against her neck.

"No, you aren't going to do anything stupid or you're dead."

She trembled with rage, couldn't help reaching out to claw his face, screaming at him, "You disgusting little creep!" He lurched against the door, out of the way of her nails. She jerked the car onto a narrow winding canyon road she knew dead-ended about a quarter of a mile upland. But she couldn't wait for that. She jerked the Mustang off the gnarly asphalt through a ditch onto an empty stretch of level rocky ground and mashed down hard on the brakes, throwing both of them forward. The momentum sent her head slamming against the steering wheel.

Mary Lisa didn't want to open her eyes, she really didn't, because she knew somewhere deep inside that Puker was still there, but she had to. Thank God he hadn't shot her. She jerked up, felt pain slice through her head and nearly passed out again. She felt wet on the side of her face and knew it was her blood.

"Hey, you coming back to reality, Mary Lisa? You were out of it a good two, three minutes. I got some good shots of you unconscious, face against the steering wheel, a trickle of blood snaking down to your neck. Real quality photos. Time to get yourself together now, Mary Lisa."

For a moment, she didn't understand. They were moving, she felt the wind on her face. Puker had shoved her over onto the passenger side. He was driving now. Thank God, he'd tossed her purse over onto the floor, at her feet. Thank you, God, thank you.

"Where are we?"

"Moseying up Coral Canyon Road. It's nice and quiet up here. I picked it because of the great views and the interesting houses. They'll be background. Hey, nice wheels. I'm glad I got some shots of you behind the wheel." He tossed her a Kleenex from a packet she kept in the glove compartment. "You're a pain in the ass, you know that? That stunt you pulled—you could have killed both of us. You knocked yourself out. Wipe off your face. I want you perfect."

Why hadn't he been hurt when she'd slammed on the brakes?

She wiped the blood off her face. Her head throbbed right over her left ear, but it didn't matter. What to do next?

"Okay, we're going to stop here. Isn't this a panorama? A lovely windswept hill with the ocean in the background, or we could use some of those houses higher up the slope. I'm getting out with the keys now, Mary Lisa. I want you to slide over here into the driver's seat and smile at me, your hands on the steering wheel. We're going to take more shots of you." He paused a moment, and she was terrified at the look in his eyes. "If you try anything again I will shoot you dead right here and leave you for the coyotes, you understand me?"

"I understand you. When did you go from annoying paparazzo to nutso psychopath?"

"I'm not a psychopath! You've pushed me and pushed me and now I've got to go further than I'd planned. Move, Mary Lisa, get behind that wheel. Now!"

He waved his gun at her. She wondered how good a shot he was, not that it mattered since he wasn't more than a foot away. She grabbed up her purse, dropped it on her lap, and moved over to sit in the driver's seat of her Mustang. Her heart was beating so loud it sounded like drums in her head. She turned to smile at him, praying he wouldn't notice her purse and wonder.

Now he was standing maybe three feet away from her, too far to hit him with the Mustang door if she pushed it open hard. "How's this, Puker?"

"That's good. Move around, turn your head this way and that, look happy, Mary Lisa. That's right, you've done this before. Give me big smiles, lots of teeth. Keep both your hands on the steering wheel." He snapped over a dozen photos of her.

While he did it, she slowly eased one hand off the steering wheel and dipped it into her purse. She felt the cold smoothness of her SIG.

"What are you doing with your hand? Dammit, bring your hand back up on the steering wheel!"

"Sure, Puker," she said, pulled up her gun and fired. His camera flew out of his hand, shattered by the bullet, and landed hard against an outcropping of jagged rocks by the roadside.

"You bitch!"

He was dancing he was so furious, looking from her to his smashed camera and waving his gun around. She fired again, and missed, unaccustomed to a moving target. Puker pulled his trigger as she flattened herself against the car seat; she heard the metallic clang of the bullet going through the car door and slamming into the leather seat.

Good, he hadn't been to the firing range. She lurched up and again aimed for his arm, but he was flailing backward, trying to find some cover and shoot at her at the same time. She missed again.

He fired back but she was down and slithering across to the passenger side door. She managed to get the door open and fell headfirst to the ground. Another bullet pinged into the car over her head. How many bullets did he have in his clip?

She scrambled on her hands and knees toward the cliff about three feet away. It was her only hope, no other cover anywhere near. How far a drop was it? It didn't matter. He could be coming around the car to put a bullet in her head.

She'd lived with terror for so long, but at that moment, she wasn't afraid, she was angry, and getting angrier by the second.

She looked back over her shoulder to see him running around the back of her car, panting hard, the gun shaking in his hand. Soon, he'd be so close, he couldn't miss. A bullet struck the ground beside her elbow, sending up a spray of dirt.

"I missed you on purpose, Mary Lisa! You stop now and don't move, or I'll put the next bullet into your head, you got me?"

"Sure, Puker, I got you."

She fired over her shoulder toward the sound of his voice, barely looking back, and heard a blessed yelp as she rolled off the edge of the cliff.

JACK heard the gunfire and thought he'd croak right there. He revved the Suzuki dual sport he'd commandeered in the Tia's Tacos parking lot and hauled ass up the narrow road. He saw the red Mustang at an angle off the road, the passenger door open, not many feet from a cliff edge. He saw Puker Hodges in the hazy sunlight standing at the edge of the cliff, a gun in his hand, looking down. Blood was streaking down his left arm.

Jack saw him raise the gun.

He roared forward, them slammed on the front and rear brakes, sending the bike into a controlled slide. When it stopped, he threw it down and started running, his gun drawn, ready to fire as soon as he was close enough.

All Mary Lisa could think about as she tumbled down the hillside was that Bernie was going to freak when he saw all these cuts and bruises no makeup would camouflage. She smashed hard against a scrub bush, felt pain roar through her, felt every bone rattle in her body. But hurt didn't matter, nothing seemed broken. Good.

"Mary Lisa!"

The twiggy branches of the scrub dug hard into her flesh but it was better than tumbling over rocky ground. She slithered farther down, putting the bush between her and Puker atop the cliff. Would he try to come down?

She was ready, but she had to see him. This time she had to do it right. He appeared at the cliff edge, staring down at her, his gun in his right hand, fanning it all around.

"Hey, you dead down there, Mary Lisa? You all broken up?"

He crouched on his knees and peered over the edge of the cliff.

Her eyes met his. Mary Lisa aimed exactly as Elizabeth had taught her and very gently caressed the trigger. He wasn't dancing around now, he was perfectly still, their eyes locked. The bullet struck him in the chest. He didn't make a sound, simply disappeared from her sight. Mary Lisa felt a punch of shock in her gut, and pulled backward for a moment. But then she jumped to her feet, ignoring the pain broadcasting from every uncovered inch of her body, and began crawling back up the cliff. She saw Jack, who nearly knocked her backward, he was trying to get down to her so quickly.

"Oh God, Jack, you came! Puker, I shot Puker."

"I know. I've got his gun. He's up there. Come on, let's get back up."

Once they heaved themselves onto level ground, Mary Lisa scrambled over to Puker. He was lying on his back, his breathing shallow. He was still alive.

She came down beside him.

He opened his eyes, looked up at her. "You broke my camera. It was my best one, a Nikon, top of the line."

"Why'd you want to kill me?"

Remarkably, he laughed, not much of a laugh because of all the liquid rattling in his throat. "I wasn't trying to kill you before, just get a little revenge and make a whole lot of money at the same time. Frightened starlet, purple prose, close-up photos of you so panicked you looked ready to freak out. Like I said, it was business. That restraining order, Mary Lisa, that wasn't fair. A guy's got to make a living, you know?"

"So there never was a Jamie Ramos?"

It looked to her like he grinned as blood dribbled out of his mouth.

From the corner of her eye, Mary Lisa saw Jack on his cell phone. She ripped off the bottom of her T-shirt and pressed it into a knot against the bullet wound. "I really can't stand you, Puker, but I don't want you to die. I don't want to be the one who killed you."

He was crying now. "I don't have my camera—a picture of this would make me a fortune."

"Yeah, right, that's the way to think. Hang in there, Puker. Help's on the way."

His eyes closed and a second later his head simply fell to the side. She pressed her palm hard against the wound. "Don't you die on me, you jerk!"

Jack shoved her away. He felt for the pulse in his throat for a very long time, raised his face to her, and shook his head. "You did what you had to, Mary Lisa. You saved yourself. I didn't get here in time. I'm proud of you. As for your gun, I'm going to bronze it and put in on the mantelpiece."

EPILOGUE

The Guiding Light has been heard or seen since 1937—how many generations?

BORN TO BE WILD

Sunday is sitting at a table at Dino's Italian Kitchen, one of her favorite restaurants, waiting for her father.

She takes a sip of her wine. She taps her fingers on the white tablecloth. Finally, she sees him striding toward her, dressed immaculately and quite expensively, looking elegant and handsome and smiling toward her. People do double takes as they recognize him, speak to each other in low voices.

When he reaches her, he leans down and kisses her cheek, lightly touches his fingertips to her hair. "You look beautiful."

She grins up at him. "So do you, and everyone in this restaurant thinks so too."

He allows the owner, Dino, to seat him himself, then accepts the wine list. "What are you drinking?"

"A lovely merlot Dino recommended."

He nodded to the flamboyant Dino. "I'll have what my daughter is having, thank you."

She doesn't pause. "What did you and my mother have to say to each other last night?"

"The fact is, I'm trying to make peace with her. No, not with your grandfather too, that would be impossible, but at least with your mother. She looks grand, doesn't she? I don't think she'll ever age."

"What does making peace mean?"

He chuckles. "So you're pinning me down, are you?"

She picks up a piece of bread, crumbles it between her fingers, sets it on her plate. "I have to," she says at last. "I've learned over the years that people slip and slide around, never coughing up the truth unless they have to, and even then they try not to."

"Is this what you do?"

"Naturally. So, what peace?"

"I asked her flat-out if she would forgive me for leaving you and her."

"But you told me you had no choice in the matter."

"There are always choices, Sunday. The fact is, I wanted out. I wanted to accept my calling. I wanted to find the meaning and purpose of my life."

"And by leaving us you found it?"

He accepts the wineglass a waiter brings him and clicks his glass to Sunday's. In his powerful deep voice, his eyes on her face, he says, "To possibilities."

She smiles at him. "Yes, to possibilities." She says again, "So, you're saying that by leaving us you found the meaning of life?"

He looks troubled, then slowly nods. "I suppose I have. Grief and loss, they help you focus on what's really important. They make you more aware of all the anguish and the sorrow in the world, make you face up to it, because otherwise they lurk inside you your whole life."

"So you suffered as you pursued your goal. But all of us suffer. Sorrow and anguish are knit into the fabric of life itself. No one has the market on it. Did you find your goal, Father?"

His eyes light up. She's called him Father. He shrugs. "Does any man ever attain his goal? Don't goals always

ift and change, become more difficult to pin down as you
ature and gain wisdom?"

"You're very good," Sunday says. "I think I'd like to or-
er. I hope you like the food."

There is silence for a moment while they peruse the
enu. He says, without looking up at her, "Do you have a
al, Sunday?"

"Why yes, I believe I'll have the spaghetti Bolognese,"
e says and gives him a false smile.

He sits forward, places his palm up on the table between
em, clearly inviting her to take his hand, but she doesn't.
'm your father. No matter what, that fact will never
ange. Don't shut me out. Don't make a mockery of what
am and what I do and what I strive so very hard to ac-
mplish. I'm only a man, Sunday, but I'm here now and I
ant you to come to accept me. As your father."

She's moved, she can't help it. She reaches out her hand
 his. Then she looks up. A beautiful young woman is
alking toward them, a woman who's very pregnant.

Sunday turns away from her, gives her father her hand.
he whispers, "Father—"

"Hey, here you are!"

He freezes, then slowly turns to face the young woman,
ho says as she tosses her hair, "I got tired of waiting. I
idn't think it would take this long."

Sunday slowly pulls her hand back. She stares up at the
oman, at the long blond hair, smooth and straight, the big
reasts now bigger with her pregnancy, incredible pale blue
yes, sexy despite the big belly. Sunday arches a brow.
And you are . . . ?"

The young woman laughs, pats her belly. "May I sit
own?"

"No, you may not. Tell me who you are."

The young woman frowns down at her. "That isn't very
olite."

"What isn't polite is interrupting two perfect strangers."

"Oh, we're not all strangers. Phillip is my husband."
he caresses his cheek with her fingers. "I suppose I'm

here to meet you." She laughs. "Isn't this delicious? You'r
older than I am and you're my stepdaughter and soo'
you're going to have a little brother."

Sunday stares at her father, devastated. Then her expres
sion changes to one of cynical, weary amusement. She give
an elegant shrug of her shoulders. She holds it, holds it—

"Clear!"

There were some cheers.

Bernie yelled out, "Wow! What a way to end the week
You can bet every single viewer will tune in for sure o
Monday. Well done, Norman, Mary Lisa, Stacy. Okay
kids, have a great weekend!"

"Let me get this damned pillow out," Stacy said
laughing.

Mary Lisa patted the pillow. "I think it looks kind o
cute," she said.

Stacy Freeman glanced over to where Jack was standing
arms crossed over his chest, watching the action. "He'
yours?"

"Yep, all mine."

Jack looked up, smiled at her. "Yes," she said again
"he's all mine."